THE ORPHAN OF THE RHINE

THE NORTHANGER ABBEY HORRID NOVELS

Castle of Wolfenbach (1793)
Eliza Parsons

Clermont (1798)
Regina Maria Roche

The Mysterious Warning (1796)
Eliza Parsons

The Necromancer; or, The Tale of the Black Forest (1794)
"Peter Teuthold"

The Midnight Bell (1798)
Francis Lathom

The Orphan of the Rhine (1798)
Eleanor Sleath

Horrid Mysteries (1796)
Carl Grosse

THE

ORPHAN

OF THE

RHINE.

𝔄 𝔏𝔬𝔪𝔞𝔫𝔠𝔢,

BY

ELEANOR SLEATH.

Sweet are the uses of adversity,
Which, like the toad, ugly and venomous,
Wears yet a precious jewel in his head.
SHAKESPEARE.

WITH A NEW INTRODUCTION BY
ELLEN MOODY

VALANCOURT BOOKS

The Orphan of the Rhine by Eleanor Sleath
First published London: William Lane, 1798
First Valancourt Books edition 2014

Introduction © 2014 by Ellen Moody
This edition © 2014 by Valancourt Books

Published by Valancourt Books, Richmond, Virginia
Publisher & Editor: James D. Jenkins
http://www.valancourtbooks.com

All Valancourt Books publications are printed on acid free paper
that meets all ANSI standards for archival quality paper.

ISBN 978-1-941147-37-5

Set in Adobe Caslon 10.5/13

CONTENTS

INTRODUCTION

"My father is now reading the 'Midnight Bell', which
he has got from the library."
— Jane to Cassandra Austen, 24 October 1798

DESPITE (until recently) a rareness that defeated even an
expert book collector like Michael Sadleir, Eleanor Sleath's
The Orphan of the Rhine (1798) has been in no danger of being
forgotten. Why? Sleath's first novel is one of the list of seven
titillatingly "horrid" novels cited by Austen in her *Northanger
Abbey* (I:6). It was the one not found or read by Sadleir when he
delivered his important paper, "The Northanger Novels" (1927),
and demonstrated that the famous seven were not just quintes-
sentially parodic titles as had been popularly assumed (Varma
xvi), but real obtainable books whose publishing history, authors
and content one could research. When the paper was published,
Sadleir's bibliographic and critical description of *The Orphan*
appeared in a postscript.

In 2000 Rictor Norton reconfirmed Sadleir's feeling that
Austen's choice was "rather deliberate than random" and that
the seven may be grouped into two representative types (Sadleir
9; Norton 76-77). Norton reprints six pages of Sleath's novel as
part of a Radcliffe "school of terror," also identified as "female
gothic" (Williams 135-40, 149-72), along with three of the others:
Eliza Parsons's *Castle of Wolfenbach, A German Story* (1793) and
The Mysterious Warning, A German Tale (1796), and (however
crude and parodic), Francis Lathom's *The Midnight Bell. A
German Story, Founded on Incidents in Real Life* (1798). Norton's
anthology includes Regina Maria Roche's *The Children of the
Abbey* rather than the novel by Roche that does appear in the
Northanger list, *Clermont, A Tale* (1798), but Norton's perspec-
tive plainly puts all Roche's novels into the Radcliffe column,
and is consonant with Sadleir's argument (10, 22) that Sleath's
novel differs only in also attempting to be a "rhapsodical sensi-

bility romance" (Sadleir, 10, 22) with no pretense to the German origins that signaled to English readers much tabooed material and graphic description of sensational and/or sexual violence inflicted on bodies found here. Yet Sleath's novel is notionally set in various places in Germany as well as Italy and Switzerland.

Close reading these texts also shows that such typologies depend on generalities that ignore major features. Norton's divisions reveal this when, as opposed to Sadleir (10), he moves *The Midnight Bell*, and two more of the Northanger list, Karl Friedrich Kahlert's *The Necromancer; or, The Tale of the Black Forest, Translated from the German of Lawrence Flammenberg* (1794), translated by Peter Will (under the pseudonym "Peter Teuthold") and Carl Grosse's *Horrid Mysteries, A Story from the German of the Marquis de Grosse* (1796), also translated by Will, into a "German school of horror," duly identified as "male gothic" (Williams 99-121). Norton's German horror column includes two early vampire novels, Godwin's *Caleb Williams*, Lewis's *Monk*, and Shelley's *Frankenstein*. Yet like Sleath's *Orphan of the Rhine* and Radcliffe's gothic novels, Kahlert's has women imprisoned, chained, and/or murdered and real stylistic power when it comes to description. *The Necromancer* resembles *Udolpho*: both are influenced by Schiller's *The Ghost-Seer* (Varma, *Necromancer* vii). *Horrid Mysteries* is overtly political (Rosicrucian) and a Fascist warning of a European-wide revolutionary conspiracy (Sadleir, 18-20, Tichelaar 59-79), but so are Radcliffe's books political (see my "Nightmare of History"), and at least four readers (Sadleir, Varma, Norton, and Muriel Tarr) have concluded that *The Orphan of the Rhine* has a serious pro-Roman Catholic "spiritual" agenda. Varma invents a biography which reinforces this conclusion (*Orphan* viii-ix).

My point is more than the once-recognized truism (Sedgwick) that most texts labelled gothic use a repetitive and (only somewhat) coherent recipe and yet have features individual to themselves that reflect the author's life from a psychoanalytic standpoint. The value of this new edition of Sleath's novel is that it gives the reader a chance to come into contact with a distinct text not accurately described anywhere. *The Orphan of the Rhine* belongs to a type outlined by Marianne Hirsch in

The Mother/Daughter Plot, one much favored in the later 18th century (Greenfield). Large swathes of Sleath's novel are given over to tranquil stories of Madame Chamont who we first meet as Julie de Rubine (an allusion to Mackenzie's novel *Julia de Roubigné*), as a mother nurturing and educating a boy, Enrîco de Montferrat, and girl baby, Laurette, whose true parentage is learned at the book's close. This boy and girl emerge as the ostensible central pair of characters who experience a Longus-like *Daphnis and Chloe* (Greek, 2nd century romance) semi-incestuous erotic childhood that becomes a shared adolescent love. The contemporary analogue occurs in Bernardin de St. Pierre's wildly popular *Paul et Virginie* (1788, Englished by Helen Maria Williams). It does take a full third of the novel before this core comes clear, and then Enrico and Laurette provide coherence to the book's main frame narrative.

Some of its paradigms do recall particular obsessions in Radcliffe: e.g., the dark father-lover who seeks to murder his daughter-niece and worldly callous aunt, and a ghost is explained away, but the one character who stays in the narrative from beginning to end is the older woman, the romance's mother. Madame Chamont stands in for Sleath. The book's back stories often parallel Madame Chamont's and project many intense retreats into solitude from the severe calamities of the social world that we find in the main narrative. Gothics lend themselves to psychoanalytical parallels, but it is intriguing to note that, like Madame Chamont, the book's true central male character is La Roque, whose real name is Conte della Croisse. Della Croisse is the most carefully delineated complicated male character who Madame Chamont comes upon early in the book, and who keeps turning up at hinge-points in the plot-design, and himself gradually presents a believably mixed personality (amoral with virtuous impulses). Like Madame Chamont, at this point Della Croisse seems a central male (it is he whom she hears being tortured); yet, like her, he becomes seemingly secondary until near the end when his fate exemplifies the book's articulated moral. Where genuinely felt anxiety is present in the book, the source is from the angle of an escaping suppliant over what's unknown on the other side of a door, a cave, inside some locked dark area and sounds that suggest mental or physical torture—curiously murders do not register anywhere as deeply as in Radcliffe or novels of "the German school," nor does rape occupy any importance. Sleath's female characters choose to marry (which means having sex and babies) and her males find compliant adulterous partners. Somewhat unusual for this era is the often-noticed insisted-upon benignity or beauty of Catholic ritual and religious types. Here and there the miseries of a particular war are alluded to in terms which recall humane Enlightenment ideals, but the characters are actuated by motives which anticipate Victorian and mystery-detective gothics: the Marchese de Montferrat, the linchpin villain of the book, is not publicly exposed or even punished lest it shame his family.

The book's most powerful passages are its many descriptive landscapes which capture some distant or still and numinous pastoral vision (with its fear and distaste for any kind of court/social intrigue) whose deepest urge is retreat. At the same time, the central debilitating flaw of the book is its weak diction. From Sleath's biography we can see she was an educated woman, from this book well-read in poetry and drama, but her prose is often composed of conventional imitative diction and relies heavily on abstractions and euphemisms which can create a vapid linguistic surface that forms a kind of barrier to the feeling Sleath seeks to communicate. She also repeatedly chooses to tell her stories rather than dramatize their incidents, so her text may fail to leave the impression intended. Sleath will say Madame Chamont's "sleep" is "transient and disturbed, fearful and uneasy visions flitted before her fancy" (59), but then does not visualize the experience or connect the dream to imagined pragmatic details in her text. She has the 1790s' powerful fears of hope-less imprisonments (through dreams too; see Bugg); again it is escape (scaling a wall) that she does best.

The tragedies, sexual scandals and constraints of Sleath's life are those of vulnerable real gentlewomen in her era and of her imagined female characters. Eleanor Carter was the child of a minor Protestant gentry family who moved from Herefordshire to Leicestershire in the 17th century. In 1792 when Eleanor was

21, she married Joseph Barnabas Sleath (a surgeon and apothecary, connected to the militia); records suggest they were happy, but their baby died in 1794; and, heavily in debt, he died four weeks later. She returned to Leicestershire to live with the family of her eldest brother, John Edward Carter, who worked to discharge the debts, and her aging mother. She fell ill. It was during this first period of her widowhood that she wrote *The Orphan of the Rhine*.

By 1801-2 Eleanor was part of a fairly numerous yet close-knit group of intellectual, literary and clerical neighbors who traveled together, exchanged letters, and worked on literary projects with each other. These included Sleath's friend Susannah Watts, who translated from French and Italian, wrote the first guide to Leicester, and is said to have been an advocate for women and against social injustice and slavery. Another member of the circle was John Dudley, vicar of Humberstone. In the earliest phase of this group (which included a trip to Bath, going to the theater), Sleath published her second novel, *Who's the Murderer? or, The Mystery of the Forest* (1802). By 1807 however, whether justifiably or not, Dudley's wife, Ann, suspected that a (perhaps adulterous) relationship had developed between Eleanor and Dudley while literary collaborators; the triangular tension became the catalyst for simmering resentments among the group and eventually polarized several individuals irrevocably: rumors spread that Eleanor had gone to London to have a child by Dudley; he separated from his wife.

One result was far fewer letters, so we know less of Eleanor's life from 1808 on. She seems to have had more time to write novels: in 1809 she published *The Bristol Heiress*, whose title suggests a domestic-realistic romance connected to the slave trade, *The Nocturnal Minstrel* (1810), and *Pyrenean Banditti* (1811). Five years later John Dudley wrote of his 1811 poem, *The Metamorphosis of Sona: A Hindu Tale*, that he thought it could be inserted in a novel of India by Eleanor ("connected to Hindusthan"). In 1815 Sleath had published *Glenowen; or, The Fairy Palace* which contains Indian material. Other records show her eldest brother died in 1813; and six months later her mother. She was bequeathed a house in High Street Leicester and received interest from two substantial bequests (totaling £3000).

We do not know where Eleanor was between 1814 and 1816, when she purchased a house for £500 in Loughborough, where a Petty Sessions court included John Dudley among its magistrates. Five miles away was Sileby where Dudley lived from 1811 after obtaining a deed of separation from Ann. We may picture Eleanor as a widow with a male friend visiting her during these years. Ann Dudley died in February 1823, and not long after, 1 April 1823, Eleanor Sleath and John Dudley were married in the Loughborough parish church. Eleanor then lived the quiet socially conventional life of a vicar's wife until 1847 when she died of liver disease at 77. (For fuller details of her life, see Czlapinsky and Wheeler.)

Jane Austen's listing of *The Orphan of the Rhine* has been on the whole beneficial for Eleanor Sleath's literary legacy. If only Mr. Austen had sat down to *The Orphan of the Rhine* that 1798 autumn night, Sleath's novel and history might not have had to wait until 1968 and the World Wide Web for copies to be available to ordinary readers. But this parodic gothic context has also distorted our view of the book and lost from view an author whose life allows us to add to a fuller spectrum of contemporary women writers than another typical division of the seemingly secure and successful, irreproachably chaste icons whose names still dominate the literary landscape (Burney, Edgeworth, Charlotte Smith) and the other, the high risk, revolutionary women writers (Mary Wollstonecraft, Mary Hays, Amelia Opie, Mary Shelley).

Ellen Moody
July 2014

A longtime lecturer at George Mason University and now teaching at American University, Dr. Ellen Moody has published on early modern to 18th-century women writers, film, and translation. She has produced e-text editions of Isabelle de Montolieu's *Caroline de Lichtfield* and Sophie Cottin's *Amelie Mansfield* and is working on an edition of Charlotte Smith's *Ethelinde; or, The Recluse of the Lake* for Valancourt Books. Her latest essay, "Epistolarity and Masculinity in

Andrew Davies's Trollope Adaptations", in *Upstairs and Downstairs: The British Historical Costume Drama on TV*, edited by Julie Taddeo and James Leggot (Scarecrow Press, 2014) will appear this fall. Her current book project is entitled *A Place of Refuge: The Jane Austen Film Canon.*

SELECTED BIBLIOGRAPHY

Austen, Jane. *Northanger Abbey*, edited with an introduction and notes by Marilyn Butler. New York: Penguin, 1995.

——. *Jane Austen's Letters*, 4th ed., edited by Deirdre Le Faye. New York: Oxford University Press, 2011.

Bugg, John. *Five Long Winters: The Trials of British Romanticism.* Stanford: Stanford University Press, 2013.

Czlapinski, Rebecca and Eric C. Wheeler. "New Sleath Biography: The Real Eleanor Sleath." May 8, 2011. Online: http://sleathsleuth.wordpress.com/2011/05/08/new-eleanor-sleath-biography. Accessed July 30, 2014.

Greenfield, Susan C. *Mothering Daughters: Novels and the Politics of Family Romance.* Detroit: Wayne State University Press, 2002.

Hirsch, Marianne. *The Mother/Daughter Plot: Narrative, Psychoanalysis, Feminism.* Bloomington: Indiana University Press, 1989.

Moody, Ellen. "The Nightmare of History in Ann Radcliffe's Landscapes," a paper delivered at South Central Region of ASECS, February 23-25, 2012. Available online at: http://www.jimandellen.org/LandscapeMemoryNightmareHistory.html

Norton, Rictor, ed. *Gothic Readings, The First Wave, 1764-1840.* London: Leicester University Press, 2000.

Parsons, Eliza. *Castle of Wolfenbach.* Edited by Devendra P. Varma. London: Folio Press, 1968.

Sadleir, Michael. *The Northanger Novels: A Footnote to Jane Austen.* Oxford: The English Association, Pamphlet No. 68. November 1927.

Sedgwick, Eve Kosofsky. *The Coherence of Gothic Conventions.* New York: Methuen, 1986.

Sutherland, John. "Michael Sadleir and His Collection of Nineteenth-Century Fiction," *Nineteenth-Century Literature*, 56:2 (2001): 145-159.

Teuthold, Peter. *The Necromancer, or, The Tale of the Black Forest*, edited by Devendra P. Varma. London: Folio Press, 1968.

Tichelaar, Tyler. *The Gothic Wanderer, From Transgression to Redemption*. Ann Arbor: Modern History Press, 2012.

Varma, Devendra P., "Introduction," in Eleanor Sleath, *The Orphan of the Rhine*, edited by Devendra P. Varma. London: Folio Press, 1968.

Williams, Anne. *Art of Darkness: A Poetics of Gothic*. Chicago: University of Chicago Press, 1995.

NOTE ON THE TEXT

The Orphan of the Rhine was originally published in four volumes by William Lane under his Minerva Press imprint in 1798. The only modern edition of the novel was a limited edition hardcover volume included in a set of the seven "horrid novels", edited by Devendra P. Varma and published by the Folio Press of London in 1968. Only two copies of the first edition are known to exist: Michael Sadleir's copy at the University of Virginia and a copy at Yale University.

The text of the present edition has been reprinted virtually verbatim from Sadleir's copy of the first edition. No attempt has been made to modernize old-fashioned or archaic spelling, grammar, or punctuation, nor has any attempt been made to regularize variant spellings such as "recompense" and "recompence". A very small number of obvious, distracting, printer's errors have been silently corrected, such as "Ceaser" for "Caesar" and "feign" for "fain". The resulting text is exactly the same as the one Jane Austen would have read without being marred by a handful of unnecessary typographical errors.

THE

ORPHAN

OF THE

RHINE.

———◆ ✳ ◆———

𝕬 𝕽𝖔𝖒𝖆𝖓𝖈𝖊,

IN FOUR VOLUMES.

───────

BY MRS. SLEATH.

───────

Sweet are the uses of adversity,
Which, like the toad, ugly and venomous,
Wears yet a precious jewel in his head.
SHAKESPEARE.

VOL. I.

═══════════

LONDON:
PRINTED AT THE
𝕸𝖎𝖓𝖊𝖗𝖛𝖆-𝕻𝖗𝖊𝖘𝖘,
FOR WILLIAM LANE, LEADENHALL-STREET
1798

ADVERTISEMENT.

The Author of the following pages presents them to the Public with a sentiment of respectful diffidence. She avows them as her first performance, and must therefore appeal to the candour and indulgence of the liberal.

As works of this kind are universally read, and, if written with discretion, are allowed by the strictest moralists to be, at least, innocent, she feels the less need of an apology for thus adding to the amply supplied treasury of literary amusement, of which this country boasts; and should her production contribute, in the smallest degree, to the entertainment of those who may honour it with a perusal, she will consider the hours spent in its composition as having been not unprofitably employed, and will deem her exertions more than adequately rewarded.

THE

Orphan of the Rhine.

CHAP. I.

—————"Thou art indeed ill-fated;
Snatch'd, when an infant, from thy nurse's arms,
And borne we know not whither.
                                        LANGHORNE.

NEAR that long tract of hills, known by the name of Mount Jura, was situated, in the year 1605, the cottage of Julie de Rubine; commanding on one side a view of Geneva and its Lake, lying north of the town, and on the other an extensive plain, covered with pine-woods and pasturage: beyond which arose, in various forms and directions, that vast range of Alps which divide Italy from Savoy, forming a natural barrier to Geneva and its little territory.

The owner of this secluded retreat, having met with some peculiar misfortunes, originating from the depravity of those with whom she was unhappily connected, had disengaged herself from the world at that period of existence when it usually presents the most alluring prospects; and accompanied by her infant son and one faithful domestic, had taken refuge in retirement.

After having passed some years in uninterrupted solitude, she was one evening returning from a monastery, near Ripaille, which formerly belonged to the hermits of St. Maurice, whither she had been at confession, and was pursuing her way through a large forest, whose vistas terminated upon the Lake, when she observed a cabriolet move along at some distance before her, which afterwards stopped at her door.

Before Julie de Rubine arrived at her cottage, the traveller, who was a female, had alighted, and on hearing her name, advanced some paces to receive her. She was a tall thin woman, of a pale, unhealthy appearance. Her dress bespoke her of the middle rank of life, and an infant that she held in her arms, which was entirely obscured in a mantle, intimated that she acted in the capacity of nurse.

After having unfolded the occasion of her visit, the stranger presented the recluse with a letter, which she informed her was from the Marchese de Montferrat. Julie de Rubine started, and appeared much affected. The messenger observed these emotions with concern, and endeavoured to remove the cause by introducing a new subject of conversation. She discoursed upon the temperature of the climate, the fineness of the weather, and related many little adventures they had met with upon the road, not forgetting to recite the difficulties they had encountered as they journeyed over the rocky steeps of Mount Cennis, on their way from Turin thither, which she assured her had cost them much labour and fatigue. Julie, who perceived the kindness of the intention, attempted to subdue the acuteness of those feelings, which had prevented her from welcoming the stranger with her accustomed courtesy; and, having in some measure succeeded, ventured to turn aside the mantle with which the infant was covered, and beheld a very beautiful female child, apparently about four months old. Having expressed her astonishment that the stranger should travel so far with so young a companion, she ordered Dorothèe, her servant, to prepare some refreshment; and taking the Marchese's letter, with a trembling hand she opened it, and read as follows:

"The Marchese de Montferrat having, after many unsuccessful inquiries, discovered the abode of Julie de Rubine, and wishing in some measure to compensate for the misfortunes he has occasioned, is willing to offer his protection to her, and also to her son, for whom he will hereafter amply provide, on condition that she will take into her care a young female infant, and perform, in every respect, the part of a mother. She is also requested not to make any inquiries relative to the child, but to rest satisfied that there are reasons, which, if known, would be deemed sufficient for the justification of his conduct, however mysterious it may appear. If Julie de Rubine agrees to these proposals, the Marchese will provide for her an asylum, in which she will find every accommodation suitable to her rank; he will also send a person to convey her to her new habitation, and will settle upon her a handsome annual sum as a provision for herself and the children. He also considers that, to avoid the effects of an impertinent curiosity, it will be at once prudent and necessary to take another name, and to assume the character of a widow. If Julie de Rubine acquits herself in this affair with that uniform propriety of conduct which she has hitherto never failed to support, she and her child have every thing to hope from his patronage; but on the contrary, if she refuses to comply with his desires, and presumes to disclose the most unimportant incident respecting this circumstance to any individual living, she has every thing to fear from his displeasure."

Amazement for the moment almost deprived the agitated Julie of reason! That the Marchese should select her from the rest of the world, to act as a mother to the orphan; her whom he had so materially injured, and that this child should be conveyed to her under circumstances so peculiar, was equally surprising and inexplicable! That it was deprived of maternal attention was beyond a doubt, or why send it to her, to perform the part of so tender a relation? It might yet have a father living, and who could that father be? An universal trembling seized her as the idea occurred—an idea which the whole of the proceeding apparently justified, that it was no other than the Marchese. She knew that he had not been long united to a woman of high rank and considerable fortune, to whom he had offered himself on an early and superficial acquaintance, when resident in the neighbourhood of Padua, whither he had spent some time in the society of a friend to whom he had been long attached. His love of gallantry was too generally known to allow the probability of his affections being long in the possession of any one; she, by melancholy experience, was convinced of the truth of this assertion: the child could then be no other than the offspring of an illicit amour. She knew that, previous to his marriage, he had seduced the affections of a young Neapolitan beauty, the daughter of a merchant, whose name was Di Capigna, less celebrated for external charms than for those seductive and elegant accomplishments, "that take the reason prisoner."

Her father, she had been informed, did not long survive the loss of his daughter's reputation, which event so seriously affected the Signora that she suddenly left the Marchese, some believing that she was dead, and others that she had thrown herself into a convent; but the truth of this singular affair was not known.

Every circumstance seemed to favour the opinion that this might be the child of the Signora Di Capigna, whose birth, added to her own distresses, probably occasioned her death. She had not indeed heard of an infant; but this, considering the secrecy with which affairs of this nature are usually conducted, was not a matter of surprise, particularly as the marriage of the Marchese must have taken place before the birth of the child. Every thing being thus collected, there no longer remained a doubt in the breast of Julie de Rubine, but that this was indeed the daughter of the Marchese, and consequently of the Signora Di Capigna.

The conclusion of the letter contained a threat, if she refused to comply with his desires; yet the pride of conscious innocence revolted at the idea of receiving pecuniary support from a man, who had stooped to the most humiliating and degrading falsehoods, merely to tarnish the brightest of all gems, a stainless reputation. But when she considered the unprotected situation of her child, her Enrîco, who would find a bitter enemy, where from the ties of nature he might reasonably expect the tenderest of friends, her own inability to provide for him, the hardships to which he might be exposed, pleaded powerfully the cause of the Marchese, and staggered her accustomed firmness. This little innocent too, sent to solicit her protection—what sorrows, what distresses, might it have to encounter, what treatment might it experience from the harsh and the mercenary! These reflections, excited by the unexampled generosity of her nature, sunk deep into her heart, and elevated her above every ignoble and selfish consideration. For herself she would have been contented to have lived and died in obscurity, and would have endured without murmuring the severest penury, rather than have thrown herself upon the liberality of one, for whom she now felt no softer sentiment than horror and resentment. But her son had no doubt a claim to his protection; on his part it might be considered as a debt, not as a bounty; and as to the infant, a handsome allowance might certainly be demanded for such a charge, without incurring an obligation; but the matter was too important to be immediately determined. Silent and deliberating, she quitted her apartment, and returned into the room, where she had left the nurse and child.

The latter was now awake, and as Julie de Rubine pressed its cheek gently to her lips, it smiled; she took its hand; it grasped her finger, and she imagined looked as if imploring her protection. Agatha, which was the name of the messenger, sent by the Marchese, observed these maternal attentions with apparent satisfaction; and discovering much humanity and softness in the deportment of the recluse, endeavoured to direct these amiable traits of character to the advantage of her employer, by dwelling with a tender concern upon the beauty and innocence of the child, from whom she lamented she was so soon to be separated. She expatiated also on the generosity of the Marchese, extolling the benevolent solicitude he had displayed in the cause of the infant, who but for him, she added, might have perished for want, as few were at once invested with power and inclination to patronize the unfortunate.

Madame de Rubine, after having complimented the stranger upon her sensibility, inquired how long the infant had remained under her protection, and was informed ever since it was born. That it was consigned to her care by Paoli, her husband, at the desire of the Marchese, with whom he had resided some years in the capacity of steward; but that whose it was, or from whence it came, she was incapable of ascertaining, though she had sometimes ventured to interrogate Paoli upon the subject; his answers being always short, undecisive, and frequently uttered with hesitation and displeasure.

She then demanded whether she herself saw the Marchese,

and if any time was fixed for her return? The former part of the question was answered with a negative; the message respecting her embassy was also conveyed by her husband, who had intimated a desire that the affair should be speedily determined, as his Lord had some thoughts of removing from the Castello St. Aubin, his present residence in the environs of Turin, to another estate to which he had recently succeeded, in consequence of the death of a near relation, who, having suddenly disappeared, was supposed to have been slain by banditti, as he was returning from a remote province to his paternal seat; which mournful event had, she added, so serious an effect upon his lady, that she scarcely survived the intelligence; and during her illness the affectionate attentions of the Marchese and Marchesa, who were sent for to assist and administer consolation, so excited her gratitude, that she bequeathed them all her valuables.

Julie then inquired if she was acquainted with the name of the nobleman whose life had been terminated by this fatal disaster, and whether he was also an Italian, and an inhabitant of Turin. But with these particulars Agatha was totally unacquainted; she had, she said, endeavoured to gain some information upon the subject, but her exertions had been at present unsuccessful, as a variety of reports had been circulated in the neighbourhood, few of which assumed the appearance of truth. She then modestly reminded Madame de Rubine of the necessity of entering into a speedy determination concerning the child; as if the proposals conveyed in the letter were rejected, she had orders to return without further delay, that it might be committed to the protection of some other, who would not scruple, in consideration of the terms proposed, to undertake the important charge.

Julie, having assured her that she would re-examine these proposals, and adopt, as soon as possible, a final resolution concerning them, observed, that the infant was again fallen asleep, and requested that it might be put to bed. Agatha, being much fatigued, agreed to the proposition; and, after having laid the little innocent to rest, and partaken of some refreshment with Dorothèe, retired herself to repose. But Madame de Rubine's mind was too much agitated and perplexed with the strange occurrences of the day, to feel the least inclination to sleep. The

Marchese's letter, which contained such promises of protection to her son, was flattering to the hopes of a fond and affectionate mother. But could a man of his character be relied upon? Might he not, from caprice, if not from a more reasonable motive, be induced at some future time suddenly to withdraw that protection, and might not this be more severely felt, than if it had never been afforded? But could she with justice suppose this possible? From his former conduct, without departing, in the smallest instance, from the native candour of her mind, she was unable to form a judgment upon his conduct decisively to his advantage. To her she was sensible he had not acquitted himself as a man of principle or of honour; but maturer years she considered might have corrected the errors of youth, and her misfortunes, united with those of the Signora Di Capigna, might have led to repentance and reformation. There had been instances of many who had entirely forsaken their offspring, exposing them without pity to all the hardships of poverty and oppression; but crimes of this nature were not become familiar to him; he seemed interested in their unprotected situations, and was anxious to defend them from the insults and cruelty of an unfeeling world.

The threat which the letter contained, appeared to have been made use of merely for the purpose of conquering those little scrupulous delicacies which might eventually stand in the way of her son's advancement. If he was not concerned in their welfare, why not have sent the infant to the care of some other; for doubtless many would have received such proposals with transport. She was pleased to find some traits of virtue in a character which resentment had for some time placed in an unfavourable light; and being accustomed to behold every circumstance with an eye of candour, she began to hope, at least, that the Marchese was become a convert.

Weary and irresolute, she retired to her apartment; but to sleep she found was impossible. Enrîco lay in a small bed by the side of her's; his slumbers were undisturbed, though a smile occasionally played upon his cherub lip. Julie, with all the fondness of parental affection, stood and gazed anxiously upon him as he slept. A tear fell upon her cheek when she reflected how soon the serenity of that angel countenance might be disturbed—at some future time what might be his sufferings! A thousand mournful presages now arose in her mind; and willing to divert her thoughts from so painful a subject, she walked pensively towards the window.

It was a calm and serene night; the moon slept upon the brow of the hill, and the whole face of nature wore an appearance of gentleness and tranquillity. She thought of the days of childhood, when she used to ramble with her father in the stillness of evening, to hear the song of the nightingale. What vicissitudes had she known since then! Could her parents have foreseen her misfortunes, what would have been their anguish; and what was now their situation! Her imagination then wandered to distant worlds; she raised her eyes towards the stars of heaven; their number, the immensity of their distance, excited her adoration and wonder! "Possibly the spirits of the departed," cried she, "may inhabit those glorious luminaries! How enviable is their situation; now how far are they placed beyond the reach of misfortune; their griefs, their inquietudes are now no more!" Full of these reflections she retired to her bed; but it was long before she forgot in sleep the strange occurrences of the day.

In the morning she arose early, and again perused the Marchese's letter. He had mentioned nothing of the melancholy story which Agatha had imperfectly related, nor of the large estates he had succeeded to in consequence of it. But this being an event in which she was not immediately concerned, any information on this subject might be deemed unnecessary.

As soon as the nurse and child arose, Madame de Rubine again took the infant into her arms, whose complexional delicacy and beauty equally attracted her admiration and astonishment. Whilst she continued to gaze upon its sweet innocent countenance, it appeared conscious of her attention; the soft sentiment of pity was already ripening into affection, and she perceived, if she parted with it, it would be with reluctance. She considered likewise it would be a companion for Enrîco, and that much domestic comfort might be reasonably expected from this lovely object of her compassion, in the stillness of uninterrupted retirement, particularly during the time of her separation from Enrîco; which, however painful the reflection was, she was convinced in the present state of affairs indispensibly requisite, as he must endeavour, by every necessary exertion, to secure promotion and independence in that department, which would eventually prove the least repugnant to his feelings and inclinations. These suggestions determined her to accept the proposals made to her by the Marchese; and, having acquainted Agatha with her intention, she addressed a few lines to him in return, in which she expressed her astonishment at this singular and unexpected adventure; at the same time assuring him that, having consented to take the child under her care, she was resolved to fulfil, in every respect, the part of a parent; that he might also depend upon her secrecy in the affair, and as he had offered her an asylum, which nothing but the welfare of the children could have induced her to accept, she must desire that he would never attempt to visit them in their retirement, as she should consider an interview of that kind as highly improper.

Agatha, being impatient to return from her embassy, besought permission to depart; which being granted, the carriage that had conveyed her hither, and was left at a small inn near the cottage, was immediately ordered. She then took an affectionate leave of the infant; and, after many tender adieus and good wishes to Madame de Rubine, set forwards on her journey.

CHAP. II.

"Seldom he smiles, and smiles in such a sort,
As if he mock'd himself, and scorn'd his spirit,
That could be mov'd to smile at any thing."
SHAKESPEARE.

Nothing material happened at the cottage till near a fortnight after the departure of Agatha, when Paoli, her husband, and the distinguished favourite of the Marchese, came to conduct Julie and the children to their destined abode. He also brought a letter from his lord, in which he expressed his entire approbation of her conduct; assuring her, at the same time, that if the secret, with which she was partially entrusted, remained inviolable, she might depend upon his friendship and protection, and expect on his part the most scrupulous attention to her desire, concerning his not visiting the retreat he had chosen for her, which was a castle on a German estate, beautifully situated near the Rhine. He also informed her, that he had given orders for every necessary preparation to be made against her arrival; and that he intended to remit her a considerable sum quarterly, which would be more than sufficient to defray every expence; and requested, that she would acquaint him, at the return of Paoli, if any part of the arrangement, which he had formed for her establishment, should not be agreeable to her wishes. He also desired that, immediately on her arrival in Germany, she would name the infant, which name he left entirely to her decision; and as to her son, she might depend upon his honour to fulfil the promises already made.

When Madame de Rubine had perused this epistle, she questioned the steward respecting her new situation, and inquired whether any servants were sent thither by the Marchese, or whether he expected her to provide them.

Paoli assured her that every thing was in readiness for their reception; that two servants were already there, an elderly woman and a man, who had been some years in the service of his lord, at the castello St. Aubin, and who were either to remain or to return, as she thought proper. The appearance of Paoli did not prejudice his fair auditress much in his favour. His deportment was stern, harsh, and forbidding, and she thought in the character of his brow she read determined villany. He seemed to behold, with the most scrutinizing eye, her every look and action, forming in the whole of his behaviour a striking contrast with the tenderness and artless simplicity of his wife. She felt uneasy in his presence, and earnestly longed for the time of his dismission to arrive. The consequence he assumed, from the known partiality of the Marchese, bordered upon rudeness, and he frequently obtruded himself into her presence contrary to the rules of good breeding, which, however, he affected to understand. He seemed to possess an infinite deal of cunning, and to be every way formed for intrigue and dark design. Being unwilling to resent this want of address, she endeavoured, as much as possible, to divert her mind from the uneasiness his unpleasant society occasioned, by nursing her little charge, and listening to the childish simplicity of Enrîco.

The ensuing week was now fixed for their departure, and Madame de Rubine and Dorothèe were busily employed in making every necessary arrangement for their journey. The few household goods she possessed, which were of the simplest kind, were divided among the neighbouring poor, by whom she was tenderly beloved.

After a residence of near four years in this beautiful retreat, the amiable Julie found she could not bid it adieu without extreme reluctance. In these calm and peaceful shades she had taken refuge from the censure of a rash unfeeling world; and had in some degree regained a tranquillity and composure of mind, which she once believed it impossible ever to recover. She had endeavoured to reconcile herself to her misfortunes, and to check, as much as in her power, the natural sensibility of her disposition, which she was convinced was too acute to admit of lasting comfort.

She knew that true happiness was only to be found in the bosom of religion and virtue, and the warmth of her affection led her to indulge in that glow of religious enthusiasm, which elevates the soul beyond every earthly pursuit, and renders it susceptible of the most worthy impressions.

On the evening preceding their departure, she wandered once more along that beautiful valley she was now soon to quit for ever; and casting her eyes over the clear expanse of waters, heaved a sigh at the recollection that she might probably, in that situation, never behold it more.

To part from these scenes, to which she had been long inured, was like parting from a beloved friend, which, though only known in the moments of sorrow, were still dear to her.

The sun had long sunk beneath the horizon, yet she still continued her walk. It was now the gay season of the vintage, but the rural sports were over, the shepherd's pipe was silent, and nothing was heard from the mountains but the distant sound of the mournful sheep-bell, and at intervals the rustling of the leaves, that faintly sighed in the evening gale.

Every object on which she gazed, wore that soft and tender melancholy so congenial to her feelings, and impelled her with an irresistible charm to linger in her favourite walks. The large plane-tree, which had so often afforded her shelter, the bank on which she used to sit selecting flowers for the playful Enrîco, were objects of regret; and it was not till the shades of night were perceptibly stealing upon the meek grey of the twilight, that she recollected the impropriety of wandering so far from her cottage alone, and at so late an hour. The danger to which this imprudent conduct had exposed her, precipitated her steps, and she was surprised on finding she had strayed so much far-ther from her little retreat, than she had at first imagined. As she advanced, it became so much darker that she was irresolute whether to proceed, or to call at one of the huts of the peasants to procure a guide; but recollecting that there were several others on the road leading to her home, she ventured to continue on her way.

On arriving at the side of the wood, near to which the cottage was situated, the moon, bursting from a cloud in its meridian splendour, partly dissipated her fears; and the melodious song of the nightingale, who was concealed in the inmost recesses of the wood, again arrested her steps. As she listened, the strain swelled still louder, and more plaintive; and she thought there was a pathos in the note she never remembered to have heard before. It seemed the language of complaint, and the frame of mind she was then in heightened the tender sensation of pity that the lay inspired.

Sitting down on a bench, which she had formed under the shade of a chesnut, she took out her pencil, and wrote the fol-lowing lines, which have certainly but little poetical merit, yet sufficiently evince that her griefs, though softened by time and the comforts of religion, had made an impression too great ever to be perfectly erased.

SONNET
TO THE NIGHTINGALE.

Hail, chantress sweet, who lov'st in woodlands drear,
 And shades unseen beneath the pale moon's ray,
To pour thy sorrows in eve's listening ear,
 And charm the nightly wanderer's lonely way;
Say, is it love that wakes the melting song?
 Or pity's tender throe, or wan despair?
If such thy woes, ah! yet the strain prolong,
 Still let thy wild notes float upon the air;
Yet spring's next visit shall, sweet bird, restore
 Those ravag'd joys that wake the thrilling lay,
Sad mem'ry's open'd wounds shall bleed no more,
 And happier love adorn the future day:
But not on me can spring one charm bestow,
Or make this pensive breast with her wild raptures glow.

Madame de Rubine had been absent on her evening walk so much longer than usual, that Dorothèe, beginning to be alarmed, was going in search of her; but was agreeably surprised on seeing her safely seated under her favourite tree. Having again reminded her of the lateness of the hour, which she had recently ceased to recollect, she thanked the affectionate girl for her attention, and returned to the cottage.

After a night spent in broken slumbers she arose, and every thing being in readiness for their journey, and Paoli impatiently waiting with the mules, they prepared to depart.

At first she was much alarmed at the necessity of the children travelling without a carriage; but the steep and craggy mountains they had to ascend rendered that mode of conveyance impossible. The mule on which Dorothèe and the infant were seated, was led by a peasant; Julie guided her own, and poor Enrîco was reluctantly left to the care of Paoli.

Having slowly descended the hill, on which the cottage was situated, they travelled along the beautiful and picturesque borders of the lake, and without any material occurrence, arrived at Lausanne, where the party was compelled to stop for a few days, being fatigued with the ruggedness of the road, and the unpleasant motion of the animals destined to convey them to their new abode.

After this salutary revival, they recommenced their journey along the finely cultivated mountains between Lausanne and Vevay. The scenery of this country, which perhaps is scarcely to be equalled, the mildness of the season, and the wild harmony of the birds that inhabited the branches of the pines, withdrew the attention of Madame de Rubine from the unpleasant conversation of Paoli, which was gloomy, morose, and artful.

Chagrined at his behaviour, she avoided mentioning any thing relative to the Marchese, and interrogated him as little as possible as to their future residence.

Dorothèe and Enrîco were less disposed to silence; they saw much in the novelty of the objects presented to them to attract their admiration, and expressed it with all the simplicity of youth and nature.

In the evening they arrived at a small post-house on the road, which was merely a cottage, though from its casual situation it had acquired some importance. As soon as the host appeared, Paoli inquired of him whether he could accommodate a party of travellers and mules with lodgings for the night. The good man seemed doubtful, and, after some minutes' conversation with his wife, informed them, that they had but two beds fit for the reception of strangers, and that one was already in use.

"This is unfortunate, indeed," cried Julie, perplexed at this unexpected disaster, "as it is impossible to proceed any further to-night with two children, and one an infant."

"I am heartily sorry," replied the host, with much apparent concern; "but what can be done in the affair? There is a gentleman in the best bed, who is so ill that my heart has ached for him ever since he has been here; and as to his daughter, poor young creature! she has taken no rest night or day since their arrival; and if he dies, which will probably be the case, she will certainly die with him!"

"It is no matter who is ill," interrupted Paoli, haughtily, "we have no leisure to hear affecting stories; if we cannot procure beds here, we must go on."

"For heaven's sake," cried Julie, "do, if possible, contrive somewhere for the children to sleep; as to Dorothèe and myself, we will submit to any thing if you will endeavour to accommodate them."

The host, pleased with the gentle manners of Madame de Rubine, which derived no inconsiderable advantage from being contrasted with the callous moroseness of the steward, assured her, that he and his wife would sit up themselves rather than they should suffer such an inconvenience; and if she would accept of their bed, which was indeed a very common one, in addition to that reserved for the use of their guests, it would give him pleasure to have it in his power to oblige them.

This proposal Paoli would willingly have accepted; but Julie's delicacy objected to making this temporary disarrangement, observing that a night's rest was too valuable to those who were condemned to arduous employment, to be sacrificed to the service of strangers.

Her arguments were, however, powerfully overruled by the host, who did not fail to convince her, that his wife and himself were better able to sustain the loss of a night's repose than they who had undergone the fatigue of a long and tedious journey.

After a little gentle reluctance, which the countenance of Paoli sternly reproved, she ventured to dismount, and was conducted into a small but decent room, enlightened with a blazed fire, which the hostess had just kindled for their reception, made of the dried stalks of the vine.

The appearance of neatness and cheerfulness, which reigned throughout this humble dwelling, animated the drooping spirits of Madame de Rubine, who was now relieved from apprehension respecting the children, for whom she experienced the most tender concern and solicitude.

Paoli himself seemed to lose something of his natural gloom; he even condescended to converse with the landlord on the manners of the country, its verdure, and of the mode of cultivating the mountains.

The hostess now appeared; who, spreading a clean coarse cloth upon the table, assured her guests, that had she known of their arrival, she would have prepared them a more comfortable meal. Their daughter, a pretty looking girl, apparently about eighteen, then entered with a small number of boiled eggs, some bread, chiefly composed of rye, and the vin du cotè, which was all the house afforded.

The bloom of Madelina, which was the name of the host's daughter, could not fail to attract the attention of our travellers. She was not tall, but elegantly shaped; her eyes possessed all the vivacity and fire which is chiefly ascribed to the Gallic brunette, mingled with a certain expression of softness and sensibility, which added much to her native loveliness. Her fine fair hair, which was remarkably luxuriant, fell in curls about her neck, and shaded a forehead of the finest proportion, which was simply ornamented with a neat straw hat and black ribbons; the mode of dress which prevails, without individual exception, among the mountain nymphs of Switzerland.

As soon as Dorothèe had conveyed her young charges to bed, Julie questioned the landlady about the gentleman her husband had mentioned, in terms so replete with compassion, being desirous of knowing whether he was indeed so ill as he had been represented, and if he had received any assistance from medicine.

"Alas! Madame," replied the hostess, "he seems to care for no advice but that of his ghostly confessor; and as to Mademoiselle, his daughter, she has scarcely partaken of any refreshment since she has been here, and weeps continually. There is none but herself to attend upon her father; and though I have frequently offered my assistance, she has seldom accepted the proposal."

"What a comfortless situation!" cried Madame de Rubine, much affected by the landlady's simple eloquence. "Ill from home, and without assistance, a young woman too, his only attendant! Can you not inform me from whence they came, and whither they are going, and is it not possible we may be of service to them? The unfortunate have an irresistible claim on our protection, and may we not obey the impulses of inclination when they are consistent with duty?"

The hostess replied, "that she knew nothing more of them than that their names were La Roque; that they arrived at the inn about four days ago, since which time the poor gentleman had been so ill, that, though his disorder was somewhat abated, his recovery was still very doubtful. That his daughter seldom quitted his apartment, except it was to prepare something of refreshment for her father, and seemed herself to be sinking under the calamity!"

"This is very singular," cried Madame de Rubine, "that a gentleman, and an invalid, should travel into a distant country attended only by his daughter! There must be something in this circumstance of a very peculiar nature; I wish it was possible to know more of it. Do commend me to the lady, and tell her, though a stranger, I feel interested in her distresses, and should be happy to have it in my power to alleviate them. Surely ceremony in an affair of this nature may be dispensed with."

"I will go to her instantly," returned the hostess, "poor young lady! I am sure so kind a message will comfort her. But would it not be better, Madame, if you was to take a night's rest before you visit them? You seem weary, and such a scene will, I fear, be too much for you."

"We must not selfishly consider our own ease," replied Julie, "when with a little exertion we may render ourselves useful to others; besides, I have heard too much already to be able to sleep, and, as we are travelling in haste, we must pursue our journey to-morrow at an early hour."

Whilst this conversation passed concerning the unfortunate La Roque, Paoli was silent; but his looks sufficiently expressed his disapprobation of her conduct. The luxury of doing good was a luxury unknown to him. Totally devoid of benevolence himself, he did not believe it really existed in the heart of another; and whilst Madame de Rubine was indulging the fond and not delusive hope, that she might soften with her tenderness the pang of misfortune, he was revolving in his mind what secret purpose of her's this was to answer, and reflecting whether it was not possible that treachery might not be concealed under the veil of humanity. From the infamy of his own conduct he formed his opinion of others; and when he could not make the intentions and actions of the greater part of the world wear a colour dark as his own, he believed himself outdone in cunning, and gave them credit for a superior degree of duplicity.

In a few minutes the hostess returned with the warmest acknowledgments of gratitude from the gentleman and his daughter, with an earnest desire of thanking her personally for her attention. "Monsieur," added she, "has just awaked from a fine refreshing sleep, and seems better; if you will permit me, I will shew you the room."

She then conducted Julie up stairs, and having led her into the interior of the apartment, introduced her as the kind stranger, and withdrew.

The young lady, who, notwithstanding the paleness of her looks, and the disorder of her dress, appeared extremely lovely, stepped forward to receive her, closing at the same time her missal, having been recently engaged in devotion, which she replaced by a small image of the Virgin, that adorned one of the angles.

As her fair visiter began to unfold the reasons that had actuated her to this singular mode of procedure, she endeavoured to express the high sense she had of the obligation; but an impulse of gratitude stifled her utterance, and the words she would have articulated, died upon her lips. She then gently undrew the curtain, and having removed a stool, on which was placed a lamp and a crucifix, led her to the side of the bed.

As she advanced, the invalid, attempting to raise himself, held out his hand to receive her; then gazing upon one of the most affecting countenances he had ever seen with mingled surprise and admiration, "May I ask, Madame," cried he, "to whom I am indebted for this unexampled benevolence, and what angel has directed you to sooth with your kindness the most forlorn and unhappy of men?"

Julie having returned this compliment to her sensibility with her usual grace, apologized for the liberty she had taken; to which she assured him she was not instigated by a principle of idle curiosity, but from having cherished the idea that she might possibly have it in her power to alleviate his sufferings. She had been informed, she added, that he had at present no medical assistance; and as business of a peculiar nature rendered it necessary for her to quit the post-house early on the following day, she intended, with his permission, to send a physician to attend him, from the nearest town.

"You are too, too good, Madame," cried the amiable young

stranger, speaking through her tears; "but my father, I fear, will never consent to it. I have urged the necessity of it without ceasing; yet he is deaf to my entreaties."

"Why, my child," interrupted La Roque, "should I endeavour to prolong a life only productive of evil? Have I not been an unnatural parent, a cruel husband? Yes," resumed he, fixing his hollow eyes upon a small picture, which was fastened round his neck with a black ribbon, "my Helena! my much injured Helena! I was thy murderer!" Then heaving a profound, convulsive sigh, he sunk again upon the pillow.

"Oh! my father," replied Mademoiselle, in a voice rendered tremulous by emotion, "how unjust, how cruel are these self-accusations! And why will you thus aggravate affliction by remorse? Reflect how conducive to health is serenity of mind, and for my sake, if not for your own, embrace the means of recovery: for though wretched at present from circumstances not in our power to prevent, let us look forwards with comfort and hope to better days."

Madame de Rubine, who, during these pathetic exclamations, had regarded Mademoiselle La Roque with a gaze of earnest inquiry, endeavoured, by the most forcible arguments she could summon to her aid, to reconcile him to the application of means to accelerate his recovery, not only for the sake of his child, who would feel so severely his loss, but from a principle of duty; assuring him, at the same time, that, if he absolutely rejected her proposal, she should depart with extreme reluctance.

Finding, from the expressive looks of the invalid, that what she had advanced was not totally disregarded, she ventured to ask, why they travelled without a servant? and requested permission to inquire in the village for a suitable person to attend them.

"Your generosity, Madame," returned La Roque, "is unbounded; and language can but feebly express the warmth of my feelings on this occasion. The servant who attended us from home was murdered by a party of banditti about nine leagues from this place, whilst we narrowly escaped with our lives! I was then ill, and the grief and apprehension this melancholy accident excited, increased my fever, which, I have some reason to hope, is now abating. Was your residence at the inn to be prolonged,

I might possibly be induced to venture upon a story long and mournful; but thus much I will unfold: My real name is not La Roque; we are taking refuge from the vilest, the most infamous of men—a wretch, who has been long resolutely determined to accomplish my destruction!"

"May I ask," cried Julie, with apparent astonishment, "who is this persecutor, and what are his intentions?"

"His intentions are," returned La Roque, "to the murder of a son to add that of a father; and was there a greater fiend than himself, I would address him by that name, it is the Marchese de Montferrat."

As he uttered these last words, Julie started, and turned pale. She had, however, presence of mind to conceal her emotion, and bade him proceed.

"It would detain you too long, Madame," replied La Roque, "and my spirits are unequal to the task; but should we ever meet again, you shall be thoroughly acquainted with the history of my misfortunes."

"That we should ever meet again is, I fear, too improbable to be depended upon," cried Madame de Rubine, hesitatingly; "yet I feel much interested in your narrative. May I ask where is your intended residence?"

"In one of the convents on the borders of Germany," returned Mademoiselle La Roque, "when my father's health will allow us to travel."

"Then it is not impossible, as I am myself going to reside in Germany, and may be fortunate enough to succeed in my inquiries."

"If then," cried the invalid, "you will so far honour me as to visit the convent, the name I mean to take is Father Francisco; and should my disorder prove fatal, my daughter will be there as sister Maria."

Mademoiselle La Roque, who was sitting by the side of the bed, attending earnestly to this discourse, wept as he reverted to the danger of his situation. The idea of parting was not become familiar to her, and covering her face with her handkerchief, she sobbed aloud.

Madame de Rubine, whose heart "was so finely tuned, and

harmonized by nature," that it vibrated at the slightest touch of human calamity, endeavoured to console her young friend, by an assurance that her fears were ill-founded respecting her father, who was visibly in a state of convalescence; signifying also her intention of sending a physician and a servant to attend him.

Having removed some slight objections that were offered by the invalid, in opposition to her benevolent proposal, she arose to depart; and taking the hand of Mademoiselle with the tenderness and familiarity of an old acquaintance, she informed her, that she would join in her prayers for the recovery of Monsieur La Roque, and would spare no effort to discover the convent to which they were retiring.

After many grateful adieus on the part of the strangers, his daughter following Julie out of the apartment, requested the favour of her name, that by mutual inquiries they might hasten a second meeting.

Not immediately prepared to reply, she hesitated, blushed, and was silent. The impropriety of mentioning a name she was so soon to disown, was too evident; to be absent from her thoughts, and the embarrassment she had already discovered, filled her with new confusion.

Yet aware of the necessity of framing a reply, she evaded the question, by informing her, that she would avail herself of every possible means of learning their place of abode, and would then take the earliest opportunity of acquainting her with every circumstance she was permitted to disclose.

Though harassed and fatigued with traversing the mountains, Julie's mind was too much discomposed by this strange unexpected adventure to allow her to hope for repose. The story she had heard was imperfect, yet the villany of the Marchese was evident; and she reflected with terror on the certainty that she had thrown herself upon the protection of a man capable of the most deliberate cruelty. She wished that her curiosity had either been gratified or unexcited; but was resolved to commence her inquiries immediately on her arrival in Germany. La Roque had mentioned their having fallen into the hands of banditti, who had murdered his servant, and that his daughter and himself had escaped with difficulty: consequently they must have been plundered by these lawless wretches, and probably had nothing left to defray their expences, which accounted in some measure for his having no person to attend upon him.

With a sensation of exalted pleasure, peculiar to the noble and disinterested mind, she recollected she was empowered to assist them; but this was an affair that required to be conducted with the greatest delicacy imaginable, and she was for some time irresolute in what manner to proceed. At last, however, she thought of an expedient which would prevent every unpleasant consequence that might otherwise arise from her benevolent intention. She had lately received fifty ducats, the quarterly portion of her income; which, on mature deliberation, she determined to inclose in a paper, and leave to be delivered by the hostess after her departure from the inn.

Then advancing slowly towards the stairs, she paused for a moment to listen if Paoli was yet retired. Finding all was silent, and remembering the lateness of the hour, and that he was probably in bed, she ventured to proceed towards the kitchen, where she discovered the host, his wife, and Dorothèe, sitting by a cheerful fire. Having asked for a pen and ink, which was instantly procured, she returned to her room, and framing an elegant apology, in which she folded up the ducats, gave it to the landlady, with orders to deliver it to Mademoiselle immediately on her quitting the inn.

In the morning she arose early, and having satisfied the kind host for his civility, put another piece of gold into the hands of his wife, desiring her to provide a servant to attend upon La Roque and his amiable daughter, and then hastened to join the rest of the party, who had already mounted their mules.

After they had each taken leave of the hospitable cottagers, they pursued their journey towards the Castle of Elfinbach, which was the name of the mansion selected for them by the Marchese de Montferrat.

CHAP. III.

"Yes, let the rich deride, the proud disdain,
These simple blessings of the lowly train;
To me more dear, congenial to my heart,
One native charm than all the gloss of art:
Spontaneous joys, where nature has its play,
The soul adopts, and owns its first-born sway;
Lightly they frolic o'er the vacant mind,
Unenvied, unmolested, unconfin'd."

GOLDSMITH.

As they advanced, the most picturesque objects of nature were presented to their view; mountains crowned with the oak, the beech, and the pine, and the most beautiful woods, groves, and lakes, interspersed with vineyards and fertile fields! To behold such a combination of beauties rivalling each other in grace, yet improving by contrast the effect of the whole, without experiencing the most pleasurable emotions, would have been scarcely possible; even Paoli appeared not to be entirely insensible of the power of sylvan attraction, for his features lost much of their accustomed austerity.

He praised the rich verdure of the landscape, listened with apparent satisfaction to the responses of the birds, which were concealed in the pine-forests, and was for the moment, or affected to be, pleased. He inquired about the strangers at the inn, what were their names, and whither they were going; and whether the melancholy account of the invalid, as delivered by the host, had not been exaggerated.

Julie in this instance mistook curiosity for humanity; from the uncontaminated purity of her own heart she formed the most liberal opinion of others, and was not a little gratified on finding in the character of Paoli, at least one trait that bore the semblance of a virtue.

But when he found that some of his interrogatories were evaded, and others answered undecisively, the look of gentleness which he had assumed, vanished, and his brow wore the cloud of disappointment and of anger.

The conversation, which this transient good-humour had animated, now sunk into silence. Madame de Rubine, who found no difficulty in ascertaining the cause, lamented that she had been deceived, though she had the internal satisfaction of knowing that it was candour, not childish credulity, that had thus momentarily obscured her better judgment.

Her spirits were, however, both soothed and invigorated by the glowing landscape before her; and she felt refreshed by the soft salute of the zephyr that wafted the perfume of the flowers which adorned the vallies.

The peasant girls were busily employed in carrying baskets of grapes from the vineyards; the chamoix, who during the extreme heat of the day had secluded themselves in the rocky glens of the precipices, or in the darkest recesses of the woods, were now skipping about them; while the loud laugh, the jest, and the song, accompanied their labours, and sometimes the wild harmony of the shepherd's pipe, attuned to the notes of the Kuhreihen*, echoed from the mountains that simple fascinating air, which is indiscriminately used by the inhabitants of the Alps, when they drive their cattle from the vallies to the cultivated tops of the eminences. As the evening advanced, the rural dance, beneath the deep shade of the trees, began, and the voices of merriment and delight were every-where heard. Those who were too ancient to join themselves in the sports, were pleased spectators of those juvenile delights, which many of them had, perhaps, reluctantly resigned, who appeared to catch something of the spirit of youth as they contemplated the happy groups before them. Uncorrupted simplicity was never more forcibly expressed, nor was ever the charm of content more successfully delineated; for the peasantry of these beautiful regions seemed to have forgotten all the cares and anxieties inseparable from humanity, in the unrestrained enjoyment of mirth and festivity.

Julie sighed as she surveyed these innocent pastimes, but it was a sigh not of envy, but regret. She recalled to her recollec-

* The herdsman's song.

tion days long past, which memory had too faithfully treasured among her stores, when she also was gay, sportive, and animated as those who were now blissfully partaking of pastoral amusement. The road being less rugged than on the preceding day, and the mountains they had to ascend less rocky, they were enabled to proceed farther than they at first intended, and in the evening arrived at a small hotel, or post-house, finely situated near the much-admired Lake of Murat, which is so justly celebrated for its crystal surface.—Here they remained during the night, and in the morning continued leisurely on their way; Paoli still silent, Madame de Rubine thoughtful, and Dorothèe and Enrîco gay and talkative.

After having previously passed through a number of those rich and beautiful fir-woods, for which this country is deservedly eminent, the travellers arrived at the town of Bern, where it was deemed necessary for them to remain resident at least for a few days, in order to recruit their strength and spirits, in which time they had an opportunity of surveying that masterpiece of Gothic architecture, the cathedral, which, for taste and greatness of design, is scarcely to be equalled in Switzerland, and of beholding those beautiful walks that run along its side, commanding, from their elevated situation, one of the most finished prospects in the world. The large number of handsome fountains too, which were variously disposed throughout the principal streets, came in for their share of admiration, as they united beauty with convenience, and gave an air of coolness and cleanliness to the appearance of the whole.

Julie recollecting that she was to take another name immediately on her arrival in Germany, after much revolving in her mind, fixed upon Chamont, and bestowed upon the infant that of Laurette. She also engaged the most skilful physician to attend La Roque; and several days having elapsed during their continuance at Bern, they proceeded on their journey.

CHAP. IV.

"High o'er the pines that, with their darkening shade,
 Surround yon craggy bank, the castle rears
 Its crumbling turrets; still its tow'ring head,
 A warlike mien, a sullen grandeur wears."

MICKLE.

It was at a late hour when the party arrived at their destined abode, and the shades of evening had conspired, with the solitude of its situation, to give an air of gloomy magnificence to the scene.

The castle, which was seated upon an eminence, about a quarter of a league from the bed of the river, seemed to have been separated by nature from the habitable world by deep and impenetrable woods. Two of the towers, which were all that remained entire, were half secreted in a forest; the others, which were mouldering into ruins, opened into a narrow, uncultivated plain, terminating in a rocky declivity, at the bottom of which flowed the Rhine, wide, deep, and silent.

Paoli, having dismounted, conveyed them through the principal portal to the door of the great hall; when heaving a massy knocker, which returned a deep-toned hollow sound, he waited for some time in visible impatience, and no one approaching, again repeated the alarm. In a few moments, the bolts being undrawn with a suspicious caution, the heavy doors were unfolded by an aged domestic, who came forwards to welcome them, and to lead them into the interior of the mansion.

They were then conducted through a spacious hall into a room newly fitted up for their reception, which seemed, from the many vestiges of ancient grandeur which remained, to have been formerly the grand saloon of the castle.

The antique furniture, consisting of many articles long fallen into disuse, and the dark wainscot composed of larch-wood, which was overhung with a number of grotesque figures, aided the gloom of its appearance, and might have awakened unpleasant sensations, had not the effect been counteracted by the cheerful blaze of a fire, which animated the sinking spirits of the travellers till the hour that called them to repose.

Julie, having enquired if necessary accommodations were made for the children, which was answered in the affirmative, partook of some refreshment; and, after lingering for a few minutes to examine the figures upon the walls, expressed a wish to retire, and was conducted by Margaritte, the old female domestic, to her room.

As she passed along the hall, which was feebly enlightened with the expiring ray of a dim and solitary lamp, she shuddered involuntarily at the gloom of its appearance, and followed her guide in pensive silence. Having ascended the stairs, and passed through the corridor, into which opened several apartments, Margaritte informed her of the one designed for herself, and wishing her a good night, left her to repose.

Thoughtful and dejected, she retired to her bed. The desolate aspect of the mansion had already affected her spirits, and as the wind howled in hollow murmurs round the turret, in which her chamber was situated, and sometimes in hollow gusts agitated the decayed tapestry with which it was hung, she looked fearfully around, and shrunk with a superstitious dread entirely new to her. It seemed as if the dreary abode, to which she was consigned, had long been forsaken by humanity, and was now become the asylum of supernatural agents; but reproving herself for this momentary weakness, and turning her thoughts towards Laurette and Enrîco, her mind dwelt with something like comfort upon the future, and she sunk into a tranquil slumber.

The sun shone in full splendour when she awoke, and reminded her that she had slept past her usual hour. Hastily arising, she endeavoured to ring the bell, that she might inquire of Dorothèe how the children had rested; but from long neglect it seemed to have forgot its office, and it was some time before she succeeded.

In a few minutes her faithful servant attended with the infant and Enrîco; whilst the innocent smiles of the former, and prattling simplicity of the latter, contributed to chase away every melancholy impression which her new situation had occasioned.

Having pressed them to her bosom with maternal tenderness, she desired breakfast to be instantly prepared, and dressed herself in haste.

The day, which was chiefly devoted to domestic arrangements, passed with unusual rapidity. The attention of Madame de Rubine was now chiefly divided between her children, and the cares of her household, which two material concerns so entirely occupied her thoughts, that she did not revert so frequently as before to the primary cause of her inquietudes.

The family, which was stationary before their arrival, consisted of Margaritte, an old female servant, the same who had directed her to her apartment on the preceding night; Lisette, who was her gran-daughter, and Ambrose, a man who had been long resident in the family of the Marchese, to whom she was introduced by the name of Chamont.

The countenance of Paoli still wore the same forbidding expression; and though Julie found it necessary to consult with him on some subjects relative to her present establishment, she still retained an unconquerable aversion to his general conversation and deportment, which gave an air of reserve to her manners, that not escaping his penetration, excited an equal degree of distrust in his breast, which he endeavoured to smother in silence.

As it was necessary, both from the desire of the Marchese, and from the age of the child committed to her care, that the baptismal rites should be performed, a friar, from a neighbouring monastery, of the Carthusian order, was applied to, who, according to the usual ceremonies of the Romish church, gave her the name of Laurette.

When this was concluded, Julie, who had not yet examined the different apartments in the castle, wandered for some time in uninterrupted silence through a long extent of desolated chambers, some of which were hung with old arras, and others wainscotted with cedar and Spanish oak. The furniture, which seemed to be nearly coeval with the building, being formed of the most durable materials, had long resisted the attacks of time; but was now, with the damps and with age, falling fast into decay. She then proceeded through a gallery to a suite of rooms that communicated with the eastern turret, the last of which opened into the oriel.

Here she observed several portraits, which appeared to have been the workmanship of some of the best Italian masters. Two of them, which were apparently more modern than the rest, chiefly engaged her attention; though even these were so covered with dust, and so injured with the damps, as to have lost much of their former beauty.

The first was the figure of a young warrior, who was supposed to have been mortally wounded in an engagement. He was supported by two grey-haired veterans; an allegorical figure of Death approached with a dart, which Valour, accoutred as Mars, opposed with his shield.

The other was the figure of a female leaning upon a tomb; it possessed uncommon beauty and expression; the hands were clasped as if in prayer; the eyes, which were dark, were directed towards heaven with peculiar sweetness, and spoke, in a language the most eloquent, the extreme sensibility of the mind.

Having gazed for some time upon these pictures with silent admiration, she proceeded through a gallery which led to the western side of the structure; in which were also several spacious and forsaken apartments that received additional gloom from the evening twilight, and made her shrink with fearful apprehension. She wondered why the Marchese had placed her and the children in this comfortless abode; or, if this was indispensible, why he had not made it more habitable? It seemed as if he was uninterested in her happiness, and careless of her fate:—the words of La Roque returned forcibly upon her mind; he had pronounced him a murderer; she shuddered at the thought, and reproved herself for not prevailing upon Mademoiselle when she led her from the room, to give her the outlines of the story; though she entertained the hope that in a short time she should be able to discover their residence, and might then be informed of the whole.

Wrapped in silent meditation, she rambled for some time through the long winding passages, without being able to find the marble staircase which she had first ascended; but was relieved from this incertitude on reaching the corridor, which she descended in haste, leaving the greater part of the mansion to be explored at some future time.

Though an air of melancholy distinguished every object around, there was much of the sublime and the beautiful in the appearance of the castle, and also in the surrounding scenery. Julie, having again crossed the hall, proceeded towards the portico, being resolved to examine more minutely the awful grandeur of its external aspect, which she had never attempted before, having been engaged in the duties of her family the greater part of the day. Walking into the inner court, which was wild and grass-grown, she stopped to observe a figure, which haste and the darkness of the evening had prevented her from perceiving on her arrival. It was a column of the Corinthian order, on whose summit was erected an equestrian statue of black marble, representing a young hero in complete armour, which, on examination, she found was designed for the same as the portrait she had observed in the oriel. It seemed to aid the solemnity of the scene, and acquired additional character from the loneliness of its situation; surrounded by lofty walls, which were overgrown with wild weeds, and the deadly night-shade, whilst the thread moss encrusted the fragments of the fallen ramparts which lay scattered at the base of the pillar, it seemed to stand as if exulting in its strength, and triumphing amid the desolation and ruin it surveyed.

She now proceeded through a gate into the outer court, which was still more wild than the former one, leading to the principal portal. The grey mist of the twilight, which now deepened and reflected upon every object a dusky hue, made her fearful of venturing through the avenues at that lonely hour, and occasioned her to return again towards the castle. As she surveyed that lofty edifice, which seemed to shrink from observation in the deep recesses of the wood, her imagination dwelt with horror upon the miseries of war, which rendered necessary those impenetrable fortresses, those massy walls that spoke of murder and imprisonment, in which the proud possessor, wrapped in selfish security, listened to the cry of anguish and the groan of death with sullen apathy.

She was roused from these reflections by the appearance of

Paoli, who had just emerged from the wood, and with his arms folded upon his breast, in the attitude of musing, was crossing the inner court. As soon as the gloom permitted him to distinguish her, he started and retreated, as a person who, conscious of guilt, recedes from the eye of observation, lest his secret designs should be displayed; but, anxious to learn for whom the statue was designed, and the pictures she had seen in the oriel, she followed him into the hall, and interrogated him concerning them. He seemed, however, averse to gratifying her curiosity; but whether this proceeded from his ignorance of the subject, or his own uncommunicative disposition, he was too great a master of dissimulation for her to discover; but though he did not give her the information she immediately desired, he indulged her with a piece of intelligence of a more interesting nature, which was, that he intended to quit the mansion on the following day. This intimation was received with pleasure not only by Julie, but also by the rest of the family, who all acknowledged themselves weary of his unprepossessing deportment and manners. When the morning arrived, whilst Paoli was preparing to depart she wrote a few lines to the Marchese, to acquaint him, that, agreeable to his former request, she had named the infant; and from his not having signified any desire of fixing upon it himself, previous to her residence in the castle, she had ventured to give it that of Laurette. She concluded this concise epistle with informing him, that she considered herself as strictly bound to fulfil the promises already made, and depended upon his honour for a future provision for Enrîco. This being folded up, and delivered to the steward, he repeated his formal adieus, and set forwards towards Italy. Julie, whose time was now uniformly devoted to the service of her little favourites, and other laudable occupations, became gradually reconciled to her new situation; and habit so powerfully prevailed, as to render scenes, which were at first beheld with an unconquerable emotion of terror, interesting and even charming. She frequently rambled in the woods, which were beautiful and wild, and sometimes on the banks of the Rhine; where, taking her pencil or her lute, she would oftentimes linger till the close of the day, till the sun having sunk beneath the horizon, was lost beyond the distant hills.

A long acquaintance with sorrow had given strength and elasticity to her mind. She had acquired by effort an advantage which Nature, though in other respects liberal, had withheld; an advantage which enabled her at once to endure misfortune, and to triumph over it.—She knew that a state of uninterrupted happiness was never intended to be the lot of mortality, and that to suffer with uniform fortitude was true dignity. This lesson, which her mother had inculcated in youth, she had cherished in maturity. The meek and unaffected piety of that excellent parent was never absent from her thoughts, and she exerted her most strenuous endeavours to emulate her virtues.

Time, though it had thrown a veil over the acute sorrow which her loss had excited, had awakened a more tender, if a less melancholy sensation, when her imagination reverted with more than filial affection to the past; and as in rural scenes the mind is more abstracted from worldly pursuits, it is also more susceptible of amiable impressions. This directed her to the recollection of every estimable precept delivered by her deceased and much-lamented parent, which had been hitherto the established rule of her conduct.

As no material incident occurred at the castle of Elfinbach for a considerable time after the arrival of the family, it may here be proper to introduce the story of Julie de Rubine, that the reader may be acquainted with the nature of these misfortunes which had occasioned her to embrace, in early youth, a life of almost total seclusion.

CHAP. V.

"Canst thou not minister to minds diseas'd,
Pluck from the memory a rooted sorrow,
Raze out the written troubles of the brain,
And with some sweet oblivious antidote,
Cleanse the foul bosom of that perilous stuff
That weighs upon the heart?"

                                    SHAKESPEARE.

Julie de Rubine was descended from an ancient and illustrious family, long resident in the southern part of France. Her father's name was Gerard, who was the only son of St. Herbert de Rubine. He had entered at an early period of life into the service of his country, and signalized himself in the victorious battles of Henry the Third; but not receiving from this Monarch those honours which he considered as the just reward of his valour, he abandoned the Court and the sword together, and retired, with an amiable wife and his only daughter, to a chateau on a small paternal estate in the province of Artois.

Nothing could be more congenial to the disposition of Madame de Rubine than the sequestered situation of this beautiful retreat. The chateau was of Gothic construction, and seemed to have withstood the attacks of ages; but the northern side of the edifice was now visibly falling to decay, and St. Gerard's mind was entirely occupied by endeavouring to make this part of the structure habitable, without destroying that appearance of ancient simplicity which formed its most striking beauty; but when this was completed, and the ardour of pursuit was over, he again experienced all that chagrin and restless dissatisfaction, which is too often the consequence of disappointed ambition.

This change Madame de Rubine beheld with extreme regret, and attempted to remove the cause with all the tenderness of a refined and inviolable affection, hoping, by the example of her own exemplary piety, she might be enabled to elevate his mind above the trifling consideration of worldly dignities; but she knew not all the distresses of the unfortunate Gerard. Previous to his seclusion from the gay circles of life he had contracted debts, that the narrowness of his annual income, which he had long vainly hoped to increase, rendered impossible to discharge; and the solicitude he felt in behalf of his amiable wife, had imprudently confined the secret to his own bosom.

He had no sooner quitted Paris than he received a letter from his principal creditor, demanding the immediate payment of a large sum. This event determined him to write to Madame Laronne, his only sister, who had been some years a widow, and was left in affluent circumstances, to acquaint her with the embarrassed situation of his affairs, and also to request the loan of a sum sufficient to discharge the debt.

But here his too sanguine expectations were again deceived. Madame Laronne assured him, that had it been possible, nothing would have contributed more to her happiness than to have given him a proof of her regard by affording pecuniary assistance; but the stile of elegance, to which she had been accustomed, was now become necessary to her happiness; and her expences were lately so considerably increased, that she was sorry to add she must endure the painful sensation which refusing his request would inevitably excite.

Grief and resentment, the natural consequence of unexpected ingratitude, now agitated the mind of the astonished Gerard. He knew that Madame Laronne's rank in life, and also her ambition, required the ostentatious display of wealth and grandeur; but he was also convinced that, without materially injuring herself, she had it sufficiently in her power immediately to relieve his necessities. When the mingled emotions of indignation and anguish had, in some measure, subsided, he seemed to have lost all his energy of soul; nothing bestowed even a transitory pleasure, and he sunk into the most alarming melancholy! Not even the conversation of Madame de Rubine, nor the undeviating gentleness of her manners, could for a moment withdraw his thoughts from the painful contemplation of his real and imaginary distresses. That smile of affection, and that look of sentiment, which once cherished her vivacity, and rewarded her tenderness, was now lost in the gloom of disappointment, disgust, and anguish.

Julie, having now entered upon her thirteenth year, was remarkably tall of her age, and elegant in her person. Her disposition was mild, frank, and benevolent; and she united, with admirable discretion, the unadorned graces of youth, with the uniform sedateness of maturer years. In obedience to the will of her father she had learned to play upon the lute, and her voice, which was exquisitely sweet, was perfectly adapted to the soft and plaintive tones of that charming instrument. During the few first months of their residence at the chateau, St. Gerard frequently rambled with her by moon-light through the beautiful woods, and sometimes over the fine range of hills which appeared so picturesque from the chateau; where he would desire her to play one of his favourite airs, selected from the sonnets of Ariosto, or expressing the melting sorrows of Petrarch.

The look of settled despondency which was so strongly portrayed on the features of the unfortunate veteran, when his new situation no longer afforded amusement and variety, did not remain unobserved by his amiable daughter, who exerted herself unceasingly to remove it by the sprightliness of her wit, the melody of her voice, or the soft pathos of her lute; but his mind, enervated by sorrow, was no longer alive to the fine touches of harmony; and frequently, in the midst of one of his favourite songs, to which he had formerly listened with all the rapture of enthusiasm, he would start as from a dream, and hasten from the room as if agitated by the appearance of some frightful demon.

His constitution, which in the early part of his life had suffered much from the severity of military discipline, now became visibly impaired; the disorder of his mind daily increased; melancholy became habitual to him, and so rapid was the progress it made in undermining his health, that Madame de Rubine began to be seriously alarmed. Advice was immediately procured, and change of air prescribed; but not to quit the chateau was the unalterable determination of Gerard. A nervous fever was the consequence of this resolution, which in a short time terminated his existence.

This shock Madame de Rubine supported with that true

dignity of soul, which gave a peculiar grace and energy to every sentiment and action. She felt severely her loss, but she felt it with the resignation of a Christian; she mingled patience with sorrow, and was enabled, through the most pure and elevated piety, to triumph over the repeated attacks of calamity. But the lovely Julie possessed not at this early period of life that exalted strength of mind, which she admired, without being able to imitate, in the character of her mother. That exquisite sensibility, which glowed upon her cheek, and spoke, in the fine language of her eyes, the tenderness of a father, she had cherished as a grace, without reflecting that, if indulged, it would degenerate into weakness, and cease to be a virtue.

Soon after the remains of St. Gerard were deposited in the chapel of the chateau, Madame de Rubine, whose health was much injured by her unceasing attention to her husband, was advised by the physician who attended her, to try the effect of a softer climate.

About this time she received a consolatory letter from Madame Laronne, with a pressing invitation to visit her at her seat near Turin; which proposal would have been accepted with gratitude, had not the coldness, bordering upon contempt, which marked her behaviour towards her brother, lessened her in the estimation of his affectionate widow. For the sake of Julie, however, she was unwilling to refuse this offered kindness; she considered that her illness might possibly prove fatal, and in that case it would be right to secure a friend for her child, though she ardently wished that friend had been any other than Madame Laronne.

Every thing was now properly arranged for the intended journey, and the time fixed for their departure, when Madame de Rubine was attacked by a malignant disorder, which threatened a speedy dissolution. It was her mind only that was masculine; for her frame being excessively slight, and delicately formed, was incapable of sustaining unusual fatigue.

Julie, who had not yet recovered from the shock occasioned by the death of her father, now felt her former loss was small, when compared with what she should experience in being parted from her beloved mother; and when she reflected upon the probability of this event, the dreadful presentiment worked so powerfully upon her feelings, as almost to deprive her of reason.

Madame de Rubine beheld the anguish of her daughter with extreme concern, which was augmented by the mournful idea of a separation, as the dangerous symptoms of her disease hourly increased; this she believed was inevitable, and being fully apprized of her situation, with that calm dignity which accompanied every action of her life, she desired that a friar from a neighbouring monastery, who was her confessor, might attend with the consecrated wafer, and read the service for the dying.

This customary ceremony being over, and the extreme unction administered, she appeared for some moments unusually agitated; but after a second interview with the monk, became more serene and tranquil. Being firmly persuaded that the awful hour was approaching that was to remove her from, and dissolve all her earthly connexions, she requested that Julie might be instantly called.

Pale and trembling, she entered the apartment, leaning upon the arm of a servant, and without attending to the common forms by addressing the holy visiter, who had just risen from a small altar erected near the window, threw herself by the side of the bed, and fixing her languid eyes upon the faded, yet interesting, countenance of her mother, burst into a flood of tears!

The venerable friar regarding her with an aspect on which pity and affection were strikingly depicted, endeavoured to console her with the comforts of religion, by reminding her of the gracious promises of protection which the doctrines of Christianity afforded, in a stile replete with simple and unaffected eloquence; but finding that her feelings were too acute to admit of premature consolation, with an air of tenderness mingled with sorrow, he withdrew.

Madame de Rubine, who beheld these emotions of severe distress with inexpressible concern, besought her to receive, and consider with gratitude, the salutary and valuable advice of the holy father.

"Remember, my child," added she, with the look and accents of a departing saint, "that this separation, though to us mournful and afflictive, is the will of the Most High God, and that we

ought to submit without a murmur to his unerring Providence!
Let us then, instead of arrogating to ourselves the right of
disputing his mercy and equity, prove, by the most implicit
obedience to his divine decrees, that we are not unworthy to be
called his servants; and give me reason to believe, my Julie, that
the lessons of fortitude, which I have so frequently given you,
have not been delivered in vain.

"I leave you, my darling alone and, almost unfriended, in a
world in which you will find much occasion for the exercise
of this estimable virtue. The only relation you will have left is
Madame Laronne; and though for many reasons she is not the
person I should have selected from all others as the guardian of
my child, yet as she is the only surviving sister of your father,
it cannot easily be dispensed with. Let me then endeavour,
if possible by timely advice, to prevent the evils which might
otherwise ensue from the precepts and example of one who may
probably have some virtues, but who, I fear, has many follies.
I must now, my love, enter upon a subject, that appears at this
crisis more than usually important: I must demand from you,
my Julie, before I leave you for ever, a solemn promise, upon the
performance of which depends both your temporal and eternal
welfare."

Here the meek sufferer paused, as if unable to proceed, whilst
her daughter, with an assumed resignation, that shaded but
imperfectly the emotions of her soul, assured her, that whatever
was the nature of the request, she was prepared to comply with
it, and would instantly ratify her resolve with the most solemn
vow.

"You are not, my dear, sufficiently aware," resumed Madame
de Rubine, "of the little respect that is paid to the religious, and
even the moral, duties of life, amid the dissipation and gaiety of
the world. Madame Laronne is a woman of rank, and undoubtedly, from a motive of kindness, but, I fear, a mistaken one, will
introduce you into the most brilliant and fashionable circles.
She will also desire, in the common acceptation of the term, to
see you advantageously married; but, though desirous of leading
you to happiness, she may unfortunately mistake the way. In her
choice of a husband for you, religion, I am convinced, will be

only a secondary consideration, and a disagreement of sentiment in this important affair has been the occasion of innumerable evils. Promise me then, my Julie, that whatever arguments may be employed to dissuade you from your purpose, never to unite yourself to a man, however estimable in point of morals, and however splendid in situation, who does not exactly agree with you in all the articles of the Catholic Faith. Say then, my child, that whatever trials and temporal distresses this resolution may involve you in, that nothing shall prevail upon you to marry a Protestant."

Julie, who equally revered with her mother the doctrines of the Church of Rome, and whose zeal in the cause of her persuasion was not less animated, readily acquiesced in the proposal; and, having assured her dying parent in a manner the most solemn and impressive, that she should consider this promise as sacred and inviolable, an exquisite expression of joy irradiated for a moment the features of Madame de Rubine, who, having uttered a few words as in prayer, sunk upon the pillow, and her spirits being greatly exhausted, fell into a slumber, from which she awoke unrefreshed, and in a few hours breathed her last!

Immediately on the decease of Madame de Rubine, the friar, who had attended her as confessor, came with a consolatory message and invitation to Julie from the prioress of an adjacent convent; but this nothing could prevail upon her to accept till the funeral rites were over, and she had paid every possible respect to the memory of her lamented relative.

In a few days the body of the deceased was entombed by the side of St. Gerard, in the chapel of the chateau, which was accompanied to the place of interment by a few of the domestics, and Julie, who attended as chief mourner.

Mindful of the lesson of resignation that her mother had so recently delivered, she attempted to appear tranquil; but the effort was ineffectual, and the service, which was pronounced with peculiar solemnity, was frequently interrupted with her convulsive sobs.

The next day, at the request of Father Austin, the confessor, she was conducted to the convent of St. Catherine, and introduced to the superior of the order, who received her with much apparent tenderness and concern, which Julie attempted to repay with the modest effusions of her gratitude.

The prioress, having been informed by the monk of the forlorn situation in which she was left, and also of the losses she had lately sustained, took the earliest opportunity of offering her an asylum until she could be more eligibly accommodated; and when she beheld her, endeavoured, with the most affecting gentleness of demeanour, to alleviate her affliction.

There was an air of solemnity in the manners of the superior, but it was tempered with mildness; and though the language of her countenance was expressive of sorrow, it was sorrow softened by resignation, reflection, and piety.

After a week's residence in the convent, Mademoiselle de Rubine, by the desire of her new friend, wrote to Madame Laronne, her aunt, to acquaint her with the death of her mother, and to inform her under whose care she was placed; requesting likewise to know, whether she was to remain under the maternal protection of the prioress, or to repair to Italy.

In a few weeks she received an answer from her aunt, in which she expressed her concern for the death of her sister, and also declared her intention of visiting the Netherlands for the purpose of conveying her into Italy, which address was concluded with many affectionate acknowledgments of unalterable regard.

The promises of support which this letter afforded, were thankfully and cordially received by the lovely Julie; yet the idea of being launched into a world, which she had been taught to believe was pregnant with vice and immorality, filled her with apprehension and uneasiness; and made her ardently wish that, instead of attending her aunt into Italy, she might be permitted to remain in the cloister, sheltered in the bosom of Religion and Virtue from the evils that threatened her in the world.

Soon after her admission into the convent, she attached herself to one of the sisters, whose name was Ursula. She was much older than herself, and from her many estimable qualities, had been recommended to her as a companion by the superior. In the society of this amiable nun, and that of her noble protectress, Julie became composed, and at times somewhat animated. Attentively observing the rules of the order, she arose early to matins, and as regularly attended at vespers, whilst the intermediate hours were chiefly engaged in assisting the prioress in embroidery, or other elegant employments, who expressed herself much gratified with her performance, and complimented her highly on the evident superiority of her taste.

After some time had elapsed in this calm, uninterrupted retirement, whose solitude was so entirely congenial to her present frame of spirits, a carriage and splendid retinue appeared at the gate, and announced the arrival of Madame Laronne.

Julie was walking in the shrubbery with sister Ursula and another lady, who was a novice, when she received an order to attend upon her aunt in the apartment of the superior.

Madame Laronne met her with many flattering appellations; but there was nothing of that genuine sensibility in her demeanour which communicates itself to the heart. When she condescended to listen to the plaint of misery, and to wipe away the tear from the cheek of the unfortunate, it was evidently more to display her own fancied superiority, than for the sake of experiencing that pure and heartfelt satisfaction, which in amiable minds accompanies the performance of a generous action.

After having continued a few weeks in the convent, which time was employed in settling the affairs of St. Gerard, she desired her niece to prepare for the intended journey, whom she rallied on her partiality to that sequestered retreat, and her strict adherence to the rules of the institution. Julie, having obtained permission to visit once more the grave of her beloved parents, which she again watered with her tears, took an affectionate leave of the prioress, her favourite Ursula, and the rest of the sisterhood; and placing herself in the carriage with Madame Laronne, they were driven from the gate.

It was in vain that Julie attempted to conceal her emotions when she cast her eyes, for the last time, upon that hospitable mansion, which had so humanely afforded her shelter; she, however, exerted her most strenuous endeavours to appear cheerful; but these efforts were painful, and sometimes ineffectual; and Madame Laronne condemned that sensibility, which having never felt, she knew not how to compassionate.

CHAP. VI.

"Far to the right where Apennine ascends,
  Bright as the summer Italy extends,
  Its upland sloping decks the mountains side,
  Woods over woods in gay theatric pride,
  While oft some temple's mould'ring top between,
  With venerable grandeur marks the scene."

GOLDSMITH.

The rich and variegated landscape that every way presented itself, had a happy but transient effect upon the spirits of Julie, and for some time diverted her mind from the painful contemplation of her own misfortunes. Amidst the vast and magnificent scenery arose mountains crested with pines, in high cultivation and verdure, some of which seemed retiring, and to have formed themselves into the most picturesque lines, whose slopes were decorated with mosses, tinted with a variety of hues, which gave a sylvan richness to their surface.

The rapidity of their motion occasioned a hasty succession of beautiful imagery; sometimes a venerable abbey, half mouldering into ruins, reared its majestic head above the thick foliage of the wood, and sometimes in the meek hour of evening, or before the sun had risen upon the eminences, the shepherd-boy, as he led his flock from the vallies, would lean upon his staff, and listen to the chaunted hymn, or early matins, as the sound floated upon the gale along the surface of the water.

As they arrived near the mansion of Madame Laronne, the magical influence of the picturesque scenery was at an end; and as Julie fixed her eyes upon the turrets of the chateau, which were gilded with the last rays of the retiring sun, a thousand melancholy presages arose in her mind, and awakened sensations of grief and terror.

The chateau was situated on an extensive lawn between two mountains, which opened to a clear and beautiful lake; the banks of the river, the lawn, and the hills, were clothed in the

finest and richest verdure, whilst the whole of the scenery appeared capable of the highest improvement; but nothing like
taste was displayed in the design. The mansion, which was lofty
and extensive, had been formerly a fortified castle, but was now
modernized with the addition of two large wings; but neither the
building nor the grounds surrounding it discovered any traces of
taste or judgment. The walks were gloomy and ill contrived, no
elevations or windings displayed to advantage the grandeur of
the mountains; nor did this appear to have been the intention
of the artist, as they seemed to have been originally designed to
lead as avenues to some fanciful but inelegant structures, which
terminated their prospect.

When Madame Laronne and Julie had alighted, they were
conducted into a spacious saloon, which was richly ornamented
with the most costly furniture and valuable paintings. The ostentatious magnificence of every thing around formed a striking
contrast with that unadorned and charming simplicity which
characterized the former dwelling of Julie, so congenial to her
feelings, and that of her mother.

Madame Laronne, anxiously displaying all the grandeur that
surrounded her, expected from her niece that tribute of applause
which she considered she had a right to demand; but was evidently mortified when Julie's countenance discovered nothing
of either pleasure or surprise as she contemplated the splendour
of her new abode.

After partaking of a slight collation with her aunt, Julie
gained permission to retire to her chamber; and a servant having
conducted her up a winding staircase, and through a long suite
of rooms, informed her which was her apartment.

It was a large half-furnished room, situated in the ancient
part of the edifice, hung with tapestry, and ornamented with
the ancient portraits of the family; she was, however, too much
fatigued, and too spiritless to examine them, and hastily un-
dressing, retired to her bed.

In the morning she arose much earlier than the rest of the
family, and amused herself for some time with observing the
pictures. The greater part of them were allegorical, but in general ill-designed and executed, much damaged by neglect, and

the colouring so materially injured by time, that the figures were scarcely perceptible.

When she had gazed for a considerable time upon these relics of ancient greatness, she opened the high Gothic casement of her window, which was adorned, on the upper part, with a variety of saints, crucifixes, and other holy devices, and cast her eyes over the fine extent of landscape with the most pleasurable emotions. The sun was just rising, but had not yet power sufficient to entirely dissipate the mists that had veiled the summits of the mountains; yet some parts of them were tinged with its faint radiance, which shed an effusion of the most soft and delicate tints.

Cheered and animated by the objects that were presented to her view, she wished to ramble through the grounds that she might examine more attentively the fine features of nature, and enjoy the first charms of the morning. Having unclosed the door, she listened for a few moments to hear if any of the family were stirring; but finding all was silent, and believing that none of the servants were at present arisen, she closed it, and taking a small volume of Metastasio from her pocket, sat down to read.

In about an hour she again opened the door, and hearing footsteps upon the stairs, ventured to proceed. It was Madame Laronne's woman, who, having conducted her to the outward gate, informed her which was the avenue that led to the principal part of the gardens. After walking slowly and thoughtfully through rows of pine and chesnut, the scene opened into a circular plain, which was decorated with a collection of statues and vases, neither of which possessed a sufficient degree of merit to invite observation.

Having taken an extensive ramble through the most considerable part of the grounds, she began to fear she had been absent too long, and returning rapidly to the chateau, found Madame Laronne in the breakfast-room impatiently awaiting her arrival.

After much uninteresting conversation on subjects little calculated to bestow pleasure on a refined and cultivated mind, which were introduced by the lady of the mansion at once to impress her niece with an idea of her importance, and to make her feel more forcibly her own dependant situation, Julie now, more than ever inclined to seek for consolation in solitude, retired to her room, and having indulged in a flood of tears, which she found it impossible to restrain, endeavoured, by serious reflection, to arm herself with courage to endure the evils of her destiny with becoming firmness. The example of her excellent mother, and the precepts she had delivered with her dying breath, recurred continually to her thoughts, tending to reassure and strengthen her mind, so as to prepare it to withstand the attacks of misfortune.

Having regained, in some measure, that enviable serenity of soul, which never long abandons the virtuous, she left her retirement, and was proceeding leisurely through the gallery, when the stopping of a carriage, announcing the arrival of visiters, arrested her steps, and determined her to return again to her apartment, and await their dismission, lest she should be obliged to attend them in the saloon.

In about an hour, on hearing the carriage roll from the door, she ventured to descend, and found Madame Laronne alone, and in high spirits, having been honoured with a visit from the Contessa di Romilini, from whom she had received an invitation for that day in the next week to a fête; which condescension, she informed Julie, was politely extended to herself, at the same time observing that all the nobility in the neighbourhood were to be present on the occasion, and that it would be necessary to prepare habits immediately suitable to the nature of the entertainment, and the company of which it was to be composed.

"But let me tell you, niece," resumed Madame Laronne, "that you must not indulge yourself in these imaginary distresses when you are introduced to circles of fashion; that pensiveness of demeanour, which you believe to be so fascinating, will be thought not only unseasonable but ridiculous, and will be considered in a young woman as a piece of unpardonable affectation. Besides, this extreme languor which you fancy so becoming and so amiable, if allowed to become habitual, will render you unfit for the society of those who may be a means of advancing your fortunes. Who do you suppose will think of addressing a girl who can do nothing but weep and sigh? Men in general are not partial to people of this cast, and indeed they are only fit to be the companions of groves and fountains."

"If my misfortunes, Madame," replied Julie, meekly, "have, as you have justly observed, rendered me unfit for the society of the fashionable part of the world, I must solicit you to dispense with my attendance, as there is but little probability of my being able to conduct myself either to your satisfaction or my own."

"I am sorry to find, niece," continued Madame Laronne, "a degree of obstinacy in your disposition, which I was not prepared to expect; but so long as you are under my protection, I am in some measure answerable for your conduct: I therefore think it right to inform you, that I shall expect, on your part, the most implicit obedience. Though your ideas of propriety and mine may not exactly accord, not to accept the invitation of the Contessa, an honour you could not reasonably expect from a person of her rank, particularly as you was not present at the time, would be considered not only as a deviation from the laws of politeness, but a breach of gratitude—an error of which I thought you people of sentiment were never to be accused."

Finding that no powers of persuasion were likely to prove effectual, Julie silently acquiesced, and the intermediate time was chiefly employed in preparing dresses suitable to the occasion.

When the expected evening arrived, which was so fondly anticipated by Madame Laronne, they were conveyed to the chateau of the Contessa di Romilini. It was a large magnificent structure, situated on the brow of a hill, which commanded a rich and extensive prospect. The architecture was a mixture of the Tuscan and Composite; the pillars, which were remarkably lofty, were finely polished and ornamented with a number of lamps of various colours, which being formed into the most beautiful wreaths, had an unspeakably fine effect. The trees that surrounded the lawn and the walks, which were long and winding, were also fancifully adorned with a profusion of lights, and garlands of flowers elegantly and artfully disposed, were carelessly hung upon the branches of the larch and the libernum. Seats were placed in the gardens and baskets of fruits, the finest that Italy could produce, were held by a number of beautiful girls, habited as wood-nymphs in a style equally simple and alluring.

The assembly was large and brilliant; all the fashion of Turin and its environs were present. Julie, being personally unknown to the lady who presided, was introduced first to the Contessa, and then to the rest of the company, who were already seated on the lawn. Nothing could be more lovely, more interesting, than her appearance. Her hair, which was somewhat darker than flaxen, waved upon her neck in the most charming profusion, decorated only with pearls formed into a garland of jessamine, which gave an air of lightness and grace perfectly correspondent with the rest of her figure. Her long mourning robe, which displayed to advantage the fine symetry of her shape, was clasped and fastened with a cestus of the same, and the whole of her form and demeanour displayed that irresistible grace and sweetness which the utmost eloquence of language can but feebly describe. Every eye was fixed upon the beautiful stranger, who, unconscious of her powers of attraction, averted her blushing cheek from the gaze of admiration with evident distress.

All the company being assembled, and the music in readiness, the dance began. Julie was led out by Signor Vescolini, the only son of the Conte della Croisse, and Madame Laronne by the Marchese de Montferrat.

In a few hours, the evening being far advanced, they repaired to the saloon, where a banquet was prepared, chiefly composed of dried fruits, cream, and sweetmeats.

Elated beyond measure at the preference shewn her by the Marchese, and anxious to cultivate an acquaintance so flattering to her ambition, Madame Laronne gave him a general invitation to visit her at her chateau, in which his relation, Signor Vescolini, was included, whose marked attentions to her niece were beheld with secret satisfaction.

It was late when the party separated for the night; yet she left with regret an entertainment which had, as was seldom the case, more than answered her most sanguine expectations. The solicitude of her partner, aided by her own vanity, had deluded her into a thousand inconsistencies. She reflected upon her beauty with triumph, without considering that, though once fascinating, it was beauty in the wane, and was in idea already a Marchesa.

Her captivating niece, who had formed no very flattering hopes of the evening's amusement, experienced more satisfaction than she believed it could produce, and felt gratified with the attention she received, without one spark of vanity being excited in her bosom.

On the morrow, by mutual agreement, the Marchese de Montferrat and the Signor Vescolini waited upon the ladies at their chateau, to inquire into the state of their healths after the fatigue of the preceding evening. As the Signor addressed himself to Mademoiselle de Rubine, there was an air of respectful tenderness in his deportment which did not elude the observation of her aunt, who would probably have felt somewhat mortified at the preference thus evidently shewn to her dependant, had not the conversation of the Marchese been chiefly directed to herself.

The remains of a fine person were still visible in Madame Laronne, notwithstanding the form which Nature had bestowed upon her, was continually distorted with unpardonable affectation. Having but just entered her fortieth year, she still retained a sufficient portion of beauty to attract regard, though the pains she employed to display and improve it, too frequently counteracted its effects.

Dress was her favourite occupation, which she studied as a science; but a false taste was perceptible in her choice of attire—a dazzling and ill judged finery, which ever renders less lovely the most delicate forms, being usually substituted in the room of that attractive simplicity which indicates a refined and elegant mind.

As the morning was fine, a walk in the gardens was proposed and acceded to, during which ramble Julie was compelled, with a slight degree of uneasiness, to endure the increasing attentions of Signor Vescolini, which she feared would not escape the penetration of her aunt, who would probably on her return rally her upon a subject, which the present tone of her spirits would render insupportable; and which determined her to absent herself on his next visit.

It was late in the day before the Marchese and the Signor arose to depart, when Madame Laronne, who in their presence had exhausted all the graces of her eloquence, again reminded them of her former invitation, which she desired them to consider as a general one; and having, with a gracious smile particularly directed to the Marchese, repeated her adieus, attended them to the gate.

Glad to be thus released from the society of her new acquaintance, Julie hastened from the room, that by this means she might escape the scrutinizing glances of her aunt, which beamed nothing of feminine tenderness, and indulge the sadness of her feelings in the solitude of her closet. In spite of every effort to the contrary, she too often reverted to the past; and when she compared her former felicity, when blessed with the counsel and society of her parents with the forlornness of her present situation, the poignancy of her affliction was scarcely supportable, and tears, that refused to be suppressed, fell fast upon her cheek. Once nurtured, protected, and caressed in the bosom of maternal affection, now consigned to the care of a haughty relation, who, notwithstanding her former professions, seemed to feel nothing of genuine regard, nor even the sentiment of pity for her misfortunes, she was lost in these melancholy reflections, when the loud tone of the dinner-bell summoned her into the dining-parlour, where Madame Laronne, with more than her accustomed dignity, was seated to receive her. As soon as the cloth was withdrawn, and the servants dismissed, she began, after a short preparatory address, to congratulate her niece upon the conquest she had made over the young Signor Vescolini. Julie blushed, but remained silent.

"His family and connexions," resumed Madame Laronne, "are unexceptionable; and though sanguine expectations are too frequently founded on error, we may sometimes innocently indulge them. At present his attentions may be directed to no other object than that of momentary amusement; but if you receive them with due gratitude and humility, it is possible it may terminate fortunately."

Disconcerted at these hasty and indelicate effusions, Julie was at first unprepared for a reply, whilst her aunt, who construed this silent embarrassment into joy for such unexpected good fortune, began to enlarge upon the subject, endeavouring at the same time to contaminate the pure principles of her heart with the precepts which had infected her own.

As soon as Mademoiselle de Rubine could command courage enough to answer, she assured Madame Laronne that, however eligible such a connexion might appear in the eyes of the world, she was convinced she could never descend to the meanness of accepting an alliance in which her heart had no interest, merely for the sake of attaining that elevation of rank and precedence which she had been taught to consider as unimportant, and which was only to be obtained by the humiliating circumstances she had mentioned; not omitting to observe, that, however the attentions of the Signor might appear to be directed to herself, those enviable distinctions to which she had recurred must eventually preclude every idea of the kind. "Can I, Madame," resumed she, raising her soft blue eyes from the ground, which were half obscured with her tears, "submit to the meanness of dissimulation for the sake of ripening into affection what may be nothing more than momentary admiration? Can I throw myself upon the generosity of a family who, from motives of ambition, may reject me, and doubly despise me for my presumption in entering it? Rather let me endure the severest mortification that neglect and penury can inflict, than lessen myself in my own estimation, and by yielding to the erroneous prejudices of the multitude, justly incur the censure of the most worthy and discerning."

"I little thought, niece," resumed Madame Laronne, "that when, in consideration of your unprotected youth, I conde-scended to take you under my care, of the difficulty attending so important a charge, or that obstinacy and caprice were so strongly featured in your character. Had the assiduities of the Signor been displeasing to me, you would have been eloquent in his praise, and would have discovered a thousand amiable qualities which have now escaped unnoticed."

"I hope, Madame," continued Julie, mildly, "that you have had no reason to pass this severe censure upon my conduct, as, should I ever form an attachment, my happiness will be materi-ally augmented by your approbation of my choice."

"But this is not an affair," replied Madame Laronne, raising her voice still higher, "in which we are likely to agree. You have, or pretend to have, an aversion to those things which only make marriage desirable, at least in the opinion of the reasonable part of the world; but I am sorry to add, niece, that you are a very romantic girl, and when it is too late, may possibly repent your error. Your mother had many strange prejudices as well as yourself, and it would have been much to her advantage if she had been enabled to conquer them."

"If I imitate her example, Madame," returned Julie, wiping an obtruding tear from her cheek, "which I hope will ever be the rule of my conduct, I shall not prove myself unworthy of your protection."

Madame Laronne was preparing to reply, but her lovely dependant, being willing to escape from so unpleasant a conference, precipitately withdrew, leaving her offended relation to vent her anger in secret. The reflection cast upon the character of her mother, whom she considered as the brightest pattern of female excellence, Mademoiselle de Rubine could but ill support. She had, indeed, formed no very high opinion of Madame Laronne's tenderness, or of the delicacy of her sentiments; but to mention this revered parent in terms of disapprobation, convinced her that she was not only destitute of sensibility, but of candour.

Not a day passed in which the Marchese de Montferrat and the Signor Vescolini did not visit the chateau. The assiduities of the latter increased; but, though Julie admired his person, which was cast in the finest mould, and was by no means insensible to his numerous accomplishments, he was unable to interest her affections. His continual solicitude displeased her, and the levity with which he treated the articles of the Romish Church, from whose tenets he had recently dissented, determined her to preserve an apparent indifference of deportment towards him, which she hoped, by offending his pride, would eventually terminate his visits.

Signor Vescolini, having received his education in Germany, had embraced the Reformed Religion through the doctrines of Luther; and Julie, after having been for some time deceived by the artifice of Madame Laronne respecting his religious opinions, was convinced, by a conversation with the Marchese, that he had relinquished what he termed his former errors; and owing to the native pliability of his disposition, had been prevailed upon, by the adherents of this celebrated reformer, to embrace Protestantism.

A few days after this discovery she was summoned into the apartment of her aunt, who informed her, to her inexpressible uneasiness, that the Signor had made a formal declaration of his passion, and moreover had solicited her interference in his behalf. Perfectly aware of the consequence of this sudden and indiscrete avowal, Julie started, and appeared much agitated.

"You have certainly been peculiarly fortunate," continued Madame Laronne, regarding her attentively as she spoke; "and, notwithstanding the unjustifiable caprice and insensibility you discovered on a former conversation, I cannot believe you mean seriously to reject such honourable proposals. I would fain not imagine it possible you could hesitate for a moment. How many young women have been obliged to accept of inferior alliances, who may boast of an equal share of beauty and discretion!"

"I am sorry to affirm, Madame," replied Julie, hesitatingly, "that there are reasons which must subject me to the painful necessity of refusing my obedience to your and the Signor's requests. The religious opinions of the person you have proposed to me as a husband are repugnant to my own, and a want of concord in that important article must ever prove hostile to domestic happiness."

"So you would actually decline a connexion with one of the first families in Italy," returned Madame Laronne, indignantly, "because the person who addresses you, happens not to be so bigoted and so ridiculous as yourself?"

Julie observing that he might be equally bigoted, even though his principles were erroneous, ventured to disclose the motive which had instigated her to this sudden rejection of a suit, she candidly acknowledged a mind less unambitious than her own, unbiassed by more weighty arguments, might have acceded to with pleasure; not doubting but when her aunt was thoroughly acquainted with the whole of the circumstance, that she would finally applaud her conduct.

A promise, administered in so solemn a manner to her last

and dearest friend, in the moment of approaching dissolution, appeared to the reflecting mind of the dutiful Julie as an unsurmountable obstacle; and she could scarcely conceive it possible that Madame Laronne, however destitute of religion herself, would presume to descant upon the subject with her accustomed levity.

But she soon discovered that this fondly-cherished hope was delusive, and that little was to be expected from the lenity of her offended relation, who perceiving that the gentle measures, as she termed them, which had hitherto been adopted, were not likely to avail, threatened to have recourse to more violent ones; not neglecting to assure her, that more misfortunes would inevitably ensue from a strict adherence to so ridiculous a vow, than from an actual breach of it. She then expatiated with equal success upon the consequences of indulged superstition, and the indispensable necessity of endeavouring to liberate the mind from the shackles of vulgar prejudices, which, she concluded with remarking, was considered by the discerning as the irrefragable testimony of an exalted mind.

Fearful of irritating her pride by a continued avowal of sentiments so dissimilar to her own, Julie did not meditate a reply; but remained with her eyes fastened upon the ground, whilst her cheek was one moment suffused with vermilion, and the next faded into the paleness of the lily, as actuated by the revolving passions of her mind.

Madame Laronne, flattering herself that her niece was reconsidering the subject, and that the arguments she had employed in defence of her favourite hypothesis, were recalling her to rationality, pursued the discourse; and to add more weight to what she had before advanced, stated the possibility of the Signor's reformation being effected, should he fail in making her a convert to his own creed, providing his attachment survived the matrimonial engagement; intimating that whatever persuasion they embraced, it was unimportant, so long as it was mutual.

Julie, finding her aunt was falling into a new error, which, if not timely prevented, might be productive of fresh evils, declared, that her resolution, however singular, was unalterable, and that she desired nothing more ardently than to have an opportunity of verbally convincing the Signor of her determination.

Astonished at the firmness of character this avowal exhibited, and mortified that her niece remained unsubdued by her arguments, and unmoved by her eloquence, Madame Laronne descended from persuasion to invective, threatening her with the most arbitrary proceedings if gentle ones continued inefficacious: then informing her, that if she consented to what would contribute to her own happiness, she was fortunate in having a relation who would guide her to the attainment of it; but if she refused, that relation would compel her to accept the only conditions which would eventually secure it. She darted an indignant look at the affrighted Julie, and withdrew.

CHAP. VII.

"Such fate to suffering worth is given,
Who long with wants and woes has striven,
By human pride or cunning driven,
    To misery's brink."
                                BURNS.

The severity which Julie experienced from Madame Laronne, and the unceasing visits of Vescolini, who seemed determined to persevere in his addresses, had a visible effect upon her health; yet believing that he was not thoroughly acquainted with her resolution, she anxiously awaited an opportunity of convincing him that she meant positively to reject the alliance, hoping that, when he was able to ascertain the primary cause of this conduct, he would be less disposed to continue his persecutions. But she knew not sufficiently the character of her lover when she cherished this delusive idea. Young, sanguine, and enterprising, every new obstacle increased his ardour, and, regardless of the consequences of such a proceeding, he was secretly persuaded that nothing but death should prevent the accomplishment of his design.

Finding that all hopes, founded on his generosity of sentiment, were likely to prove abortive, since no honourable motive could instigate him to abandon the pursuit, she began to lose all esteem for his character, and to reflect upon this authoritative mode of procedure with mingled disgust and aversion.

The Marchese, whose attentions to Madame Laronne were less marked than on the commencement of their acquaintance, was still a constant visiter at the chateau; and Julie observed that he was now become unusually thoughtful without in the least suspecting the cause, though in conversation he was visibly abstracted from the subject in which he had engaged, and he frequently gazed upon her with a degree of silent and tender earnestness that heightened her distress. This change, though it might have been easily penetrated by an uninterested spectator, was unmarked by Madame Laronne, who was too much blinded by an excess of unprecedented vanity to imagine that the Marchese could behold any other than herself with an eye of approbation.

As Julie's indisposition now daily increased, she spent many hours in her apartment, which was one of the most substantial comforts allowed her under her augmenting afflictions. She was sometimes fortunately excused from attending upon her aunt's parties, which were frequent and uninteresting, and declined, as much as possible, all visits of ceremony.

One evening, Madame Laronne being engaged at a route, to which the Marchese was also invited, Julie was left alone in her absence to meditate upon her own misfortunes, as well as to endeavour to arm her mind as much as she was able against the accumulating adversities of her fate.

As soon as her haughty protectress had left the chateau, she took a long and solitary walk along the margin of the lake. It was a still and beautiful evening; every object seemed to repose in uninterrupted silence and tranquillity. The sun, retiring from the horizon, was setting beyond the distant hills. Not a bird broke the stillness of the night; not a breeze disturbed the universal calm of nature; not a sound was borne upon the air, save a bell from an adjacent convent, which was solemnly tolling for vespers, "that the day, which had been ushered in with blessings, might be closed with the effusions of gratitude."

As she gazed upon that venerable pile, which was tinged with the last ray of the retiring orb, she lamented she had not been consigned to a similar abode, and reverted with tender regret to that in which she had found so hospitable an asylum. Having yielded to a flood of tears, she endeavoured to recal her mind from these painful contemplations; but the attempt was inefficacious; the cruelty of her aunt, the perseverance of Vescolini, and her own defenceless situation, were invincible bars to returning peace.

The moon, now sailing majestically through the concave, was shedding her mildest light upon the surface of the water, which warned her of the approach of night, and precipitated her steps towards the mansion; but not without an intention of extending her walk along the gardens in this serene hour of moon-light.

Having reached the chateau, she took her lute, which had lain neglected in one corner of her apartment, and repairing to a grotto that terminated one of the principal avenues, played her service to the virgin.

As the last notes, which were warbled with a peculiar taste and sweetness, died into cadence, she fancied she distinguished the sound of advancing footsteps, and willing to discover the intruder, hastily arose from the place; but not being able to discern any one, and finding all was again silent, she believed it to be only an illusion, and again resumed her seat. The moon, now shining with redoubled lustre, deepened the contrasting gloom of the walks, which were so effectually shaded from its benign influence by the protuberant branches of the chesnut, that her beams could only play on the tops of the boughs. Again she thought she heard the approach of footsteps, and a faint rustling among the leaves, and starting from her seat, hurried to the door of the grotto, where she beheld, in the same instant, the shadow of plumes waving upon the grass. Believing it could be no other than Vescolini, an emotion of terror took possession of her frame, and, without waiting to be assured whether she was right or not in the conjecture, she quitted the recess.

It was the Marchese de Montferrat, who, having learned from Madame Laronne that Julie was prevented by indisposition from joining the party, to which he had repaired in the hope of meeting with her, had suddenly retreated from this scene of splendour and gaiety soon after its commencement, and had wandered about in pursuit of her. Finding she was not at the chateau, he had rambled for a considerable time along the grounds; and being still unsuccessful in his undertaking, was alarmed lest any thing had happened, till he was at once relieved from the anguish of fear and suspense by the wild harmony of her song, to which he had listened attentively with the most pleasurable emotions till the sound died away upon the air, and was succeeded by a mournful silence.

Julie, being assured that the Marchese was of Madame Laronne's party, was not less surprised than agitated at this intrusion; and supposing that some material occurrence had occasioned it, eagerly demanded if any thing had happened to her aunt.

Having dissipated her apprehensions, and made an inquiry concerning her health, he began, in a stile at once the most seductive and impressive, to assure her, that he had long sedulously sought for an opportunity of soliciting her attention on a subject the most serious and important.

After this preparatory address, he proceeded to inform her that Vescolini, contrary to the nice dictates of honour, intended to have recourse to the most infamous mode of conduct, if she refused to yield to his entreaties; and that Madame Laronne was so earnestly engaged in his interest, that every thing was to be dreaded without timely interference. This, he added, had influenced him to quit rather precipitately the society into which he had entered, as the probability of her being sacrificed to a man who had proved himself not only destitute of religion, but of honour, was insupportable and dreadful.

He then endeavoured, with all the eloquence he could command, to prevail upon her to accept of his protection, since the means of preventing the machinations of her enemies could only be accomplished by instant flight; which arguments he attempted to enforce by an avowal of his regard, and a declaration that his life would be joyfully hazarded in her defence.

Julie, who had listened to this discourse with mingled confusion and astonishment, replied with more warmth than was natural to her disposition, but with the firmness inseparable from rectitude, and the delicacy peculiar to her sex; which tended to convince the Marchese that nothing could induce her to rush voluntarily into an act of imprudence, which might hereafter be attended with the severest remorse; and, though she acknowledged the high sense she entertained of the honour he was anxious to confer, desired, if he valued her esteem, he would desist from farther solicitation. She was then hastening towards the chateau, when the Marchese, throwing himself at her feet, again besought her attention.

"Say but that you pity me," continued he, respectfully taking her hand, which she instantly withdrew, "that you forgive this premature declaration, and promise that no arguments shall persuade you to bestow yourself upon a man who has proved himself unworthy of your favour."

Julie, having given him an answer sufficiently satisfactory concerning Vescolini, whom she now began to reflect upon with increasing indignation, quickened her steps towards the mansion, and had just reached the edge of the lawn, pursued by the Marchese, when Madame Laronne's carriage appeared at the gate.

Alarmed at her unexpected arrival, she ran to the side of the carriage, and inquired if she was indisposed, or what had occasioned her return, with that affectionate tenderness of deportment natural to her character, whilst the Marchese endeavoured to escape unobserved through the vista, which opened on the lawn, till perceiving he was already discovered by the person whose notice he was visibly anxious to elude, he was compelled to emerge from his obscurity.

Madame Laronne, having observed an alteration in the looks of her imaginary lover, when she had mentioned the indisposition of Mademoiselle de Rubine, and having also remarked that soon afterwards he had suddenly disappeared, began to feel herself neglected by the only individual in the company whose attention she was anxious to secure, and by comparing the present with the past, and reverting to some little occurrences which her vanity had prevented her from considering before, suspected her niece as the cause. She had a presentiment that he was with her during her continuance at the route, and being determined to ascertain the truth of the surmise, had pleaded a sudden indisposition as an excuse to return to her chateau.

Confused and chagrined at this discovery, the Marchese, though not often off his guard, was unable to acquit himself with his accustomed address; and after inquiring into the state of her health as he led her from the carriage, which was answered with an air of unusual formality, an awkward silence ensued. Conscious of the integrity and purity of her conduct, Julie met the angry glances of her aunt with patient firmness, who exerted herself to conceal her mortification whilst in the presence of the Marchese.

As soon as he had retired, Julie perceiving from the countenance of Madame Laronne, that she had but little to expect from the candour and clemency of her offended relative, sat for some moments in silent dread. "Your taste for solitude is at last well accounted for," cried the irritated lady, darting a look of severity at her innocent niece; "I little thought when I consented to take you under my protection, that my kindness would have been repaid with such flagrant ingratitude; but since the liberty I have allowed you in the disposal of your time has induced you to form assignations which may lead to the most dangerous consequences, I am resolved to prevent the bad effects of a conduct which prudence would blush to reflect upon, to hasten your marriage with the Signor; granting you a month only to conquer your ridiculous scruples, during which interval I shall insist upon you confining yourself to your chamber, excepting the evenings when you will be permitted to have a private conference with your lover."

Finding that no powers of persuasion were likely to soften the invincible cruelty of Madame Laronne, Julie retired from her presence, and, after some time spent in devotion with more than usual earnestness, she endeavoured to find comfort in repose. But the subject of her dreams had a reference to the past; her sleep was transient and disturbed, for fearful and uneasy visions fleeted before her fancy.

In the morning she arose long before her accustomed hour, and cast her eyes over her ancient and gloomy apartment, which was now become her prison, with a painful sensation, though even this was felicity when compared with the prospects of the future.

Several days were passed by Mademoiselle de Rubine in this dreary confinement, in which time she received no message or visit from Madame Laronne, who avoided giving her any opportunity of repeating her entreaties. Dorothèe, one of the inferior domestics, who had received orders to convey her food into the chamber, glanced upon her a look of tender concern as she was performing her office, which Julie, long unused to the language of sympathy, did not fail to return.

"This is a poor forlorn looking place, Mademoiselle," cried the simple-hearted girl, looking fearfully around as she spread the cloth upon the table for supper; "I little thought Madame would have fixed upon this for your apartment, that looks for all the world as if it was haunted by spirits, when there are so many handsome ones in the chateau!"

Julie, being awakened from her reverie by these words, which were uttered in an accent of condolence, was going to reply, when a message from her aunt summoned her into the saloon.

Weak and trembling she descended the stairs, and a glow of resentment crimsoned her cheek, when on entering the room she beheld, instead of Madame Laronne, the Signor Vescolini. Amazed and disconcerted, she was hastily retreating, when he caught her hand to prevent her retiring, and closing the door, led her to a chair. As soon as she was seated, he repeated his former professions, lamenting at the same time that measures, seemingly so arbitrary, could not be dispensed with; assuring her, that when he had attained the completion of his happiness, he would endeavour to insure her's by the most unremitting attention to her desires; and, though he could not so far divest himself of every thing repugnant to her inclinations as to embrace the tenets of the Romish Church, he would allow her the free exercise of her religion, and would engage a confessor to attend her.

Julie, who rejected his proposals with dignity and energy, informed him, that if he desired to make any alteration in her sentiments respecting himself, that this could only be accomplished by his desisting from further persecution, which, as her resolution was irrevocably fixed, would be at once conducive to his honour and her peace.

Pacing the room for some minutes with a perturbed air, and

then gazing wildly upon her face, he declared that nothing on earth should alter his determination; and, though he had much rather use persuasion than force, if one would not prove effectual, the other must.

"In a fortnight from this time," resumed he, emphatically, "you become my wife; and as business of a peculiar nature will detain me from this place during the interval, I must request you will employ it in attempting to reconcile yourself to a destiny that is unavoidable. Madame Laronne will see you no more till the ceremony is performed."

The truth of the Marchese's assertion being now proved, Julie was unable for the moment to utter a reply. She endeavoured to arise, but could not; her limbs trembled—her voice failed—an ashy paleness overspread her face—and she sunk into a state of insensibility!

Vescolini, having caught her in his arms, rang the bell for some water, which soon acted as a restorative; and wiping a tear from his eye, uttered some incoherent expressions as he pressed her hand to his breast, and suffered her to be conveyed from the room.

The next morning, her agitation being in some measure subsided, she began to reflect seriously upon her situation, and to consider if by any means she could prevent the success of the Signor's designs. Her first resolve was, to send a note to Madame Laronne, to desire she would indulge her with an interview, which intention was speedily executed. To this an answer was returned, which was perfectly consistent with her former conduct; it contained an assurance of the request being granted, on her promise of acceding to the proposals of Signor Vescolini, but on no other conditions, and a conviction that, if she still continued to decline the alliance, she had nothing to expect from her compassion.

Several days had elapsed after this event, in which time Julie was not permitted to see any of the family except Dorothèe. During this period of suspense, the extreme agitation of her mind so seriously affected her health, that the rose had forsaken her cheek, though without considerably impairing her beauty, having left in its stead a bewitching softness of complexion, a kind of interesting dejection, which was infinitely more charming and attractive than the most striking animation of colour.

One week of that fortnight which was to seal her inevitable doom, was now past, and still no probable means of preventing the success of these authoritative measures appeared. To escape unassisted from the chateau was impracticable, and to stay (in the present situation of affairs) would be attended with unavoidable misery; yet, possessing much sanguineness of disposition, she did not yield, without reflection, to the despondency of the moment. Some unexpected assistance she still hoped might be administered, though no object was presented to her imagination to justify and confirm the supposition.

This comfort, however delusive in its consequences, was cherished as a divine emanation, and with spirits more tranquillized than before, she partook of the evening's repast, whilst Dorothèe, availing herself of her permission, kindled a fire in the apartment, as the night was unusually chill; and the hollow gusts of wind, penetrating through the crevices of the walls, which were but partially covered with the faded and decayed tapestry, made her shrink with cold.

Having drawn close to the fire, whose cheerful blaze enlivened the gloominess of her extensive apartment, she thought in the pauses of the wind she perceived the whispering of voices on the stairs. The sound was indistinct; but on advancing towards the door, she easily distinguished that of the Marchese, who, before she had time for resistance, entered the room.

Alarmed at this intrusion, she uttered an involuntary scream, and attempted to retire; but this he so resolutely opposed, that she was compelled to desist. When he had in some degree quieted her apprehensions, he acquainted her with the purport of his visit, which was to convey some important and necessary intelligence respecting the intentions of Signor Vescolini, who had determined, with the assistance of Madame Laronne, to remove her either by force or stratagem from the chateau at the expiration of three days, and to oblige her to assent to the nuptials. How he had obtained this information he seemed unwilling to disclose; but from what had already occurred, the intimation was too probable to admit of a doubt as to the truth of it; and the shortness of the intervening time appeared to preclude all possibility of escape.

The Marchese, who beheld every movement of her soul in the expression of her countenance, so tenderly interested himself in her concerns, and applauded so warmly that uniform piety and rectitude of mind which had hitherto withstood the attacks of severity and artifice, that, though Julie continually besought him to resign her to her destiny, she was not insensible to the sympathy he discovered, which she assured him would be ever gratefully retained in her memory.

He then ventured to repeat his former proposals, urging the necessity of the measure with all the arts of persuasion he could summon to his aid, which, he added, would insure his happiness, and, he presumed to flatter himself, her own. That, if she would consent to accept of his protection, a carriage should be stationed at a convenient distance from the chateau, which would convey her with all imaginable speed to the Castello St. Aubin, where the ceremony, which was to complete his felicity, might be instantly performed.

Though Julie at first strenuously opposed a proceeding which, on a cursory survey, appeared rash and imprudent, she was finally influenced by a mode of behaviour, which, but for the circumstance of his having forced himself into her room, was at once amiable and respectful; and ventured to promise, if he would immediately quit the apartment, she would reconsider his proposals, and acquaint him with the result of her reflections on the ensuing day.

As soon as the Marchese had retired, Mademoiselle de Rubine being again alone, began to ruminate in silence upon this singular adventure. The person who was solicitous to obtain her regard, had hitherto conducted himself in her presence with the strictest propriety and decorum. In respect to religion he was decidedly of that persuasion in which she had been educated, and early taught to believe was essential both to her temporal and eternal interests. His figure was rather agreeable to her than otherwise; in manners he was peculiarly elegant and alluring, whilst in point of rank, which was only a secondary consideration, it was a match which she imagined as far transcended her merit as expectations. To escape unassisted from the power of Vescolini was impossible, and even could it be effected, without a protector to act in her defence, she was still liable to insult and persecution.

These arguments determined her to accept the offers of the Marchese, could she be so fortunate as to prevail upon her favourite domestic to attend her. This being easily accomplished, she awaited the evening, when she was to deliver her final answer to him agreeable to her promise, with a kind of fearful impatience.

Madame Laronne had so carefully concealed from Mademoiselle de Rubine her extraordinary prepossession in favour of the Marchese, that the most distant suspicion of this partiality never occurred to her thoughts, or she might have concluded, from the present as well as the past, that jealousy was the foundation of this arbitrary conduct.

When the time, in which her final decision was to be conveyed to the Marchese, arrived, being anxious to spare herself the confusion of another interview, Julie wrote a note to acquaint him with the whole of her determination, which was carefully delivered by Dorothèe. Another was instantly returned, informing her that a carriage would be in readiness to receive them beyond the walls of the mansion, at an appointed hour, on the succeeding evening.

The intervening time was passed by Mademoiselle de Rubine in extreme agitation of mind; she, however, endeavoured to combat her fears, and when the hour of their departure approached, had reasoned herself into some degree of composure.

Having with much difficulty escaped from the chateau, she ran, attended by Dorothèe, to the appointed spot; and the Marchese, after placing them in the carriage, seated himself by their side, and commanded the postillion to proceed.

In a few hours they reached the Castello St. Aubin, the residence of the Marchese, and a priest being in readiness, the nuptials were solemnized.

As soon as this ceremony was performed, he acquainted Julie, that, owing to his not having at present informed his friends of the connexion, it was necessary for them to remove to another of his seats till the affair should be unfolded. To this proposition Julie readily assented, and was soon afterwards conveyed to a hunting villa, in a very remote situation, half concealed in a wood.

Here the augmenting tenderness of the Marchese, aided by his amiable and polished manners, soon ripened what was only esteem into the most lasting affection; but the happiness of Mademoiselle de Rubine was always of a transient nature. After the few first months had elapsed, his attentions visibly declined; he was continually forming excuses to absent himself, and at last nearly forsook the retreat. He was forever engaged in parties of pleasure, in gaming, and expensive diversions; and when he visited the villa, conducted himself towards Julie with a chilling indifference of demeanour, which was perceived with inexpressible uneasiness.

Yet still she retained some hopes that when the tender interest of a father was united with that of a husband, his former affection might be awakened, and his home endeared; but in this she was also deceived;—he still pleaded engagements; nor could the infantine innocence of Enrîco withdraw him from folly and dissipation.

Unable to endure the pressure of this severe and unexpected calamity, she at last ventured to inquire of the Marchese in what way she had been so unfortunate as to forfeit his regard, and if there was no possible means of regaining it? But what was her grief and astonishment when he informed her that their nuptials were not solemnized by a priest, and that the marriage was consequently illegal!

For a considerable time after she had received this intelligence Julie was too ill to bear a removal; but as soon as her health was sufficiently re-established, she took an eternal adieu of the Marchese, and with the child and Dorothèe, after much fatigue and many difficulties, repaired to the cottage on the borders of the Lake of Geneva.

CHAP. VIII.

"I care not, Fortune, what you from me take,
  You cannot rob me of free Nature's grace;
  You cannot shut the windows of the sky,
  Thro' which Aurora shews her brightening face;
  You cannot bar my constant feet to trace
  The woods and lawns by living streams at eve;
  Let health my nerves and finer fibres brace,
  Of Fancy, Reason, Virtue, nought can me bereave."

THOMSON.

Several years passed in an uninterrupted tranquillity at the castle of Elfinbach, and its peaceful inhabitants, being perfectly reconciled to their situation, had not a wish ungratified. No visiter, except Paoli, broke in upon their solitude, and his visits being those of business and necessity, were hastily terminated.

The amiable manners of Julie, whose real name will hereafter be disguised under that of Chamont, and the uniform sweetness of her disposition, so endeared her to her dependants, that the domestics were cheerful and assiduous to oblige; and as she contemplated the happy countenances around her, she felt that delightful sensation arising from the performance of duty, which is frequently the only temporal reward of virtue; but is, notwithstanding, a reward so considerable, that the mind, which has once experienced its effects, would not exchange it for every other advantage independent of it.

Ambrose, who had been long tutored in the family of the Marchese, did not possess that openness of character which distinguished the rest of the household. A mixture of selfishness and cunning was evident in his disposition, which could not elude the penetration of an accurate observer, though upon the whole he appeared quiet and inoffensive; and, if he did not secure the esteem of his associates, he managed so as to escape their censure.

Nothing could be more simple, more innocent, than the life

of Madame Chamont, which was occupied in the education of her children, in family arrangements, and every other worthy employment which her station required.

Both Enrîco and Laurette displayed early in life quickness of parts and gracefulness of demeanour, which were united with the most amiable inclinations of which the human mind is susceptible. It was impossible for any thing to exceed their mutual affection; one was never to be seen without the other; in play, or in study, they were equally inseparable; nor could one taste of any enjoyment, of which the other might not partake.

Enrîco possessed spirit, and energy of soul, sufficient to encounter the greatest difficulties. He was sometimes impatient of controul, and impetuous in his replies; but a fault was scarcely committed before it was followed by repentance, and an earnest desire of removing the consequent uneasiness of his mother by the most endearing caresses.

Laurette was blessed with an equal share of sensibility, but was gentle and timid. Her manners were so invariably amiable, that she never excited anger; when she did fall into an error, which was seldom the case, a look of disapprobation was sufficient to recal her to a sense of her duty, and an acknowledgment of her fault. Her charming instructress had never imposed herself upon her as her mother, neither had she intimated anything relative to the mysterious manner in which she had been conveyed to her; but had taught her to believe that she was an orphan, protected by the Marchese de Montferrat, to whom she was under infinite obligations, and whose kindness she must repay with the obedience of a child.

Nor was Enrîco informed of the circumstances of his birth, his affectionate parent having concealed from him, with equal discretion, what she did not cease to reflect upon with unutterable anguish; though sometimes in infantine simplicity he would touch upon the subject, and ask some questions respecting his father, his innocent interrogatories being only answered by tears and blushes, he had soon penetration enough to discover they had awakened mournful recollections, and a sufficient degree of prudence to discontinue the inquiry.

Father Benedicta, a friar, who belonged to a monastery of

Carthusians, not far from the castle of Elfinbach, and who was Madame Chamont's confessor, assisted her in the education of the children. He was a man that had spent the early part of his life in the bustle and gaiety of the world, in which he was supposed to have suffered much from disappointment; but what were the misfortunes that had occasioned this almost total seclusion from society, and from which he had taken refuge in the gloom of a cloister, were unknown even to the fraternity; but they were thought to be of a peculiar and mournful nature. Yet, though removed from the pleasures, he was sensible to the charities of life. To the unfortunate, the afflicted, or the dying, he was a never-failing source of support and assistance; he never heard of a calamity in which he did not take an interest, or a request, if virtuous, that he did not immediately grant. But the uniform austerities of his own life were beyond the strictest rules of his order, and it was only from the tender concern that he discovered for the welfare of others, that he was supposed to feel any "touch of humanity."

He overlooked the conduct of Enrîco and Laurette with the mild benignity of a saint; instructed them in the principles of religion, as well as in the classics, and watched the unfolding of each infant virtue with parental tenderness.

From the instructive conversation of this holy Father, Madame Chamont reaped many advantages; he was her friend and adviser, as well as her confessor, acquitting himself always to her satisfaction in every undertaking; though his increasing affection for his pupils, exclusively considered, was of itself sufficient to secure her esteem.

Of this Monk she made an inquiry concerning La Roque; but no Friar of the name of Francisco had arrived at his monastery. At her request he wrote to the Superiors of several others, but every attempt of gaining intelligence upon the subject proved ineffectual, which made her apprehend that either his illness had proved fatal, or that he had fallen into the hands of his persecutors. His mournful, his interesting expressions, the stingings of remorse that attended the recollection of his sufferings, excited her compassion whenever she reflected upon them, and awakened new curiosity to be acquainted with the sequel.

The undisturbed felicity which was experienced by Madame Chamont in the bosom of her family, and in the exercise of religion and virtue, was of a more pure and animated nature than any she had enjoyed since the death of her parents. No society was to her like that of her children, no hours passed so pleasantly as those dedicated to their improvement and amusement; whilst on their part affection was so entirely divested of fear, that they were never so happy as when in her presence.

The mornings were chiefly devoted to study, and the evenings to beautiful rambles in the woods, or along the margin of the river, and sometimes to the adjacent villages, where they were enabled to feel that tranquil delight arising from the practice of benevolence—the luxury of succouring the unfortunate, and of giving an expression of joy to the face long accustomed to sadness.

The study of botany was one of Madame Chamont's favourite employments, in which she had made some proficiency, which occasioned her to spend many hours in the fields, improving herself in this useful and elegant science. On these expeditions her young pupils were ever ready to attend her, and taking an osier basket on her arm, she would frequently wander with them in the stillness of the evening amid scenes the most romantic and picturesque, where, seated upon a hillock, or under the broad shade of a chesnut, she would weave a garland for Enrîco, or a chaplet to adorn the beautiful hair of Laurette; and frequently they would exchange the fertile and cultivated charms of Nature for her unadorned and more majestic works; sometimes they would ascend the steep crags of the mountains, where all was wild, waste, and rude, yet in its naked simplicity grand, stupendous, and sublime. Here they would contemplate the awful beauty of the scene, the retiring hills half lost in the distant horizon, and the spires of some neighbouring abbies just appearing amid the deep gloom of the woods, and hearken to the faint sound of the vesper bell, borne at intervals upon the wing of the breeze; and sometimes, when not a breath of air disturbed the universal calm, or shook the light foliage of the leaves, the distant chaunt of the Nuns would be heard, now swelling into holy rapture, and now sinking into sweet and mournful cadence, till softened by distance, or lost in the rising flutter of the gale, it died away upon the ear.

To the admirer of Nature every object she presents becomes interesting; the variety of her charms relieves the mind from satiety, and, in the enjoyment of her beauties, the soul of the enthusiast becomes elevated above the narrow boundaries of the world: he sees the Creator in his works, and adores in silence the perfection of the whole. At times a disposition of this cast will be inclined to melancholy; but it is a sublime and tender melancholy, which he would not resign for all the pleasures which gaiety could bestow, or wealth procure. To such impressions as these the mind of Madame Chamont was peculiarly susceptible, and she perceived this pensive sensation steal upon her spirits, at that season above all others, when the rich bloom of the landscape begins to fade, when the glow of vegetation and the flush of maturity are past, and the whole scenery exhibits a more saddened, but a more interesting appearance.

To these simple and innocent delights Enrîco and Laurette discovered an early attachment, which their amiable protectress beheld with satisfaction. She knew the necessity of employment, being well aware of the danger attending inactivity and indolence. She taught them to value every moment of their existence, not allowing them to pass without due improvement. Reading was a favourite occupation, and Madame Chamont did not neglect the selecting such books for their perusal as were capable of conveying both instruction and amusement, the reading of which might be considered not so much a task as a recreation. Enrîco was partial to historical writings, and having been permitted to examine, at an early age, the most eminent authors in that species of composition, was soon well acquainted with the works of the most celebrated Grecian and Latin historians. He was also an ardent lover of ancient poetry, particularly of the epic kind. Homer, Lucan, and Virgil, were perused with juvenile transport; nor was the much admired Gerusalemme of Tasso disregarded: his soul was fired with the illustrious atchievements of Rinaldo, and he burned with an irresistible desire of attaining military honours. Madame Chamont, who discovered his inclinations before he was conscious of having betrayed them, endeavoured at first to check a propensity which she had not a sufficient portion of fortitude to reflect upon with calmness: but finding that his happiness depended upon the success of his hopes, opposition appeared like cruelty; and having heard from Paoli that the Marchese wished to provide for him in the army, where his interest could not fail of being successful, she began to reason herself into compliance. She considered that if his disposition had a strong bias to a military life, he would not have an equal chance of rising to eminence in any other profession; and that this disposition, aided by the powerful interest of the Marchese, would doubtless raise him to high preferment. Thus the fondness overcame the fears of the mother, and she acquiesced in the proposition.

When this affair was determined upon, the Marchese being apprized of Enrîco's wishes, procured him a commission in the army of Maximilian, Duke of Bavaria, and Paoli attending to conduct him from the castle, he took an affectionate adieu of his mother and Laurette, and proceeded on his journey.

For some time after the departure of Enrîco every countenance expressed concern and inquietude. Dorothèe, who had been his nurse from his infancy, was inconsolable for his loss, and continued to weep incessantly; but being gradually reconciled to what was unavoidable, the family regained their serenity.

In a short time Madame Chamont received a letter from him, which contained the most pleasing intelligence, that he was well and happy. He spoke tenderly of his dear companion, his little Laurette, and desired she might be told that he would never forget her. This account of the health and welfare of Enrîco was received by his excellent parent with the most lively rapture; and though sometimes this temporary absence would cast a shade of sorrow upon her countenance, which all her firmness could not enable her to subdue, she would anticipate the future glory of her son; her sanguine imagination would follow him through all the intricacies of his destiny, and represent him covered with honours, and glowing in the pride of martial glory.

With redoubled attention Madame Chamont now devoted herself to the education of her lovely charge. She instructed her without any assistance in the French and Italian languages, as well as in drawing and music. She also cultivated her taste for poetry, of which she was passionately fond.

The songs of Laurette were generally of the plaintive kind, which she accompanied with her lute with exquisite taste and judgment; though she sometimes exerted herself in a lively air to dissipate the tender dejection which was perceptible in the demeanour of Madame Chamont, when her thoughts reverted too anxiously to her son, who felt she was amply repaid for all the attention she had bestowed upon her orphan charge, by her undeviating assiduity to please, and the sweetness of disposition she displayed.

The absence of Enrîco had for some time affected the spirits of Laurette. She could ill support the loss of him who had been the companion of her infancy, the sharer in her amusements and her studies, and for whom she felt more than a sisterly affection.

Laurette in person was at the age of fourteen, in which time she had nearly completed her growth, rather above the middle size. Her form was of the most perfect symmetry, her complexion rather delicate than blooming; her eyes were dark, sparkling, and tender, and when directed upwards, had an expression of sweetness, and sometimes of melancholy, that was at once charming and interesting. When silent, there was a certain softness in her countenance that was infinitely fascinating; and when animated by the expression that her conversation diffused, it was equally captivating and alluring. Though her cheek did not always display the full and glowing tint of the rose, yet exercise, or an emotion of surprise, awakened the most delicate bloom, and gave a dazzling lustre to her beauty.

> Whene'er with soft serenity she smil'd,
>> Or caught the orient blush of quick surprise,
> How sweetly mutable, how brightly wild,
>> The liquid lustre darted from her eyes!
>
> MASON.

One of the rooms in the eastern part of the building, which was entirely appropriated to herself, contained her music, books, drawing implements, and embroidery. The windows of this room opened upon a lawn, that was terminated by groves of laurel, fir, and flowering ash. Here she spent many hours in the morning, improving herself, with the assistance of Madame Chamont, in useful and elegant employments. She usually arose early, and rambled for some time unattended through wild and unfrequented walks, where too frequently the image of Enrîco would recur to her imagination, and melt her into tears. These rambles were inexpressibly grateful to her at that charming season when all Nature is rising as from her grave into perfect vegetation and verdure, when the embryo leaves are just unfolding their beauties to the sun, and all breathe harmony, delight, and rapture! It was after one of these little romantic excursions that she penned the following lines, which was the first effort of her muse:

SONNET TO SPRING.

Come, lovely nymph, with all thy flow'ry train,
　　And let thy herald gem these mountains hoar;
With fragrant violets deck this lonely plain,
　　And bid rude Winter's whirlwind howl no more.
Thy soft approach the hawthorn buds declare,
　　That scent, with odours sweet, the passing gale,
And, clad in snowy vest, the lily fair,
　　Hides her meek beauties in the humid vale.
Oh! come, thou nymph divine, delightful Spring!
　　With all thy graces, all thy melting lays,
And mild Content, thy sweet companion, bring,
　　She that in sylvan shades and woodlands strays:
Whose angel form, health's blushing sweets disclose,
And on whose beauteous lip the eastern ruby glows.

Laurette's time was not so entirely devoted to music, reading, or the study of languages, as to preclude the duties of society, nor the tender and benevolent offices of charity. She frequently visited the sick, the infirm, and the aged, and to work for the peasantry that inhabited the border of the river, was a favourite occupation.

In one of these cottages was a poor widow, who was left with a numerous family, without any other means of support than what was afforded by her own industry. Here Madame Chamont and Laurette oftentimes resorted to soften the acuteness of distress, and to relieve the hardships of poverty. By their hands the younger part of the family were entirely clothed, who no sooner beheld their benefactresses, than they flocked around them with the most endearing tenderness; their presence diffused universal pleasure, and never was the sentiment of gratitude more eloquently expressed than in the countenance of the widow. Those who have experienced the luxurious sensation of contributing to the happiness of their fellow-creatures will form some estimate of that heartfelt satisfaction, which animated the amiable visiters as they contemplated the objects of their benevolence; and will allow, that it is a luxury too pure, and too refined, to exist in the midst of folly and dissipation, and, like other virtues, usually retires from the bustle of the world to the silent walks of domestic life.

CHAP. IX.

"How happy is the blameless vestal's lot,
The world forgetting, by the world forgot;
Eternal sun-shine of the spotless mind,
Each prayer accepted, and each wish resign'd;
Labour and rest, that equal periods keep,
Obedient slumbers, that can wake and weep;
Desires composed, affections ever even,
Tears that delight, and sighs that waft to heaven."

POPE.

The only female acquaintance cultivated by Madame Chamont in her retirement was the Superior of a convent of penitent Nuns, of the order of St. Francis, to whom she was recommended by Father Benedicta. This Abbess was a woman of high birth and education. Her aspect was entirely divested of that stately reserve, which usually accompanies undisputed authority. Her conduct was irreproachable, and she blended judiciously all the elegances of refinement with maternal tenderness. She loved the Nuns as her children, entering into all their concerns and distresses with the lively interest of a friend, extending her sympathy to all that were in need of it, her charity to the friendless, and her succour to the oppressed. Her looks, her words, were those of comfort and compassion, and her precepts, being delivered with plainness and energy, never failed to persuade. Misfortune had given pensiveness to her demeanour without throwing any thing of gloom around. The whole of her countenance was expressive of the most fervent piety; no appearance of bigotry disgraced it, for her religion was that of the heart, that of sentiment rather than of theory, which taught her to cherish every virtue that dignifies the human mind, to instigate by example, and to reward with affection.

To such perfections as these Madame Chamont could not be insensible; and on a first interview there was nothing she more ardently desired than to be included amongst the number of her friends. She was not long denied this enviable privilege; for the holy Benedicta had advanced much in her favour, and her own insinuating address had done more. The lady Abbess found in the graceful ease of her manners, a charm every way congenial to her mind. She saw she had suffered, for time and reflection had not yet erased the mark of sorrow from her countenance; yet this was not its only character—gentleness, meekness, and resignation, were blended with the harsher lines of calamity, each uniting to soften what could not be eradicated.

She was soon admitted into the cloister as an intimate, and spent many hours in the society of her new acquaintance, who received her with inexpressible tenderness, never allowing her to depart without a promise to shorten her next absence. The difference of their years did not preclude the advances of friendship of the most noble and interesting kind, though in this the Abbess had considerably the advantage. But age had given nothing of gloom to her deportment, having rather added to, than detracted from, its natural grace. She soon loved Madame Chamont as her daughter, cherished her as a friend, and felt unusually animated in her presence. Some of the Nuns beheld her with no symptoms of pleasure; the attentions of their noble protectress, which had hitherto been confined to themselves, were, they imagined, transferred to a stranger; and though respect for their much-revered lady prevented them from murmuring, they could not entirely conceal the cause of their chagrin.

At every meeting the two friends were more delighted with each other than before, and this attachment led them to indulge in the luxury of mutual confidence. The lady Abbess related to Madame Chamont the most memorable events of her past life; they were melancholy, but not uninteresting, and her gentle auditress, who listened to her with the most lively concern, shed many tears at the recital; the substance of which was as follows:

THE STORY OF THE ABBESS.

The Superior of the convent of the penitent Nuns, of the order of St. Francis, was of Gallic extraction, being the only daughter of the Compte de Vendome, who was a General Officer in the service of the Prince of Conde, when that renowned warrior fought the famous battle of Jarnac with the Duke of Anjou.

His valour was the boast of his country, the admiration of Europe, making him revered as an ally, and equally dreaded as an enemy! After being celebrated, and almost idolized in France for the signal victories he had gained, his hitherto successful armies were routed by an attack from an unexpected quarter, and the enemy being joined by numbers too powerful for resistance, they were called upon to surrender.

The Compte, unwilling to lessen his former fame by what he termed a shameful acquiescence, resolutely refused to obey, chusing rather to die in the field than to tarnish his spotless reputation by relinquishing his arms. Some of the soldiers preferring captivity to death, consented to the proposition, whilst others, who had caught somewhat of that martial ardour that animated the invincible soul of their leader, persisted in a refusal. The fight now became more desperate; the enemy was joined by a detachment conveniently ambushed near the place; the field was soon covered with the dead and the wounded, and the father of the amiable Abbess, after having defended himself bravely for a long time, was at last overpowered and slain!

This melancholy news was soon communicated to the Comptessa with all imaginable delicacy, but she did not long survive the recital. She had been for some time in a weak state, and this was a shock she was unable to sustain. Immediately on her decease, Adela, her only surviving child, was consigned to the care of her guardian, Monsieur de Santong, who resided in a distant part of the province. He was a widower, of reduced fortunes; with one son, who was finishing his education at one of the public seminaries in Paris.

Monsieur was a man of stern and severe deportment, in disposition at once haughty and morose, and his manners were so little calculated to please, that Adela, having never since her birth left the side of her mother, shrunk with terror from his gaze.

Before the Comte de Vendome quitted his beloved home, to undertake his last fatal expedition, he settled all his temporal affairs, leaving his daughter to the protection of this his only surviving relative, on the death of her mother, should this event take place before she was disposed of in marriage.

Monsieur de Santong, having been long disgusted with the world, had retired from the haunts of society to a small estate that he possessed in a remote and dreary situation, where he lived as peaceful and undisturbed as if consigned to his grave. Previous to his seclusion, he had mixed occasionally with people of various descriptions, but without being able to select any one with whom he could remain in habits of intimacy. He was a man of parts, without gaining the respect that usually adheres to science, because he expected undue regard; and in spite of the gravity of his appearance, the eccentricities of his conduct frequently made him the sport of witticism: by the learned he was rejected for his obstinacy, by the gay for his severity, and by the candid for his misanthropy. Thus, after the death of his wife, and the departure of his son, who was educated under the eye of one of his mother's relatives in the metropolis, he was left a lonely and solitary being, in whom no one was interested; few gave themselves the trouble to inquire whether he was still in existence, and those who did, lamented, when answered in the affirmative, that the useless were permitted to survive the worthy.

His relation, the Compte de Vendome, was, perhaps, the only person of his acquaintance by whom he was not thoroughly despised, though the sentiments and disposition of this justly-esteemed nobleman were so diametrically opposite to his. The application and activity inseparable from a military capacity, had indeed prevented a continual intercourse, and the connexion subsisting between the families had silenced many out of respect to the much-revered Compte, who might otherwise have uttered much to Monsieur de Santong's disadvantage. He had more than once visited Monsieur before he took refuge in retirement; and, from the observations he was enabled to make, was convinced that his knowledge was profound, though obscured by caprice; and finding nothing to alledge against him but his inordinate love of praise, and his eccentric indulgences, he fixed upon him as the guardian of his Adela, should she be deprived of her parents before that sacred trust should devolve to another.

The fair orphan, being not more than seven years of age, received from Monsieur de Santong the first rudiments of her education. She was not allowed, for reasons never to be penetrated, to receive it in its usual form, in the shades of a cloister, though the mansion in which she resided was equally dreary and secluded. Society, or unexpected events, never retarded her progress, which enabled her soon to become conversant in every branch of elegant literature, and to be well acquainted with the classics, without being compelled to receive their beauties through the medium of her mother tongue.

Monsieur de Santong, who, next to his own son, loved her as much as he was capable of loving any one, beheld the proficiency she made with surprise and pleasure; and when in conversation with her, relaxed so much from his accustomed severity, that she became imperceptibly more at ease in his presence; yet her youthful imagination would frequently wander beyond the walls of the chateau, and portray scenes of gaiety and happiness in the world, which the original would not have equalled.

But, upon the whole, the life of Adela passed less unpleasantly than might have been imagined. A lively French woman, who was the director of the domestic affairs, interested herself much in her happiness, and saved her from many moments of despondency. Her name was Agnes; she had received a respectable education at Moulines under the care of an aunt, and after meeting with some misfortunes in life, respecting pecuniary affairs, had accepted a superior kind of service in the family of Monsieur de Santong.

In the society of this young woman, who possessed much genuine good humour, she frequently rambled a considerable distance from the mansion when the occupations of the day were over, and amused herself with surveying the landscape which her secluded situation commanded. But books were her chief amusements, and these were never denied her. Those selected by her guardian for her instruction and entertainment were mostly of the learned kind, though she was sometimes supplied with lighter works by the assistance of Agnes, from which she reaped less solid advantage.

Several years were passed in this manner without any material incident, till the arrival of the younger Santong, who had just completed his studies, occasioned an alteration in affairs.

He came attended by a schoolfellow, his principal companion, who was introduced by the name of Clairville to Monsieur, who received him with an air of coldness bordering upon rudeness. The young chevalier, who did not fail to remark the unpleasant consequence of his visit, appeared chagrined and uneasy, which Adela perceiving, endeavoured to remove by every attention she was empowered to bestow. In this she succeeded. His thoughts were soon abstracted from this slight cause of distress, but were directed to a subject more dangerous to his peace. He loved Adela the moment he beheld her, and without asking permission of his reason for doing so: well aware of the distance at which fortune had thrown him, he would have submitted, for the first time, to have solicited her favours, could wealth have secured the possession of his wishes.

Every interview increased his regard; he soon lived but for Adela, who was by no means insensible to his merit; and from the native openness of her disposition, felt no inclination to conceal from the observation of others the sentiment she indulged in his favour.

The young Santong, who was evidently as much inferior to his friend in mind as in person, beheld the decided preference shewn to him by his fair relation with a degree of dissatisfaction and displeasure, which he sometimes failed to disguise. He had bestowed upon the person and accomplishments of Adela no common attention; but her birth and splendid possessions were still more alluring in his eyes. His father had intimated his intention of uniting him with his ward, whose early seclusion from the world must have prevented the possibility of any other attachment. He had acceded with rapture to the proposal before he was introduced to her, and no sooner beheld her than he considered her as his future bride. Had his own vanity been less, he would have avoided throwing a handsome young chevalier in her way, whose mind was not less perfect than his person, and whose soul was formed for all the delicacies and refinements of the tender passions.

Adela, being a stranger to disguise, would frequently, in the absence of Clairville, speak eloquently in his praise in the presence of Monsieur and the younger Santong, and perceived, not without astonishment, the apparent coldness with which her guardian repressed her innocent encomiums, and the flashes of anger that occasionally darted from the eyes of his offended son. But unsuspicious of the cause, she still continued to talk of him with that ardour of friendship, which declared to the more experienced observer how tenderly she was attached to the object of her commendation. Clairville, who felt the awkwardness of his situation, endeavoured to reconcile himself to the thoughts of quitting the chateau; but the idea of never again beholding her, in whose fate he was so strongly interested, and of the probability of her being soon disposed of to his more fortunate rival, sunk upon his heart, and he became pensive and disconsolate. Every day brought with it fresh proof that the affections of his friend were estranged from him, and that common courtesy only prevented him from accelerating his departure. Conscious of this, he began internally to despise himself for having so long yielded to the weakness of his feelings, and resolved to regain his own esteem by naming an early day for his return to the metropolis. Having once determined upon this mode of conduct, he hastened to fulfil his intentions, and on the following morning, seeing his friend walking alone in the shrubbery, he joined him with the resolution of executing his purpose.

The young Santong did not immediately observe him, being lost in musing, till the voice of the once-respected chevalier roused him from his stupor; and turning towards him, he accosted him with an expression of kindness that overcame him with surprise and pleasure.

Contrary to his original determination, he did not instantly make known his intention; and being soon afterwards joined by Adela and Monsieur de Santong, he continued to defer it.

The conversation now became general, and more than usually lively; the young Comptessa discoursed with her accustomed sprightliness, whilst the eyes of her lover, announcing every feeling of his soul, conveyed a tender and earnest expression as they became riveted upon her's. Not far from the mansion was an extensive wood; and Santong having heard that it contained a large quantity of game, proposed to de Clairville, as the morning was fine, to spend a few hours in the diversion of shooting. His friend agreed to the proposal, though not without some reluctance, as it would deprive him of the society of Adela, and they began their excursion.

As soon as they were gone, the fair recluse retired pensively to her library, willing to beguile the moments of absence with her books, her usual resources in the moments of uneasiness. She felt, without knowing why, an unusual depression of spirits, which she made many efforts to dissipate, but without success. She reflected, with dissatisfaction, on the solicitous attentions of Santong, who, she easily perceived, was designed by her guardian for her future husband. She compared him with the noble, the insinuating stranger, and for the first time discovered the partiality which the merit of the latter had inspired. He had never openly declared his passion for her; but his expressive manners could not be misconstrued, and he was apparently withheld, only by respectful diffidence, from making a verbal confession.

Nothing appeared so dreadful to her as a marriage with Santong; yet how was it to be avoided, if her guardian insisted upon her compliance? How could she presume to oppose him, to whose will she had hitherto yielded the most implicit obedience? She knew that he was severe in his disposition, terrible in his displeasure, and capable of adopting the most resolute measures, and of performing the most daring actions. As to the younger Santong, he appeared to her somewhat prejudiced mind to be deficient in every amiable qualification of the heart. She wondered why the Chevalier de Clairville, who seemed to possess every moral and elevated virtue, had enlisted him among the number of his intimates, since there was certainly no reciprocity of sentiment to unite them in the bonds of affection.

The young sportsmen, having been absent some hours, and nothing happening to break the train of her reflections, she took a walk towards the skirts of the wood, and having reached a heathy mountain, seated herself upon a piece of broken rock, and continued to muse on the subject which had so recently occupied her thoughts. She had not been long in this situation before the report of a gun, proceeding from the wood, convinced her they were returning from their excursion. She started from her place without knowing whither she was going, and advancing rapidly towards the spot from whence the sound was heard, a dreadful scream alarmed her, and in the next moment she beheld young Santong and the servant, who had attended them in their expedition, bearing the bleeding, and apparently almost lifeless form of the Chevalier de Clairville!

What a sight was this for Adela, the tender, the adoring Adela, to sustain! But surprise and anguish soon depriving her of sensation, she sunk into a state of insensibility. The cries of the servant (for Santong, transfixed in horror, was unable to utter a sound) reached the chateau, and the domestics, with anxious and terrified looks, crowded around them. Adela, who was long before she discovered any symptom of returning life, was conveyed to her room, where every method was employed to restore and console her; but a fever and delirium were the consequence of this dreadful alarm, which threatened to terminate her existence. The physician that attended de Clairville was called in to her assistance, who pronounced her to be in a state of danger; at the same time desired that she might be kept as tranquil as possible, as the only chance of success depended upon the recomposing of her spirits. This induced her attendants to delude her, in the intervals of reason, with the most flattering information respecting the chevalier. The physician was also from necessity compelled to aid the deception, by assuring her that his wounds were not mortal, and that from their favourable appearance every thing was to be hoped.

This joyful intelligence tended to accelerate her recovery, and as soon as she was enabled to bear a repetition of the subject, inquired how the accident had happened? But of this she could hear no satisfactory account. The young Santong was alone acquainted with the particulars, and he being in a state little short of distraction, was not in a situation to answer inquiries.

As soon as Adela was sufficiently recovered from her illness to endure the sight of de Clairville, he requested permission to see her. What they might mutually suffer from so trying an interview, induced the worthy physician to deny him the privilege; but as the necessity of refusing a dying request is, perhaps, one of the severest inflictions that benevolence can endure, he at last yielded, though not unreluctantly, to his wishes.

As soon as Adela was informed of his desire, she quitted her room, for the first time since she entered it, and proceeded, supported by Agnes, to the side of his bed.

But what were her feelings when, instead of finding him in a state of convalescence as she had been taught to expect, she beheld him with the image of death stamped upon his countenance, saw his lips quivering as if on the eve of closing for ever, and heard his short convulsive breathings, with every other symptom of approaching dissolution! The moment she fixed her eyes on the faded form before her, a cold trembling seized her: she had but just power to repress the scream that was escaping her, and afraid she should relapse into insensibility before she should catch the last accents of his voice, clung still closer to Agnes. The dying chevalier, though unable to articulate, extended his feeble hand to grasp her's, with a look so tender, so mournful, so touching, that her grief arose to agony!

Incapable of moving, she still continued by his side, with her eyes fixed wildly upon his face, with such an expression of anguish, that none present could refrain from tears! At last the wan countenance on which she gazed assumed a more ghastly paleness, the films obscured his sight, the pulse that had long beat feebly, fluttered, and then ceased for ever, and that captivating, that once graceful form, became stiffened in death! Adela's distress was now too acute to be suppressed, and disengaging herself from Agnes, who could no longer restrain her, she fell breathless on the bed! A deep silence, as of the grave, ensued, which was only interrupted occasionally by the loud sobs of Monsieur de Santong, who had remained in speechless sorrow at the farther end of the room during this pathetic scene, unobserved by the unfortunate sufferers. It was too much for human nature to endure with firmness, and the stern, and before impenetrable, heart of the misanthropist melted at the touches of sympathy!

As soon as the account of de Clairville's dissolution reached the ears of his son, he flew into the room with the desperation of a maniac, declaring himself his murderer. His cries recalled Adela to existence, who, regarding him with speechless horror as he uttered the dreadful truth, threw herself into the arms of her attendant, and was conveyed to her apartment.

It was several days after this mournful event before she was in a situation to see any one except her physician and confessor, and during that period the remorse and distraction of Santong portended the loss of his senses! He raved continually of Adela, besought his father to plead for his forgiveness, and then resign him as a murderer to the laws of his country. He acknowledged that it was jealousy alone that had instigated him to the horrid deed, having observed the attachment that had subsisted between his friend and the young Comptessa ever since its commencement, particularly the tender looks they had exchanged on the morning that had witnessed his guilt, which, he added, had given fresh fuel to that unbridled resentment, which was before too violent to be concealed or subdued.

Though Adela had been brought by this trying calamity nearly to the brink of the grave, youth, united to a good constitution, finally triumphed, and in a few weeks she was enabled to sit up in her room, and to converse with her confessor.

Monsieur de Santong, who had made daily inquiries concerning his unhappy ward ever since the death of de Clairville, ventured, at the request of his son, to solicit an audience. Having gained the permission he desired, he was ushered into the room, and, with an aspect on which pity and distress were strikingly depicted, placed himself on a chair by her side. Adela received him with a placid and sorrowful air; but when he began to plead for his son, the assassin of the noble chevalier, a slight blush of resentment tinged her cheek, and she surveyed him with a look of mingled astonishment and displeasure. But when he assured her that his son did not aspire to her love, but only besought her forgiveness, and had convinced her that the atrocious crime his unfortunate child had committed was not the effect of deliberate and premeditated cruelty, the expression of her countenance changed, and compassion gave new softness to its character. A heart that could deny its pardon to a wretch, suffering all the agonies of guilt and remorse, must have been made of sterner materials than was that of Adela; and she bestowed it in accents so gentle, that, though the younger Santong never presumed to obtrude himself into her presence, when he received an account of it from his father, he became more tranquil.

The wretched culprit did not continue much longer at the chateau; and though despondency had prompted the request concerning a resignation to the civil laws of his country, other considerations determined him to purchase a dispensation from the Pope, and to close his existence in some religious retirement. Monsieur de Santong did not oppose his inclinations; this heavy calamity, inflicted upon him by the violence of unregulated passions, had an effect upon his mind as powerful as it was instantaneous. He was now no longer proud, vain, or inaccessible; his favourite project, that of uniting his son to the heiress of the noble house of Vendome, was at an end, and every earthly pursuit seemed to have expired with it. Grief had the happy effect of convincing him that he was not beyond the reach of misfortune, and by teaching him the insufficiency of immoderate acquirements, had conveyed a lesson of humility and wisdom. When the chevalier was first introduced to him, he imagined, in his fine person and insinuating address, he discovered a formidable rival for his son. He saw his perfections with dissatisfaction, because he believed they could not fail to attract the regard of the youthful and blooming Adela; but now that he had paid so dear for his rivalship, he felt nothing of prejudice lingering at his heart, and cherished a kind of melancholy esteem for his memory. This sudden transition, from moroseness to kindness, indicated that his former misanthropy was rather the effect of circumstance than a natural inclination of the mind; for from this time he became the mild guardian, the compassionate and tender father; and could he have prevailed upon himself to have returned to society, might have become the estimable friend.

As soon as Adela was recovered, she formed a resolution of secluding herself in a convent, and took an early opportunity of informing Monsieur de Santong of her design. Amazed at her intention, he offered some slight objections, which she speedily removed, and then consented to inquire for a situation suitable to her wishes.

About a week after she had made known her determination, the unhappy Santong repaired to his monastery, which was somewhere in the southern part of France; and on the succeeding day the Comptessa de Vendome was conducted by her guardian to the convent, which, in obedience to her former desire, he had selected for her residence: it contained a society of Carmelite Nuns of one of the strictest orders in the country. Here she was admitted as a boarder; but owing to its not meeting with her entire approbation, did not continue her abode in this place. There was not one among the sisterhood with whom she could connect herself; for the Lady of the convent was reserved, haughty, and mercenary, and the Nuns seemed invariably to emulate her example.

This influenced her intentions of not remaining in so unpleasant a society during life, and led her to adopt a resolution of quitting it as soon as she could inform herself of another more congenial to her taste. Having executed her design, she left France, and removing into Germany, entered into a convent of Penitent Nuns, of the order of St. Francis. Here she spent several years as a sister; and after the death of the Abbess, having endowed this religious asylum with her vast possessions, was preferred to the honour of succeeding her as Superior.——

When this little affecting narrative was concluded, which was illustrated with many elevated sentiments and tender incidents, which, unless recited with the grace and eloquence of the amiable narrator, might fail to interest the reader, she drew a small gem from her bosom, which contained the name of the chevalier, wrought with his hair: it was suspended by a small string of rubies, and was worn continually round her neck. As she gazed upon this precious relic, a throbbing emotion disturbed her usually serene features; she sighed, pressed it mournfully to her heart, and seemed to be insensible to every thing for the moment but the recollection of her long-indulged sorrows.

Madame Chamont, who had listened to her with a painful interest, bent over the arm of the chair on which her friend was sitting, and mingled her tears with her's, till their attention was recalled from melancholy reflection by the appearance of a Nun who came to present a piece of embroidery to the Abbess, which she had newly finished. As she advanced towards the Superior with a pensive and dignified air, she bent gracefully to Madame Chamont, and drawing aside her veil, discovered to her one of the most lovely faces she had ever seen. It was pale, and marked with sorrow; but there was a certain expression of softness and resignation in her fine Grecian features—an air of meek, corrected sadness, that could not be perused without pity and affection. As soon as she had delivered her work, and had received the grateful commendation of the Abbess, she drew her veil again over her face, and retired.

As soon as she was gone, Madame Chamont, willing to withdraw her revered friend from the luxury of too tender remembrances, praised the singular beauty of the sister, and requested to be informed of her name. "It is sister Cecilia," returned the Superior, "one of the most devout Nuns of the order. She never enters into any of our amusements, except at the holy festivals, and seems to dedicate the whole of her life to prayer and religious exercises. She confines herself almost entirely to her cell, seldom enters into conversation with any other than her confessor, and preserves a life of uniform reserve and austerity.

"She is the only one of the sisterhood with whose story I am unacquainted, though she has been in the society upwards of fourteen years; nor have any of the Nuns, not even those for whom she possesses the most decided regard, been able to gain admission into her confidence. Yet, though she has preserved this invariable reserve, none of the inhabitants of the cloister are more tenderly, more universally beloved. She is the first to shew consolation and kindness to all who are in need of it; her breast is the temple of benevolence, the seat of truth and of virtue. Her charity is as unbounded as her other excellencies, and she seems capable of no other enjoyment than what she derives from the source of religion, and the happiness of her fellow-creatures. Besides these solid and estimable virtues, she possesses many charming accomplishments, which, but for their being con-nected with the stable principles, the intrinsic excellencies of the mind, might be justly deemed of little value. Nature has bestowed upon her, amongst her other gifts, a rich and excursive fancy; the devout pieces, which are used not unfrequently on the most solemn occasions, attuned to the notes of the organ, are chiefly of her composing; and for grace, delicacy, and energy of thought, may be said to be nearly unequalled. In music she is an avowed proficient, and the needle-work she has just brought for my inspection," resumed the Abbess, "is an indisputable proof of her taste in that elegant department."

There was something in this account, united with the exalted, yet meek devotion, that characterized the appearance of the Nun, so affecting to Madame Chamont, that, when the Superior had finished, she still listened, in hopes of hearing a farther account of her. But her informer had related all that she knew of her, except that she was a Neapolitan, and that it was believed she had suffered some severe irremediable calamity previous to her retirement from the world.

Madame Chamont's curiosity was now more than ever awakened; she thought of the Signora di Capigna, the supposed mother of Laurette, and anxiety to be informed of the truth of this surmise arose to the most painful impatience. The more she mused upon the subject, the more probable it appeared, that the devout Cecilia was no other than the once celebrated Neapolitan, the fair unfortunate victim of early seduction, who, after the death of her father, was believed either to have died of grief, or to have sought a remedy for it in some religious seclusion. When she considered every thing the Abbess had uttered, her grief, her silence respecting her family and name, her penitential devotions, the length of time since she had entered into the convent answering so nearly to the age of Laurette, her Italian origin—every circumstance seemed to convince her that the conjecture was not founded on error, which determined her, if possible, to gain further intelligence; but the difficulty of accomplishing her design repressed the energy of the enterprize; was it likely that the fair Nun, who had denied her confidence to so many with whom she was in habits of intimacy, and even to the Superior herself, should impart it to a stranger, one whom she had scarcely seen, and who had no possible claim on her regard or attention?

As soon as she had quitted the convent, she returned silently towards the castle, meditating as she went upon this new incident. If this was really the Signora de Capigna, and her idea concerning Laurette was a just one, she was doubtless ignorant respecting her offspring, who had probably been conveyed from her without her consent or knowledge. The actions of the Marchese were so veiled in mystery, that it was impossible to comprehend, or to account for them. But the propriety of acquainting sister Cecilia with the situation of her child, if by any means Laurette could be proved to be her's, appeared, every time she reflected upon it, more striking. After much consideration, she formed the resolution of sending a few lines to the Nun by Father Benedicta, who was confessor of the convent.

Some days passed before she had an opportunity of accomplishing her design, not being able to gain an interview with him in private; but having written a letter to be in readiness, in which she avoided mentioning any thing of herself or her charge, merely asking if she ever had a daughter, and was ignorant of her fate, she committed it to the care of the Father. The holy Benedicta eyed the direction, which was written in Italian, with a look expressive of surprise; and then placing it silently in the folds of his habit, bowed meekly, and withdrew. It was not long before the Monk returned again to the castle, and as soon as he was admitted into the presence of Madame Chamont, presented her with an answer to her epistle, which she instantly opened. It contained many grateful acknowledgments, elegantly and delicately expressed, and, without any reference to her own peculiar misfortunes, informed her she never had a daughter. The conclusion, expressive of the devout spirit of the writer, breathed a solemn benediction, commending her with impressive fervency to the protection of Heaven. The signature, which bore no other name than that of Cecilia, a penitent Nun of the order of St. Francis, seemed to have been written with a disordered hand, and to have been watered with her tears.

Satisfied that this either was not Signora di Capigna, or that Laurette was not the daughter of that unfortunate beauty, she made no further attempt to investigate the subject; and whether from chance or design she was unable to ascertain, the Nun never more entered the apartment of the Abbess when Madame Chamont was there.

CHAP. X.

"Down many a winding step, mid dungeons dank,
 Where anguish wails aloud, and fetters clank
 To caves bestrew'd with many a mouldering bone,
 And cells, whose echos only learn to groan,
 Where no kind bars a whispering friend disclose,
 No sun-beam enters, and no zephyr blows,
 He treads."

DARWIN.

A considerable time had elapsed since the departure of Enrîco, and no recent account of him having arrived at the castle, a thousand mournful conjectures destroyed the repose of Madame Chamont and Laurette, who began to believe that he was either taken captive, or was slain by his more fortunate foes, while bravely fighting the cause of the great Maximilian. These dreadful apprehensions drew tears incessantly from the eyes of his affectionate mother, whilst her beautiful pupil, who endeavoured to appear cheerful in the presence of her protectress, often retired to her apartment, or into the secret recesses of the woods, to weep and suffer in silence.

The imagined fate of the young warrior was yet undecided, when Paoli once more arrived at the mansion. From him they indulged a hope of gaining some information respecting the Bavarian armies; but this proving delusive, the family again sunk into sorrow and deep dejection.

Madame Chamont's mind was so extremely agitated with these distressing surmises, that, unable to sleep, she frequently forsook her bed before the sun had risen upon the mountains, and wandered for some hours unattended in the solitudes of the forest; hoping, in the contemplation of external objects, that she might be able to divert her thoughts from a subject that was attended with the severest anguish.

One morning, having extended her walk much longer than usual, she found herself in a part of the domain which she had never visited before. It was more wild and picturesque than any thing she had ever seen; an appearance of uncultivated grandeur was delineated in the prospect it commanded, an air of desolation that was in unison with her feelings, and to the frame of mind she was then in, was infinitely more grateful than the more soft and glowing landscape.

As she continued her ramble through the most woody part of the grounds, one object above all others engaged her attention, and excited her surprise.

This was a small square tower that once belonged to the fortification wall of the castle, which had formerly spread along a vast extent of ground, including the principal part of the forest; the design of which was evidently that, in case of a siege, a sufficient quantity of cattle might be pastured to supply the inhabitants during the attack. This solitary turret, which, with the aid of a buttress, had strengthened one of the angles of the exterior polygon, was all that remained of the out-work, and even this was falling to decay. It was overtopped with long grass, briery, and the enchanter's nightshade; and being almost immersed in the deep gloom of the woods, seemed to have become the residence of birds of prey.

Curiosity impelling her to examine the inside of the fabric, she entered what had once been a door, and was proceeding through the arch on the opposite side, when the sound of voices issuing from below struck her with terror and dismay. The first idea that presented itself, which the extreme solitude of the situation seemed to favour, was, that it was the resort of a party of banditti, which made her irresolute whether to stop for a few minutes to be convinced if she was right in her conjecture, or to hasten from a place which threatened her with danger, and return towards the mansion. Whilst she was thus hesitating, she perceived, at the most remote part of the structure, a small iron door, and on one side of it, nearly at the bottom, a narrow grated aperture. An irresistible impulse impelled her to kneel down, that she might be able to observe to what part of the building this entrance led; but the light this window admitted was so feeble, that she could but just distinguish a small extent of passage, which apparently terminated in a flight of stone steps.

In a state of inconceivable dread she listened for some moments to be assured from whence the voices proceeded; but the deep sighing of the wind among the trees prevented her from discriminating any other sound. Anxious to be assured who were the people thus strangely secluded in the subterranean recesses of this gloomy abode, and to be acquainted with the purpose of their concealment, she advanced fearfully towards the door, and examining it attentively, endeavoured to discover some way of opening it; but no visible means appearing, she pressed forcibly against it, and to her utter astonishment it unclosed. Thus enabled to gratify a curiosity which was augmented by the small prospect of gratification the first view of it had presented, she walked slowly through the passage, and was within a few paces of the stairs when a deep groan, which was instantly succeeded by the clinking of a chain, overcame her with horror and amazement. Fear having suspended her faculties, she stood for a few seconds motionless as a statue, totally unable either to proceed or to return, till a loud voice, elevated as in anger, recovered her from her stupor, which being answered in the low, mournful accents of entreaty, convinced her that some unhappy being was suffering in that unfrequented and dreary solitude; but, as the turret belonged immediately to the castle, who could be the tyrant, and who the prisoner, was strange beyond conjecture.

As soon as she was enabled to conquer the terror this incident had occasioned, she again advanced towards the stairs, and in the pauses of the wind heard these words distinctly pronounced, in a voice which she immediately knew to be Paoli's:—

"You have had a sufficient time allowed you, and as death is inevitable, and nothing can procure even a temporary respite, you have only to chuse the means. I leave this place to-day. The moments are precious, therefore be hasty in your determination."

These incoherent expressions were enough to assure her that some person was confined in that place for the purpose of being murdered. Almost fainting with apprehension, she receded as far as the entrance, and holding the iron door with her hand, was irresolute whether to return again towards the steps, or to hurry from the spot. As she stood for a few moments endeavouring to overcome the agony that this strange adventure had excited, as well as to consider if it was not possible, by timely interference, to avert the fate that awaited this victim of perhaps unjust resentment, she heard a noise like the undrawing of rusty bolts, which was followed by the sound of footsteps, apparently proceeding towards her.

Knowing this could be no other than Paoli, she closed the door that led into the passage, and rapidly retreating, concealed herself in the thick foliage of the trees that surrounded the lonely turret; but in such a situation, that she must unavoidably see him pass.

In a few minutes he quitted the tower; and having turned into the glade, was hastily putting something into his pocket, when the rustling of the trees, under which Madame Chamont had secreted herself to elude being noticed by him, made him start involuntarily, and what he was attempting to secure fell upon the ground. The grass preventing any noise, he was unconscious of his loss, and, seemingly satisfied with being undiscovered, walked speedily away.

Paoli having reached a considerable distance, Madame Chamont emerged from her obscurity, and on gaining the spot the steward had recently left, beheld, to her unutterable joy, a small rusty key, which she had no doubt belonged to the dungeon where the sufferer was confined.

For some time she was undetermined whether immediately

to release the unfortunate captive from his state of misery and perplexity, or to return to the castle, and to perform that office of humanity as soon as Paoli had quitted it, who had just intimated an intention of commencing his journey without further delay. On mature deliberation the latter plan was adopted; as, should the careful steward be aware of his loss before his arrival at the mansion, he would probably return in hopes of being able to recover it, in which case her generous designs would not only be frustrated, but instant death, or new and unheard-of torture might be inflicted upon the ill-fated object of her compassion.

This being resolved upon, she returned towards the castle elated at the thoughts of being able to release a fellow-creature from the grasp of inflexible tyranny, and secretly determining not to acquaint Laurette with the adventure, as it was impossible that an affair of that kind could be executed without the knowledge and consent of the Marchese; consequently, was she to be informed of this singular circumstance, she would reflect upon him, whom she had every reason to believe was the author of her being, with horror and aversion.

As soon as she had reached the outer court, she beheld her beautiful charge, with the airy lightness of a sylph, advancing to meet her; an emotion of joy played upon her features, and the usual salutations being over, she presented her with a letter from Enrîco.

Madame Chamont's feelings on this occasion can better be imagined than described. The intelligence the epistle conveyed was of the most pleasing kind; he spoke highly of his Colonel, the Marchese de Martilini, and rapturously of the way of life in which he had engaged. He also informed them that, as his regiment, at the close of the year, was likely to be stationed in a less remote province, he entertained some hopes of being permitted to pay his respects to his beloved mother and his dear Laurette, at the expiration of a few months.

Thus effectually relieved from a painful inquietude, Madame Chamont, though she could not forbear slightly censuring the negligence that had given rise to it, felt a degree of tranquillity and animation which she had been long unused to.

As soon as she arrived at the castle, she found Paoli was

already returned; and being assured, from his manner, that he had not seen her in the forest, scrupulously avoided mentioning any thing in his presence relative to her excursion.

Immediately on his departure she resolved, though enervated with the terror this occurrence had excited, to visit the solitary tower, and to liberate the unfortunate captive. The more she considered this singular incident, the more mysterious it appeared. If the Marchese had received any material injury from the prisoner, why not resign him to the laws of his country? Or, if the offence was of too venial a nature for justice to punish with death, or sufferance, why confine him at so vast a distance from his own residence, when assassination, or torture, might have been inflicted with equal secrecy and success in the dungeons of the Castello St. Aubin? What Paoli had uttered before he quitted his victim was expressive of the most arbitrary conduct; for though it allowed him the choice of means, this affected clemency was counteracted by a repetition of threats, which could not fail to appal the most resolute mind. He mentioned, during this conference, his intention of leaving the castle immediately, and the necessity of a hasty determination respecting the method of accomplishing the design; yet the matter seemed not to have been decided; no violent measures had at present been adopted, no screams of terror, or of agonizing torture, had pierced the deep solitude of the woods. The unfortunate being was then assuredly alive, though probably left to perish by poison, or the pining miseries of famine. More than once it occurred to her thoughts that it might possibly be La Roque; yet the length of time that had elapsed since her meeting with him at the post-house, did not justify the opinion, as, had he so long escaped falling into the hands of his enemy, he would surely, before this time, have placed himself beyond the reach of his malice.

The clinking of a chain, so distinctly heard from the place, convinced her of the difficulty of her enterprize; but recollecting that amongst a quantity of old lumber, in one of the chambers in the northern buildings, she had observed several files, and other instruments, which might be useful in the undertaking, she hastened to find them.

Having obtained the means of admission, she entered this range of apartments, which, from superstition, or some more rational motive, were kept constantly fastened, and in one of the most desolate-looking rooms, discovered the objects of her search. They were thrown into a remote corner, with a considerable number of broken helmets, shields, corselets, and other military accoutrements, with some fragments of different kinds of tapestry, and a large heap of rusty keys, which seemed to have remained in a state of inactivity for many years. After availing herself of these treasures, whilst Laurette was employed in her morning amusements and exercises, with a hurried step and palpitating heart she bent her way towards the tower.

When she arrived at the entrance, she looked fearfully round, lest any one should observe her; but no one approaching, and no sound, not even the flutter of the breeze, disturbing the awful stillness of the place, she ventured to proceed. The iron door, as on a former occasion, gave way to a forcible pressure, and having reached the passage, that only admitted the light of a small grated aperture, she distinguished the flight of steps which she had perceived before. Beyond this all was dark; but having with much difficulty groped her way till she had obtained the bottom of the stairs, she proceeded through a vast extent of passage, and was then enabled to observe, by the feeble ray of a lamp that glimmered through a crevice in the wall, a door which, from the appearance of the light, seemed to be that leading into the dungeon.

As she paused for a moment, to find the key, a deep sigh, that might be said to breathe the language of despair, broke the sepulchral kind of stillness that had hitherto prevailed.

Having, with much difficulty, applied the key to the door, she withdrew the bolts, which the wretched inhabitant of this dark abyss supposing to be a prelude to death, or some new calamity, answered with a scream. "Whoever you are," cried Madame Chamont, in a low disordered voice, "whom guilt or misfortune have brought to this miserable abode, I beseech you to be comforted." Having uttered these words, she listened for a moment, but all was again silent; no sound was returned, which made it probable that her words were unheard, or disregarded. Much strength

was requisite in the accomplishment of her purpose, for the lock
was so rusted by time and neglect, that it was impossible for so
feeble and delicate a hand to make it (without painful exertion)
perform its long-forgotten office. By repeated efforts she was,
however, enabled to put her designs in execution, and opening
the door, which turned sullenly on its grating hinges, she beheld,
in one corner of the dungeon, a pale, emaciated figure seated
upon straw. An emotion of terror seemed to have deprived him
of reason, which prevented him from attending to the compassionate exclamation of his deliverer; and having covered his face
with his hands, he did not perceive her approach till she was
within a few steps of the place where he was sitting. A second
address, however, uttered in the plaintive accents of pity, roused
him from his stupor, and discovered to Madame Chamont the
features of La Roque, who, instead of the messenger of death
which his affrighted imagination had portrayed, beheld the still
beautiful form of his former benefactress.

After quieting his apprehensions, by convincing him of the
possibility of effecting an escape, she raised the lamp from the
ground, and having used many ineffectual efforts to release him
from his fetters, finally succeeded in her design.

The effusions of his gratitude for some time deprived the
astonished La Roque of utterance; but his feelings being now
too violent to be restrained, he burst into a flood of tears. Joy
and compassion operated as powerfully in the mind of Madame
Chamont, who having, after many arduous endeavours, entirely
accomplished his deliverance, assisted in raising him from the
ground, and led him from the dungeon.

Those who have been long secluded from the beauties of
Nature in a miserable subterranean abode, can only form an adequate conception of the raptures experienced by La Roque on
his sudden emancipation from captivity. A few minutes before,
he was in continual expectation of a miserable death, hopeless,
and, as he believed, beyond the reach of compassion; now he was
restored to a world from which he imagined himself separated
for ever, was permitted to behold the beautiful face of Nature,
to hear again the melody of the birds, and to feel the enlivening
breath of the zephyr; yet so much was he enervated by confine-

ment, and his ancles were so weakened by manacles, that he was unable to walk without support.

Madame Chamont, who at first thought only of the means of deliverance, now foresaw difficulties which her mind had not been collected enough to have contemplated before. She had now conducted La Roque from his dreadful abode, but in what manner he was to be disposed of was an idea that never occurred to her before. After having suffered much from the dark vapours of a dungeon, from the miserable confinement of chains and fetters, with the addition of spare and meagre diet, he wanted assistance and support. This rendered it impossible for him to prosecute his journey without needful rest and refreshment; yet how was this to be procured, since it could not be accomplished without assistance, and this would be attended not only with difficulty, but with danger? She was resolved, however, to procure him some food without further delay, and having seated him upon a projection of stone in the turret, gave him a promise that she would speedily return, and hurried towards the castle.

As she went, she began to reflect upon the necessity of coming to a speedy resolution in this important affair, as to the manner of proceeding in it; for should the loss of the key be discovered, it might occasion the return of Paoli, which would render abortive every scheme she had devised for the preservation of the prisoner.

After much consideration, she found it would be impossible to convey La Roque to his place of destination without some one to assist her in the enterprise; and knowing the prudence and secrecy of her faithful Dorothèe, resolved to make her a confidante in the undertaking. This matter being settled, she proceeded towards the mansion with redoubled alacrity; and having acquainted her servant with the adventure, desired that she would take some food and wine to La Roque in the turret of the forest. The good woman, whose tenderness and compassion were equally awakened, cheerfully obeyed the summons, whilst Madame Chamont retired to her apartment to consider of the most effectual way of rendering herself serviceable to the much-injured La Roque, that he might be immediately placed in security, and herself avoid detection. She saw the policy of a hasty removal, yet was anxious that he should first recover from that state of weakness and indisposition, to which grief and imprisonment had reduced him.

Whilst she still continued to muse upon this affecting incident, without being able to adopt any plan for her future conduct, the arrival of Father Benedicta, her confessor, broke in upon her reflections.

As she surveyed the placid countenance of this holy Father, lighted up by the smile of benevolence, and glowing with universal philanthropy, the idea of soliciting his protection instantly occurred to her. With his assistance La Roque might take refuge in the monastery till he was in a condition to travel, and in the habit of a Friar, which could easily be procured, might be secure from the possibility of discovery.

This plan appeared so much more eligible than any she had before conceived, that she was resolved to put it into execution. As soon as the Monk was seated, having first expatiated upon the duties of charity, she informed him that an unfortunate stranger, whom she had lately met with under peculiar circumstances, which were at present somewhat veiled in mystery, had much interested her compassion. That there were reasons, with which she was herself partly unacquainted, why he must be secluded from observation till he could prosecute the remaining part of his journey without farther injury to his health; and from the exemplary piety and general benevolence of her revered Father, she had flattered herself that he would, if possible, offer him an asylum till that period arrived. She forbore mentioning any thing of the Marchese, and even of Paoli, and entirely avoided the subject of his imprisonment.

Father Benedicta, who regarded her, during this discourse, with a look of tenderness and admiration that encouraged her to proceed, easily discovered, from the timid hesitation of her manner, that she was not only much concerned in the fate of the stranger, but that there was something connected with the affair which prudence forbade her to reveal.

Having desisted from any inquiry that might tend to heighten her anxiety, he readily assented to her desire of affording him a place of security, appointing an hour in which he would meet them at the end of the eastern rampart, for the purpose of conducting him to the cloister.

As soon as the Friar was departed, Madame Chamont formed an excuse to Laurette for her absence, and then returned towards the tower, where she found La Roque considerably revived by the salutary relief which the castle had afforded, and anxious to assure her of the extent of his gratitude.

Having seated herself by his side, she informed him of her newly concerted scheme of placing him in the monastery under the patronage and protection of Father Benedicta, whose benevolent acquiescence had delivered her, she added, from much apprehension and perplexity on his account, from which place he might escape in the dress of the order; and should his flight be discovered by the return of the steward, he might be easily defended from the vigilance of his pursuers in so holy a disguise.

This proposal, that promised at once secrecy and security, was accepted with transport; and La Roque being evidently much recovered by the attentions bestowed upon him since his confinement, Madame Chamont made some inquiries concerning his daughter, who she learned was consigned to the care of a generous protector; and then reminded him of the promise made to her at the post-house of relating his story, at the same time desiring him to desist if he found himself unequal to the task.

Having acknowledged the justice of the claim, and given his assent to the proposition, he hesitated for a few moments, as if to acquire additional fortitude; and then checking a tear, the obtrusion of which seemed to have been occasioned by the recollection of some recent calamity, he thus began his narration.

END OF THE FIRST VOLUME.

THE

ORPHAN

OF THE

RHINE.

———➤ ✳ ◀———

𝔄 𝔕𝔬𝔪𝔞𝔫𝔠𝔢,

IN FOUR VOLUMES.

———

BY MRS. SLEATH.

———

Sweet are the uses of adversity,
Which, like the toad, ugly and venomous,
Wears yet a precious jewel in his head.

SHAKESPEARE.

VOL. II.

═══════════

LONDON:

PRINTED AT THE

𝔐𝔦𝔫𝔢𝔯𝔳𝔞-𝔓𝔯𝔢𝔰𝔰,

FOR WILLIAM LANE, LEADENHALL-STREET

1798

CHAP. I.

—————"List a brief tale,
And when 'tis told, Oh! that my heart would break,
The bloody proclamation to escape."

SHAKESPEARE.

"MY real name, which from unavoidable circumstances I have for some time disguised under that of La Roque, is Conte della Croisse." Madame Chamont started, and with much difficulty concealing her emotions, La Roque proceeded:—

"Being early in life deprived of my parents, I was consigned by my father to the guardianship of the late Marchese de Montferrat; and, immediately on his decease, quitted Naples, the ancient seat of my ancestors, and repaired to the environs of Turin.

"Being too young to know the extent of my loss, the affectionate behaviour of the Marchese, and still gentler attentions of the Marchesa, soon relieved me from unpleasant recollections, and restored me to my former felicity. Masters were procured to instruct me in the classics and different sciences; as it was the particular request of my dying father, who had an unconquerable aversion to public seminaries, that my education should be a private one.

"My time, now chiefly devoted to literary pursuits, fled rapidly away; and my guardian beheld the progress I made with satisfaction and complacency.

"The family at the Castello St. Aubin, consisted of the Marchese, the Marchesa, one daughter (who was somewhat younger than myself), and a large number of domestics.

"The hospitality and generosity inseparable from the inhabitants of this princely abode, was become proverbial. Every countenance expressed disinterested affection, content, and innocence; and every breast was animated with truth, sincerity, and virtue.

"The first serious uneasiness I experienced, after the loss of my parents, was occasioned by the death of the Marchesa, who died, much regretted, in consequence of a fever that proved fatal after a few days illness. The Marchese was for some time inconsolable for her loss, and instead of mixing as usual with the world, abandoned himself to solitude; till an habitual melancholy was stealing gradually upon his mind, which threatened the most unhappy consequences.

"Whilst he was yet yielding to the influence of unavailing regret, he received a visit from a relation who had been some years abroad, and for whom he had conceived a peculiar regard. This unexpected event had so happy an effect upon him, that with much persuasion, he consented to accompany his friend on an expedition to Verona, for the recovery of his health and spirits.

"He had not been there long before he was struck with the singular beauty of a young Signora, much his inferior in point of rank and fortune, but whose person, he imagined, resembled that of the once lovely Marchesa. Opportunity threw her frequently in his way, and, finding her affections were disengaged, he offered her his hand, which she readily accepted; and the marriage being solemnized during the Marchese's continuance at Verona, they returned to the Castello.

"It was easy to discover, even on a transient acquaintance, that the mind of the young Marchesa was much inferior to that of her predecessor; with whose manners, the haughtiness of disposition she early displayed, formed a striking contrast. She did not long, however, enjoy her newly acquired dignities; but having given birth to a son about a year after her marriage, soon afterwards expired.

"About this period, Helena, the daughter of my guardian, having completed her education at Naples, returned to the Castello. Her vivacity and sweetness of demeanour soon dissipated the clouds that shaded the brow of the Marchese, and diffused universal tranquillity around. During the infancy of the young Signor, her brother, she attended to him with the undeviating affection of a parent; and the family, under her gentle authority, were re-instated in their original felicity.

"To have been continually in the presence of the beautiful Helena without feeling the power of her attractions, would justly have exposed me to the imputation of stoicism; a short time convinced me that I had too little of that cold philosophy in my heart to be insensible to the modest graces of her person, or the angelic sweetness of her disposition. I had soon the consolation of discovering that our feelings were mutual, and had the satisfaction of perceiving that the Marchese beheld this growing attachment with approbation.

"The period was now arrived in which some knowledge of the world was supposed to be requisite; and, accompanied by another young nobleman, whose name was Berlotto, I made the tour of Europe.

"Having visited several of the principal Courts, and seen the most valuable vestiges of antiquity, my companion became weary of the expedition, and expressed his impatience to return; but as much remained to be seen, which was sufficiently interesting to merit observation, and as yet my thirst for information was ungratified, I was deaf to the intreaties he employed for the accomplishment of his desire, till an alarming account of the declining health of the Marchese altered my resolution.

"On my arrival at the Castello St. Aubin I found him much worse than I had reason to apprehend; and soon afterwards the progress of his disorder was so rapid as to preclude the probability of a recovery. Perfectly sensible of his danger, he summoned me to the side of his bed; and, warmly commending the young Signor to my friendship and protection, soon afterwards expired.

"It was now necessary to exert all the fortitude that Nature had bestowed upon me, as well to rouse myself from the state of despondency that succeeded the death of so valuable a friend, as to mitigate the sorrows of the affectionate Helena. During the illness of the Marchese, a female relation of his was sent for to the Castello, who was now resident in the family. She was past the bloom of youth; but possessed some accomplishments and much good-humour, and seemed anxious to afford consolation.

"When the time of mourning was expired, and grief had in some measure yielded to the certain effects of time, finding that Helena still continued to receive my attentions with courtesy,

I ventured to declare my love. She was too frank, too innocent for disguise; and, confessing a mutual attachment, gave me her hand at once, to reward and to confirm my virtues.

"After this event, as the time of my minority was expired, we repaired to Naples; and, in that city, enjoyed more pure and uninterrupted felicity than usually falls to the lot of mortality.

"The young Signor, now Marchese de Montferrat, soon after the celebration of our nuptials, was removed to a public school in the vicinity; and from the proficiency he made in all the branches of literature, and the early genius he displayed, attained every mark of distinction to which he had ambitiously aspired. But, as he arrived towards manhood, it was easy to discover that his mind possessed more brilliancy than energy; and through the exterior accomplishments of the gentleman, an accurate observer might distinguish some qualities, which, though early veiled in dissimulation, were unpromising as well to the man as to the scholar.—He wished to appear virtuous, without doing violence to his inclinations by becoming so; refusing to deny himself the smallest gratification to obtain, what is much more estimable than popular applause, the approbation of his own heart. Wearing publicly the semblance of goodness, he so far succeeded in his desires as to impose himself upon the greater part of the world, who are only superficial observers, as a miracle of worth and honour.

"About a year after our marriage, the happiness we had hitherto enjoyed was augmented by the birth of a son; which event was celebrated by a *fête*, given at a beautiful villa in the environs of Naples, to which, as a summer residence, we frequently resorted.

"On this occasion, several of the Neapolitan Nobles were present, and, amongst others, the Conte de Pietro, who was introduced to me by an acquaintance with whom I had been lately in habits of intimacy, having newly arrived in the province.

"This much-esteemed courtier was just returned from his travels; and, compared with many that were present, who had seen life with equal advantages, displayed many shining perfections—in conversation he was polite, easy, and communicative; and there was an air of unreserve, and at the same time, of dignity in his manners, which could not fail to attract the admiration of congenial minds. The deference he paid to my opinion in every subject of discourse, and the warmth with which he applauded every sentiment I expressed, could not fail of exciting somewhat of vanity in my breast, when I perceived the countenances of others soliciting his regard without equal success.—From this æra I date most of my succeeding misfortunes. We had early conceived a partiality for each other; and I naturally considered a man of his easy address, fashionable accomplishments, and literary attainments, as a most valuable acquisition to my domestic happiness.

"The affluence of his circumstances enabled him to indulge himself unrestrainedly in those pleasures to which he was the most addicted, and allowed him the gratification of performing many acts of benevolence, which considerably exalted him in my estimation.

"The dissipation of the metropolis was every way suited to the gaiety of his mind, where his rank, his person, and his lively parts quickly introduced him into the first assemblies; gaining him universal applause in all places of public resort which he honoured with his attention.

"With the other sex he was a general favourite; for he was by no means insensible to the attractions of beauty, though he might be said to be incapable of a sincere and honourable attachment. No dissimulation, however, veiled for a moment his natural character: he was ostentatious in his gallantries, and open in his amours. He smiled when I expatiated on the happiness arising from the endearments of a beloved wife and a beautiful offspring; for his attentions having been confined to the gay, the light, and the dissipated, he knew not the value of an inviolable attachment. Anxious to lead me from those home-bred pleasures that my Helena had endeared to me, he used many arguments for the accomplishment of his purpose; and though at first they were firmly opposed, yet, becoming by degrees too powerful for resistance, they at length finally succeeded.

"When the mind once deviates from the path of virtue, it soon becomes reconciled to vice; and the habits of life into which I was continually led, began imperceptibly to destroy my natural feelings of rectitude, and to take from depravity the restraints of conscience.

"From a long course of perpetual and, I may add, guilty indulgences, what had formerly afforded the most serene satisfaction, became tasteless and disgusting; since the most worthy occupations were exchanged for debauchery, and that time, which used formerly to be devoted to the welfare of my family, was divided between the Theatre, the Opera, and the Gaming-house.

"The Contessa's attachment to the country occasioned her to reside chiefly at the villa; and, as she partook but little of the amusements of Naples, she was for some time spared the uneasiness which a knowledge of my excesses would have inevitably produced. At first she expressed some degree of pleasure at my having found entertainment in society; but when my absences became more frequent, though she forbore reproaches, her countenance sufficiently testified her disapprobation of my conduct.

"A daughter was now added to our family; after which event my wife was for some weeks so ill that her life was supposed to be in danger, during which time my anxiety was so great that I never quitted her room; but, contrary to my expectation, the disease, when arrived at the crisis, took a favourable turn, and she recovered. My joy at this moment was beyond all bounds; for a sense of her condition had recalled me to reason, and I felt anxious, by convincing her of my affection, to atone for the errors of my past conduct.

"No sooner was she restored to my wishes, than I received a visit from the Conte de Pietro, who congratulated me on this happy event; and observing that I looked ill, and that too much confinement had injured my health, endeavoured to prevail upon me to accompany him on an excursion to Padua. At first I persisted in rejecting the proposal; but Helena, whose mind was reassured by the attention I had paid her in retirement, and with the tender anxiety I had discovered on her account, prevailed upon me to accept of it, and in a few days we commenced our journey.

CHAP. II.

——————"Hark!
Waked—from according lyres the sweet strain flows
In symphony divine; from air to air,
The trembling numbers fly, swift bursts away
The flow of joy."

LANGHORNE.

"Not many days after my arrival in Padua, as I was walking with De Pietro, by the side of the Brenta, our steps were arrested by the tones of a lute, accompanied by a female voice, which breathed such exquisite sweetness that we were unable to move from the spot. Whilst we still continued to listen, in wrapt and silent attention, the strain ceased, the plaintive notes of the instrument died into silence, and, in a few moments, we perceived a gondola, from which the melodious accents proceeded, approaching towards the margin of the river. Anxious to behold the musician and songstress who had possessed such powers of enchantment over us, we still lingered on the banks till the gondoliers rested upon their oars, and we beheld two females come on shore, who were escorted by a young Signor apparently of the middle rank of life.—They were both veiled; but the graceful figure of the younger, for the other seemed to have passed the summer of her days, chiefly attracted our regard. Fancy had portrayed a face not less beautiful than the form to which it belonged; and I was anxious to be assured whether she had not been too profuse of her colouring, when a ruder breeze from the water wafted aside the light texture of her veil, and discovered the original.

"It was a face that could not be gazed upon with indifference; it did not possess the insipid uniformity of perfect beauty; but there was something in it infinitely more attractive than the most exact harmony of feature could have bestowed, divested of that inexpressible charm, which gave animation and loveliness to the whole. The blush that suffused her cheek, at being thus unexpectedly exposed to the rude gaze of admiration, gave new graces to her person. Having directed her eyes upwards, which were dazzlingly bright, she drew her veil over her face, with a look that expressed somewhat of distress; and taking the arm of her companion, hastened along the banks of the river.

"The Conte having intimated a desire to follow them to their home, I gladly consented to attend him; and, keeping a respectful distance, we followed slowly behind.

"Our way lay, for a considerable time, along the borders of the Brenta; and during this pursuit the beautiful stranger frequently turned, as if to discern whether we were near them; and then, in apparent confusion, hastened her steps, as if anxious to elude our observation.

"Having ascended the cliff, contrary to our expectation, they took a road which did not lead into the city; and the young Signor that attended them, who appeared to be only a schoolboy, having resigned the lute which he had carried for the beautiful songstress, took a contrary direction.

"Our curiosity was now too much excited to enable us to relinquish a project, whose novelty was attended with so much pleasure; and having proceeded through a vista, we reached the confines of a simple but elegant villa, whose situation was equally secluded and picturesque:—It was seated upon a gentle acclivity; and being nearly surrounded with groves of citron, acacia, and mountain ash, which were tastefully interspersed with a number of variegated shrubs peculiar to the climate of Italy, formed one of the most delightful landscapes we had ever seen.

"Having arrived within a few paces of a gate, leading into a kind of shrubbery, which seemed to be a private entrance, the laws of politeness would have compelled us to recede, had not the necessity of this conduct been prevented by a trifling occurrence:

"A snake, which had concealed itself in the grass, had assailed the ancle of the youngest Signora, and the alarm this circumstance occasioned was so excessive, that I had no sooner flown to her assistance, and accomplished her release from this venomous attack, than she fell senseless in my arms. A rivulet that wandered among the recesses of the shade, inclosing this sylvan retreat, supplied us with water, and soon afterwards, to my unspeakable satisfaction, she recovered.

"When this was effected, the elder lady abounded in the most eloquent expressions of gratitude, whilst the young one thanked me rather with her looks than with her words.

"Having supported the fair invalid into the mansion, we were ushered into a room genteelly, but not expensively furnished, where we were courteously accommodated with seats; and when the alarm was dispelled that this little accident had produced, had the consolation of seeing the countenance of the interesting stranger animated with smiles, and sparkling with intelligence. She called me her deliverer; and when addressing herself to me, there was a bewitching softness in her eyes, a fascination in her voice and manners, that would have warmed a heart less susceptible than mine. In those moments even Helena was forgot; and, as the Conte stedfastly observed my emotions, there was an air of triumph in his countenance when I adverted to the incident that had obtained for us the gratification we desired, which did not escape my notice.

"Laurentina, which was the name of the syren, at the desire of Signora Beritola, who was her aunt, presented us with some fruit, the produce of her garden; and then, at our joint solicitation, took her lute, which she again touched with exquisite expression, and performed some of the finest Italian compositions with inimitable grace and sweetness.

"The hours flew so rapidly away that it was late before we departed; which we could not prevail upon ourselves to accelerate without requesting permission to repeat our visit at a more convenient season.

"In this we succeeded; and so well availed ourselves of this indulgence, that not a day passed in which we did not repair together, or severally, to the villa of Salazzar.

"Laurentina possessed wit, sentiment, and tenderness—every thing I valued most, and least expected to find united with such youth and beauty; and was apparently so much interested in my appearance, and so much flattered by my attentions and conversation, that I felt unusually delighted in her presence. Every interview tended to increase her partiality in my favour, as well as to convince me that my attachment to her person and accomplishments was become too powerful for resistance, and that her society was necessary to my happiness, if not to my existence.

"After about a fortnight's residence in the city, the Conte de Pietro discontinued his visits to the villa; observing with a sarcastic smile, at which I was not so much offended as I ought to have been, that though Laurentina was as beautiful as an angel, he was too much my friend to endeavour to deprive me of so inestimable a jewel; then assuring me that if I continued the siege, she would not long continue inexorable. He proceeded to inform me of some traits in the character of her aunt, Signora Beritola, particularly that of avarice, which might eventually prove favourable to my wishes; and of some hints which he had received from a native of Padua respecting the conduct of Laurentina. They were of a nature to encourage hope, and I felt still more elevated at the discovery.

"The ascendancy over me that the Conte possessed, was increased by a more powerful attraction than what had hitherto cemented our affections—from the infatuated regard which my own vanity and susceptibility, as much as her own art and loveliness had made me experience for Laurentina.

"When under the dominion of passion we are insensible to the influence of reason, Vice, on a nearer acquaintance, loses her deformity; and the mind abating in its vigour, and being no longer able to resist the force of temptation, finally espouses her cause.

"Having given a thousand imaginary perfections to the object of my admiration, of which I could not easily divest her, the enterprize in which I had engaged, on a transient survey appeared to me more difficult than it eventually proved, which the extreme innocence of Laurentina's looks and manners contributed to increase, at the same time that it established the affection I had conceived for her on a firmer basis.

"The unbounded hospitality with which I had been treated by Signora Beritola, ever since the commencement of our acquaintance, aided by the respectful politeness that accompanied her attentions, were circumstances favourable to my wishes;

particularly as I had never imposed myself upon her niece as an unmarried man, and she was too much a woman of the world to mistake the warm addresses of the lover, for the temperate assiduity of the friend.

"Having some reason to believe, from what I had heard from De Pietro, that she would not oppose my designs upon her beautiful dependant, I requested an audience with her in private; and, after avowing my passion for Laurentina, proposed a handsome addition to her own fortune, with a considerable settlement upon her niece, on her consent to accompany me to Naples. I lamented that it was not in my power to offer her my hand; but did not neglect to assure her that unremitting attention should be paid to her desires, since the affection her merit had excited would find its chief gratification in ensuring her felicity.

"At first she objected to the proposition with a degree of earnestness, which, considering what was past, and the report I had heard previous to this declaration, filled me with surprise and consternation; but the largeness of my offers eventually silenced her scruples, and she promised to exert her influence in my cause.

"I did not long suffer the tortures of suspense; but the conditions were such that, if I had not proceeded too far to recede, would have recalled me to the path of rectitude: they were, that if, during the lifetime of Laurentina, I should be left in a state of widowhood, I was to repair her injured reputation by making her Contessa della Croisse, should I have no reason to suspect her fidelity.

"This promise was to be delivered to Signora Beritola in writing;—I complied, but shuddered as I penned it. The image of my Helena was presented to my imagination at the moment when I was going to desert her; the meek, the unoffending innocence of her conduct, her purity, her tenderness, the unaffected graces of her person appeared as rising up in judgment against me, and staggered my resolution. But one empassioned look from the insidious Laurentina, one word from her, uttered in the tremulous accents of genuine affection, were sufficient to silence the eloquent pleadings of reason, and to stifle the impulses of virtue and compassion.

"The time now drew near in which we were to quit Padua, and already had I received several letters from my wife which gently chided my absence; and having previously taken lodgings for Laurentina, in one of the principal streets in the city, for her immediate reception, we proceeded towards Naples. With a heart not much at ease, I placed my fair favourite in her new situation, and repaired to the villa.

"Those who have lost that calm dignity of mind that accompanies conscious rectitude, will only form an adequate idea of my feelings. When I met those artless expressions of unalterable regard which marked the deportment of Helena, I felt a sensation of anguish at that moment more keen than I had ever experienced, and would have given worlds to have regained that integrity of soul which I was now capable of estimating—that internal satisfaction which is the offspring of uncorrupted virtue. Reflection now became torture; and, unable to escape from it whilst thus exposed to its influence, I sought to bury it in dissipation.

"The conversation of Helena could only bestow a charm on minds serene and angel-like as her's; and what had formerly so largely contributed to my happiness, now became my aversion; I felt my inferiority, and wished to hide it from all, and even from myself.

"My time was now chiefly divided between Laurentina and the Conte de Pietro; for the former I took a house in one of the squares, which was furnished with much expence and magnificence suitable to her taste and inclination.

"To conceal Laurentina from the knowledge of the Contessa, was a matter which was attended with but little difficulty; since her mind was too pure for suspicion and jealousy, and it was easy for a less able dissembler than myself to deceive her. Independent of this, I had also an experienced assistant in the Conte, who frequently, in her presence, delivered a lecture upon the wise government of wives; in which there was something so smart, and yet so unoffending, that it was impossible not to be pleased with him.

"But when my absences became still more frequent, the mild dejection of her looks testified her uneasiness at my conduct, whilst I was compelled to hide the pang of distress and the stingings of remorse, under an affected appearance of gaiety.

"When nearly two years had elapsed, I found my expenses were so materially increased, having also lost many considerable sums at the gaming-table, that I began to be seriously alarmed. Laurentina, under a character which she had artfully assumed for the accomplishment of my destruction, disguised many of her sex's frailties: she was passionately fond of equipage and shew, and was not only elegant, but magnificent in her attire. The profusion of jewels she demanded were adequate to the expences of my household; and finding that my situation was becoming desperate, I hinted the affair to De Pietro, who advised me to forsake Laurentina.

"Though from the uneasy sensations I had experienced ever since the commencement of my folly, a separation would assuredly have been desirable; but there appeared a degree of cruelty in this method of proceeding which I could not immediately reconcile to my feelings. The Conte anticipated my meaning, and took some pains to convince me, that amours of that kind did not require that delicacy of sentiment which I believed to be requisite; for having made a settlement upon the Signora, her person and accomplishments, he added, would easily procure her another lover; and she might possibly be a gainer by the change.

"The idea of her encouraging the addresses of another, my passion was not sufficiently cooled to reflect upon without emotion, and I replied, with some warmth, that I did not believe it possible that the affections of Laurentina could be transferred; and having been the means of wounding her reputation, I considered myself indisputably bound to protect her. The Conte regarded me with a look of surprise and dissatisfaction, and then asked, with an assumed gravity of appearance, whether I did not suppose Laurentina had other admirers, who were equally favoured with her attention?—I was too much irritated by this question not to betray somewhat of anger; and assured him, with a degree of impetuosity too natural to my character, that nothing less than ocular demonstration should convince me that she ever admitted any other visiters.

"The violence of my emotions during this discourse, too plainly evinced that I was still the slave of an unfortunate attachment; and De Pietro, with his usual address, finding the subject was a painful one, endeavoured to change it; but that which he introduced was foreign to my heart, and I could not join in it.

"When again alone, I began to reflect upon my situation with redoubled energy; and, after much consideration, resolved immediately to visit Laurentina, and to inform her, that the immense sums she had squandered, threatened me with the most serious consequences; and that it was necessary for her sake, as well as for my own, that new measures should be adopted.

"Thus determined, I was hastening to execute my design when, having arrived within a few steps of the door, I was agreeably surprised on meeting with my old travelling companion, Signor Berlotte, who expressed much pleasure at this unexpected event.

"He had not been many hours in the city; and having been informed at Venice, where he was detained some time on business of an important nature, that I had quitted Naples, he had not yet, he added, extended his enquiries respecting my present place of residence; but as it was now his intention to remain some months in that city, his happiness, he assured me, would be materially augmented by my society.

"Though, in the early part of my life, I entertained no very high opinion of the character of Berlotte, knowing that his sentiments were mean, and his abilities contracted; yet allowing that years and reflection might have refined the one, and expanded the other, though I did not express myself on this occasion with equal warmth and ardour, I was not insensible to his professions of friendship, or undesirous of cultivating it.

"Having walked with him as far as the hotel, I requested that his visits might be frequent and without ceremony; and, after giving him my address, hasted back to Laurentina.

"Not expecting me at so early an hour, my visits being usually nocturnal ones, I was told she was absent. Believing that she was only gone on some trifling business, without regarding the answer, and meaning to wait her return, I walked on to the saloon.

"Having entered this room, the first object that engaged my attention was a small miniature portrait, suspended over the chimney-piece by a chain of gold: It was the figure of a young Signor in a military habit, of a noble and dignified appearance. The countenance was fine, open, and impressive, and had at once an air of grandeur and of sweetness. That this was some favoured lover of Laurentina's, was an idea that instantly occurred, and brought with it all the tortures of jealousy and resentment. The words of De Pietro returned to my recollection, who I now believed was acquainted with her inconstancy, and was only prevented from disclosing it by an unreasonable warmth, which determined me, on a next interview with him, to interrogate him concerning her.

"When the first emotions of surprise and anger had subsided, I again took the picture from its place, and was gazing upon it attentively, when Laurentina entered.

"She started in visible confusion on observing me; but in a moment recollecting herself, assumed an appearance of composure that filled me with astonishment, since the miniature was still in my hand, which I considered as a testimony of her falsehood.

"This, however, she seemed not to regard; but was advancing towards me with one of those fascinating smiles, which had so often deceived me, when I demanded, in an authoritative tone, for whom that portrait was designed? She was too able a practitioner in the art of dissembling, to suffer the least hesitation to betray her, and replied emphatically, her brother. I regarded her earnestly as she spoke, but the undaunted serenity of her countenance was unchanged; and having expressed my surprise that I had never heard her speak of her brother, she informed me that he had entered into the service of his country very early in life, and having been some years abroad, he had sent her that picture as a memento, which had lately been conveyed to her by Signora Beritola.

"There was too much of the appearance of truth in this recital to justify suspicion, which made me anxious, by the gentleness of my manners, to atone for the want of confidence I had betrayed, as well as to reward the patience with which she had supported it.

"This was no time for expatiating on the necessity of adopting a plan of economy, being too much humbled by her artifice to propose any thing on that subject; and having an engagement at the villa, I left her with many expressions of tenderness, and hasted to fulfil it.

"The circumstance of the picture, and the conversation of the Conte, in spite of all my efforts to the contrary, would frequently return to my memory, and awaken unpleasant surmises. There was indeed nothing improbable in the story of its being the portrait of her brother, nor had I any reason, at present, to doubt her veracity; yet it by no means amounted to conviction.

"Berlotte was now frequently at the villa, and generously made one in our parties, on private as well as public occasions, though he was far from being a general favourite. There was indeed nothing prepossessing in his appearance; and he was justly suspected of shallowness and affectation.

"My wife, who was candour itself, could not sometimes forbear uttering something to his disadvantage; his confidence distressed her, and his conversation at once wounded her feelings, and excited disgust.

"I now anxiously sought an opportunity of questioning the Conte concerning Laurentina; and was not long before I succeeded. I found that nothing material could be alledged against her; but I was still chagrined and unhappy. De Pietro observed my uneasiness, and being convinced that a state of suspense is, of all others, the least supportable, asked me if I would submit to a stratagem, that would at once either remove or realize my suspicions. Having assured him that I would gladly embrace any means that could be adopted with honour, he proposed, that when I next visited Laurentina, I should inform her that business of importance made me under the necessity of quitting Naples for a few weeks. That on the supposition that I had put my intentions in execution, she would consider herself at liberty to follow her own inclinations; and in the mean time, avoiding detection, I might observe her actions in those places of public resort to which she was the most attached.

"This proposal was no sooner made than agreed to; and having acquainted Laurentina with my design of leaving the city for a few weeks, on an affair of importance, I became a spy upon her conduct.

"The masquerade was, I knew, a favourite diversion; and as this was one of which the Contessa never partook, and a place of more security than any other, I frequently spent my evenings there with Laurentina, and determined to make my first trial there.

"I had not been long in this place before a number of dominos entered the room. To ascertain her by her dress was I knew impossible, as she seldom appeared twice in the same. But a figure of more than ordinary elegance, who entered leaning upon the arm of a young Signor in a blue domino, soon attracted my regard; and this, on a near view, I conceived to be the object of my search. The jewels that braided her hair, which I had lately presented to her, convinced me of the truth of the conjecture; and the suspicion that the person who attended her was a lover, was soon lost in conviction.

"It was with much difficulty that I was enabled to forbear discovering myself to her, and of upbraiding her with the infamy of her proceedings.

"My endeavours to overhear any part of the conversation were unsuccessful, as it was invariably delivered in a whisper; yet I still followed, in hopes of hearing something of which I might openly accuse her, till the rest of the company unmasking, they suddenly retreated.

CHAP. III.

——————"Know'st thou not,
That when the searching eye of heav'n is hid
Behind the globe, and lights the lower world,
Then thieves and robbers range abroad unseen,
In murders and in outrage, bloody here?
But when from under this terrestrial ball
He fires the proud tops of the Eastern pines,
And darts his light through ev'ry guilty hole,
Then treasons, murders, and detested sins,
The cloak of night being pluck'd from off their backs,
Stand bare and naked, trembling at themselves."

SHAKESPEARE.

"The various emotions of rage, jealousy, and remorse that the conviction of her falsehood had awakened, for some time deprived me of the power of action; and in a frame of mind little short of distraction, I returned again to the villa.

"The ruin to which her artifice was leading me, now flashed upon my mind; the altered looks of the Contessa added keenness to my affliction, and I felt all the miseries of guilt and anguish.

"Several days passed before I had fixed upon any mode of proceeding respecting Laurentina; in which time the agitation of my mind was so great, that my situation was thought to be alarming.

"Affairs were in this train when a Monk of the Crucifix Order arrived at the villa, who having intimated that his business was of moment, requested an audience.

"Being admitted into a private apartment, after strictly enjoining me to secrecy as to what he was about to relate, in a manner not less singular than impressive, he proceeded to inform me of a piece of treachery, which had been unfolded to him at the confessional of the Order of the Holy Cross.

"Who the penitent was by whom the confession was made, was, he added, unknown to him; and even could it have been ascertained, the rules of the church absolutely forbade a discovery. But that a female had attended on the preceding day, who appeared to suffer much from the horrors of an awakened conscience; and, after an endeavour on his part to console her with promises of forgiveness on a candid avowal of her sins, she began to disclose the cause of her remorse.

"She had, she said, yielded to the solicitations of a young man, that was employed by a courtezan, whose name was Laurentina Beritola, to administer poison to the Contessa della Croisse. That he had addressed her as a lover, and had so far insinuated himself into her affections and wrought upon her by his promises, that she had finally consented. Since which time she had suffered such dreadful, such uneasy sensations, that she was resolved to abandon the project. And the idea of having agreed to participate in a crime of such magnitude, returned so forcibly upon her mind, that she had hasted to the Confessional, at once to disburthen her conscience, and to obtain absolution.

"As it appeared probable to the Father that, without timely interference, some other person would be employed to commit this atrocious murder, he had, he continued, taken the earliest opportunity of apprizing me of it.

"He then repeated his former injunctions respecting my secrecy in what he had unfolded; since, if known, not even the necessity of the case would excuse his disobedience to the ecclesiastical laws: the nature of a confession never being permitted to be made public, unless the priest to whom it is made, is called upon by the Courts of the Inquisition to prove something which cannot otherwise be known in cases where, for capital offences, the culprit is either punishable according to the severe rules of that institution, or is given up to the civil powers, as in cases of murder, or of any other crime not bearing the imputation of sacrilege.

"Surprise, horror, and resentment almost deprived me of utterance; but when the first tumults had subsided, and the Monk had quitted the villa, I loaded the authoress of my misfortunes with the most bitter invectives; and having already formed a resolution never more to enter her doors; but to make an assignation with her that I might convince her I was not ignorant of her perfidy and ingratitude, I repaired to an hotel.

"From this place I wrote a billet, in which I desired that she would meet me in a retired spot in the evening, having something of importance to communicate to her in private. In this I avoided mentioning her name, and having given it to my valet, with orders for him to convey it immediately as directed, hastened to the Conte de Pietro's.

"He was from home, and finding that he was not expected till the evening, I was for some time irresolute how to dispose of myself, not being sufficiently tranquil to be able to see Helena, who expressed much anxiety about my health, without adding to her distress; which determined me, after some consideration, to return again to the hotel, and to wait there the hour in which I had appointed to meet Laurentina.

"Never shall I forget with what sensations I quitted this place, when I went to fulfil the engagement—when I went to accuse the fair cause of all my griefs and inquietude of premeditated guilt, and, by one desperate exertion, to tear myself from her presence for ever.

The destined spot was near the borders of the sea; it yet wanted some minutes of the time, and seating myself upon a fragment of rock, in a state of mind not easy to describe, I listened to the moaning waves of the ocean with divided attention, till the murmur of voices at a distance roused me from my place. I started, without considering that it was unlikely that she would bring an attendant; and, before I had time for conjecture, perceived that the voices approached nearer to the spot, and soon afterwards distinguished these words, which were pronounced in low and tremulous accents:

'His frequent visits have distressed me more than I can express; and I must, if possible, be released from them. You know how much I have suffered, and that he is now more than ever my aversion.'

"The answer was nearly lost in the flutter of the breeze; but I could easily discover it was the voice of a man.

"In a few moments the female advanced towards me; I did not suppose it could be any other than Laurentina, though her features were not perceptible, for her veil and the deepening shades of the twilight completely concealed them from my view.

"Having now a fresh proof of her ingratitude, as I felt assured that I was the subject of their discourse, my rage increased to such a height at the idea of having been so long the dupe of an infamous designing woman, that nothing less than the death she meditated against the most amiable of her sex, seemed adequate to her crime. Thus being worked into a fit of desperation by the violence of contending passions, without reverting to the cause, I obeyed the impulse of my feelings, and instantly drawing my stilette from my cloak, plunged it into her heart.

"She fell!—but just Heaven! what was the horror of my situation when I heard my own name pronounced, in a voice which was not Laurentina's, but which I immediately recognized as that of my wife, my much-injured Helena!

"This dreadful conviction was succeeded by a state of insensibility, from which it was long before I awoke to a sense of my irremediable crimes and misfortunes; when I did, I found myself in the hotel which I usually frequented, attended by De Pietro and the Marchese de Montferrat.

"As soon as the powers of recollection were returned, I asked eagerly for my wife; their looks told me she was no more; and I relapsed into a state little short of distraction.

"My death was hourly expected, but the measure of my woes was not yet full, and I recovered. I then declared the fatal mistake which had occasioned this mournful catastrophe, and found, from the confession of a servant, who sometimes carried letters to Laurentina, that he had received a bribe from Berlotte to deliver the next into his hands; who having artfully altered it, to suit it better to his purpose, inclosed it in a cover, and directing it to the Contessa della Croisse, ordered it to be conveyed to the villa.

"She had expressed her surprise at this strange appointment in the presence of her brother, the Marchese de Montferrat, who offered to accompany her, in a carriage, within a few yards of the place, as to walk so far in her weak state was impossible, and to wait her return at a convenient distance.

"This accounted for the voices I had heard, and the subject of the discourse; doubtless Berlotte, who had long secretly endeavoured to insinuate himself into the affections of Helena, as the most effectual way, attempted to convince her of my falsehood.

"When the violent effects of overwhelming distress had in some degree subsided, I found, upon enquiry, that this melancholy affair had been managed with so much secrecy by the Conte and Marchese de Montferrat, that it was not generally understood. The rumour that prevailed was, that the Contessa della Croisse was assassinated when walking unattended by the Bay of Naples, and it was supposed, though the cause could not be investigated, that it was perpetrated by one of those inhuman wretches who are too frequently hired for that dreadful purpose.

"It was long before I had courage to enquire for my children; when I did, I learned that Vescolini, my son, was placed under the care of one of his mother's relations in Germany; and that my daughter was entered as a boarder in a neighbouring convent.

"The grief of the Conte de Pietro, who considered himself as the primary cause of my misfortunes, though it was more calm, was but little inferior to my own. What he before termed innocent amusement, and attempted to palliate by the appellation of youthful levities, he now discovered might lead to the most serious consequences, and be productive of the most fatal effects. A short time after this event, which had so materially affected his peace, he formed the design of entering into a monastery of Carthusians, and soon afterwards put it into execution.

"I would gladly have retired with him from the world, and have submitted with him to the severe discipline of the Holy Fathers, and had once adopted the resolution, but it was shaken by the entreaties of the Conte.

"He bade me to consider my children, to watch over their educations, particularly that of my son; and to guard him from those fatal errors which had caused such severe calamity, and which inevitably lead to lasting misery.

"During my illness he attended me with the greatest care and humanity, never allowing Laurentina or any thing relative to the subject to be mentioned in my hearing, till I was sufficiently recovered to bear it with calmness; and then informed me that she was, by his orders, conveyed to her former place of residence, and that the settlement which she demanded, he had ordered to be paid.

"Persisting in his resolution of abandoning the world, he began to make every necessary preparation; and having wrested a promise from me not to avenge myself on Berlotte or Laurentina, but to leave them to the tortures of a guilty conscience, he hastily quitted Naples, which was become no longer supportable, and endeavoured to take refuge from inquietude in the gloom of a monastery.

"When my health was so far re-established as to enable me to leave my room, and dismiss my physician, I began to form some plan for my future conduct. Society was now become irksome to me; every object reminded me of her I had lost, and I finally resolved to quit the scene of my guilt and my sorrows, and to bury myself in a castello situated amid the solitudes of the Apennines. This to me appeared more eligible than even a monastic life, since here I should find interesting companions in my children, who were all that could make life desirable.

"This resolution being fixed, I acquainted the young Marchese with my intention, whose recent rectitude of conduct had considerably exalted him in my esteem. At first he objected to the plan with some warmth, but finding, from a second review of the subject, the propriety of the measure, he offered his assistance in the regulation of my affairs.

"The immense debts I had contracted during my connection with Laurentina, I found, upon enquiry, had been discharged by the Conte de Pietro previous to his seclusion; and, also, that he had settled the greater part of his princely fortune upon my son, which was made over to a person, selected as a guardian in trust, till he should arrive at years of maturity.

"Fearing that, by coming to the knowledge of this affair, I should endeavour to frustrate his generous design, he had left Naples precipitately, without even informing me, or any of his associates, of his place of destination.

"Vescolini being still in Germany, I wrote to acquaint his relation with the plan I had projected, and to request his return; but the arguments he made use of to prevail upon me to permit him to remain under his protection, at least for the present, were so persuasive that I consented to his wishes.

"My daughter, my little Helena, whom I had not seen since

the commencement of my misfortunes, I ordered to be conveyed from her convent; and soon afterwards, attended by a small number of domestics, we proceeded on our journey by slow and easy stages, till we arrived at this long forsaken mansion, which had been for many centuries the abode of the Contes della Croisse.

"Here many years passed in uninterrupted retirement. My son's visits, though not frequent, were long; the education of my daughter employed much of my leisure; and though moments of dejection would occasionally intrude, my griefs in some measure had yielded to the influence of time, and I began to taste something like tranquillity.

"The Marchese de Montferrat having finished his minority, took possession of the Castello St. Aubin; and some time after this event, Vescolini being on a visit to this relation, accidentally saw a young beauty that was under the care of Madame Laronne, a widow of quality, who occupied a chateau in the neighbourhood of Turin, with whom he became instantly enamoured. Her charms were also too powerful for the Marchese to withstand, who soon became a passionate admirer."

Here Madame Chamont heaved a deep sigh, and covered her face with her handkerchief, to hide the blushes and tears this narration excited, whilst La Roque proceeded:

"I knew that during my son's residence in Germany he had embraced what is sometimes termed the Reformed Religion; and found, upon enquiry, that the lady he addressed was a Catholic, which had instigated her to discourage his attention, and finally to reject the alliance. Being at too great a distance from Turin to obtain a thorough knowledge of the affair, and having previously determined not to influence my son in a matter of such importance to his future happiness, I awaited the result without further enquiry.

"But, merciful Heaven! what was my grief and my astonishment when I was informed that Vescolini was assassinated in the streets of Naples by one of the Lazarone; whither he had repaired to arrange his affairs before his intended marriage.

"Who was the author of this bloody deed was for some time unknown; but being at last discovered by an inhabitant of that city, through the confession of the wretch employed, I was informed that the villain who had stooped to this base, cruel, and dishonourable method of gratifying an unconquerable passion, was the Marchese de Montferrat."

Madame Chamont, being now no longer able to restrain her emotions, sobbed aloud; whilst La Roque, who was unacquainted with the cause, regarded her with redoubled tenderness, and hastily drying the tears that fell in torrents from his eyes, continued his recital.

"Scarcely could I credit the assertion, till undeniable proofs rendering unbelief obstinacy, I could no longer be deceived.

"In the desperation of the moment I resolved to see him immediately, and publicly accuse him of these infamous proceedings; but a fever, the consequence of extreme agitation of mind, prevented my design. Yet though disabled from verbally declaring my resentment, as soon as I had regained strength enough for the purpose, I wrote to assure him that the crime he had committed was of too great magnitude to sink into oblivion, and that it called aloud for justice.

"This menace had the effect I might have expected; he had satisfied the Ecclesiastical Powers, and having of course nothing to fear from the Civil, now vowed vengeance against his accuser. Soon after this I received a letter from a person whose name was concealed, but who I supposed was the Marchese's former steward, because I knew him to be a benevolent character, informing me that my life was in danger so long as I continued in my present abode; and that if I was anxious to preserve my existence, I must take another name, and remove my family from the Apennines, without further delay.

"Having availed myself of this intelligence, I assumed the name and character of a Frenchman, the better to disguise me from notice; I hastened with my daughter into Germany, meaning to have taken refuge in a convent.

"With the circumstance of our being assaulted by banditti you are already acquainted; and it was from your bounty we were enabled to proceed, which I hope soon to have an opportunity of doubly repaying."

Madame Chamont having assured him that she would never

allow him to repay the trifle it gave her so much pleasure to
bestow, requested that he would relate what happened to them
after having quitted the inn; and inform her, since he had so
long escaped the vigilance of those who were in pursuit of him,
by what strange chance he had at last fallen into the hands of
his persecutors.

CHAP. IV.

"To thee, yon Abbey, dark and lone,
  Where ivy chains each mould'ring stone,
  That nods o'er many a martyr's tomb,
  May cast a formidable gloom;
  Yet some there are, that free from fear,
  Could wander through these cloisters drear,
  And dauntless view, or seem to view,
  As faintly flash the lightnings blue,
  Thin shiv'ring ghosts from yawning charnels throng,
  And glance, with silent sweep, the shaggy vaults along."

MASON.

"Having, Madame," continued La Roque, "by the assistance of
the physician, whom you benevolently ordered to attend me,
sufficiently recovered from my indisposition, with the addition of a servant we set off from the inn, and for several days
performed our journey with ease and safety; till my daughter,
whose constitution was ever delicate, began to experience some
symptoms of the disorder with which I had lingered. In the
evening she became so much worse that I began to be alarmed,
and we were compelled to stop once more at a small cottage on
the road.

"A few days, however, so far recovered her, that we were
enabled to pursue our journey; and being anxious to retrieve
the time we had lost, we travelled with all imaginable speed till
we arrived at the edge of a forest, whose woods seemed as if
destined for the abode of banditti; when night closing in upon
us, we had not courage to proceed.

"We were now at too considerable a distance from the last inn

to be able to return, and no other human habitation appearing
to offer us shelter, we were for some time undetermined what
course to pursue. At length the sky became suddenly overcast
with unusual darkness; the wind rising in sudden gusts, swept
along the mountains, and seemed to portend an approaching
storm.

"In a few minutes the thunder rolled awfully over our heads,
the forked lightnings ran dreadfully along the sky, and convinced
us of the danger of continuing exposed to the fury of the elements, or of taking refuge in the woods.

"We were in this alarming situation when a sudden light from
the heavens discovered to us what seemed to be the remains
of an Abbey, which was not sufficiently in ruins to deny us an
hospitable shelter.

"Elated by the hopes of finding safety in this desolate abode,
which appeared to have been long forgotten by humanity, we
hastened to the spot. Having entered the gate-way, our path
was obstructed by large fragments of the broken edifice, which
lay either hurled from the summit by the fury of the winds, or
scattered by the decaying hand of Time; but our case was too
desperate to remain long irresolute, and we ventured to proceed.

"Having burst open the door, which was too old to make a
formidable resistance, we entered a spacious hall, the roof of
which was so exposed to the severity of the tempest as not to
wear an appearance of safety.

"We then, with fearful steps, hastened through a long aisle;
and, at the end of this, perceived, by a sudden flash of light that
darted through the half decayed casements, a flight of steps.
This was a discovery that afforded us much consolation, and we
advanced with alacrity, till having descended them, we found
ourselves involved in total darkness, there being no grate to
admit even a partial glimmering of light. The mournful obscurity that veiled us, the loud blasts that howled dismally around
the pile, and the thunder that echoed amongst the rocks, filled
us with terrifying apprehensions, making us unable either to
return to that part we had quitted, or to continue our pursuit.

"The fortitude of Helena, which had hitherto so wonderfully supported her, now almost forsook her; and Nicola, our

affrighted servant, joined with her in entreaties for us not to proceed.

"Having felt about the walls, which were dropping with the damps, I at last perceived a door, which opened without difficulty into a place that offered an asylum from the violence of the storm.

"Here we remained till it gradually abated, and at last entirely subsided, and then ascended the steps.

"It was long past midnight when we left our subterranean abode, and we waited with some degree of impatience the approach of morning. At length the grey mists stole meekly over the summits of the mountains; all nature seemed restored to its accustomed serenity; and the rising sun, bursting from the glowing horizon in unusual splendour, animated our drooping frames, and restored us to new life and vigour.

"On examining our new situation, I found that a considerable part of it was still habitable, and that there was also a sufficient quantity of furniture for our immediate use, though much impaired by time, and covered with dust and cobwebs.

"This was an asylum that promised peace and security to unfortunate fugitives like us; and, upon mature consideration, I determined if there was any town or village that could supply us with food, within a few miles of the place, to remain there for the present. This scheme I imparted to Helena, whose looks told me that she had not so effectually quieted her fears as to relish the proposal; but, as she always submitted her will to my judgment, she did not seriously oppose it, and I persisted in my intention.

"Having cautiously provided ourselves with a quantity of provisions before we proceeded from the post-house, we had yet suffered nothing from the attacks of hunger; but the principal thing remained yet to be proved, which was, whether more could be procured at a convenient distance. It was also a matter of doubt, whether it would be better to send Nicola on this expedition, or to go myself, as it was possible that the blunders of a servant might betray us; yet should it be a town of any eminence, it might be imprudent to venture there myself.

"I was yet irresolute what course to pursue, when walking

thoughtfully along the gallery, I observed a door in the corner, which I did not recollect having entered before. Curiosity induced me to explore this part of the building, which I found upon examination opened into an entire suite of rooms, containing nothing like furniture except a large iron chest.

"This object immediately engaged my attention, and brought with it the idea that it probably contained the booty of robbers, till having lifted up the lid, I beheld to my astonishment the complete habit of a monk; which consisted of a white cassock, a scapulary and hood of the same colour, a plited cloak, a cowl, and a pair of sandals.

"Having examined these different articles of dress, which were all perfect, though they seemed to have remained for some years in their present situation, I determined, in the evening, to cloak myself in these newly acquired vestments, and to sally forth in quest of provisions.

"My first step was to take a view of the face of the country from one of the neighbouring mountains, that I might be assured there was some town or village within a few miles of the Abbey; as, should there be none, it would be proper to defer the execution of my design till the succeeding day.

"Having reached the summit of a rocky acclivity, which promised an extent of prospect, I found that a great part consisted of forest ground, intermingled with woods and lakes, but in general wild and uncultivated; inhabited chiefly by fishermen and goatherds, whose simple cottages just peeping beneath the deep foliage of the trees, added much to the beauty of the landscape.

"The other side of the country was more fertile: several towns, villages, and monasteries appeared within the reach of vision, which, from contrast, received additional grandeur and beauty; but a little hamlet that skirted a lonely precipice, which seemed to be but a few miles from our abode, chiefly engaged my attention. It appeared to have no connection with any other town from the distance at which it was placed from all others, and to be distinguished for the loneliness of its situation.

"Pleased with the observations I had made, which flattered me with peace and security, I hastened to put my intentions into practice. Having invested myself in my new habiliments, I ordered my mule to be prepared; and, taking an osier-basket upon my arm, I threw the cowl over my face, and proceeded towards the village.

"I had no difficulty either in finding the place which I sought, or in procuring food; but I could not help observing that the inhabitants seemed to be somewhat alarmed at my appearance, and felt the awkwardness of my situation.

"There was certainly nothing very extraordinary in the figure of a white friar; but the circumstance of being mounted on a mule, and coming in quest of food to a village so little frequented, and so totally uncivilized, was sufficient to awaken curiosity, and to lead to conjecture.

"As soon as my business was dispatched I returned again towards the abbey, so well satisfied with my expedition, that I resolved not to leave it; and having again mentioned the affair to Helena, who began to be more reconciled to the plan, she soon acceded with pleasure to the proposal.

"It was not long before I discovered that the forest contained a large quantity of wild fowl and venison, which we esteemed delicacies; and that it also abounded in chamoix and wild goats, whose flesh and milk were very acceptable in our retirement; and having provided myself with a gun, we were soon amply supplied with provision.

"Some years had passed in uninterrupted quiet, till an unexpected adventure occasioned a change of situation.

"As we were partaking of the morning's refreshment, in an apartment adjoining the hall, we were alarmed with the cry of hounds, and in a few minutes, before we had time for resistance, a stag darted into the room.

"This circumstance so much alarmed Helena, that she screamed and fell lifeless into my arms; before I could recover her, two of the hunters, who were in pursuit of the animal, entered the place in which it had taken refuge, attended by a number of dogs, whose cries resounding through the building, recalled Helena to life.

"If I was surprised at the appearance of strangers, they were no less astonished to find the abbey was become once more the abode of humanity; and, with many apologies for their intrusion, flew to the assistance of Helena.

"The amiable solicitude they discovered for my daughter could not be returned with indifference, and I requested them to accept of some refreshment. They gladly acquiesced in the proposal; and, in the pleasure that their conversation diffused, I lost for the moment the fears of detection.

"I soon discovered that they were people of rank, as their conversation was elegant, and their deportments dignified. Having acquitted themselves with infinite grace and propriety, they asked permission to repeat their visit; which being unreluctantly acceded to, they departed.

"Though in cultivating an acquaintance of this kind, there appeared some probability of its leading to a discovery, I felt an irresistible inclination to gratify myself in this particular, and was resolved to run some hazard to obtain that pleasure.

"In a few days they availed themselves of the permission I had so willingly granted, and again arrived at the abbey.

"Helena being engaged in her household concerns, was not present; but as the youngest of my guests enquired after the health of my daughter, I observed a blush steal across his cheek, and a degree of hesitation in his manner, which convinced me that the beauty of Helena, though seen only in the languor of illness, was not beheld with indifference.

"I did not know whether to be pleased or otherwise at this discovery, till I found that he was one of the first private Noblemen in Germany; that the gentleman who accompanied him was his guardian; and that they were not only men of rank, but of unsullied reputation.

"At present I had hinted nothing of my rank, neither had I related any thing of my story, but only that I was unfortunate, and from some wayward circumstances, was compelled to remain in obscurity.

"It was not long before I perceived that the insinuating manners of Count Saalfield, which was the name of the stranger, had won the affections of my daughter; and I beheld it with concern, till he requested the honour of her hand, and engaged me to plead in his behalf.

"As this was an opportunity of settling my child eligibly in life, by uniting her to a person equal to her in rank, superior in fortune, and every way worthy of her regard, I could not reasonably object to it; and a time was soon fixed for their nuptials.

"It was not till the eve of the day appointed for the celebration of this event, that I informed the Count to whom he was going to be united; which intelligence seemed to excite more surprise than pleasure; for it was the virtues of my daughter that had won his esteem, and this could not be augmented by a knowledge of her rank and connections.

"Before this marriage could be solemnized, we were necessitated to quit the hospitable retreat which had so long afforded security. Custom had long reconciled me to its solitudes, and I left it with regret.

"The length of time which had elapsed since I retired from the Apennines, seemed to justify the supposition that time had quieted the fears and softened the resentment of the Marchese de Montferrat; and I was less afraid of mixing with the world than before; though I cautiously avoided dropping any hints which might lead to the knowledge of my family and connections, and was still known only by the name of La Roque.

"Having drawn a considerable sum out of the hands of my banker immediately on my arrival at Augsburg, which was the residence of Count Saalfield, I took a small seat at a convenient distance from his castle, where I remained near two years, experiencing more tranquillity than I ever expected to enjoy; till walking one evening in the city, unarmed and unattended, I was attacked by two ruffians, one of which I soon discovered to be Paoli, who having fixed a gag upon my mouth to prevent my crying for assistance, placed me in a vehicle ready stationed for the purpose, which conveyed me with inconceivable rapidity to this place.

"As soon as I was consigned to the dungeon, I was informed that I must die; and the only indulgence that would be allowed me, was to chuse the means.

"Dreadful as was the prospect of perishing by famine, I chose this in preference to any other death that was offered me; and was vainly endeavouring to reconcile myself to my destiny, when the arm of Providence graciously interposed in my defence, and sent you, Madame, for my deliverer."

CHAP. V.

"Now o'er the braid from fancy's loom,
The rich tints breathe a deeper gloom,
While consecrated domes beneath,
Midst hoary shrines and caves of death,
Secluded from the eye of day,
She bids her pensive vot'ry stray;
Brooding o'er monumental cells,
Where awe diffusing silence dwells,
Save when along the lofty fane,
Devotion wakes her hallow'd strain."

SALMAGUNDI.

La Roque, having concluded his narration, was conducted by Madame Chamont, agreeable to the appointment of the Monk, to the end of the eastern rampart.

Though she had ill succeeded in the endeavour of concealing her emotions during this pathetic recital; yet that Madame Chamont, by which name only she was known to him, was Julie de Rubine, that unfortunate beauty who was the innocent cause of the death of Signor Vescolini, was a suspicion that never occurred to the agitated mind of La Roque. And as she prudently avoided mentioning any thing relative to her knowledge of the Marchese, he had no reason to suppose, even had his mind been sufficiently tranquillized to have reflected, that her story was in the least connected with his own.

Father Benedicta, who was faithful to the hour he had proposed, was in readiness to receive them; and, the better to disguise the object of his compassion from the gaze of curiosity, had conveyed a habit of his order.

As La Roque advanced towards the Monk, with a mournful yet dignified air, the benevolent Father sprung forwards to receive him, who, after regarding him for a moment with a look of silent interrogation, threw back his hood upon his shoulders; whilst La Roque, who instantly recognized a long lost friend disguised under the habit of a Carthusian, rushed into his arms.

Surprise and joy for some time deprived them of utterance, till the name of De Pietro escaping the lips of La Roque, convinced Madame Chamont that the penitent Father, who was now become eminent for that meekness, piety, and virtuous resignation which dignify the Christian character, was no other than the once brilliant Italian, whose dangerous example and seductive accomplishments had ensnared the affectionate, the once noble Della Croisse, and had finally annihilated his happiness.

When the first transports of joy, grief, and astonishment, which were alternately expressed in the countenances of La Roque and the Monk, were in some degree subsided, the former was arrayed in the holy vestment of a Carthusian; and after taking an affectionate adieu of Madame Chamont, which was accompanied with an expression of gratitude which words could not have conveyed, he put himself under the protection of his newly discovered friend, and repaired to the monastery.

Pensive, thoughtful, and dejected, Madame Chamont continued on her way towards the castle; musing as she went upon this singular adventure, which now engrossed all her attention.

Having entered the gate leading into the outer court, she missed a bracelet from her arm. It was one which contained the portrait of her father, and she felt distressed and chagrined at the loss.

Thinking it probable that she might have dropped it in her way from the tower, with hurried steps and a perturbed air she returned again towards the forest.

After walking along the whole extent of the battlements, and through the deep recesses of the wood which secreted the turret, without success, she began to lose all hopes of recovering it, till recollecting that she might have lost it when liberating La Roque from his fetters, she descended once more into the dungeon.

The dim and nearly extinguished lamp that glimmered from a remote corner of the abyss, throwing a melancholy gleam upon the dark and mouldering walls, just served as a guide for her steps; having raised it from the ground, she looked carefully around, but not discovering the object of her search, she replaced the light, meaning to examine those parts of the castle where she remembered to have been in the morning.

When passing by the door of the chapel, it occurred to her that she might have dropped it on assembling with the rest of the family at *matins*; and that the surprising incidents of the day, which had so strangely affected her mind, had prevented her from discovering her loss before. But afraid lest Laurette should be alarmed at her long absence, she determined first to partake of some refreshment with her, and to endeavour at least to revive her deeply depressed spirits, and then to explore the chapel.

The ill-assumed appearance of serenity with which Madame Chamont attempted to conceal the grief La Roque's adventures had revived, and which the recent loss of the picture had increased, appeared too unnatural to escape the notice of Laurette, who watched every movement of her countenance with an earnest anxiety.

The inexorable cruelty of the Marchese, the heart-rending sorrows of La Roque, the murder of Vescolini, herself the primary cause, flashed upon her mind in spite of every effort to the contrary, and heaved her bosom with convulsive throbbings.

As soon as dinner was removed, she repaired to her apartment; and, as was her custom when any new griefs or misfortunes assailed her, bowed her knee before a small altar that was erected for the purpose, and addressed herself to Heaven, in the hope that, with the divine assistance, she might be enabled to triumph over the severest attacks of human misery.

With spirits somewhat more composed she descended the stairs, and proceeded, with a slow and measured step, towards the chapel.

It was a fine and cloudless evening, and no sound but the sighing of the wind amongst the trees, broke the stillness that prevailed. The sun was just quitting the hemisphere; its appearance was at once sublime and beautiful, which induced her to pause for a moment to survey it: now richly illuminating the western canopy with a crimson glow, and then trembling awhile at the extremity of the horizon, and at last sinking from the sight beyond the summits of the mountains.

Having opened the door of the chapel, she fixed her eyes

upon the ground, and walked slowly through the aisles, in hopes of discovering the bracelet; but being still unsuccessful in the pursuit, and believing it to be irrecoverably gone, she began to reconcile herself to the loss.

At the corner of the chapel was a door which she had before frequently observed, but without any hopes of being able to ascertain whither it led, as it was always fastened whenever she had attempted to open it; from which circumstance it appeared probable that it belonged to the burial vault, in which the ancient inhabitants of the castle were entombed.

As she passed this door, which terminated one of the eastern aisles, she perceived that it was not entirely closed, and curiosity induced her to examine it.

Having opened it without difficulty, she descended a winding flight of steps, and proceeding through a stone arch, whose strength seemed to defy the arm of Time, entered a spacious building, which, instead of being merely a receptacle for coffins, as her imagination had suggested, appeared to have been originally used as a chapel; as the monuments which it contained were more costly and ornamented than those in the place which had latterly been appropriated to purposes of devotion, and were evidently much more ancient. This surmise seemed still more probable, when she considered that the part of the edifice which was used as a chapel, was more modern than the rest of the structure; and that neither the doors nor the windows were strictly gothic, like those belonging to the other parts of the castle. A small grated window at the farther end of the place, which dimly admitted the light, discovered to her the last abode of man, and spoke of the vanity of human greatness.

It was dreary and of vast extent; the walls, which were once white, were now discoloured with the damps, and were mouldering fast into decay.

At the upper end of the abyss were erected two statues, now headless, which though not sufficiently entire to betray the original design, gave additional melancholy to the scene.

Having lingered for some time amid the graves, whose proud arches contained all that remained of former greatness, and whose inscriptions were too much effaced to convey the intended lesson to mortality; she felt herself impressed with a solemn awe, and an emotion of fear, which she could neither account for, nor subdue, directed her towards the grated aperture.

The sky was clear and serene, and nothing but the light trembling of the leaves, heard at intervals in the breeze, disturbed the silence of the place. It was a moment sacred to meditation, and wrapped in sublime contemplations, she beheld the deepening veil of the twilight, which had just shaded the meek blue of the heavens, stealing upon the surrounding scenery. As she gazed, the first pale star trembled in the eastern sky, and the moon rising slowly above the tops of the trees, sailed majestically through the concave; all lower objects the height of the window had excluded, except the foliage of the trees that waved mournfully over the place, and replied to the moaning of the rising blast.

Unwilling to quit a scene so congenial to her feelings, and anxious to examine the stately monuments that arose above the remains of former greatness, she determined to convey a light to the place, since it was now too dark to distinguish them, and another opportunity of satisfying her curiosity she considered might not speedily occur.

This design was no sooner formed than executed; having procured a lamp, unobserved by any of the family, she again returned to the chapel, and descending the stairs, as before, entered the vaulted building.

Having observed with the most earnest attention the stately busts that adorned the niches, the heavy gloom of the impending monuments, and the cross-bones, saints, crucifixes, and various other devices suitable to the nature of the place, which were once painted on the walls, but which time had now nearly obliterated, she felt an uneasy sensation stealing upon her mind; and, as the partial gleam of the lamp fell upon the ghastly countenances of the marble figures before her, she started involuntarily from the view. Ashamed of having given way to this momentary weakness, she seated herself upon a fallen stone near the entrance, and, setting down the lamp by her side, cast her eyes calmly around, as if determined to conquer the fears that assailed her, and then taking her pencil from her pocket, wrote the following lines:

TO MELANCHOLY.

Oh! thou, the maid, in sable weeds array'd,
Who haunt'st the darksome caverns, dreary shade,
Or wrapp'd in musing deep, mid charnels pale,
Meet'st in thy sunless realms the humid gale,
That sullen murmurs, and then loudly blows,
Disturbing Silence from her deep repose;
Whilst in the mournful, dreaded midnight hour,
The hermit owl screams from yon mould'ring tower,
Or flaps his boding wing, the death room nigh,
Waking grim Horror with his funeral cry.
Hence, horrid dame, with all thy spectre train,
And let Hope's star illume this breast again;
Not with that dazzling, that delusive ray,
Which oft misleads the youthful Pilgrim's way;
But that pure beam that burns serenely bright,
And leads to visions of eternal light.

Having raised the lamp from the steps, she arose, and perceiving that it was nearly extinguished, was retiring in haste; when casting her eyes over this extensive and gloomy abode, to take a last survey of the whole, she thought she distinguished, by the expiring gleam of the lamp, a tall white figure, who having emerged slowly from behind one of the gigantic statues at the remotest part of the building, glided into an obscure corner.

The alarm that this strange appearance, whether real or imaginary, occasioned, was so great that Madame Chamont was for some moments unable to move; but in a short time again collecting her spirits, yet at the same time not daring to turn her eyes to that part of the chapel where the phantom had appeared, she gained the steps she had descended; willing to persuade herself it was only an illusion, yet not daring to be convinced, when she thought she heard a faint rustling, as of garments, which was succeeded by the sound of distant footsteps. Fear added swiftness to her flight, but before she could reach the top of the stairs, the lamp, which had been some time glimmering in the socket, expired and left her in total darkness.

Having with much difficulty reached the door leading into the chapel, exhausted and almost sinking with terror, she paused for breath, and was for some moments unable to proceed, however dreadful her present situation.

The aspect being an eastern one, the moon shining full into the window partly dissipated her fears, and she again stopped to listen if all was still. In the same minute the rustling sound which she had heard upon the stairs returned; and, without closing the door which she had entered, with the swiftness of an arrow she darted through the aisles, not slackening her pace till she had reached that part of the building communicating with the chapel; then turning once more to be assured that no one was following her, she saw, by the partial beam of the moon, a tall stately figure moving slowly by the window without the chapel.

Having reached a door which was open to admit her, she stopped at the entrance, and following the phantom with her eyes, saw it sweep mournfully along the corner of the edifice, and then glide into the deep recesses of the wood.

This strange occurrence so much alarmed Madame Chamont, that it was some time before she could recompose her spirits; and being too much fatigued to endure conversation, she excused herself to Laurette, whose looks anxiously enquired the cause of these emotions, and retired to her bed. But her mind was not sufficiently tranquillized to admit of rest; the strange appearance she had seen, continually occurred to her memory, and when she sunk into forgetfulness, her dreams were confused, wild, and horrible. Sometimes the image of Vescolini would present itself to her fancy, covered with blood, and gasping in the agonies of death; at others, the ill-fated La Roque loaded with chains, weak, pale, and emaciated, torn from his tenderest connections, and consigned to a dungeon as to his grave.

These terrible imaginations and dreadful realities worked too powerfully upon her mind not to occasion indisposition, and she awoke in the morning weak and unrefreshed. Her griefs were not of a nature to be softened by friendly participation; for prudence forbidding her to reveal them, condemned her to suffer in silence.

Laurette discovering that some hidden sorrow was preying upon the spirits of her revered protectress, exerted every effort she was mistress of to remove it; these gentle attentions were usually rewarded with a smile, but it was a smile that expressed more of melancholy than of pleasure, and which was frequently followed with a tear.

Near a week had passed since La Roque's departure from the tower, before Father Benedicta again visited the castle. By him Madame Chamont was informed, that he had quitted the monastery on the preceding day, and was continuing his journey towards Augsburg, being anxious to relieve his daughter from that state of suspense and apprehension to which his absence had reduced her.

When the holy Benedicta mentioned the name of his friend, there was a swell in his language which spoke the tenderest affection, and the deep and heartfelt sighs that accompanied the subject whenever he was mentioned, convinced her of the sincerity of his repentance; and in the penitent Benedicta she forgot the once dissipated De Pietro.

CHAP. VI.

"Oh! how this spring of love resembleth
  Th' uncertain glory of an April day,
  Which now shews all the beauty of the sun,
  And by and by a cloud takes all away."
                                        SHAKESPEARE.

Some months had elapsed since La Roque's departure from the tower, before Madame Chamont was sufficiently recovered from the shock her feelings had sustained, to be enabled to partake of those simple and elegant amusements, which were formerly so conducive to her happiness; till the unexpected arrival of Enrîco, who declined mentioning any thing of his intended visit, that joy might be augmented by surprise, restored her once more to felicity.

The rapturous sensations which this meeting occasioned, must be left to the imagination of those who are blessed with sensibility exquisite as their's, and are capable of experiencing those fine, those delicate emotions which are the offspring of a genuine affection.

After an absence of near two years from the Castle, the person of Enrîco was considerably improved. He had nearly entered his eighteenth year, was tall and finely proportioned; his eyes were full of fire, yet occasionally tender; and his countenance, which was frank, open, and manly, being animated with the most lively expression, betrayed every movement of his soul.

But the form of Laurette was more visibly improved than even that of Enrîco. Being some years younger, she had just attained the age when the playful simplicity of childhood is exchanged for the more fascinating charms of the lovely girl. The peculiar elegance of her mind, which her amiable monitress had refined and cultivated with unceasing attention, was finely portrayed in her features, which were soft, pensive, and interesting; and though not exactly answering to the description of a perfect beauty, possessed a something which beauty alone could not have bestowed.

The presence of the young Chevalier diffused universal gladness throughout the mansion. The domestics, who had conceived for him an early regard, were anxious to convince him of their esteem, by the most marked and assiduous attentions, which he never failed to repay with that insinuating gentleness of demeanor which is frequently more eloquent than words.

Dorothèe, who loved him with a degree of tenderness but little inferior to that of a parent, could not restrain the tears which surprise and transport had excited on his arrival; and would frequently pause longer than her duty required, to hear him enumerate the difficulties he had encountered, the hardships he had undergone, and the dangers to which he had been exposed.

But the pleasures which his profession afforded was a topic still more productive of delight; and Madame Chamont, who listened to him with undivided attention, beheld with satisfaction, that the mind of her son was too strong to suffer either from the intoxication of success, or the depression of disappointment.

When the subject was of a kind to awaken pity, Enrîco marked with affectionate concern the intelligent looks of Laurette. He saw the blush overspread her cheek, then fade, and as suddenly disappear, as conversation unfolded the powers and energies of her soul. The lifted eye directed upwards in the language of sympathy, and the tear that trembled beneath its lid, which gave new softness, expression, and character to her appearance, he beheld with a degree of admiration which he found it impossible to conceal.

As the only amusements which this sequestered situation afforded were of the most simple kind, they were usually enjoyed in the open air; under the thick shade of an oak or a plane tree, they would frequently pass many hours listening to the harmony of the birds, and, in the calm serenity of the evening, would extend their rambles along the most wild and unfrequented paths, till the bat flitted silently by them, and the cottage lights seen at intervals between the dark foliage of the trees, reminded them of the approach of night; whilst the music of the nightingale, immersed in the deep gloom of the woods, broke softly upon the stillness of the hour.

In these little excursions Laurette would sometimes seat herself upon a stile or a fragment of rock, and taking her lute, which she knew how to touch with exquisite pathos, would play some charming air which she accompanied with her voice, till the soul of Enrîco was lost in an extasy of delight, from which he was reluctantly awakened.

But their favourite walk was through a thick grove of beeches and laburnums, that led to a little sequestered dell; there the distant murmur of a waterfall gave a soothing tranquillity to the scene, whose monotony was only occasionally interrupted by the lively tones of the oboe, or the pipe of the shepherd, who having led his flock from their pastures, had retired from the immediate scene of his labours and his cares, and placing himself at the root of an elm or an acacia, beguiled the moments with a song.

Such were the innocent delights of the rural inhabitants of this lonely retreat; to Enrîco they had the additional advantage of novelty; but when he recollected that he must soon relinquish them, must leave Laurette, his revered parent, all that was dear to him, perhaps for ever, a sigh would agitate his breast, and an involuntary tear would oftentimes start into his eye.

Madame Chamont was not insensible to these emotions, nor unsuspicious of the cause; she observed, with tender anxiety, the looks of her son when the subject of his departure was touched upon, and saw the colour fade from the cheek of Laurette as the necessity of it was mentioned, with evident concern. The suspicion that she was the daughter of the Marchese de Montferrat, and consequently nearly allied to Enrîco, was a sufficient cause for distress; and as every circumstance she had collected seemed to confirm the justice of the supposition, the evidence, upon the whole, nearly amounted to conviction.

This growing tenderness, if not opposed, might ripen, she considered, into a deep and lasting attachment; yet to give a hint of disapprobation, without adding a reason sufficient to justify such a proceeding, would seem arbitrary and capricious, and from its not being conducted with an appearance of openness, might probably fail in the design.

To a young and susceptible mind like that of Enrîco, the beauty and accomplishments of Laurette could not be indifferent; and when he compared her with many of her sex whom he had accidentally seen on his travels, whose manners contrasted with hers were coarse or unnatural; her superiority was too evident not to attract his admiration, and that admiration was of too exalted and refined a nature not to terminate in a softer passion.

Yet this increasing affection, though it might have been easily discovered by a common observer, was for some time concealed from the objects by whom it was mutually inspired. They felt they were uneasy in each other's absence without suspecting the cause, and looked forwards to the moment of departure with painful inquietude.

The subject was too unpleasant to be unnecessarily introduced, yet time flew rapidly away, and after a month spent in this enviable retreat, he was in hourly expectation of an order from his Colonel to summon him to join his regiment. This, notwithstanding his military ardour, his thirst for honour and immortal glory, he now dreaded as the approach of death; since it would tear him from society which was become necessary to his happiness, from quiet, innocence, and rural life.

Yet constrained by situation to submit, without murmuring, to his destiny, he combated as much as possible the sensibility that assailed him, endeavouring to mitigate what he could not subdue, the poignancy of uneasy reflections, by the cold, and frequently ineffectual, dictates of reason.

Fearing lest his passion for retirement, which was endeared to him by objects too tenderly beloved, should extinguish every vigorous, active, and noble principle of his mind, he frequently retired voluntarily from the presence of Laurette; and, in the vain attempt of reconciling himself to this approaching separation, would walk alone upon the borders of the wood; hoping, by this method of communication with himself, that he might be enabled to recall the natural fortitude of his mind, which had yielded without reflection to the impulse of a premature attachment.

Yet though he wished so far to conquer his feelings as not to sink into effeminacy, and to disgrace the soldier, he did not wish to be insensible to the virtues and graces of Laurette, which, on a nearer examination of his heart, he discovered to be the indissoluble spell that had bound his affections to the place.

Was it possible that he could have beheld her perfections with indifference, he would have sunk in his own estimation; he did not wish not to love her; but he wished to love her with that moderation which would not interfere with the performance of his duty; and should he be so fortunate as to conciliate her regard, to look forward to her as the invaluable reward of his perseverance and virtue.

Unconscious of what was passing in the mind of Enrîco, Laurette, in these temporary absences, sometimes appeared pensive and dispirited; she observed after his return from the wood, which was always his walk when alone, an air of thoughtfulness in his deportment, and oftentimes of dejection, that awakened solicitude, and led to anxious enquiry.

Madame Chamont, who was a silent, but not an unconcerned spectator of what was passing, was often absorbed in musing and abstraction, whilst yet in their presence; but this being natural to her disposition was disregarded, as the suspicion that their attachment was the cause, never occurred to the minds of the lovers.

But these little absences arising from melancholy reflection, though frequent, were not lasting; a lively air, a ramble in the forest, or the artless tale of a cottage girl, delivered with that genuine simplicity of expression which will continue to interest whilst nature has a charm, was sufficient to restore them to animation, and even to gaiety.

How rapturous were the sensations of Enrîco when sometimes alone with Laurette, he would linger amid the lonely recesses of the mountains, and would point out to her the peculiar beauties of the landscape; beauties which she had before observed, but never with such charming sensations. How soon did the sun appear to sink upon the bosom of the waters, and the night shades to fall upon the surrounding objects. And how lovely did she seem to him amid scenes so picturesque; how delicate, how undescribable were the emotions her beauty and innocence inspired.

Hurried away by a sanguine and warm imagination, he would sometimes indulge hopes which a more experienced mind would have rejected as fallacious; and at other times a causeless anxiety would prey upon his spirits, and suspend every faculty of his soul.

After a six weeks residence in the castle, the dreaded order, which had been daily expected, arrived, and he now perceived, more than ever, the necessity of conquering those feelings which, though in themselves amiable, and the object that excited them every way worthy, might, considering his situation, have a dangerous tendency.

Induced by the most honourable motive to preserve a perpetual silence upon the subject, he had never yet verbally hinted to Laurette his prepossession in her favour, and he resolutely determined not to make an open declaration of his passion, either to her or to his mother, but to strive to render himself agreeable to both, by those ardent and vigorous exertions in his military capacity, which might eventually lead to independence and to happiness.

Though to subdue the sentiment of affection, which occasioned this intellectual weakness, was impracticable, he succeeded in the endeavour of concealing it; and was congratulating himself on the success attending it till the evening preceding his departure, when some of those mournful presages, which too frequently assail minds of extreme sensibility, threw him somewhat off his guard.

He was then sitting with Laurette in an oriel window, commanding an extensive view, in the serene hour of moonlight; when the idea presented itself that he might probably never more be placed in so enviable a situation, since a few hours must inevitably separate him from his dearest connections, and that death, or some wayward circumstances, might prevent the fruition of those fondly indulged hopes which had hitherto supported him.

Agitated by this surmise, he seized the hand of Laurette, and pressing it to his lips with an impassioned exclamation, an immediate disclosure of his sentiments would have succeeded, had not the retiring diffidence of her manners checked the momentary impulse, and given him up to the guidance of discretion.

When the time of departure arrived, which was early on the following morning, a severe trial awaited him. The uneasiness expressed in his looks was understood by his mother, who mingled tears with embraces; whilst Laurette, whose feelings were not less awakened or acute, was condemned by the laws of delicacy, which are sometimes severe and arbitrary, to conceal them under an appearance of tranquillity.

Having torn himself from a scene too tender for his present frame of mind, with a breast throbbing with emotion, he waved his hand to Madame Chamont and Laurette, whose eyes anxiously followed him through the portal, and departed from the castle.

That tender and interesting kind of dejection that steals upon the spirits after the departure of a beloved friend, we often fondly indulge; it is one of those amiable propensities that the heart cherishes and approves. When under the dominion of this pleasing melancholy, we love to retire from observation, to recollect every parting expression, and to feed upon the remembrance of the past; every affecting incident connected with those we have lost, every interesting situation in which we have seen them, recurs to the memory, and excites moving and pensive reflections.

It was this affectionate impulse that led Madame Chamont beneath the spreading branches of an oak, where, in the society of Enrîco, she had often sat secluded from the influence of a mid-day sun; and where they had sometimes partaken of a simple repast.

It was this stealing tenderness that sooths whilst it wounds, that directed Laurette to the side of a foaming rivulet, which fell in a natural cascade from a rocky acclivity, to whose murmurs they had often listened with the most pleasurable emotions when they visited the lonely dell.

But here she found it impossible to remain without enduring the most poignant regret. Tears, which she was unable to restrain, fell fast upon her cheek, and she was compelled to retire from the spot she had chosen, that she might exchange it for one less mournful and sequestered.

Enrîco had not been gone many days from the castle before the arrival of Paoli was announced. So unpleasant a visiter was not considered as an acquisition to the happiness of its inhabitants, which occasioned him to be received by all, though not with incivility, yet with coldness. His presence was always a restraint upon the conduct of Madame Chamont, but at this time fear also was mingled with aversion.

The circumstance of La Roque's delivery, though she reflected upon it with satisfaction and self-complacency, was not unattended with certain presages, which neither reason nor fortitude could subdue; that he would repair to the turret, and also to the dungeon, in the expectation of finding the body of his prisoner, she considered as highly probable; that he would be both surprised and irritated at the disappointment, and would take some pains to discover the author of it, was equally certain; but that the suspicion should fall upon her, or any of the family, she was willing to hope was unlikely.

CHAP. VII.

"The midnight clock has told: and hark! the bell
  Of Death beats slow; heard ye the note profound?
It pauses now, and now with rising knell,
  Flings to the hollow gale its sullen sound."

MASON.

The strange variety of events that had recently occupied the thoughts of Madame Chamont, prevented her from paying her respects to the Lady Abbess so frequently as had been her custom; who beginning to feel uneasy at her absence, sent a message by Father Benedicta to invite her to the convent. Not more anxious to obtain that consolation which the conversation of the Superior afforded, than to be released from the society of the steward, whose haughtiness of deportment rather increased than diminished, she readily acquiesced; and Laurette, who was usually the companion of her walks, was allowed to accompany her on her visit.

The features of the venerable Abbess were animated with a smile as she came forward to receive them, but an expression of deep dejection soon afterwards succeeded.

Believing that she had met with some new cause of distress, Madame Chamont would have requested permission to have shared it with her; but fearful of intruding upon the sacredness of her sorrow, she remained silent with her eyes fixed upon the ground, till the Superior, in a voice which she could scarcely command, informed her that the sister Cecilia was so ill, that all hopes, founded on human assistance, were likely to prove inefficacious. "But as her life," resumed the Abbess, "has displayed an example of the most uniform piety, penitence, and submission; so her serenity at the approach of death indicates that the hope of acceptance she has cherished is not founded on error. If you will attend me to her cell," continued the Superior, "you will witness the most perfect tranquillity in the midst of exquisite suffering."

Madame Chamont, who had every reason to believe that the beautiful vestal had of late carefully avoided meeting with her, though she could not easily account for it, would have excused herself from visiting her cell; observing, that the presence of a stranger, in the last moments of existence, might be considered as an intrusion. But every objection that she offered was instantly removed by the Abbess, who seemed so anxiously to desire her attendance, that she was compelled to yield to the proposition.

As they were proceeding along the cloisters on their way to the chamber, they were met by a nun, who advancing hastily towards the Superior, informed her that for the last two hours the sister Cecilia had been rapidly declining; and, as the moment of her departure was supposed to be near, her Confessor was in waiting to perform the usual ceremony for the repose of her soul.

The Abbess replied only with a sigh, and a look directed eloquently towards heaven, and then taking the hand of Madame Chamont, with the fond affection of a mother, led her to a small door between two columns which opened into the apartment.

Here on a mattress, at the end of the room, lay sister Cecilia. She was attended by two nuns, who were seated on stools by her side, and who, by the silent movement of their lips, appeared to be engaged in devotion.

Beneath a dim gothic casement on the eastern side of the apartment, stood Father Benedicta. He held a missal in his hand, and seemed to be so entirely abstracted from worldly affairs as not to observe their entrance.

The fair sufferer, who was apparently too near death to feel any acute pain, cast a glance of filial tenderness upon the Abbess, and another, not less affectionate, towards Madame Chamont. Her fine blue eyes were not so radiant as before her illness, but in other respects she was but little altered; her features still retained the same interesting expression, and though overspread with that livid hue, which indicates approaching dissolution, were still lovely.

"Daughter," said the Superior, seating herself on the bed by her side, "I have brought Madame Chamont to see you; I thought a visit from her would not be unpleasant."

The nun smiled serenely, and then, with a motion of her hand, invited her to come forwards; whilst the Abbess walked towards the window where the Confessor was stationed.

"Perhaps I have been unkind to you," cried sister Cecilia, addressing herself to Madame Chamont, in low and mournful accents; "you have discovered a tender interest in my misfortunes, and I have hitherto denied you my confidence. You wrote to ask me if I ever had a daughter, or had cause to lament the loss of one? The answer I returned was as true as it was concise—I never had one. But had I not previously taken a vow never to disclose any incident of my past life to any other than my Confessor, the amiable sympathy you discovered for my irremediable calamities, would have induced me to reveal them; but this sacred vow, which has long bound me to secrecy, reaches but to the confines of the grave. Father Benedicta is acquainted with my story, and has my permission to give you any information you may desire upon this subject immediately on my decease."

Madame Chamont thanked the nun gratefully for her attention, who being much exhausted by this slight exertion, uttered a benediction, and then closing her eyes, fell into a gentle doze.

As soon as she awaked from this short slumber, the sisterhood were summoned, by the ringing of a bell, to attend the mass.

The Monk was now arrayed in his priestly robes, and the ceremony was performed with a degree of solemnity that was at once awful and impressive.

Madame Chamont attended to these pious rites with a devout enthusiasm peculiar to her character; they reminded her of the last moments of her revered mother, and sighs, which she was unable to subdue, frequently convulsed her bosom.

As soon as these holy acts of devotion were concluded, the Lady Abbess and the rest of the assembly, except the nuns whose business it was to attend upon the dying, arose to depart. But the former being recalled by the Monk, at the request of the sister Cecilia, remained in the apartment, whilst Madame Chamont retired in procession with the rest of the nuns.

Had she not been withheld by earthly connections, how willingly would Madame Chamont have committed herself to this holy retirement. The placid countenances of the sisters, the gentleness, the humility of their deportments, the air of solemnity that dignified their movements, were so grateful to her feelings, that she was tempted to believe, from a transient review of the subject, that peace was only to be enjoyed in the solitude of a cloister.

The deepening shades of the evening now convinced her of the necessity of quitting the convent, and calling for Laurette, who had remained below in the Abbess's parlour, they returned to the castle.

The next day the Father Benedicta was commissioned by the Superior, to inform Madame Chamont of the death of sister Cecilia, which event had taken place a few hours after her departure; and also to request, if her spirits were equal to the task, that she would attend the funeral of the nun, which was fixed for the evening of the ensuing day.

Seduced by that pleasing melancholy which scenes of solemnity inspire, she assented to the proposal; and calling the Monk into a saloon which was unoccupied, she besought him to acquaint her with some circumstances relative to the departed sister, particularly that of her name and former residence.

"Her name," replied the Father, "which I am now permitted to disclose, is Di Capigna."

Madame Chamont started; a blush passed suddenly across her cheek, but instantly disappeared, leaving it more wan than before.

"Her place of residence," resumed the Father, "before the commencement of her misfortunes, was Naples." Madame Chamont's countenance became still paler; whilst, without appearing to observe her emotions, the Monk continued.

"She formed an attachment in early youth, an attachment not more unfortunate than dangerous. Her lover was an Italian Noble of high rank and immense possessions, but of libertine unstable principles; he had been long initiated in all the arts of intrigue; and being entirely divested of that energy of soul which resists evil inclinations, became a slave to every passion that tyrannizes in the heart of man. He seduced her affections under the appearance of sincerity, and finally prevailed upon her to relinquish the protection of her only surviving parent, and to become an inmate of his mansion.

"The father of the misguided Signora was no sooner informed of his daughter's dishonour, than it began to have an alarming effect upon his constitution: he raved incessantly of his child, though he persisted in refusing to see her; and soon afterwards fell a victim to his own and his daughter's calamities.

"The Signora was no sooner acquainted with his death, which she was conscious of having hastened, than she fled from her lover, and suddenly became the most austere of penitents. She undertook a pilgrimage to the Chapel of Loretto, and afterwards consigned her youth, beauty, and almost matchless accomplishments to the shades of a cloister.

"It is now upwards of fourteen years," resumed the Father, "since she entered into the convent; and whatever irregularities may have marked her former conduct, her penitence, her tears, and her sufferings have been sufficient to expiate them.—Yes, her late exemplary life," continued the Monk, after a momentary pause, "whatever errors she may have committed previous to her retirement, we may venture to hope, with humility, will ensure her eternal felicity."

The conversation was here interrupted by the presence of Laurette, who advancing towards the Father with an easy and sprightly air, drew her chair near his, and seated herself by his side.

The holy Benedicta, who loved her with parental affection, gazed placidly upon her beautiful face, and then taking her hand, continued—

"The death of the sister Cecilia presents to all, particularly to the young and the sanguine, an awfully important lesson; let us consider it, my daughters, and endeavour to profit by it:— She was once rich, lovely, and celebrated; but, by one act of unrestrained error, became miserable, despised, and abject. A whole life of austerity was scarcely sufficient to purify her contaminated soul, and to prepare it for that unknown change that awaits us all. The sting of conscience is, perhaps, the most acute pang which the regenerated mind can endure. It is a wound we carry unhealed to the grave; and at the hour of separation, when the parting spirit requires every aid that conscious integrity can bestow, is, unless softened by the interposition of divine grace, more dreadfully afflictive than at any other period of existence."

Madame Chamont perceiving that the latter part of this discourse was delivered in a faltering voice, raised her tearful eyes from the ground, on which they had long been riveted, and fixing them upon the countenance of the Father, saw it was distorted by emotion: he seemed to feel acutely the terrible sensation he had been describing, and finding himself observed, embarrassment deprived him of the power of proceeding.

But the pang of remorse was not of long continuance; hope re-animated his breast, and the same placid expression which his features usually wore, returned with more affecting interest.

He was unconscious of Madame Chamont's being informed of his story, though he knew that she had released his friend from captivity, and consequently that she had made herself acquainted with some of the most remarkable events of La Roque's past life. Perhaps there was nothing that the Father so ardently desired as to conceal from the knowledge of the world the dissipated follies of his youth, though the cause of this reluctance to reveal them could not be easily ascertained; as of all men he was the most meek, humble, and unassuming, the least apprehensive of censure, and by no means solicitous to secure the applause of the multitude. To his God only, he was accountable for his actions, and not to frail humanity. In his service he preserved an uniform austerity of life, suffering all the mortifications and bodily inflictions which the severity of his order required. By this method he endeavoured to erase from his mind the melancholy remembrance of the past; or, if it could not be forgotten, at least to blunt the poignancy of his feelings with the comforts of religion, attended by the elevated, and not presumptive hope, that the atonement was accepted.

When the Monk had regained his composure, he continued the subject till the chime of the vesper-bell, which was heard faintly on the wind, warned him of the hour of prayer, and precipitated his departure from the castle.

On the succeeding day Madame Chamont prepared, at the

request of her friend, to attend the funeral of the sister Cecilia; and putting on a long black robe, with a veil of the same colour, but little different either in form or texture to those worn by the order of Penitents, she took her missal, her crucifix, and her rosary, and repaired to the convent.

She was met at the gate by a friar, who usually attended for the purpose of opening it, and on enquiry for the Abbess, was directed to the Refectoire, where the nuns, who had taken the eternal veil, were already assembled.

They all arose on her entrance, and courteously offered her a seat by the fire, which, as the evening was cold and damp, she consented to accept. When the first salutations were over, a mournful silence ensued, which was interrupted at intervals by deep and heartfelt sighs, proceeding from the farther end of the room.

Curiosity induced Madame Chamont to turn; it was Father Benedicta, who had taken a place in a remote corner, to conceal what he mistook for weakness, but what was really the effect of his humanity.

The hollow tolling of the bell, and the entrance of four lay brothers, who passed hastily through the room, and departed at a contrary door, announced the moment was at hand in which the remains of the beautiful penitent was to be consigned to its last cold and cheerless abode.

As soon as these religious men had passed through the Refectoire, the Superior gave orders for the assembly to remove to the edge of the chapel-yard, to wait there till the body was disposed in the order in which it was to be conveyed, and to be in readiness to attend it from thence to the place of destination.

Having arrived within the gate of the burial-ground, they stopped, and in a few minutes beheld the melancholy procession stealing solemnly towards the spot. The coffin was supported by the four lay brothers from the Carthusian Monastery, who were commissioned to attend for the purpose; a friar walked before, holding in one hand a crucifix of ebony, and in the other a small image of the Virgin; six of the same order moved slowly behind bearing torches, followed by the novices and boarders of the convent; these advanced at a short distance, bearing baskets of myrtle, laurel, and other evergreens, to decorate the new-made grave of their departed sister.

The procession was now joined by the Lady Abbess, Madame Chamont, and the train of nuns, who proceeded between the corpse and the following monks, till they reached the door of the chapel; here they were met by Father Benedicta, who being the sister Cecilia's Confessor, was requested to officiate at the last mournful office, that of interment.

Having arrived at the interior of the edifice, the coffin was deposited in a recess scooped out in the wall for similar occasions, beneath the image of a Magdalen in the act of penitence. The chapel was dimly lighted, except near the altar, which was splendidly adorned with a profusion of valuable paintings and consecrated tapers. At some distance from this stood the venerable Father: a gleam of light, which fell upon his face, marked the shadowy lines of sorrow softened by resignation; the hood which he usually wore being thrown back upon his shoulders, as soon as the service was begun, the whole of his countenance was visible and impressive. At first his voice was low and faltering; but, as he resumed the discourse, his words regained their accustomed solemnity of expression, his features no longer retained the cloud of dejection, but assumed the vivid glow of hope and confidence.

An exhortation to survivors succeeded, delivered with all the moving graces of eloquence: every auditor listened with reverence as the holy Father proceeded, and felt impressed with the spirit and fire of devotion as he continued to expatiate upon the beauty of holiness, and the misery inseparable from vice and immorality.

As soon as this was concluded, the nuns, who had seated themselves in the aisles during the ceremony, attended by the monks and the rest of the congregation, advanced towards the burial-ground, whither the deceased was borne, in the same order as before, till they reached the edge of the grave. As they passed along the chapel on their way towards the place, strains, almost divine, echoed through the cloisters, which being aided by the voices of the choir, had a charmingly sublime effect, tending to preclude as unholy every earthly idea, and to wrap the mind in deep religious musings.

When the procession arrived at the consecrated spot, the tones of the organ were still heard, and the voices that accompanied it, being softened by distance, sounded to the ear of enthusiasm like the chaunt of angels.

Madame Chamont listened with undescribable sensations till the notes died into silence, and the Father made a sign for the coffin to be committed to the earth. A short prayer was then delivered with much fervency and emphasis, which was often interrupted by the sobs of the audience, who loved the sister Cecilia with the most refined affection and tenderness. Madame Chamont's tears flowed fast; and as she returned towards the convent, her feelings became so acute that she was compelled to take the arm of a nun for support.

As it was nearly dark when the funeral rites were concluded, the Abbess used many arguments to prevail upon her friend to continue with her during the night; but unwilling to leave her young charge, who she considered might be uneasy at her absence, declined the proposal; and, attended by one of the superior domestics of the convent, walked thoughtfully towards the castle.

Deeply impressed by the awful scene she had witnessed, Madame Chamont retired early to her room, and feeling little inclination to sleep, placed herself in a large antique chair which was fixed at the side of her bed, and taking her pen, her customary resource in the moments of dejection, she endeavoured to beguile the solitary hours by inscribing the following lines to the memory of the unfortunate Signora Di Capigna:

DIRGE.

Meek Flower, untimely doom'd to fade,
 Ere half thy op'ning sweets were known,
To pine in drear Misfortune's shade,
 Alike forgotten and unknown.

Tho' rob'd in more than mortal charms,
 To quit thy peerless earthly frame,
To waste thy sweets in Death's cold arms,
 That slowly, but relentless came.

Ah! what avails the vermeil dye,
　　The charm that Beauty's step attends;
The ruby lips, the halcyon eye,
　　And ev'ry grace that Nature lends;

Since all must meet the direful blow:
　　Nor could thy powers, Oh! Genius, save;
For thee the tear shall ever flow,
　　To grace thy silent, early grave.

And there no thistle rude shall grow,
　　No weedy flower of baleful hues;
But there the mournful poppy blow,
　　And bathe thy turf with opiate dews.

No spectre wan shall haunt the way,
　　Nor screaming owl with boding cry;
But Cynthia's bird, of sweetest lay,
　　Shall sooth the zephyr's evening sigh.

When Madame Chamont had finished this little plaintive memorial, she began to ruminate upon the subject of Father Benedicta's discourse on the evening preceding the funeral. As the beautiful nun was indisputably proved to be the Signora Di Capigna, agreeable to her former supposition; from her own declaration she was assuredly not the mother of Laurette, as she had verbally confessed, within a few hours of her death, that she never had a daughter; which was perfectly consistent with the assertion which her letter contained previous to this event. This certainly communicated a slight gleam of satisfaction to her mind; for if Laurette was not the daughter of this unfortunate nun, it appeared highly probable that she was the orphan child of some deceased friend of the Marchese's, whom pity had induced him to patronize; and possibly, should time and reflection fix the attachment between her and Enrîco upon a still firmer basis, no adverse circumstances might prevent their union.

CHAP. VIII.

————————"Oh! Conspiracy!
Sham'st thou to shew thy dang'rous brow by night,
When evils are most free? Oh! then by day
Where wilt thou find a cavern dark enough
To mask thy monstrous visage?"

SHAKESPEARE.

Paoli had not been long resident in the castle before Madame
Chamont was convinced, that the uneasy apprehensions she had
experienced previous to his arrival, were not groundless; and
that the noble part she had taken in liberating the unfortunate
from the grasp of oppression, an unforeseen accident had early
discovered.

The sullen reserve which had hitherto marked the behaviour
of the steward, and was peculiar to his character, was soon after
his arrival augmented; and he frequently fixed his eyes upon
Madame Chamont, when he accidentally and unavoidably met
her, with a look conveying a shrewd and malicious expression.
This she perceived with some appearance of emotion; whilst her
tormentor, who seemed to derive pleasure from her embarrassment, endeavoured, as much as possible, to increase that distress
he was conscious of having excited, with a repetition of his
former conduct.

That he had already visited the dungeon, and that his suspicions were directed to her, nearly amounted to conviction;
but why he should suspect her, as the immediate cause of La
Roque's escape from captivity, without some recent information
which might lead to the conjecture, was at once strange and
unaccountable. But from this state of surmise and perplexity
she was soon afterwards relieved, by the certainty that a full
discovery was the consequence of a trifling inadvertency; which
convinced her that she had every thing to fear from the rage of
her enemies, and that on her part the most strenuous exertions
of heroic fortitude were necessary.

The bracelet which she had dropped from her arm, whose loss she lamented because adorned by the portrait of her father, was found by Paoli amid the files and other instruments which she had employed in the accomplishment of her design, in the dungeon of the turret.

This he secured and presented to her when she was amusing herself in the selection of some of the finest flowers which the gardens produced, to ornament the windows of the oriel; informing her from whence he had taken it, and demanding, in an imperious and authoritative tone, for what purpose she had visited the tower.

Being unprepared for an answer, Madame Chamont did not immediately reply; nor could the conscious rectitude of her conduct, which had hitherto dignified her misfortunes, prevent her from feeling some portion of that acute pain, which is inseparable from the performance of decided wrong.

The hesitation of her manner, and the paleness of her looks were a sufficient confirmation of the truth of the conjecture; and the haughty steward, having thus openly avowed the circumstance which had led to the supposition, after eyeing her with a malignant sneer, that insulted and wounded her feelings more than the severest invective, retired from her presence, with the self-important air of a man who congratulates himself upon some new and valuable discovery.

Soon after this event, Ambrose was dispatched with a letter to the nearest town, addressed to the Marchese; which Paoli informed Madame Chamont was respecting some business which was to be transacted before his return into Italy, which could not be conducted without the directions of his Lord; and at the same time avoiding any hint that could justify the opinion that it had any relation to herself.

Some weeks passed without any material occurrence; in which time the steward, in the presence of Madame Chamont, still preserved that stately kind of reserve, which necessarily forbids the communication of sentiment; seeming to regard the family at the castle as people of an inferior order, whose welfare and happiness were entirely dependant upon himself, and over whom he was permitted to exercise an unlimited power.

This behaviour could not pass without the deserved imputation of arrogance; and Madame Chamont, who possessed a
delicate sense of propriety, and had been early taught to make
reflections upon character, though she did not allow herself to
yield to the impulse of a quick resentment, was not insensible to
the indignity that was offered her, and anticipated, with somewhat of impatience, the moment of his departure.

A letter from the Marchese, that was directed to Paoli, in
answer to that which had been recently conveyed to him, was
now brought to the castle. The joy evidently expressed in the
countenance of the steward, on the perusal of it, could not pass
unobserved; but the contents, or even the subject of the epistle,
was carefully concealed.

Madame Chamont, who was too well acquainted with the
disposition of the Marchese, not to be assured that she had much
to fear from his resentment, should he arrive at the knowledge
of La Roque's release, which she had every reason to believe
would be the case, that she felt depressed and uneasy whenever
this was the subject of her thoughts; and so terrifying were her
apprehensions at times, that nothing but the applause of her
own heart, that internal reward of virtue, could have supported
her under them.

It was not without some astonishment that she perceived
a considerable alteration in the manners of Paoli soon after
the receipt of the letter: He appeared at some times unusually
animated, joined frequently in conversation, and lost much of
that haughtiness of demeanour which had hitherto precluded
the advances of freedom.

To account for this sudden alteration was no very easy task,
though Madame Chamont could not forbear surmising, that
it was assumed for the concealment of some deep design; but
from whatever motive it proceeded, it contributed much to the
comfort of that part of the family who were entirely unsuspicious of the cause.

Laurette, whose heart was still occupied by the image of Enrîco, took every opportunity of being alone, when her necessary
assistance in the household concerns did not render her presence
indispensable, that she might ramble alone and unobserved in

those walks which his society had endeared; where she frequently remained till the close of the day, recollecting every sentiment he had expressed, every object he had admired, and soothing herself with the hope that she still lived in his remembrance.

One evening, after having wandered for some time through the groves and shrubberies surrounding the mansion, which were wild, lonely, and beautiful, she was tempted to prolong her walk, and striking into a new path, which apparently led into a wood not immediately connected with the castle, she felt an irresistible inclination to follow the track, and proceeded in it rapidly.

Having reached the precincts of the wood, she heard the trampling of mules as advancing towards the spot, and stopped for a few moments to distinguish whither they were going. She had not remained long in this situation before voices were heard, which seemed to approach nearer, and were soon afterwards succeeded by loud bursts of laughter, evidently proceeding from intoxication. Alarmed at the consequence of venturing so far unattended, she receded from the borders of the forest, and being afraid lest she should be overtaken before she could arrive at a place of security, ran swiftly towards home.

As soon as she had entered the gate leading into the second court, the tolling of the vesper bell, which informed her she had been absent too long, directed her towards the chapel.

The family were already assembled to render thanks for the blessings of the day; and, as she placed herself in the aisle where the congregation were kneeling, Madame Chamont's looks seemed gently to reproach her inattention to the hour. Laurette felt severely the reproof, and secretly determining not to merit it again, joined in devotion with more than her accustomed earnestness.

As soon as vespers were concluded, Paoli requested that Madame Chamont would indulge him with a few moments' conversation in private, as he wished to consult with her respecting some repairs that were wanting on the other side of the edifice. Our heroine fixed her eyes upon her governess as the proposal was made, and perceived that she appeared much concerned, though the cause was unknown to her, and that she seemed unwilling to comply. After having made some objections, chiefly arising from the lateness of the evening, which the steward removed by observing that the moon was unusually bright, and that the distance was so trifling as to preclude the possibility of danger, she assented; Laurette, who innocently besought permission to attend them, was repulsed by a frown from Paoli, and not daring to dispute his authority, returned to the interior of the castle.

As the evening was cold and rather damp, she ordered a fire to be made in the saloon; and taking one of her favourite authors from her store of books that were arranged in an antique piece of furniture, designed for the purpose, she sat down by the cheerful blaze, and endeavoured to amuse herself with reading.

When nearly an hour had elapsed, she began to be alarmed at Madame Chamont's absence, which appeared protracted beyond the time which business required; and desiring Dorothèe to accompany her, walked by the side of the rampart wall till she had reached the northern buildings, the way she recollected they had taken.

The melancholy stillness that universally prevailed, increased the uneasy sensation that was stealing upon her spirits; and as she looked anxiously around without distinguishing those she was in search of, her fears began to augment, and she felt irresolute in what manner to act.

The apparent dissatisfaction and reluctance with which Madame Chamont had yielded to the steward's proposal, recurred frequently to her thoughts, though she was unable to form any conjecture as to the reason of it, since there was nothing very surprising or singular in the request.

Yet, notwithstanding the probability of his having something to communicate in private, which could not well be dispensed with, she was not unacquainted with the malignant disposition of the steward; and had oftentimes beheld with astonishment the causeless aversion he seemed to have conceived for her amiable protectress, ever since she had been capable of forming a judgment upon the subject.

Having pursued their way for a considerable time without better success, they mutually agreed to return, and to send Ambrose immediately in search of them.

This was no sooner determined than they saw Paoli walking by the side of the wood. He was alone, and unconscious of observation, was moving slowly and thoughtfully along.

Dorothèe being anxious to know what was become of her lady, called to him, and roused him from his reverie. As he turned and advanced towards them, he betrayed some symptoms of confusion; but recollecting himself, proceeded to inform them that as he was conducting Madame Chamont along the northern side of the battlements, a party of banditti rushed suddenly from the wood, and, regardless of her cries, or the threats and remonstrances that he had uttered, seized upon her with violence, and placing her upon a mule, in spite of every effort he had exerted to effectuate her release, fled instantly away. The alarm this strange adventure occasioned had, he added, so entirely deprived him of the power of action, that he was undetermined what mode to pursue; and was meditating on the most probable method of overtaking them, when he was roused from these reflections by the voice of Dorothèe.

Laurette, being overcome with grief and apprehension, was insensible to the latter part of the discourse, for she had fainted in the arms of her attendant, who, after many attempts to recal her to life, was obliged, with the assistance of the steward, to convey her into the castle.

Dorothèe, though she had more command over her feelings, was not less affected, and besought Paoli to send Ambrose immediately, accompanied by some of the peasantry, in pursuit of the ruffians. To this proposal he readily assented, though there appeared but little probability of success; and Ambrose, with a party of men armed and mounted, were instantly dispatched.

However unlikely it was that a few simple cottagers, headed by an old servant, who was equally unskilled in the use of arms, should succeed in an attack against a band of robbers, it was a hope that conveyed a solace to the bosom of Laurette, and after many intreaties she was at last prevailed upon to retire to her bed.

CHAP. IX.

————"Patience and Sorrow strove
Which should express her goodliest; you have seen
Sunshine and rain at once; her smiles and tears
Were like a better May; those happy smiles
That played on her ripe lip, seemed not to know
What guests were in her eyes, which parted thence
As pearls from diamonds dropped; in brief
Sorrow would be a vanity most lov'd,
If all could so become it."

                                        SHAKESPEARE.

Laurette arose early in the morning unrefreshed by sleep, and being informed that the party in pursuit of the robbers were not yet returned, remained in a state of anxious expectation. Dorothèe, and the rest of the domestics, whose hopes were less sanguine, wept incessantly at their loss; though they carefully concealed from Laurette this appearance of sorrow, lest it should lead to the suspicion that the case was hopeless.

It was not till the evening of the ensuing day that Ambrose and the peasantry returned, without having gained any satisfactory intelligence of the fate of Madame Chamont. All the information they were enabled to obtain, was at a small village inn, about a league and a half from the castle, where they were told that a lady, who seemed to be a person of rank, had stopped for a few moments in the society of three men of a strange suspicious appearance. They were unable to give an accurate description of her person, as she was covered with a veil of unusual thickness, which descended nearly to her feet; but, from the little observation they had been able to make, she seemed to be above the middle size; that during their stay at the door of the inn, she had betrayed no symptom of fear or indisposition; and one of the men, of a less ferocious deportment than the others, having assured her in a low voice that she had nothing to apprehend, each of the men took a glass of spirits, without alighting from their mules, and galloped from the place.

As no hint respecting their future destination had escaped them whilst they were refreshing themselves, the party in pursuit were, for a short time, undetermined which way to proceed; but, as danger might be augmented by delay, they finally resolved to follow the beaten track, and to make a second enquiry at the next town. Here they arrived at the break of day but were unable to gain any hint that could lead to the knowledge they desired. They then pursued their journey for a considerable way, without better success; and as there appeared but little chance of overtaking them, or of gaining farther intelligence upon the subject, they mutually agreed to return.

Laurette, now finding that the feeble hope which had sustained her was delusive, felt the keenest affliction, and it was long before a cessation of sorrow allowed time for reflection, or the animated exertions of fortitude. To indulge in unavailing regret was, she had frequently been told, vain and impious; but this was a trial which youth and inexperience could with difficulty support. Every object reminded her of her valuable friend, and she found it impossible to resist the pressure of her grief, which now affected her spirits, and undermined her health.

A letter from Enrîco, which at an earlier period would have been received with the most innocent effusions of rapture, now tended to increase her uneasiness; it was directed to Madame Chamont, but having been always allowed the privilege of perusing his epistles, she ventured to open it.

As the tender, the dutiful expressions with which it abounded met her eye, her tears flowed silently and fast; but when she got to that part of the letter which treated of the danger of his situation, and informed her that he expected soon to be called into action, her feelings could no longer be restrained, and she wept and sobbed aloud.

Paoli, who at first affected to interest himself in her distress, now either totally disregarded her, as a being unworthy of his attention, or reproached her with severity for the indulgence of it.

The only consolation afforded her was derived from the conversation of Dorothèe, whose solicitude to remove her concern mitigated the severity of her own.

The suspicion that Paoli was indirectly an auxiliary in the

affair, would sometimes occur to the imagination of Laurette, though she could not effectually reconcile it to her reason or the native candour of her mind. The voices that excited alarm, which she supposed to be those of the ruffians, and the circumstance of the steward's requesting the society of Madame Chamont alone, and at that silent hour, and his walking apparently from the wood from whence those voices proceeded, was food for conjecture; and a mind less pure and inexperienced than her own, would have resolutely decided against him. But she knew the value of that virtue which places the actions of others in the most favourable light, and willingly rejects every thing that tends to criminate, if it falls short of conviction.

Had she been acquainted with La Roque's confinement and escape from the dungeon, which was carefully concealed from her, or had heard of the bracelet which was found there by the steward, sufficient evidence would have been collected to justify the opinion.

The only consolation that now offered itself, was the probability of Madame Chamont's being still alive, and in a place of safety; for as one of the men had assured her she had nothing to fear, there appeared not to be any design upon her life.

Her silence and apparent tranquillity at the inn could not easily be accounted for; but from whatever cause it proceeded, it wore an aspect by no means unfavourable.

These circumstances she continued to reflect upon with hope; and as the possibility of meeting again with her beloved friend was presented to her young and sanguine imagination, her spirits gradually revived.

When the mind has once escaped from the influence of over-whelming calamity, it endeavours to extract comfort from surrounding objects at once to apply a balm to the wounds it has endured, and to compensate for the losses it has sustained. So Laurette attempted to divert the melancholy that assailed her by constant and unremitting employment; at first her former amusements were irksome and uninteresting, in a short time they became more supportable, and finally, as the reward of effort, assumed the power of pleasing.

Though the lovely orphan was too much intimidated to

venture far from the castle alone, she continued to stroll as usual in the gardens, whose wild and desolate appearance was in unison with her feelings, and sometimes, under the shade of her favourite tree, where she had so often sat with Enrîco, would resign herself to the influence of melancholy reflections.

One evening as she was returning from this spot, and had arrived at the smaller gate which led directly to the mansion, she observed Lisette, seemingly much affrighted, darting along the side of the edifice. Anxious to be made acquainted with her cause of alarm, she called to her, and desired her to stop. The girl, not immediately hearing her, did not slacken her pace, till Laurette's repeating the call occasioned her to turn.

Having made some enquiries, which the affrighted servant was too much terrified to answer, she led her into the hall, and observing that she looked unusually pale, called instantly for assistance. As soon as Lisette revived, she informed them, that as she was returning from one of the cottages on the margin of the river, whither she had been to convey some food to a poor woman that was ill, according to her usual custom in cases of a similar nature, she perceived a tall dreadful looking figure gliding by the side of the rampart. She was too much agitated, she added, to observe it minutely; but it appeared much taller than any human being she had ever seen, and very ghastly.

As soon as she had arrived within a few steps of the court, she saw the same figure, which she was assured could be no other than an apparition, stealing along the avenue. Having turned hastily back, she had, she said, the courage to look behind, and saw the spectre pursuing her, who having waved its hand mournfully, as if beckoning her to follow it, vanished suddenly from her sight. In a few moments a terrible scream, which was more loud and dreadful than any thing she had ever heard, and which was succeeded by a strange noise or fluttering in the air, so considerably augmented her alarm as almost to deprive her of her senses.

When a little recovered from the astonishment which this horrible phantom had excited, she was, she said, hastening towards home, when the voice of her young lady, which she believed to be that of the spirit, increased her terror.

Laurette could not forbear smiling at the latter part of the recital, and though she could not account for the strange unnatural appearance she described, she was persuaded that the screams and flutterings in the air which had so powerfully affected the girl's fancy, were occasioned by the sudden flight of a number of owls that inhabited the tops of the turrets. But it was difficult to convince Lisette that it could otherwise be accounted for than by the interposition of supernatural agency.

Father Benedicta, who had frequently been at the castle since the departure of Madame Chamont, having been informed of the strange incident that had been the cause of it, expressed much surprise and uneasiness. As he was not ignorant of Della Croisse's escape from captivity being effected by her means, he naturally suspected the Marchese to be the primary cause. He knew that under an inscrutable disguise he was capable of executing the most daring villany; though accustomed to think with candour, and act with gentleness, the mild precepts of his religion did not render Father Benedicta insensible to the vices of others, neither had they obliterated all traces of former resentment.

He reflected with concern upon the unprotected situation of Laurette, and endeavoured to dissuade her from the indulgence of unavailing sorrow. As she appeared to derive comfort from his society, his visits were more frequently repeated than before the commencement of her misfortunes, and he had the satisfaction of finding, that when he expatiated upon the indispensable necessity of guarding against that intellectual weakness, which is sometimes dignified with the name of sensibility, and of the incontestible advantages arising from an undiminished fortitude, that she listened to him not only with attention, but with gratitude.

Though the Father had resolved to discover, if possible, whither Madame Chamont was conveyed, and by what authority she was forced from the castle, he executed his intentions with secrecy, lest it should occasion the indulgence of unwarranted hope. Yet though he extended his enquiries with perseverance and solicitude, they were ineffectual, and he was finally compelled to relinquish an enterprize that was attended with so little success.

Laurette was for some time irresolute whether to write to
Enrîco immediately, to inform him of this unhappy event, or
to defer it till some future period. The former plan seemed to
be the most eligible, as his endeavours would be exerted in the
cause; but the mournful intelligence she had to communicate,
so entirely deprived her of the power of action, that though she
several times began to frame an epistle, she was long before she
accomplished her design.

The idea that probably before the arrival of that letter Enrîco
might be no more, would sometimes present itself to her disordered fancy, with a thousand dreadful accompaniments: She
saw him, in her terrified imagination, borne bleeding and lifeless
from the field; her heart sickened at the thought, till a shower
of tears that fell in large drops upon the paper, which she had
prepared for the purpose of writing to him, relieved her almost
bursting bosom.

She recollected every amiable qualification he possessed, his
graceful, his dignified deportment, the uniform delicacy of his
manners, his tenderness, and filial affection. When she remembered these, and the expression of his countenance at the parting
interview, and saw the groves through which they had walked,
and the flowers they had together admired, her feelings were
too painful to be endured, and she quitted abruptly the place, as
if desirous of escaping from the memorials of her former happiness.

A letter from the Marchese to his steward now arrived at the
castle, which contained an account of the death of the Marchesa.
She had suffered much from a lingering and severe illness, with
which she had been afflicted some time. Having been separated
from her husband soon after her marriage, she had resided,
during this state of premature widowhood, in a mansion on a
German estate, in a distant part of the country.

The Marchese, who had been long weary of his present residence, the Castello St. Aubin, determined immediately on the
decease of his lady, to have the mansion where she had resided
repaired and modernized for his reception.

This occasioned the removal of Paoli, who had orders to visit
the estate, to observe what repairs might be requisite, and to

employ a sufficient number of hands to accomplish the work with all possible expedition. Having informed Laurette of these particulars, and of his intention of returning as soon as the business was transacted, the steward made some little necessary arrangements, and commenced his journey.

Laurette, in the meantime, dedicated her hours to the most worthy and useful employments, and with the assistance of the good Friar, the Father Benedicta, was soon enabled to reflect upon the past, and to anticipate the future, with some degree of tranquillity.

Her virtues were of the most active kind: she employed means of being acquainted with the necessities of the indigent, and experienced the delightful gratification of contributing to their comforts.

This diffusive humanity, which acquired additional excellence from its being united with youth and beauty, so exalted her in the estimation of those who were its objects, that they mingled admiration with gratitude; and though they lamented the loss of their former benefactress, who had so suddenly and so strangely disappeared, they soon discovered that her young charge possessed all those valuable and endearing qualifications which had rendered her so deservedly beloved.

Though Laurette, in the course of her reading, had met with some fictitious tales of distress, those abounding in tender description, and that irresistibly affect the fancy, were in some measure prohibited. Madame Chamont, though she had retired early from society, and of course had mixed but little with the world, was sufficiently acquainted with the human heart to be convinced that works of this kind might have a dangerous tendency. She therefore discountenanced in her young pupil that unlimited indulgence, in the passive feelings of sensibility, which inevitably unfits the mind for any undertaking that requires firm and vigorous exertion; she knew that, when deeply affected by tales of imaginary woe, the mind too often sinks into imbecility; and when abstracted from the influence of romantic delusion, it beholds real objects of compassion divested of those false and glowing colours in which they have been exhibited by the song of the Poet, or the pen of the Novelist—it beholds them without that sympathetic interest which would extend the arm of active benevolence for their relief.

CHAP. X.

I'll read you matter deep and dangerous,
As full of peril and adventurous spirit
As to o'erwalk a current, roaring loud,
On the unstedfast footing of a spear.

The gentle mind of Laurette, though strengthened by effort, was yet tenderly alive to mournful impressions, which solitude and the native softness of her disposition rendered sometimes irresistible. The silence of Enrîco increased her apprehensions, and though she endeavoured to dissipate her fears, and to sweeten with hope the cup of affliction, her anguish was sometimes too keen to be subdued, and her life became a series of sufferance and exertion.

Paoli's absence being protracted beyond what he had intimated as necessary, it began to be a matter of doubt whether it was his intention to return, or to remain stationary in the family of the Marchese; till the trampling of hoofs, heard in the silence of evening, put an end to conjecture.

Laurette was sitting in her apartment when he arrived, endeavouring to find comfort in employment, when a message from the steward, which was delivered by Lisette, summoned her into the saloon, where he was in waiting to receive her. As soon as she entered, he presented her with a letter. She was unacquainted with the hand-writing, but, on opening it, found it bore the signature of the Marchese de Montferrat. So unexpected a circumstance covered her with confusion, and she perused it with apparent emotion.

He expressed much astonishment at the intelligence that had been recently conveyed to him concerning the departure of Madame Chamont, and also informed her that it was his intention to remove her, in a few weeks, from her present residence to a less ancient castle, that was preparing for himself, in the principality of Saltzburg. He was, he added, by unforeseen events, prevented from repairing thither immediately himself; but, as it would soon be in readiness for her reception, he had given orders for his steward to convey her to the mansion, where it was his intention for her to remain during the winter season. He concluded with desiring her not to regret the loss of her protectress, as all possible means of discovering the authors of so unjustifiable a proceeding should be instantly employed.

Laurette examined the contents of this letter with mingled distress and astonishment. To leave that beloved retreat, which had been her home from earliest infancy; to be allowed to ramble no more over those beautiful mountains, which had been the scenes of youthful festivity, and which were endeared to her by the remembrance of former happiness, was a subject of painful reflection; but when she recollected that the felicity which she had once experienced in those delightful shades was annihilated, and that those who had shared it with her were separated from her, perhaps for ever, she endeavoured to reconcile herself to a destiny which, from the unlimited power which the Marchese possessed over her, she considered as unavoidable.

Paoli, in the meantime, began to make every necessary preparation for a speedy removal. And as it appeared probable to Laurette that he was to remain in the castle mentioned by the Marchese in the absence of his lord, she endeavoured, though with little hopes of success, to soften the native moroseness of his disposition with the undeviating sweetness of her own. But though she frequently attempted to engage him in conversation, she usually failed in her design; for his mind was so entirely absorbed in its own reflections and concerns, that he seemed scarcely conscious of her presence. Yet as the suspicion which she once faintly entertained, respecting his having entered into a conspiracy with the ruffians who had forced Madame Chamont into the woods, was now entirely removed, she beheld him with less aversion.

As the time drew near which was to separate her from the scenes of her earliest happiness, she found it difficult to support that serene tranquillity of soul which she so ardently desired to retain, though she did not fail to exert every effort in her power to preserve that uniformity of conduct she had been taught to estimate and admire.

When Father Benedicta again repeated his visit, Laurette informed him of the letter she had received from the Marchese, and also of his intention of removing her to another castle in a distant part of the country, whither she was soon to be conveyed.

The surprise and uneasiness expressed in the countenance of the Father when the intelligence was communicated, could not pass unobserved by his lovely young pupil, who beheld him with a silent and fixed attention.

He asked eagerly under whose protection she was to be placed, and whether the Marchese was to reside on this estate during her continuance there.

Assured of the sincerity of his friendship, and grateful for the interest he had ever discovered in her concerns, Laurette presented him with the letter. Having perused it, he sighed, shook his head mournfully, and, as if anxious to escape from enquiry, arose to depart: "I shall see you again, my child," cried the Monk tenderly, as she followed him towards the door.

Laurette regarded him stedfastly as he spoke, and thought she perceived a tear steal down his placid cheek. She would have enquired the cause, but her heart was too full for utterance, and having attended him to the portal, she watched him as he proceeded along the avenue till he was lost in distance, and then returning to the saloon, placed herself in one of the recesses of the windows, and indulged the acuteness of her feelings in secret.

It was evident from the words of the Friar, as well as from the tone in which they were delivered, that there was something either in the stile of the epistle, or in the proposal it contained, that did not accord with his ideas of propriety. She wished she had been collected enough to have requested the avowal of his sentiments, and looked forwards to another interview with somewhat of impatience.

The Marchese she had never seen, consequently, though he had offered her his castle, he was uninfluenced by affection. She had been taught to believe that he was her only surviving friend and protector; yet, as he had never conciliated her esteem by winning offices of kindness, her gratitude was unmingled with tenderness.

The mysterious silence that had been preserved concerning her birth, she had often considered with surprise; she was called Laurette, but no other name was added; and when she ventured to extend her enquiries, her questions were either evaded, or remained entirely unanswered. When blessed with the protection of Madame Chamont, the subject was attended with curiosity, and not with regret; but now that protection was withdrawn, it returned forcibly upon her mind. She had been told she was an orphan, but every hint that could tend to a farther knowledge of this mystery was carefully avoided.

These reflections, which the forlornness of her situation suggested, added to the uncertainty of the fate of Madame Chamont and Enrîco, so entirely occupied her thoughts, that the taciturnity of the steward, and the presaging gloom of his aspect were unobserved, or beheld with indifference. But on being assured that Dorothèe and Lisette were to attend her to her place of destination, her spirits became suddenly reanimated and she began to prepare for her journey with redoubled alacrity.

As to ramble alone in the wood, or along the solitary glens of the mountains, was a charm the most suited to her mind, she yielded to the impulse of her feelings, and often, in the meek hour of twilight, would gaze with a tranquil kind of melancholy upon those dear, those much-loved scenes she was soon to resign for ever.

One evening, on her return from one of these lonely excursions, she seated herself against a window in the room which she always called her own, because it contained the implements of her studies and her amusements.

When wrapped in pensive reflections, as she was gazing upon the moon gliding silently along through a clear and cloudless sky, she observed a white figure, somewhat answering to the description that Lisette had given of the phantom which had occasioned her alarm, move slowly beneath the arch of the window.

Though Laurette had before treated this appearance as an illusion, she now felt a superstitious dread stealing upon her mind. Fear, for a moment, arrested her faculties, but an effort of fortitude releasing them, she arose and opened the casement. In a few minutes the same figure emerged from the deep shade of the trees, and approached towards the window.

She started and was retreating, till the sound of her own name, uttered in a deep and hollow tone, rivetted her to the spot. She stopped—it was again repeated, and venturing to raise her eyes towards the object of her terror, she beheld a person standing before her, of a pale and melancholy aspect, clad in the habit of a monk; he was tall and of a singular physiognomy, he wore no cowl nor even a cloak, and his dress being entirely white, except a narrow black scapulary, added much to the ghastliness of his appearance.

As he moved towards the casement, he waved his hand, in token for her to stop, and again repeating the name of Laurette, with deeper emphasis, "Beware," cried he, "of the Marchese de Montferrat."

Laurette trembled, but was unable to articulate; she scarcely knew whether the being addressing her was human or super-natural; a sensation of mingled terror and awe almost overcame her, and it was with difficulty that she could prevent herself from falling.

The Monk, not seeming to regard her emotion, drew a miniature from beneath his garment, and then surveying her for a moment in silence, added—

"Will you, in consideration of my holy office, utter a solemn promise, which nothing shall prevail upon you to violate, never to disclose to any individual living what I am about to relate?"

Laurette's tremor increased; but not being allowed time for reflection, and having no idea that a person in the garb of a religious could act so inconsistently with that devout character as to exact a promise which she could not make with impunity, she gave her answer in the affirmative.

"Will you swear then," resumed the Father, raising his voice still higher, which acquired deeper energy of expression as he proceeded, "by the ever spotless and holy Maria, by the accepted souls of the departed, and by the blessed assembly of the Saints and Martyrs, to keep this vow inviolable, till I shall call upon you to attest the truth of what I shall hereafter declare, at some future and, perchance, far distant period."

Laurette tremblingly assented to the proposition, and the Father repeating the form in which he wished it to be delivered, she pronounced it after him.

When this impressive vow was recited agreeable to the desire of the Father, he presented Laurette with the miniature which he held suspended by a chain of brilliants, and then softening his voice, added, "Take this, it is the portrait of thy mother; wear it as an invaluable gift, and to-morrow, as soon as vespers are concluded, meet me at the equestrian statue in the inner court. Recollect the solemnity of your promise, and I will unfold to you an important secret."

She was going to reply, but before she was sufficiently collected, he had glided amongst the trees, and had disappeared.

"The portrait of my mother!" cried Laurette, fixing her eyes upon the picture with a look of undescribable astonishment, "is it possible; and have I then a parent living?" But in an instant remembering that the delivery of the miniature by no means implied that she was still in existence, a slight degree of disappointment was communicated to her heart.

Dorothèe, who entered the room to kindle a fire, broke unwelcomely upon her solitude; but mindful of the injunctions of her mysterious visiter, Laurette arose, and, after secreting the portrait, assumed an appearance of composure.

As soon as she was again alone, and her thoughts were somewhat recomposed, she began to muse upon this singular occurrence. If this was the person who had excited so much alarm in the bosom of Lisette, it was strange that his nocturnal rambles had not been regularly continued, as since that time no one had been seen about the grounds in the least answering to that description; and as the subject of his visits was undoubtedly herself, and the secret he had to declare was of so important a nature, it was natural to suppose, instead of avoiding her, he would have loitered within the boundaries of the mansion, in the hope of meeting with her.

The solemn manner in which these words were pronounced, "Beware of the Marchese de Montferrat!" struck her with dismay.

To beware of him whom she had been taught to revere as a parent, and to look forwards to as the patron of her future days, was not more astonishing than afflictive. The admonition seemed to presage some impending evil from which it was impossible to fly; and the dread of what she might have to encounter, alone and unfriended, now entirely occupied her thoughts, tending to make her fear more than ever the approach of that hour which was to separate her from the much-loved scenes of her earliest youth.

As she examined the features of the portrait, rendered infinitely more touching by the sweet pensive cast of the countenance, she thought she had somewhere seen a painting that strongly characterized it; and as the castle contained all that had ever fallen under her observation, she was resolved to regard them more attentively, and, if possible, to trace the resemblance.

The chain, by which the miniature was suspended, did not fail to attract her admiration; she had never seen any thing of the sort, and the jewels, though small, being of the most valuable kind, possessed unusual brilliancy and lustre.

As Laurette wished to ruminate in secret upon this singular adventure, she retired to her room earlier than was her custom, at once to abridge the moments of suspense, and to lose the society of Paoli. But though weary and indisposed, she was unable to sleep, and arose in the morning but little refreshed.

Her first resolve was to examine the portraits, which were very numerous, and much defaced by time and neglect. She had wandered over the greatest part of the castle, except the northern side of the building which remained always unopened, before she recollected the paintings in the oriel, which were more modern, and consequently less injured than the rest.

Here she examined the picture which had attracted the attention of Madame Chamont soon after her arrival at the mansion. It represented the figure of a female leaning upon a tomb, the countenance of which bore some resemblance to the miniature; the latter, indeed, appeared somewhat younger, and, if possible, still more beautiful. It possessed the same softness of expression, but there was less of melancholy; a smile beamed from the eyes, which were dark, and full of the most animated sweetness, while the light brown tresses that shaded the forehead, and waved carelessly upon the neck, completed the character of beauty.

But for whom the portrait was designed, which she imagined was so lively a representation of that presented by the Monk, she had never been informed; though she remembered having once questioned Margaritte concerning it. But as her only hope of gaining intelligence upon the subject depended upon the expected interview in the evening, she awaited the hour with increasing solicitude.

CHAP. XI.

"With what a leaden and retarding weight
Does expectation load the wing of Time!"
                                    MASON.

Willing to divert her thoughts from a subject in which she was too nearly interested, Laurette attempted, though without success, to find amusement in employment: She took up her lute, but her fingers were unable to perform their office; the notes she awakened were low, spiritless, and inharmonious, and it was replaced with languor and dissatisfaction. Her embroidery and books were equally ineffectual to bestow the charm of content, and the more frequently this strange incident recurred to her mind, the more insupportable were the moments of suspense. That attractive composure of demeanour, which formerly added the most winning softness to her motions, had in some degree forsaken her; she reflected, with concern, upon her promise to the Father, and seemed equally to dread and to desire the expected interview.

As soon as dinner was removed, she arose and quitted the room, meaning to ramble though the shrubberies; but as the afternoon was a remarkably fine one, she determined to endeavour, at least, to calm the more painful emotions by visiting the cottages that bordered the river, whose simple and industrious inhabitants had been always the objects of her bounty.

Having relieved the necessities of those who apparently suf-

fered the most from the hardships of poverty, and listened with
peculiar kindness to the infantine prattle of the children, who
were each anxious to gain a smile or a kiss from their lovely
benefactress, she continued her walk.

The loneliness of the road she had chosen was ill adapted to
her present frame of mind, as it failed, for want of variety in its
scenery, to fix her attention, and to recal her from that harassing
anxiety which enervates, and unfits for action.

The singular aspect of the Monk, his abrupt stile of addressing her, the secret he had to disclose so dreadfully important as
his manner had indicated, were circumstances ever present to
her thoughts. Sometimes it occurred to her that the expected
discovery related to Madame Chamont, and that the person
who had so strangely introduced himself, having by some means
become acquainted with the violent measures that had been
adopted in forcing her from her abode, and of the primary cause
of them, intended, by making it known to those who were the
most nearly concerned in her welfare, to prevent the unhappy
consequences that might otherwise ensue. But this, on a second review, appeared unlikely; if the Monk had obtained any
knowledge upon this subject, he would doubtless have embraced
some other means of conveying this necessary intelligence at an
earlier period, and of rendering her such advice and assistance,
as to the manner of proceeding, as would have been consistent
with his holy character and office.

What he had to unfold must then relate merely to herself,
something probably concerning her birth. This opinion the delivery of the picture seemed to corroborate; but who it could be
that had acquired information upon a subject which had hitherto been so mysteriously concealed, and by what means he had
gained possession of the picture, which he declared to be the
portrait of her mother, were points equally surprising and unaccountable.

The shades of night that fell fast upon the surrounding objects, now warning her of the approaching hour, quickened her
steps towards the castle.

The soft stillness of the evening that seemed to breathe peace
and tranquillity, tended to revive her depressed spirits, enabling

her to reflect upon the appointment she had made with more composure and serenity.

As soon as she entered the hall, the shrill tone of the vesper-bell reminded her of her mysterious visiter, and summoned her to nocturnal prayer.

When the service was concluded, and the family were retired from the chapel, with trembling steps and a palpitating heart she prepared to meet the Monk, according to her engagement.

Having waited for a few minutes in the outward court, in hopes of seeing Paoli enter the castle, she observed, with some emotion, that he turned into the wood that secreted the eastern side of the edifice. But as he sometimes rambled alone in the evening for a considerable time, she began to flatter herself into the opinion that he would not return from his excursion during her conference with the Father.

She had no sooner entered the smaller court, and placed her-self by the column, than she perceived the mysterious Monk, with a thoughtful and dejected air, moving slowly through the avenue.

When he had arrived at the vista he stopped, crossed himself, and then numbering his Paternosters and Ave Marias on his rosary, a ceremony which Laurette's impatience would at that moment gladly have spared, he hastened to the appointed place.

A hood was added to his dress, which he threw back the instant he recognized Laurette, and a small crucifix of silver was suspended on his breast.

Having advanced within a few paces of the column—"I am come," said he, fixing his eyes upon her with a mild and stedfast gaze, "to warn you of the dangers that threaten you—to save you from misery, and perchance from death. I am come also," added he, sighing deeply, and clasping his hands together, with a look directed meekly towards heaven, "to acquaint you with the wrongs you have endured, and to unveil the hidden myster-ies of your birth. Listen to me, my child; on this moment, this important moment, depends your future destiny."

Laurette trembled, and looking fearfully around, whilst the Father was repeating his injunctions of secrecy in the same manner as on the preceding day, she beheld Paoli embowered in some trees that projected from the side of the wood, apparently listening to their discourse. Fear almost deprived her of utterance: "We are observed," cried she, in tremulous and broken accents, "leave me, holy Father, I beseech you—to-morrow at this hour."

She could proceed no farther; the Monk glided amongst the trees, but his motion was not sufficiently rapid to elude the observation of Paoli, who finding himself discovered, rushed instantly from the wood.

Having demanded, in an imperious tone, with whom she was conversing, and what was the subject of their conference, and Laurette, amazed at his presumption and arrogance, resolutely refusing to answer, he seized her rudely by the arm, and led her into the saloon.

Here he again repeated his command, but finding that neither this nor menaces were likely to prove effectual, as she replied to his interrogatories with a degree of firmness which he termed the most daring obstinacy, he desired her to prepare for her departure from the castle on the following morning.

This was a blow the gentle spirits of Laurette could with difficulty support; yet no alternative remained. She was too well acquainted with the disposition of the steward to believe he would yield to intreaty, and she was also convinced, from the judgment she had formed of his character, that if she ventured to expostulate with him, or to enquire by what authority he was capacitated to remove her from her present residence, without the knowledge and acquiescence of the Marchese, before the expiration of the time proposed, that by thus appearing to doubt his consequence in the eye of his Lord, he would only, by more arbitrary proceedings, endeavour to convince her of the unlimited extent of his power.

Being assured that all hopes of receiving the information she so ardently desired, respecting her birth and connection, were now entirely frustrated, she felt all the bitterness of disappointment and perplexity; as she was perfectly convinced that was she even permitted to remain a few weeks longer at the castle, she would doubtless be so strictly watched by the suspicious eye of Paoli during the interval, as to render a second interview with the Monk impracticable.

The night was passed by Laurette in a state of restless anxiety; what she had heard from the Father increased her uneasiness, and nothing but the rectitude of her intentions, and the conscious innocence of her conduct, could have sustained her under this new cause of distress.

CHAP. XII.

> "At night returning, every labour sped,
> He sits him down the monarch of a shed,
> Smiles by his chearful fire, and round surveys
> His children's looks, that brighten at the blaze;
> While his lov'd partner, boastful of her hoard,
> Displays her cleanly platter on the board;
> And haply too, some pilgrim thither led,
> With many a tale repays the nightly bed."
>
> GOLDSMITH.

The sun had scarce risen upon the mountains before Laurette, by the desire of the steward, was awakened from a soft slumber into which she had recently fallen, with orders for her to prepare for an immediate departure.

Dorothèe, who was the unwilling messenger of these unpleasant tidings, unable to bear the idea of this temporary separation, as it was determined on the preceding night that she and Lisette were not to accompany them, but to remain at the castle till the return of Ambrose; Laurette, feeling more collected than she had been since her interview with the Monk, assumed an appearance of serenity, and having conversed with her faithful servant for some time, as she sat by the side of the bed, with the most affecting tenderness, she gave some necessary orders concerning her wardrobe, her books, and what other things she wished to have conveyed to her future residence, and then ordering breakfast to be served in her apartment, prepared to obey the summons.

She had scarcely partaken of the morning's repast before she was informed that the mules were in readiness, and that Paoli and Ambrose were already impatiently awaiting her arrival.

Having taken a tender adieu of the kind Margaritte, who

was too old to be a follower of her fortunes, and had therefore determined to return to the cottage she formerly possessed in an adjacent village; she presented her with her five last remaining rix-dollars, as the reward of her services; and waving her hand to her poor pensioners, who crowded about her to give and to receive a last farewel, she held her handkerchief to her eyes, as if afraid to trust herself with a last look at the only home she had ever known, and advanced towards the gate.

Being placed upon the mule that was guided by the steward, Ambrose mounted the lesser one, and after some resistance on the part of the latter, who had been for some time unaccustomed to discipline, they pursued their journey.

It was a fine autumnal morning, and as the travellers advanced, the face of Nature, which at the early hour they had chosen, wore a lowering and unpromising aspect, now gradually brightened. The mists, which had veiled the tops of the eminences, were suddenly dispersed, and the sun, no longer watery and dim, spread over the landscape a soft and silvery light.

The birds, whose responses were at first low, now swelled into choral harmony; every object seemed to partake of the general joy; all was melody, delight, and ecstasy.

Laurette meditated on them in silence, lamenting at the same time that she could not join in these universal expressions of rapture, which would have afforded her inconceivable pleasure, had melancholy anticipation been banished from her heart.

The same gloomy reserve marked the behaviour of Paoli that was peculiar to his character; sometimes he turned to Laurette, and asked her some questions concerning the road, and whether the motion was too slow or too rapid, and then, without attending to the answer, relapsed into his former state of silence and thoughtfulness.

There were several small inns on the road that afforded them rest and provisions, whose inhabitants frequently extended their civility beyond the common bounds of hospitality, seeming anxious to accommodate them with every necessary which their situation as travellers required.

It was not till the evening of the third day that they arrived near the boundaries of Saltzburg, when Laurette was informed

by the steward, who appeared somewhat to relax from his reserve, that they were within two days' journey of the castle of
Luenburg, which was the name of her future abode.

The beauty of the landscape now visibly improved; the boundless and variegated plains, innumerable lakes, rivers, brooks, and
valleys of tremendous depth, encompassed with huge rocks
of granite, which, being contrasted with the dark woods that
waved from the cultivated mountains, had an unspeakable fine
effect, and could not be gazed upon without the most sublime
and exquisite sensations.

Every thing was presented to the eye in these beautiful regions which the most fertile and picturesque imagination could
conceive; and Laurette, recalled from the contemplation of her
own peculiar distresses, beheld some of the finest scenery in
nature with indescribable astonishment.

Every beauty was augmented by contrast; sometimes the hut
of a shepherd, or the cottage of a goatherd, situated upon the
hanging brow of a precipice, caught her eye, shaded only by the
foliated branches of the oak from the inclemency of the weather.
The roads in this mountainous country being in general good,
they proceeded on their journey with less fatigue than would
otherwise have been the case. The most dreadful abysses were
rendered passable by the assistance of wooden bridges, which
were hung in chains, some apparently so loosely as to impress
on the mind an alarming idea of danger. But of their safety our
travellers were assured by the peasantry, who asserted that an
accident very rarely happened from this mode of conveyance,
as the heaviest carriages had been known to pass over without
receiving any injury but what might be occasioned by a violent
gust of wind, or a sudden fall of snow in the spring.

Having left the town of Saltzburg on the right, they proceeded on their way with redoubled speed, in hopes of being
able to reach the next tolerable inn, which Paoli recollected was
at some distance from the place.

But as the evening was approaching, and Laurette was somewhat fatigued and indisposed, it was mutually agreed that the
party should endeavour to get accommodations at one of the
cottages that lay scattered upon the road.

One peculiar for its neatness riveted their attention, and Ambrose being dispatched with a message, Laurette and Paoli stopped at the bottom of the hill on which it was situated, to await the success of his embassy.

In a short time the owner of this little retreat, attended by his daughter, with all that diffusive hospitality which is characteristic of the peasantry of Saltzburg, mingled with a certain degree of courtesy that seemed not to be wholly the gift of nature, appeared to conduct them to the cottage.

All that Laurette had ever read of rural simplicity, content, and innocence, and all that her imagination, though somewhat warm and romantic, had formed, fell short of that which was presented to her in the family of the cottager.

Zierman, which was the name of her host, having led them into a small neat room, whose casement was embowered with the honeysuckle and the eglantine, and which commanded a prospect of pastoral beauty almost unequalled, left our heroine and the steward alone, whilst he went to assist Ambrose in finding a place of security for his mules, and to order refreshment for his guests.

In a few minutes he returned with some fruit, cream, and a thin kind of wine, which was all that the cottage afforded.

Having partaken of this hospitable meal, which was animated with a smile of unfeigned welcome, the spirits of the travellers were recruited; and as Paoli conversed with the peasant, who seemed, though placed in obscurity, to possess some knowledge of men and manners, Laurette amused herself with observing the beautiful variety of every thing around.

The little garden cultivated with care, that was surrounded with a hedge blooming with briar-roses and wild honeysuckles, discovered not only the simplicity but the taste of its owner; beyond which arose hills formed into the most picturesque lines, and covered with delightful verdure, which acquired an appearance of the most flourishing vegetation from being contrasted with those tremendous mountains, whose summits, penetrating the clouds, were veiled in awful obscurity.

Much as she had been accustomed to admire the wild and extensive scenery which her former residence commanded, the infinite diversity of objects which were visible from this secluded retreat, could not be contemplated without the sublimest emotions.

When Paoli and his host had conversed for some time upon common subjects, the latter began to recite some particulars relative to himself and his family, which were interesting, because in relating them he discovered a sensibility of mind not usually found in that sphere of life, the hard and laborious employments of which preclude the cultivation of the nicer feelings.

Paoli, who neither understood nor internally applauded these amiable traits of character which Laurette observed with increasing admiration, apparently listened to the discourse, though his intellectual powers were probably more profitably employed in the contemplation of some favourite project.

"It is now ten years," added the old man, with a sigh, and a tear which he endeavoured to repress, "since I lost my wife; she died suddenly, and for some time this cottage, which was once so dear to me, and in which I had enjoyed so many hours of repose and happiness, was by this unexpected event rendered insupportable, which determined me to remove from it to another occupied by my daughter, that is situated about a league and a half from this place; hoping to take refuge from uneasiness in the society of my only child, who was united to a young farmer, to whom she had been long attached, a few months before the death of her mother.

"There I remained some time, till my natural affection to my little paternal inheritance returning, I felt an irresistible inclination to revisit it. Having obviated some objections on the part of my daughter and her husband, I at length prevailed upon them to accompany me here; and in their society, and in the amusement their little family affords, I have regained that habitual cheerfulness of temper which I am persuaded is one of the first blessings of life."

Here Zierman was interrupted by the entrance of Ulrica, his daughter, with two of her children, whom Laurette remembered having seen and admired as she ascended the hill, when they were engaged in play with their companions in the glens of the mountains.

As soon as Ulrica entered, she repeated the same friendly welcome with which the party were at first received, and then seating herself by the side of her young guest, to whom she more particularly addressed herself, occasionally joined in conversation.

Laurette being now materially recovered from her fatigue by the salutary rest and refreshment that had been administered, requested permission to walk to the end of the garden, which terminated in a kind of natural terrace, that she might be gratified with the beauty of the prospect. The hostess agreed to the proposition, and attended her to the place.

It commanded an infinitude of objects of the most interesting and attractive kind: on the right was a beautiful lake retiring amongst the hills into remote distance, whose silvery appearance, contrasted with the dark woods that frequently interrupted its course, had a very charming effect. On the left, appeared a range of rocks of an enormous size, some of which, projecting forwards, frowned over the Saltza, that rushed impetuously through the cliffs with the foam of a cataract; except the noise of this boisterous stream, which, from its being softened by distance, occasioned only a gentle murmur, no other sound was to be heard, save the tones of a flute, resounding from the valleys or from the brow of a precipice, to assemble the sheep around the huts of the peasants.

As Laurette took a survey of this beautiful country, she was tempted to believe that happiness was exclusively the portion of the shepherd and the goatherd, and would at that moment gladly have resigned all future advantages for a similar situation, could those she had lost have been restored to her.

Having thanked Ulrica for her attention with the most insinuating courtesy of manners, Laurette made some general enquiries concerning the families of the mountaineers whose picturesque habitations had so romantic an appearance, and then returned towards the cottage.

Here she found Paoli and his host regaling themselves with some wine and grapes which the son-in-law of the latter had presented to them in her absence, and of which, on being politely offered to her on her entrance, she consented to partake.

The moon now shone full into the casement, and every sound being hushed, except the light trembling of the leaves that overshadowed the cottage, Laurette intimated a wish to retire, and was conducted by her hostess to her room.

As she paused for a moment at the window of the apartment to enjoy the serenity of the scene, the notes of a guitar, accompanied by a female voice that breathed the most affecting sweetness, fixed her to the spot. The air, which was a melancholy one, seemed to have been awakened by no common sorrow, and throwing open the casement, she stood for some time to be assured from whence it proceeded, and to indulge herself in the soft sensation of sympathy which the song inspired.

As she still listened, the strain died away upon the air, and all was again silent; but after a momentary pause it swelled louder, and seemed to approach nearer towards the cottage.

In hopes of being able to get a sight of the harmonist, she still lingered at the window, but, contrary to her expectation, the music seemed to retreat again towards the woods, and was soon heard no more.

Ulrica, who re-entered the room to enquire if she could render her any farther assistance, gave her some intelligence relative to the musician, who she learned was a young woman who had met with a disappointment in the tender passion, which had occasioned the loss of her senses.

"I know but little of the story, Madame," resumed Ulrica, "but I believe my father can inform you of the whole. All that I have heard is, that she is the daughter of a goatherd, and that she lives in a small hut on one of the neighbouring mountains;—her name is Ida; her lover, I think, died on the day fixed for their marriage; but there are many mournful circumstances attending the story which I am partly unacquainted with, for it is now several years since they happened, and at that time I was not resident in the neighbourhood. But ever since the commencement of her misfortunes she has wandered about in the woods, singing so sweetly that I have heard my father say, before it was known to be Ida, it was reported that the woods were haunted."

"And does no one attend her," asked Laurette, "in her nocturnal rambles?"

"Yes, her father or her brother follows her at some distance," returned the hostess; "but she will not allow them to break in upon her solitude; if it was known to her that she was watched, she would become desperate; so that they are compelled to indulge her in this unfortunate propensity, which frequently deprives them of rest, because her father, who adores her, will not allow her to be confined. In the day-time she usually remains in her hut, though I have sometimes seen her in the glens of the rocks culling flowers from the interstices, and forming them into garlands, and then sing so sadly, that I have been unable to refrain from weeping.

"But it is a mournful story, Madame," continued Ulrica, observing that her fair auditor appeared much affected; "let us change the subject."

Laurette forced a smile upon her features, and desiring that she might no longer detain her, since it was a late hour, and the rest of the family were in bed, wished her a good night, and endeavoured to forget her own sorrows, and those of the unfortunate Ida, in repose.

As soon as the morning appeared, the travellers arose from their slumbers, and after a simple repast, returned thanks to the cottagers for their hospitable reception, who would accept no pecuniary reward for their services, and then continued their journey.

It was not till the evening that they arrived within sight of the place of their destination, and Laurette's heart sunk within her when the first turret was partially seen through the dark foliage of the woods with which it was surrounded.

As they advanced nearer, the body of the edifice gradually emerged from the gloom, and the moon, throwing her soft light upon its summit, discovered a magnificent abode, which, from comparison with the desolate looking mansion they had left, appeared to the young and astonished eyes of Laurette like the residence of an eastern prince.

CHAP. XIII.

"Bear me, embowering shades, between,
Through many a glade and vista green;
Whate'er can captivate the sight,
Elysian lawns and prospects bright;
Give me, fair Fancy, to pervade
Chambers in pictur'd pomp array'd,
Peopling whose stately walls, I view
The godlike forms that Raphael drew;
I seem to see his magic hand
Wield the wond'rous pencil wand,
Whose touches animation give,
And bid the insensate canvas live."

SALMAGUNDI.

As soon as the travellers had alighted, Paoli conducted Laurette to a private-door, and having ordered a female-servant to convey her into the interior of the castle, left her whilst he gave some necessary orders to Ambrose respecting the mules.

Our heroine in the meantime proceeded through a long extent of passage, dimly lighted by a lamp, which terminated in a spiral stair-case. As soon as she had ascended the steps, the woman who attended her opened a door leading into an anti-chamber, which was furnished with much taste and magnificence, where, to her inexpressible astonishment, she beheld a lady, apparently about forty, genteelly and rather elegantly dressed, seated upon a sofa.

Laurette being somewhat embarrassed at the appearance of the stranger, who herself betrayed some symptoms of surprise, endeavoured to apologize for her intrusion, and to explain the occasion of it.

Signora d'Orso, which was the name of the lady, having acquitted herself with much grace and propriety, led her to a seat, and observing that she looked faint, rang the bell for refreshment.

The courteous manners of the stranger, whose aspect bespoke her a woman of rank, soon dissipated the uneasy sensations of her guest, who was early relieved from the suspicion that her arrival was unexpected, though it was evident that it was precipitated without orders from the Marchese.

The air of tender dejection that marked the features of Laurette, and the peculiar elegance of her deportment, rendered still more interesting by that gentle diffidence of manner, occasioned by the exquisite sensibility of a mind yet new to the world, so insinuated her into the affections of the Signora, that admiration was mingled with pity, and she felt an irresistible desire to be more particularly acquainted with her story, of which she had heard something, but not distinctively, and to conciliate her regard. Yet being influenced by the native gentleness of her heart, she forbore to make an immediate enquiry, lest it should lead to melancholy remembrances; and having prevailed upon her to partake of a repast that was prepared for her, finding that rest was more than ordinarily requisite, she conducted her to her apartment.

Laurette, when alone, began to ruminate upon an incident which, though unlooked for, was attended with some degree of pleasure. Her first conjecture was, that the lady who presided at the castle in the absence of its owner, was related to the Marchese; and this opinion the air of fashion that distinguished her, and the circumstances of her being at the mansion previous to his arrival, to prepare it for his reception, seemed to justify. But that Paoli, who consequently must have been apprized of the affair, should have preserved so strict a silence upon the subject, notwithstanding his disposition was naturally uncommunicative, was a matter of astonishment.

In the morning Signora d'Orso entered her room, and having made some general enquiries concerning her health, which were answered with the most captivating sweetness, they descended into the breakfast room.

Though Laurette exerted herself as much as possible to wear an appearance of cheerfulness, she frequently sunk into fits of abstraction. The uncertain fate of her lamented friend, whose loss had so long wounded her repose, the mysterious silence of Enrîco, whose dangerous enterprize her fears had so materially augmented, preyed upon her heart; and now that she was removed from the castle, it seemed as if she was separated for ever from every vestige of her former happiness. Yet to appear uneasy in the presence of her new acquaintance, whose solicitude to please could not be misconstrued, would, she considered, wear an appearance of ingratitude, or at least of indifference, which might injure her in the estimation of a person apparently so little deserving of neglect or inattention.

This reflection instigated her to endeavour, at least, to conceal that regret which she found it was impossible to erase, under an assumed tranquillity of deportment; but in this attempt she succeeded so ill that the Signora, who possessed much penetration, united to a sound judgment and a thorough knowledge of the world, easily discovered that she was unhappy; and though partly acquainted with the cause, arising from her own forlorn and dependant situation, which, joined to the uncertainty of her birth, a mind of sensibility could not reflect upon without pain, she believed there was some more recent occasion of inquietude, and curiosity, as well as pity, was excited in her bosom.

As soon as breakfast was over, the Signora proposed a walk in the gardens, observing, that since they were at present condemned to solitude, they must accommodate themselves to what was unavoidable, and extract comfort, if not happiness, from the means that were offered them.

"There are some paintings also in the castle," resumed the Signora, "which are worthy of notice; and if you will permit me, I will conduct you through the principal apartments, and we will then take a stroll through the grounds."

Charmed with the gentle attentions of her new friend, Laurette unreluctantly assented to the proposal; and throwing an embroidered scarf over her shoulders, followed the Signora through the corridor.

Several of the rooms were in an unfinished state, but those that were completed were extremely magnificent, and much taste was displayed in the decoration: some of them were hung with damask, others with costly tapestry, and the inferior ones with gilt leather. The furniture corresponded with these, and appeared so much superior to any thing Laurette had ever seen, that she could not forbear expressing her surprise. The Signora smiled at the simplicity of her remarks, and anticipated her astonishment when she should behold the grand saloons and principal rooms in the castle.

Having taken a general survey of the upper apartments, they proceeded towards the northern gallery, which was ornamented with several paintings from sacred history by the first masters of the Lombard school, as Titian, Paul Veronese, and Tintoret, under which were placed a number of ancient and valuable busts, particularly those of the Emperors Trajan, Otho, Tibullus, and Augustus Cæsar.

They then descended the marble stair-case, and proceeded through a long vaulted passage, which led immediately to the great hall. Here a scene of wonders was presented to the astonished eyes of Laurette; it was spacious and of vast extent; the floor was of marble; the walls, in which were several recesses, were painted in fresco; the ceiling, exhibiting a scene from the Odyssy of Homer, was supported by twenty composite pillars, whose bandelets were of silver; the recesses were adorned with statues from the antique of granite, porphyry, and parian marble.

At the upper end of the hall was erected a stately organ, composed of ebony, beautifully inlaid with ivory, and decorated with a variety of ornaments. The curtain was of purple satin, fringed and drawn up with tassels of gold; the pipes and pedals were of silver, and the upper keys of the finest ivory.

The Signora having opened it, touched a few simple notes; the tones were full and harmonious, and the effect was heightened by echo. Laurette, to whom this instrument was new, requested that she would favour her with a song; to this she immediately assented, and taking a place at the organ, played and sung the following air:

THE SYLPHS.
A Rondeau.

From your wild aerial pleasures,
Sister spirits, haste away,
Join the dance, in frolic measures,
'Mid dark woods, in shadows grey.

On the zephyrs' pinion sailing
   Swift we'll cleave the ambient air,
Catch the od'rous sweets, exhaling
   From each herb and flow'ret fair.

Now our wild course earthward bending,
   Where the sportive sun-beams play;
On the viewless winds descending
   Through the silvery floods of day.

'Mid deep shades and glens advancing,
   Where sequester'd mortals dwell,
Round the purple orchis dancing,
   Or the lily's pendant bell.

From your wild aerial pleasures,
   Sister Spirits, haste away,
Join the dance in frolic measures,
   'Mid dark woods, in shadows grey.

Laurette having complimented the Signora upon a performance that discovered much taste and judgment, was conducted
by her into the saloons, and other magnificent rooms in the
castle, which were adorned with a profusion of rare and valuable pictures by the most celebrated of the Italian painters, and
some that exhibited the bold and masterly strokes of the Roman
pencil.

All here appeared like the work of enchantment; the windows, descending to the floors, opened into balconies, in which
were placed vases containing roses, myrtle, and amaranthus that
distilled delicious fragrance; beyond these the most gay and
beautiful parterres, lawns, groves, and winding streams, being
aided by the natural grandeur of the scenery, presented to the
eye of the enthusiast a combination of beauties which Fancy
herself could not so successfully have delineated.

From the principal saloon they proceeded through a glass
door, which opened into the pleasure-ground. Here our lovely
heroine, whose astonishment could be only equalled by her admiration, was conducted to several grottos, cascades, and beautiful declivities, where so little method was observed by the artist,

that they appeared like the work of Nature when in one of her most wild and fanciful moods.

The timidity natural to minds of quick and delicate perception, which had hitherto repressed the communication of sentiment, now imperceptibly yielded to reciprocal affection; and the Signora, ardently desirous of exciting an interest in the heart of her young and amiable guest, began to relate several incidents of her past life, endeavouring by her example to betray her into a similar and mutual confidence.

Laurette listened with attention; and some symptoms of curiosity appearing in her looks, the Signora continued.

"My life, which has been hitherto almost invariably marked with ill-fortune, can boast no great variety of incident; yet, though my story is uniformly sad, it may not be altogether uninteresting; and a mind that has been taught by reflection to think and to feel, will not contemplate the misfortunes I have endured without an emotion of pity."

Laurette, to whom the latter part of this discourse was particularly addressed, bowed gracefully; and still more desirous of being acquainted with a story, which though its prelude promised little to entertain, yet much to interest, besought her to proceed.

The Signora hesitated some moments, as if to recollect or to arrange some circumstances of her narrative, and then began as follows.

END OF THE SECOND VOLUME.

THE

ORPHAN

OF THE

RHINE.

———➤ ✳ ◄———

𝕬 𝕽𝖔𝖒𝖆𝖓𝖈𝖊,

IN FOUR VOLUMES.

———

BY MRS. SLEATH.

———

Sweet are the uses of adversity,
Which, like the toad, ugly and venomous,
Wears yet a precious jewel in his head.
SHAKESPEARE.

VOL. III.

LONDON:
PRINTED AT THE
𝕸𝖎𝖓𝖊𝖗𝖛𝖆-𝕻𝖗𝖊𝖘𝖘,
FOR WILLIAM LANE, LEADENHALL-STREET
1798

CHAP. I.

"The beauteous maid that bids the world adieu,
Oft of that world will snatch a fond review,
Oft at the shrine neglect her beads, to trace
Some social scene, some dear familiar face,
Forgot when first a father's stern controul
Chas'd the gay visions of her op'ning soul;
And e'er with iron-tongue the vesper-bell,
Bursts thro' the cyprus walk, the convent cell
Oft will her warm and wayward heart revive,
To love and joy still tremblingly alive."

ROGERS.

"MY father, whose name was Ruberto, was lineally descended from a younger branch of the noble and once honourable house of Manini. The misfortunes of this family, which are well known, rendered it necessary for my grandfather, the unhappy victim of Court intrigue, to take refuge in obscurity. When the policy of this measure first appeared, he felt the severity of his fortunes with the keenest energy. To be compelled to quit his paternal inheritance in Naples, long the residence of his ancestors, was to him dreadful as a Siberian banishment; yet no alternative remained, and after many struggles, too powerful to be immediately overcome, he repaired with his wife, who was also a person of high birth and a numerous family, of which my father was the eldest, to a chateau on the borders of France.

"Thus trained in obscurity, and disguised under an assumed name, the children of the unfortunate Manini were deprived of the advantages of birth, though not of education, as my grandfather instructed them in the learned languages, and other branches of literature, with unceasing attention; but at the same time that he assisted them in classical acquirements, he instilled into them principles that were at enmity with the social virtues.

"After some years, a political revolution occasioned a change of circumstances; and my grandfather, whose character was finally cleared from the false aspersions of his enemies, returned once more to his paternal seat, and was restored to his former dignities. This sudden transition from disgrace to favour, from obscurity to comparative splendour, wrought so violent an effect upon his mind, that he, who could once think nobly, and act vigorously, now became weak, vain, and luxurious, a slave to passions he once boldly resisted, and to vices which he felt no longer an inclination to oppose. He believed, because he had met with some insincerity where he had the least expected it, that all were vicious and ungrateful. With this conviction he renounced all former friendships, he rather wished to excite envy than esteem, and as the most effectual way of attracting the observation of the multitude, enlarged his mansion, and increased his household.

"One expence naturally led to another, till his fortune, his peace, and the future prospects of his children were eventually sacrificed. In a few years this unfortunate and misguided courtier died insolvent; his widow did not long survive him; his three sons were provided for in the army, and his daughters forced into a convent, that the family might not be disgraced by inferior alliances.

"My father was united, early in life, to a woman, elegant in her manners, and amiable in her disposition. She was beautiful, but beauty was her least perfection, for she possessed, in an eminent degree, all those virtues and graces by which the female character is adorned and dignified;—she was a native of Italy, and an only child; her fortune was small, but her family respectable. Her parents dying in her minority, left their fair daughter to the guardianship of an uncle, who was distantly related to my father, which led to the connection that afterwards formed all the happiness and misery of their future lives.

"Soon after this marriage, which took place a short time after the commencement of the acquaintance, my father's regiment being called into action for the purpose of quelling a rebel troop of Condottieri, he was necessitated to leave Mantua that he might join a detachment in a distant part of the province, who were in readiness to march against the foe.

"During this state of separation, which was equally afflictive to both, my mother remained under the protection of Signor Montesico, her uncle and former guardian, at his residence, which was a small but elegant villa on the banks of the Po. My birth rapidly succeeded this event, and my mother's attention was now entirely confined to the care and education of her daughter; so much so that she seldom quitted her solitude, and seemed to be insensible to every pleasure or amusement but what I was empowered to bestow.

"Several years passed before the return of my father; and a report of his death being circulated, which his unusual silence tended to confirm, my mother resigned herself for some time to unavailing grief; but recollecting the defenceless situation of her child, she exerted herself to endure what could not be remedied, and in time regained some portion of her former tranquillity.

"As no doubt remained concerning the truth of the report, she assumed the dress of a widow, and with redoubled assiduity dedicated her time and her thoughts to my instruction and improvement.

"But the serenity she had acquired was soon afterwards disturbed by the death of Signor Montesico, who expired suddenly in a fit, without having received the benefit of the sacrament, or the other customary solemnities of the church. As he died without a will, his property, which would otherwise have been my mother's, descended to the male heir.

"Poverty, and other accumulated distresses, now threatened to destroy the small remains of comfort which had hitherto been afforded; but my mother, who possessed firmness sufficient to withstand the severest attacks of misfortune, did not suffer herself to sink under them; but having followed her venerable protector to the grave, and paid every mark of respect to his memory which pecuniary embarrassments would permit her to bestow, she prepared to quit the villa Santieri, which had been her home almost from infancy, and to repair to the interior of the city. But she was prevented from putting her design immediately in execution by the arrival of Signor Gualando, the rightful heir to the estates of her deceased friend, who came to assert his claim to the personal, as well as landed, property of Signor Montesico.

"Something relative to the arrangement of his affairs rendered frequent conversations with my mother indispensible, previous to her quitting the villa. She was too beautiful not to attract his admiration, and too amiable not to ensure his esteem. The soft melancholy that pervaded her features, the easy dignity of her figure, and the winning graces of her manners, inspired the most lively sentiment in her favour.

"He felt that he loved her, but that love was so tempered with esteem that it was long before delicacy allowed an avowal of his passion.

"At first he steadily opposed our leaving the villa, having no intention of continuing there himself, as he possessed a considerable estate, independent of this, in the neighbourhood of Pisa, the present residence of his family. But my mother strictly adhered to her first resolution, and soon afterwards, agreeable to her original intention, removed into the city.

"She was frequently visited in her new abode by Signor Gualando, whom necessary business detained some time in Mantua, who finally made her an offer of his person and fortune.

"Though my mother had no remaining doubt concerning her widowhood, she prudently declined the proposal, having already formed a resolution never to enter into a second engagement.

"The disappointment and uneasiness which a knowledge of this determination inflicted upon the Signor, cannot easily be described; not only his spirits, but his health, seemed to yield to the force of his attachment, which was too serious to allow him to relinquish the pursuit, and too ardent not to expose him to real distress. Yet not absolutely despairing of success, he ventured to continue his visits under the sanction of friendship, and was meditating on the most effectual method of insinuating himself into the affections of the beautiful widow, as she was generally called, when the unexpected return of my father, who had been confined five years in a fortress by the forces of the triumphant Condottieri, terminated all his future hopes.

"The Signor Gualando was alone with my mother on his arrival, and, in the attitude of intreaty, was pressing his suit with all the eloquence of an inviolable regard, when my father, whom no motive of prudence could restrain from precipitating himself into the presence of his wife, burst into the room.

"The rapturous surprise experienced by my mother when she

beheld the long lost object of her affections, whose imaginary death she had so long and so tenderly lamented, can better be conceived than described. My father was sensible to the first impulse of joy, but far different emotions succeeded. From this moment his mind became a prey to violent and contending passions, which reason could neither bridle nor subdue. In the Signor Gualando he believed he beheld the favoured lover of his wife, to whom, supposing herself at liberty, she would shortly have been united, had not his unexpected and unhoped-for return rendered it impracticable. Though, from the natural expressions of transport which were portrayed in the countenance of my mother, and the innocent effusions of unfeigned rapture that succeeded, a mind collected and unimpassioned would have decided otherwise; yet too much was he blinded by an excess of jealousy to be enabled to observe the one, or to feel the just value of the other.

"From this æra a gloomy reserve characterised his deportment towards his wife, which no effort of tenderness, on her part, could soften or dispel; though she cautiously avoided giving him any cause of suspicion, by abstracting herself from society, and devoting every moment of her time to domestic duties.

"Signor Gualando, in the mean time, suffered all the chagrin and mental uneasiness which love and disappointment could inflict. He saw the necessity of tearing himself from the object of his regard, and of combating these feelings by the most strenuous exertions in his power; and, after repeated conflicts with himself, was enabled to put his prudent resolutions into practice, and returned to his former abode.

"The behaviour of my father, which was alternately sullen and severe, was so injurious to the peace of my mother, that her natural vivacity disappeared, and her health rapidly declined. Her cruel companion beheld this change without either pity or remorse; he imputed it to chagrin for the loss of her lover, not to his unmerited severity; and this reflection, as distressing as it was unjust, marked his appearance and manners with increasing asperity.

"In a short time this patient victim of groundless and unjustifiable resentment, was removed from a state of sufferance and oppression to receive the reward of uncorrupted innocence; and left him, who was insensible of her value when living, to feel and lament her loss.

"As at this period I was not more than twelve years of age, my father, who had no female relation living, was for some time irresolute in what manner to dispose of me. At length he determined to board me in a convent of Celestinas, which was about a league and a half from Mantua, whither he promised to convey me at the expiration of the time which he had fixed.

"That boundless love of variety, which is inseparable from youth and inexperience, made me readily agree to the proposal; and my father having previously entered into a contract with the Superior to admit me as a boarder, I was conducted by him to the convent.

"The Lady Abbess received me with a stately kind of politeness but little adapted to my sentiments or my years; and the nuns eyed me with a kind of eager curiosity, which, young as I was, filled me with confusion and displeasure.

"When my father had left me, which he appeared to do with little regret, I felt the forlornness of my situation with redoubled energy. I seemed to have awakened to a new state of existence, and to be placed among beings of another order, which made it long before I was sufficiently reconciled to my new abode to be able to enumerate its comforts.

"But as the mind naturally submits to necessity, and endeavours to accommodate itself to those circumstances that are unavoidable, in time I became tranquil and even gay; though I believe my satisfaction chiefly arose from the too sanguine expectations I had indulged of the future, when, being liberated from confinement, I should be restored to society.

"With these hopes, which I conceived were shortly to be realized, the hours fled rapidly away, and having no idea of continuing in the convent longer than the time proposed, I felt the tenderest pity and commiseration for those whom pride, bigotry, or other adverse circumstances had condemned to perpetual retirement.

"Many of the sisters were young, and some of them were extremely lovely. The dress of the order, which consisted of a loose white robe simply confined at the bosom, and ornamented with a blue cloak, and scapulary of the same colour, added grace to beauty; and had they not been characterized by a certain air of discontent and dejection, they would have appeared infinitely charming. But few had voluntarily resigned themselves to a conventual life, and the hopelessness of their situations was a source of continual dissatisfaction and regret.

"Whenever I contemplated features whose harmony and expression, if lighted up by the animated smile of contentment and benevolence, would have possessed undescribable powers of attraction, I mingled a degree of silent indignation with my pity at the violated rights of human nature, at once trampled on and overborne by creatures, formed and endued with so many delicate and exalted affections. Can it be the will of heaven, thought I, that beings, who are endeared to each other by so many tender connections, should embrace a system which is unquestionably subversive of all the ties of humanity? Is it virtue to fly from the possibility of exercising those amiable principles which are implanted in our natures for the noblest purposes, and to relinquish those innocent sources of amusement and delight, that are bountifully bestowed upon us to give value to our existence? It cannot be—we are assuredly designed to be the mutual support and comfort of each other; and as by mixing with the world our sphere of action is enlarged, it is indisputably our duty to continue in it.

"But pardon me, Madame," continued the Signora, "I confess I have been guilty of an egotism, and am now amusing you rather with sentiment than narrative; but I will resume my story, and conclude it as briefly as possible."

Laurette replied only with a smile, and the Signora proceeded.

"Two years had elapsed before my father again visited the convent, who I now believed was come to obtain my dismission. But what were my feelings when he acquainted me with his determination, which was, that I was to remain in the convent, and immediately to take the veil as a novice! My anguish was now too acute to be concealed, and, throwing myself at his feet, I besought him not to doom me to eternal regret—not to exclude me from the blessings of nature, but to allow me to return with him.

"The sternness that was gathering on his brow convinced me that I had nothing to hope; and the peremptory tone in which his former resolution was repeated, terrified me into silence; and knowing that resistance would be in vain, and being fearful of exasperating him with a refusal, I appeared to acquiesce. When he left me, his countenance somewhat relaxed from its severity; and after an assurance that he would see me again before the ceremony was performed, he quitted the convent.

"The recollection of my sufferings when I was apprized of my unalterable destiny, returns, even at this distant period, forcibly to my thoughts, and brings with it a train of correspondent ideas. At one time I resolved to disobey, and to purchase liberty at the expense of duty and every moral obligation; at another, to submit patiently to what was unavoidable, and to endeavour, at least, to alleviate the sense of my uneasiness with the rectitude of my conduct.

"Had persuasion been used instead of those arbitrary means which had been adopted, and had that persuasion been directed by reason, I could have yielded myself a sacrifice, however painful the task; but as no motive could be alledged to justify measures so repugnant to my inclinations, they appeared so despotic and capricious that I could neither reconcile them to my feelings or my understanding.

"The stately distance that was uniformly preserved by the Abbess, precluded the possibility of winning her over to my interest; and though I more than once determined to solicit her interference in my behalf, her looks, her voice, and her manners were sufficient to awe me into silence.

"Some of the sisters apparently pitied my situation, whilst others secretly triumphed in my disappointment; for there were some that, though trained to habits of hourly devotion, were destitute of sensibility and every amiable principle of the mind.

"It was on the eve of the vigil of San Marco that my father again repeated his visit, and as it is usual at this festival for nuns to be professed, I naturally imagined that he had received some previous intimation of it from the Superior, and was come at once to enforce and to witness my vows.

"No powers of language can do justice to my feelings at that

moment; for though as a novice I was not absolutely a prisoner
for life, yet placing but little confidence in the paternal tenderness of my father, and being perfectly aware of the watchfulness
of the Lady Abbess, any successful attempt of effectuating an
escape from captivity would, I knew, be impracticable, before
the expiration of the year, when the other veil would follow
of course. Thus situated, I resolved, though with no sanguine
hopes of success, to soften, if possible, the native ferocity of my
father's temper; and, if every spark of affection was not entirely
extinguished in his breast, to strive to rekindle and call it into
action.

"As soon as I was admitted into his presence, which was
not till the Abbess had retired, I endeavoured to execute my
intention by appealing to his compassion; and, contrary to my
expectation, he heard me with complacency;—and whether it
was my altered looks, for my complexion was much faded by
sorrow, or the result of a previous conversation with the Superior, that occasioned it, I was unable to ascertain; but, after fixing
his eyes upon mine, which were streaming with tears, with an
expression of earnestness not unmingled with pity, after a few
gentle reproaches he granted me his permission to accompany
him home, and to remain resident there till my health was re-
established; though he took some pains to convince me that
his former resolution was unchanged; but in compliance with
my unjustifiable prejudices, as he termed it, he would grant me
the indulgence of postponing the performance of it till another
opportunity.

"Even this indulgence, though not augmented by a promise
of its permanency, so much exceeded my expectation, that, in
the ecstatic emotions of the moment, I loaded him with the
effusions of my gratitude; and having yielded to the intreaties
of the Abbess to wait the celebration of the festival, which was
crowded with friars, pilgrims, and other professed devotees, we
quitted this religious asylum, whose massy walls and solitary cells
heard only the sigh of regret and the groan of mental anguish,
and repaired to Mantua.

"As I gazed upon the venerable spires of the convent retiring
into distance, which were half lost amid the rocks that sur-

rounded them, I secretly determined not to enter it again, since I believed that misery and confinement were inseparable.

"Every object which I regarded, and every sound that I heard, had now the advantage of novelty; the hills covered with verdure, the flowers that embroidered the vallies, the low warblings of the birds from the deep shade of the woods, all were in unison with my feelings, and I felt as if just called into existence to enjoy the sublimities of nature. With the vanity inseparable from youth and inexperience, I anticipated the pleasures of society, anxious to display the few accomplishments I had acquired, and to be convinced of their value.

"My solicitude to please being frequently carried to excess, my father did not fail to observe, with concern, a propensity that threatened to render his favourite scheme of professing me abortive. This induced him resolutely to oppose my mixing with the world, which he constantly represented as teeming with misfortune, folly, and insincerity.

"The only persons who were in habits of intimacy in the family, were Father Alberto, a Jesuit, who was my father's Confessor; Signor Lamberto, a man of fortune and connections resident in Mautna, and Lorenzo d'Orso, a young officer, who was committed to his care by his last surviving parent, a short time before his death, which happened in consequence of a wound received in a desperate engagement, a few months after he had been raised by merit to the rank of Mareschal, not without some hopes that a future provision might be the effect of this politic arrangement, should this veteran, who had lately retired from the toil and uncertainty inseparable from a military life, continue single, or die without heirs.

"Signor Lamberto was not so rigid in his principles as my father, and being informed of the decided aversion I had expressed to the solitude of a cloister, and of his inexorable determination to oblige me to take the vow, used some arguments to dissuade him from his purpose. But they were overruled by the more powerful ones urged by the Jesuit, who was my father's friend and adviser on every occasion, and who contrived, from interested motives, to convince him that his eternal salvation depended upon the sacrifice of his daughter; who, if allowed to remain with him, would so far influence his affections as to withdraw them from the only true source of all consolation.

"To be continually in the society of the Signor d'Orso without feeling a prepossession in his favour, would have been impossible. His manners were easy and elegant, his figure was more than ordinarily graceful, and his countenance expressive of a certain ingenuousness of mind, which could not be contemplated without affection. I had not been many weeks in the city before we mutually felt and acknowledged our attachment, though it was necessary to conceal it from my father, his Confessor, and even from Signor Lamberto; who, was every objection to be removed on the part of my friends, would, we had every reason to believe, vigorously oppose an alliance which, in the indigent situation of his dependant, could not be justified by prudence. But though we attempted to disguise our affection under an assumed appearance of indifference, we were so narrowly watched by the scrutinizing eyes of the Jesuit, who contrived to overhear our conversation when we imagined ourselves in secrecy, that my father was early apprized of it.

"Perfectly aware of the extent of my punishment, and more than ever averse to a conventual life, which would inevitably separate me for ever from the amiable object of my early love, I at last consented to accept the protection of Signor d'Orso, and to unite my destiny with his.

"My father, in the mean time, placing no confidence in the dutiful acquiescence of his daughter, probably from a consciousness that he had never deserved it, resolved to accelerate my departure, as the most effectual method of preventing any future intercourse between us, and desired me to prepare to accompany him to the convent on the following week; at the same time commanding me not to quit my apartment during the interval, on pain of his everlasting displeasure.

"Thus secluded from the possibility of obtaining another interview with Lorenzo, I abandoned myself to despair; and since, in the despondency of the moment, I believed the fate that awaited me was irreversible, wished, for the first time, that I had never quitted my prison, since I should now return to it with redoubled reluctance.

"By means of a confidential servant, a method of informing the Signor of my confinement was with some difficulty effected; who I discovered by a letter, which was immediately conveyed, was actually meditating my escape.

"This, by the assistance of the domestics, who were bribed to our interests, notwithstanding the vigilance of my father and his Jesuitical Confessor, was finally accomplished: a ladder of ropes was placed beneath the window of my apartment, which I unreluctantly descended, and a vehicle being stationed at a convenient distance from the mansion, I placed myself in it, without asking whither I was going, and was conveyed rapidly away.

"It was the intention of the Signor to take a cross-road, lest a premature alarm might occasion pursuit, and to alight at one of the monasteries in the road, where a priest might be procured, and the ceremony be performed.

"It was long past midnight when we commenced our journey; but the moon shining with unclouded radiance, enabled us to prosecute it with speed, till her light became gradually pale, and the grey mists of the morning rose slowly upon the summits of the hills.

"Having arrived at a lonely and apparently deserted village, situated at the foot of a mountain, we enquired for the nearest convent, and was directed to one about a league from the place.

"Here we arrived when the Monks were returning from matins. It was a society of Augustines, and having engaged a Friar of the Order to officiate, the marriage was solemnized.

"As we had no fixed residence to return to, nor any friend or relation to receive us, we mutually agreed to drive on to the next town that could offer us accommodation, and to remain there till we could fix upon some plan for our future conduct.

"Here we arrived early in the day; and as soon as my scattered thoughts were somewhat collected, I wrote to my father, at once to solicit his forgiveness and his patronage. Lorenzo also wrote to Signor Lamberto, but our letters were disregarded; another and another were written, but without success; and having no hopes of obtaining the attention we requested, we determined to relinquish the pursuit.

"Near a month elapsed in this situation, when Lorenzo received orders to join his regiment, that was stationed in a remote province, whither, after some little preparation, I accompanied him.

"The journey was accomplished with little fatigue; and soon afterwards we had the satisfaction of being placed in a state of security and comfort, in which we experienced all the happiness that life could bestow. Our circumstances were indeed limited, but we managed so as to make not only a decent, but a respectable appearance, and might be said to be rich in each other's affection.

"Some years had passed in unclouded tranquillity, without any interesting event, except the birth of a son, who bore the name as well as the resemblance of his father, but of whom death early deprived me. Scarcely was I recovered from the indisposition this loss had occasioned, before our regiment was ordered into another part of the kingdom, to secure it from the invasion of the enemy, which obliged us to remove with all possible speed.

"Alas! I knew not then it was destined to become the seat of war, and being anxious to recover my spirits, exulted in the variety a change of situation would afford.

"But not to weary you with too long a detail, the regiment was soon afterwards engaged in a close action, and Lorenzo d'Orso fell!

"Gracious heaven! what were my sufferings at that dreadful moment when I was informed that he was amongst the number of the fallen; though, to soften the intelligence, I was told he was only wounded. Frantic with despair, I flew into the field with the wildness of distraction, though it was night, and I had no one but a servant to attend me thither. After examining for a considerable time the mangled forms of the vanquished; which were so covered with blood as to render the features scarcely perceptible, I discovered the object of my search. But he was dead; the breath seemed newly to have forsaken the body, and his limbs were not yet stiff in death.

"In an agony, not to be described, I pressed him to my heart; and it was long before the people, whom my cries had attracted, could tear me from the place. A fever and delirium succeeded, which brought me to the brink of the grave; but the natural goodness of my constitution finally resisting the attack, I was gradually restored.

"As soon as the disorder of my mind was in some degree removed, I formed a resolution of returning to Mantua, for the purpose of soliciting the protection of my father, who, I now believed, would receive me with compassion and affection. When the physician who attended me, pronounced me able to travel without endangering my safety, I availed myself of his permission, and soon put my design into execution.

"After a few days' journey, which was performed with less fatigue than was expected, I arrived within the territories of Naples, and from thence proceeded, by easy stages, to Mantua.

"Here I learned, to my inexpressible grief and disappointment, that my father had been dead some time; and, on extending my enquiries concerning the disposal of his property, was informed that he had bequeathed the whole of it, which was indeed nothing very considerable, to the Jesuit, his Confessor.

"Having now no other means of subsistence than what my own exertions could procure, I had recourse to the embroidering of silks, to supply the convents and principal nobility of the place; which, from some skill in the art, more than supplied me with the actual necessaries of life.

"Near two years had elapsed without any incident worthy of attention, when a cessation of hostilities, which was somewhat suddenly effected, occasioned a visit from the Marchese de Martilini; who, having been acquainted with my misfortunes, and the injustice of my father, requested my acceptance of a sum sufficient to elevate me above want and dependance. This, knowing the exalted character of the bestower, I gratefully accepted; and, on the death of the Marchese de Montferrat, which happened some years after this event, consented, at the request of my patron, to accept of this situation, till one more eligible could be procured. Here I hope, in the capacity of Casiera*, to enjoy at least peace and tranquillity.

"I have not at present been introduced to the Marchese de Montferrat; but as the castle will soon be in readiness for his

* Housekeeper.

reception, it is not probable that he will continue much longer in Italy. He has already honoured me with two letters respecting the repairs, and the disposal of the pictures, statues, vases, and other ornamental effects, in which he has discovered much taste and sentiment.

"In his last letter he mentioned a young person of the name of Laurette, who was shortly to be placed under my protection, with whose person, he added, he was yet unacquainted, though he had maintained and patronised her from infancy. This, I acknowledge, excited my curiosity, and instigated me to extend my enquiries among the servants, from whom I could gain no satisfactory intelligence upon the subject."—

Here the Signora was silent; and Laurette, who had listened with a painful interest to this brief yet mournful narrative, in return for such unlimited confidence, proceeded to inform her new friend of some particulars relative to herself. The incidents of her life were few and simple; but the tone and manner in which they were delivered, and the tears that accompanied the recollection of infantine felicity, gave importance to the most trivial event, and won the esteem of her auditor.

When she arrived at that part of her story which treated of the sudden departure of her more than parent, the attention of the Signora was fixed in astonishment; and when the name of Enrîco escaped her lips, the blush that suffused her cheek, and the tremulous accent in which the words were delivered, declared how tenderly she was interested in his concerns, and breathed more than sisterly affection.

The Signora, who observed these emotions with the most re-fined compassion, endeavoured to console her with an assurance that she would make some immediate enquiries respecting the fate of the young chevalier, desiring her at the same time to look up and be comforted; not to give way to causeless suggestions, but to continue to rely on the protection of that Supreme Power, which she had never wilfully offended, and who consequently would never abandon her.

Those who know what it is to suffer, and to have those suffer-ings alleviated by the sympathy of friendship, will conceive the delightful sensation that was imparted to the bosom of Laurette in thus finding, contrary to her expectation, a person inclined to bestow that consolation which her present feelings required, in a stile the most grateful to her heart, and in whom, from what had recently passed, she had reason to believe she might entirely confide.

The only part of her narrative which Laurette had concealed, was the extraordinary appearance and behaviour of the mysterious Monk, with the delivery of the picture. This circumstance she had strictly promised to conceal; and though it returned frequently and forcibly to her thoughts, accompanied with the most dreadful presages, she resolved, agreeably to the solemn vow she had taken in the presence of the father, never to disclose it.

CHAP. II.

"Oft at the silent shadowy close of day,
When the tir'd grove has sung its parting lay,
When pensive Twilight, in her dusky car,
Comes slowly on to meet the evening star,
Above, below, aerial murmurs swell,
From hanging wood, brown heath, and bushy dell,
A thousand nameless rills, that shun the sight,
Stealing soft music on the ear of Night;
So oft the finer movements of the soul,
That shun the sphere of Pleasure's gay controul,
In the still shades of calm Seclusion rise,
And breathe their sweet seraphic harmonies."
ROGERS.

Laurette had not been long resident in the castle of Luenburg, before Paoli received an order from the Marchese to hasten his return into Italy; who having made some necessary arrangements, and given general orders to the Signora, prepared to depart.

His attention was so wholly directed to the business of rendering the mansion a fit residence for his Lord, and he so seldom obtruded himself into the presence of the ladies, that Laurette was scarcely conscious that he was an inhabitant of the place.

When he entered the saloon to bid them adieu, being anxious to know when Dorothèe and Lisette were to be conveyed thither, she ventured to follow him through the hall to make some enquiries concerning them, and was informed, to her inexpressible uneasiness, that they were already discharged; the Marchese having recently given orders for none of her former domestics to attend her.

There was something in this circumstance so unkind, as well as capricious, that had not her mind been occupied by nearer interests, she would have felt severely the having been once flattered by assurances which were probably never intended to be realized.

Though hope, the usual attendant on youth and inexperience, sometimes brightened the future prospects of our heroine, she often yielded to despondency; and though grateful for the comforts her present situation afforded, which exceeded her most sanguine expectations, she did not cease to reflect upon the past with the most poignant regret and anxiety.

The picture, which was delivered by the Monk, she wore continually in her bosom, carefully concealing it from observation, according to her promise, and secretly cherishing it as an invaluable relic, consecrated by the solemn manner in which it was bestowed and endeared as being the portrait of her mother.

Though the conversation of the Signora d'Orso, which was at once animated and interesting, excited in the gentle mind of Laurette the most lively emotions of gratitude, the exertion which was requisite of wearing the aspect of cheerfulness, was often times painful, which occasioned her to seize every opportunity of abstracting herself from the rest of the family, when it could be done without a breach of propriety, that she might wander alone through the grounds attached to the castle, which were not more beautiful than extensive.

One evening, when the Signora was engaged in giving directions to the persons employed in the repairs, concerning the ornamental parts of the workmanship, Laurette was induced by the fineness of the weather to ramble in an adjacent forest; and having reached a distant part of it, seated herself upon a gentle eminence, to enjoy the prospect it commanded. The evening was serene and cloudless—no sound, except the song of the nightingale that was warbling its last farewel, or the soft note of a far distant oboe, broke upon the calmness that prevailed. These tended to recal to her memory the imagery of the past, and, absorbed in tender reflections, she paused till every sound was hushed, till even the night bird had forsaken his accustomed haunts, and all was silence and repose.

Her mind was now tenderly susceptible of the finest impressions, and the melancholy stillness that pervaded the woods, only occasionally agitated by the last sigh of the zephyr, aided the poetic enthusiasm that was stealing upon her spirits, and resigning herself to the luxury of sadly pleasing emotions, she composed the following lines:

AN ELEGY
ON THE CLOSE OF THE YEAR.

Where are the wreaths that Spring's young fingers wove,
    Each op'ning bud, which she had gemm'd with dew;
Hypaticas that blush'd in every grove,
    The heath flower, and the violet meekly blue.

No more beneath the woodbine's trembling shade,
    Peeps the wan primrose from its silken cell;
No more the wild rose blooms along the glade,
    Or modest cowslip hangs her golden bell;

Yet though no shrubs the Alpine steeps adorn,
    Though Spring and Summer's smiling reign be past,
I love to linger in these shades forlorn,
    And listen to the rude Autumnal blast.

And chief, when Evening hangs her glooms profound
    On every pine-clad hill and valley fair;
When the noctule* begins his nightly round,
    In mazy circles, through the liquid air;

Then oft I climb some mountain's hoary side,
    Whose craggy base the silent water laves,
And mark the wand'ring Naides, as they glide
    To meet the Sea Nymphs in their coral caves;

*Bat.

Or seek the moss-grown cavern's inmost dell,
    The tangl'd wood walk, or the forest drear;
Where, as soft, dying gales at distance swell,
    Methinks the Spirit of the rock I hear.

And when meek Eve, with matron step retires
    With humid tresses newly bath'd in dews;
Then Fancy visionary dreams inspires,
    Veiling each object in unreal hues.

Her magic wand bids fairy forms advance,
    Forms that have slept in lily bells the day,
In frolics wild to celebrate the dance,
    Beneath the silver moon-beam's trembling ray;

To keep their vigils far from mortal ken,
    By side of fringed brook, or shadowy glade,
Or in some rushy cavern's hallow'd glen,
    Till Day's bright orb the realms of Night pervade.

Then swift they fly, nor can e'en Fancy's power,
    With all her magic spells, prolong their stay,
Till Cynthia's train leads on the silent hour,
    And Night's sad minstrel tunes his parting lay.

Ah! so, before cold Reason's sober gaze,
    Youth's fairy visions fade and disappear;
Dark Winter thus her chilling form displays,
    Blasting the produce of the blooming year.

Yet Spring again shall dress her groves with flow'rs,
    Perfum'd and tinted by a hand divine;
And Music's voice delight the laughing hours;
    But when will happiness again be mine?

The deepening shades of the evening at length reminded her of her distance from the castle, and that she had a long and lonely wilderness to pass, which made it necessary for her to return with all possible speed to the path she had quitted, which was the direct road to the mansion, before it was too dark to be able to distinguish the way.

When she had reached the gate that marked the boundaries

of the pleasure grounds, being nearly exhausted with fatigue, she paused for a moment to recover herself, and as she was now well acquainted with the road, to take a survey of the beautiful range of hills that bounded the horizon, and the rich, though half-foliated woods that skirted the mountains.

Lost in the contemplation of these picturesque objects, she proceeded leisurely along till having imperceptibly arrived at the vista, which opened upon the lawn, her attention was recalled from the illusions of fancy, to whose captivating power she had resigned herself, by the voices of two people, apparently in earnest discourse, but whose persons were concealed amid the trees of the avenue.

In the direction she had taken it was probable she must have passed very near to them; but they were too much engaged in their own concerns to perceive her approach, and the grass preventing her footsteps from being heard, as she moved lightly beneath the shade of the trees, occasioned their being unconscious of any observer.

It naturally occurred to her, that they were some of the servants belonging to the castle; but, lest strangers might have intruded themselves into these extensive domains, she emerged precipitately from the gloom of the avenues, and bounded swiftly over the lawn.

In a moment she heard steps pursuing her, and before she had recovered from her alarm, the sound of her own name, uttered by a well-known voice, drew her attention upon the person who pronounced it. Turning hastily around, she beheld, to her astonishment, a young chevalier in a military habit, who immediately came up to her; and, before she was restored to recollection, found herself in the arms of a stranger, in whom she afterwards recognized the person of Enrîco.

Surprise and joy operated so powerfully upon her feelings, that she was near fainting; which made it some time before she was conscious of her situation, or of the extent of her happiness.

When amazement had in some degree subsided, Laurette fixed her eyes upon Enrîco with an earnest and tender gaze, and, as the partial beams of the moon fell upon his face, observed that he looked unusually pale, and that his once animated features wore an expression of deep dejection, which it was not difficult to interpret.

As soon as she had courage to introduce the subject, which had been productive of so much uneasiness, she ventured to ask if he had received the letter containing the melancholy intelligence respecting Madame Chamont, and what had occasioned his unexpected arrival.

Enrîco sighed deeply, and then proceeded to inform her, that on account of his regiment having shifted its quarters, her letter did not arrive till some weeks after the date; but that immediately on the receipt of it, he obtained permission of his Colonel to absent himself; and, attended by Anselmo, his servant, took the direct road to the Castle of Elfinbach.

"You have been at the Castle, then," interrupted Laurette, not instantly considering the improbability of his being able to receive information relative to her present place of residence by any other means; as, at the time she addressed him, she was herself unacquainted with the intentions of the Marchese, and consequently had mentioned nothing of her removal. Enrîco answered her question with an affirmative, and having hesitated for a moment, continued—

"Though hopeless as to receiving any satisfactory intelligence concerning my much-injured parent, which might serve as a clue to guide me in pursuit, I resolved to hasten to the Castle; by these means to soften, if I could not eradicate my grief, and to convince myself whether you, my Laurette—my more than sister, was in safety. But what was my disappointment and distress when I found the mansion silent and deserted, and every vestige of my former happiness removed and annihilated?

"It was night when I arrived; and the air of extreme desolation that it exhibited, had my mind been sufficiently collected, or abstracted from more painful interests, would have struck me forcibly; but my feelings were too much and too tenderly wounded, to regard local circumstances.

"Having reached the principal gate, I rapped violently, but without success; no passing footstep answered to the summons, and surprise and impatience succeeded. I then alighted from my horse, and desiring Anselmo to follow my example, we fastened the animals to a tree, and then walked round the courts, in hopes of being able to gain admittance at the western side of the structure; but here our sanguine expectations were again deceived. I called, but no voice returned an answer but the echo of my own, which being aided by the loud rising of the blast, that swept in hollow gusts along the mountains, had a mournful and solemn effect.

"Impatience now yielded to the most excruciating anguish; I began to imagine that you also was separated from me for ever. My heart beat quick—my feeble limbs could scarcely support my agitated frame—and throwing myself on a piece of the fallen rampart, I yielded to the despondency that was stealing upon my mind.

"The clouds now passing rapidly over the sky, seemed to portend an approaching storm; which Anselmo observing, reminding me at the same time of the danger to which our present situation would expose us, ventured to request my permission to release the horses from their confinement; stating the necessity of our endeavouring to accommodate ourselves for the night at one of the cottages by the side of the river, as, by this method of proceeding, we might obtain shelter from the storm, and be enabled to pursue our enquiries at leisure on the following day.

"This advice, however reasonable, was suddenly rejected, as I still flattered myself a possibility existed that the castle might be still inhabited, though nothing appeared to justify the opinion. Anselmo objected to the probability of the proposition, declaring that the repeated alarms he had given were sufficient to have awakened the dead; and besought me to consider my own safety while it was yet in my power, and, plunged in unavailing despair, not to brave the fury of the storm which was gathering fast over our heads.

"Having finally yielded, though reluctantly, to his entreaties, I determined to make another attempt, and wheeling round the quadrangle again, rapped loudly at the gate. But all was yet silent;—I called, but no answer was returned; and a stillness, as of the grave, ensued. Still more chagrined, though the hope that had inspired this last effort was too feeble to admit of extreme disappointment, I walked silently towards the oak, to whose trunk the horses were bound, and began to liberate them.

"Anselmo, who had anticipated my second unsuccessful undertaking, proposed, that since we had so little chance of obtaining admittance into the interior of the mansion, for us to make the best of our way, since we had a wild and dreary forest to pass, and a wood that appeared like the abode of robbers; observing, that if it was really the case, our only chance of escape depended upon the threatening aspect of the heavens, which might induce those outlaws, by whom these solitudes are infested, to take refuge in their caves.

"Whilst I still continued to meditate upon the past, without forming any plan for the future, Anselmo, after having employed many fruitless endeavours to engage me in conversation, directed my attention towards a tall edifice, which was partially seen as the light issued from the sky, which he imagined to be a fane; remarking that if it was any thing that could offer us an asylum, we were fortunate in having made the discovery, as it would prevent the necessity of encountering the peril and danger of traversing the wood, in whose tangled thickets we might possibly be so entirely bewildered as to lose the track.

"Though I was too much lost in uneasy conjecture to be apprehensive of consequences, and was too little inclined to attend to the loquacity of Anselmo, to listen to the former part of his discourse; I turned involuntarily towards the mountain to which he had pointed, and beheld, by a second ray of light that flashed from the heavens, the spires of a convent, which were half lost to the eye amid surrounding foliage. Instantly it occurred to me that it was the convent of St. Angelo, belonging to the Carthusians, which determined me to make up to it immediately and to enquire for Father Benedicta.

"The extreme perturbation of my mind accounted, in some measure, for my not having recollected the propriety of this step before; as information respecting the former inhabitants of the castle might, with more appearance of probability, be obtained by this means, than by any other that had been offered. Somewhat animated by this reflection, we redoubled our speed, regardless of the storm that broke in thunder over our heads, or the almost universal darkness that prevailed.

"When we had arrived near the boundaries of the forest, Anselmo's horse took fright, and threw him, with inconceivable force, against a piece of broken rock. The scream he uttered on falling, and the deep groan that succeeded, made me apprehensive of the worst. I called, but he was unable to answer; the groans continued, but were fainter, and being convinced that he was materially injured by the blow he had sustained, if not already dying, I dismounted and hurried to the spot from whence these melancholy sounds proceeded, though I was so enveloped in darkness that it was with difficulty I could grope my way.

"The lightnings had ceased, but the thunder continued to roll, though distantly, among the rocks, and the rain fell in torrents around. Having, after many arduous endeavours, raised him from the ground, being anxious to be assured he was still in existence, I demanded in what manner he was afflicted. He spoke faintly, that his head only had suffered, but the blow he feared was mortal. I put my hand upon his forehead, it streamed with blood; and, being desirous of preventing too copious an effusion, bound my handkerchief around his head, and assisted in placing him on my horse.

"Recollecting that there was a hut, whose possessor I had formerly known, at no very considerable distance from the place, I resolved to convey him thither; though from the length of time that had elapsed since I had last seen it, I was not assured of its exact situation.

"We were, however, fortunate in finding the place we sought; and, though the family had long forgotten the cares of the day in the tranquillity of repose, we roused them to the exertion of benevolence.

"Having procured something of a cordial nature, by means of the cottagers, to restore the fleeting spirits of Anselmo, I ordered him to be put to bed, but not till I had examined his wound, which my skill in surgery, though slight, was sufficient to convince me was not likely to have a dangerous tendency. But being unwilling to rely upon my own judgment in so important a matter, lest it should prove to be erroneous, I dispatched a peasant to the next village, where I was informed that a surgeon of some eminence resided, to procure assistance.

"The good fellow, who appeared to possess many excellent qualities, readily undertook the care of my servant; and mounting my horse (that which had caused Anselmo's misfortune having escaped), galloped towards the village.

"It was near midnight when the cottager returned attended by the surgeon, whose countenance I stedfastly regarded as he examined the wound, which I had soon the satisfaction of hearing him declare was not mortal, no contusion having been effected; though he averred that a slight fever would probably be the consequence of the accident, which would render an early removal impracticable without a prospect of further danger.

"The storm was now past; the light clouds dispersed rapidly towards the horizon, and the moon gleaming palely from the sky, made me anxious to pursue the way leading to the monastery; and having convinced Anselmo that he was in good hands, and given him assurances that I would be with him at an early hour on the following day, I committed him to the care of the peasants, and quitted the cottage.

"The rude winds were now hushed, and the undisturbed tranquillity that succeeded the boisterous warring of the elements, assisted the melancholy of my reflections. Having descended into the valley, I looked anxiously towards the mountain where the spires of the convent had appeared, but they were lost in the gloom of the woods; and finding it was impossible to obtain even a partial view of the edifice, I began to apprehend I had taken a wrong path, and was on the eve of determining to bend my way towards the cottage I had left, and to wait there for the returning light of the morning, when the midnight chaunt of the Monks broke softly upon the stillness of the night, and directed me towards the place from whence it issued.

"As soon as I had struck into the glen that wound up the steep ascent of the eminence, the meek and holy strain swelled louder, paused, then sunk into deeper cadence, and in a few moments was heard no more.

"Fearing lest I should not be able to reach the monastery before the Monks returned from the chapel, I redoubled my speed, knowing that admittance could not be easily obtained, should the fathers have returned to their cells before I could introduce myself to their notice.

"When I had arrived at the outer gate, I perceived they were just crossing the chapel yard; and, hanging the bridle of my horse round the trunk of a chesnut-tree, I waited in hopes of being able to distinguish Father Benedicta, to whom I could instantly make myself known, and explain the occasion of this visit. But the faces of the Monks were so shrouded in their cowls, that not a feature was exposed to observation.

"The Superior walked first, and the rest of the order in procession. They had nearly reached the arched door leading into the court, before I had determined in what manner to address them; when finding I was at present unperceived, I resolved to let them pass quietly into the abbey. This done, I rapped loudly at the gate, and one of the lay brothers appearing, I enquired for Father Benedicta.

"Without returning an answer, the person whom I addressed retired, but soon afterwards came attended by a Monk, who, I felt assured, by his gait and figure, was him for whom I had enquired. Believing I could not be mistaken in this particular, I was advancing forwards to meet him, and to express my satisfaction on seeing him, when he threw back his cowl, and discovered a countenance meek, placid, and full of devout expression, but it was not Father Benedicta's.

"The Monk bowed courteously, and seemed to await my introduction; I informed him that I was a benighted traveller who had met with some singular misfortunes, and had been induced, by the known benevolence of the fraternity, to request a lodging for the night. The Monk again bowing, I declared my name, and repeated my enquiries for Father Benedicta.

"Our brother is ill," replied the Monk, mildly, "and has not been able to attend public devotions for some days; but if you will have the goodness to step into the Refectoire, I will visit his cell, and will inform him of your name, and the circumstances you have mentioned." Then ordering a servant to take care of my horse, he desired me to follow him.

"Having entered the Refectoire, he offered me a seat by the fire, and hastened to acquaint the Father with my arrival. I was soon ordered to attend him, and accompanied my conductor to his cell.

"At the farther end of this little apartment was the holy Benedicta, who had newly arisen from a mattress, probably for the purpose of performing his midnight devotions. He appeared pale and emaciated, but serene and cheerful. He arose on my entrance, and instantly recollecting me, sprang forwards to receive me with an expression of affection which words would have imperfectly conveyed.

"His looks and manner affected me so powerfully that I was unable to speak, and sitting down by his side, I covered my face with my handkerchief to conceal my emotions; when these had somewhat subsided, I observed that his features were lighted up by a smile of more than usual tranquillity, and he began to converse upon common topics of discourse. I saw he wished to lead me from the subject of my griefs, and I wished to flatter him with the hope that he had succeeded."—

Laurette, who had listened with tender anxiety to this little narrative, here interrupted Enrîco, by asking if the Father Benedicta was indeed very ill, and if his disorder was supposed to be of a dangerous nature? On being assured that it was generally believed to be otherwise throughout the monastery, she demanded eagerly, whether the Monk had mentioned any thing relative to herself, or the Marchese de Montferrat? Enrîco's countenance visibly changed as she repeated the question, and he appeared for the moment unable to reply.

"You hesitate," resumed Laurette, tenderly, "and consequently have heard something you are unwilling to disclose;—but if you feel for me as for a sister, agreeably to your former professions, I conjure you to make me acquainted with it?"

"If I feel for you as for a sister!" repeated Enrîco, "Oh! Laurette, is it possible you can be ignorant of my sentiments?" But in a moment recollecting that he had never openly avowed them, he checked himself; whilst Laurette, confused, and anxious to change the conversation, asked whether he had been into the castle previous to his meeting with her, and if he had been introduced to the Signora? To this he answered that he had seen the Marchese's casiera, whom he supposed to be the lady mentioned, and was directed by her to that part of the grounds where, she observed, her young guest usually walked when alone.

A silence of some minutes then ensued, which Laurette at length broke, by asking whether his servant was sufficiently recovered to be able to attend him hither.

"He is somewhere hereabouts," returned Enrîco, "and will soon be here to answer for himself. Anxious as I was to see you, I could not leave the poor fellow alone in so melancholy a situation; which occasioned me to prolong my continuance in the monastery, till the surgeon who attended him assured me that he was in a situation to travel without endangering his health."

"You had then frequent conferences with the Monk?" returned Laurette.

Enrîco assured her that he had; but it required little penetration to discover that there was something connected with the subject he was desirous to avoid. The discourse then turned upon Madame Chamont, but this was too distressing to be continued.—Enrîco had gained no intelligence respecting her, as Father Benedicta's exertions had been at present unsuccessful.

The Signora, who now crossed the court to remind them of the lateness of the hour, a circumstance that never occurred to them before, summoned her guests into the saloon, where a simple, but elegant, repast was prepared.

The conversation now became more animated, though less interesting, than before; and the Signora joined in it with much spirit and sentiment; she related many incidents concerning some of the most celebrated families in Italy, and displayed much wit and vivacity.

Enrîco insensibly became pleased with her, and, had not his attention been so entirely engrossed by the companion of his earliest days, she might have been a candidate for admiration.

It was late when the party retired to their beds; and Enrîco and Laurette were both too deeply interested in the occurrences of the day, and too much inclined to reflection, to yield immediately to the impulse of nature, by seeking forgetfulness in repose.

CHAP. III.

"Oh! let me still with simple Nature live,
  My lowly field-flowers at her altar lay;
Enjoy the blessings that she meant to give,
  And calmly waste th' inoffensive day.

"When waves the grey light o'er the mountain's brow,
  Then let me meet the morn's first beauteous ray;
Carelessly wander from my sylvan shed
  And catch the sweet breath of the op'ning day."
LANGHORNE.

Enrîco arose early in the morning, and as no part of the family was stirring, except the inferior domestics, endeavoured for some time to amuse himself with strolling about the gardens. As the residence of the lovely Laurette, scenes that might otherwise have been contemplated without any extraordinary emotions, excited an interest in his breast, and he wandered about the castle, wrapped in that pleasing kind of melancholy which is peculiar to refined and cultivated minds.

Often as he paced silently the terrace-walk that led to the inner court, he turned an enquiring eye towards the upper apartments, in hopes of seeing Laurette at the casement; but she was at present invisible, and he could not forbear secretly chiding her for losing the beauty of the morning. Still anxious to beguile the moments of separation, he walked towards the western lawn, and having reached the centre, attempted to open the door of the pavilion; but it was fastened, which made him for a short time irresolute in what manner to dispose of himself.

At length he determined to return towards the mansion, and to procure the key; this being delivered to him by the porter, he again walked pensively along the lawn, and before he applied the key to the door of the pavilion, stopped to examine this magnificent structure with more attention than he had before bestowed on it.

It was of Corinthian architecture, and ornamented with

much taste and splendour. It appeared not to have been coeval with the castle, which was originally Gothic, though some part of the edifice was so materially modernized that, except the embattled parapets, the chapel, which was half in ruins, and the narrow pointed arch of the window, it retained little of its primitive appearance.

The portico of the pavilion was composed of various coloured marbles, and the pillars which supported it were of the finest porphyry. The interior of the building was not inferior in magnificence, and displayed an infinite superiority in point of taste and beauty. It consisted of three apartments elegantly furnished; one as a banqueting room, which being lofty and extensive, exhibited a profusion of rare and valuable ornaments; the ceiling was richly adorned with paintings by the most celebrated masters; and the floor covered with a carpet of purple damask, which was beautifully embroidered with silver, in fanciful and elegant devices. The walls being in fine relief, were decorated with gilded trophies, whilst the canopies and other ornaments harmonized with the splendour and magnificence that pervaded the other parts of this superb apartment.

Behind this were two other rooms, smaller but not less beautiful than the one he had examined. They were terminated by glass doors opening into a shrubbery, whose entrance was guarded by two statues from the antique, which were half lost to the eye amid the trees and flowering shrubs that surrounded them. The floors of these apartments were covered with tapestry, representing scenes from Lucan, Tasso, and Ovid. The walls were adorned with historical and fanciful devices, and the upper part of them decorated with valuable pictures by the first Italian painters. One was a descending angel, by Pietro Perugino; another a Madonna, by Raphael.

As Enrîco gazed attentively upon the latter, which exhibited the astonishing genius and cultivated taste of the inimitable artist, he thought he discovered a charm that was familiar to his fancy. The lifted eye, the melancholy, yet captivating, smile that was stealing upon the features, he imagined so strikingly resembled the lovely object of his affections, that he was unable to move from the spot.

Whilst he was regarding this performance with the admiration it merited, Laurette entered the room, and finding his attention was entirely absorbed in the contemplation of the picture, she seated herself, without accosting him, on a small settee, which was placed near the door, and amused herself with penciling a flower, which she had selected for the purpose on her way thither.

When a few minutes had elapsed, finding that he still continued to observe the Madonna with a fixed and earnest attention, she laid aside her pencil, and advancing towards him, demanded why he continued to examine that picture so minutely, when there were so many paintings in the pavilion which were equally worthy of admiration?

Enrîco, though effectually roused from his reverie, did not immediately reply; whilst Laurette turning her beautiful eyes alternately upon him and the picture, repeated the enquiry.

"Because it resembles," returned Enrîco, in a voice faltering with emotion, "my too charming sister; she whose image is ever present to my mind, and who is dearer to me than my existence."

Laurette blushed deeply, but was silent and Enrîco proceeded:

"Did you know what I have suffered, and what I still suffer on your account, you would not deny me a part of that angelic pity and commiseration which I have seen you bestow upon objects less deserving of it.—I have long imposed upon myself," resumed he, still more agitated, yet endeavouring to stifle his emotions, "a severe restraint;—hitherto I have listened to, and obeyed the dictates of prudence which instigated me to forbear verbally acknowledging an attachment which must eventually form all the happiness or torment of my future life. But doubts and melancholy presages recur frequently and forcibly to my thoughts which neither reason nor reflection can subdue. I would fain find a solace for my present inquietude by anticipating the future, with those enthusiastic hopes which are peculiar to youth and inexperience; but that future presents only grief and disappointment to my disordered fancy.

"Whilst you are here, Laurette," continued Enrîco, pressing her unreluctant hand to his breast, "you are under the protection of the Marchese de Montferrat; a man who has had art enough to impose himself upon the superficial part of the world, as one of its most perfect characters. I cannot absolutely assert that I am acquainted with any material crimes that can be alledged against him; but from some hints, inadvertently dropped by those who have received better information upon the subject, I am convinced that there are reasons to justify the suspicion that he is not what he pretends to be."

Finding that Laurette continued to listen to him with eager attention, he requested that she would take a seat upon the sofa, and, placing himself by her side, proceeded:

"The Marchese is yet passionately attached to the pleasures and luxuries of life, and his ample possessions at once gratify, and give unlimited range to his desires; he is unaccustomed to controul, and cannot submit to be shackled by discretion, when it is at enmity with his inclinations.—Is such a man the proper guardian of youth and beauty? or is it possible that he, who has hitherto never resisted their power, can behold them with decided indifference. Besides he has recently been released from a matrimonial connection, in which his heart had no interest, and may possibly earnestly desire to contract another less repugnant to his feelings and inclinations."

"Why, Enrîco," interrupted Laurette, "do you thus resign yourself to unavailing despondency? why voluntarily yield to the impulse of a quick and warm indignation, which at once enslaves and obscures your better judgment?—Is it likely that the Marchese de Montferrat should behold with decided preference a poor dependant orphan, whose birth is veiled from all but himself in impenetrable mystery, and whose youth must preclude the probability of his thinking of her but as a child?"

Enrîco was meditating a reply, when a summons for breakfast prevented a continuation of the subject.

As soon as they entered the castle they were met by the Signora, who had prepared the morning's repast, and had been some time in waiting to receive them. Having rallied them good-naturedly on their early rising, she proposed a walk, after breakfast, to an adjacent village, which, from its elevated situation, commanded an extensive prospect. Laurette and Enrîco readily acceding to her wishes, it was agreed that a female servant should attend them, for the purpose of conveying a basket of fruit, sweetmeats, and other articles of food, that the party might not be obliged to return before the evening.

The Signora's favourite woman was also permitted to accompany them on their excursion, more in the capacity of a companion than a domestic. She was an Italian, and before the arrival of Laurette, was admitted as a familiar into those apartments which were appropriated to the use of her mistress, and was considered as her companion and confidante. Since then she had been less conversant with the Signora, who was more strongly attached to her new acquaintance, but was still highly esteemed and beloved.

It was yet early in the autumn, and the weather remarkably fine. The road leading to the village was for a considerable way through a lone and beautiful wood, chiefly composed of oak, flowering ash, and wild juniper; it skirted a neighbouring mountain which rose gradually from the gloom, whose summit was crested with the village, which was the object of their ramble. Its aspect was wild and picturesque, whilst the profusion of trees that half screened it from observation, being contrasted with the bare rocks and huge masses of granite, with which they were surrounded, had a singular and beautiful appearance.

By winding round an obscure path, encircling the foot of the mountain, they might have avoided a steep and rugged ascent, but they preferred the unfrequented glade they had chosen, accessible only to the foot of the enthusiast and the goatherd. Here they lingered amid the points of the rocks, selecting mosses and flowers from the interstices, till the sun, in its noon-tide radiance, spread over the variegated scenery that full profusion of light and shade, which is deemed the most favourable to landscape.

As they advanced within a few paces of the summit, the Signora's foot unfortunately slipped; and had not Enrîco, whose solicitude was equally extended to all that were in need of it, caught her in his arms, she must have fallen, and such a fall would consequently have been attended with danger.

A slight hurt was however the result of this trifling accident; her ancle was sprained, but being unwilling to give pain to others by the expression of her own, she concealed it; and thanking

Enrîco for his attention, agreed to accept of his arm the rest of the way.

Before they arrived at the village it was considerably worse, and she was under the necessity of stopping at one of the huts, which were dispersed over the brow of the mountain, to procure an embrocation. An hospitable cottager received them with a hearty welcome, and as the Signora's ancle was much swelled, and the pain still more acute, it was thought necessary for the party to postpone the execution of their design; and, as it was impossible for her to return without a conveyance, it was proposed that Enrîco and Laurette should return to the castle, and send Ambrose or Anselmo with a horse; as no carriage could be procured at a convenient distance.

This, however, the Signora earnestly opposed till they had taken a view of the country from the extremity of the eminence, and had seen every thing worthy of observation; at the same time informing them that it was her intention to remain in the cottage till the evening, if her hospitable hostess, addressing herself to the woman of the house, would permit her to remain there.

The cottager acceded, with much good humour, to the request; and leaving the room for a few minutes, presented them on her return with some newly-gathered grapes, which her husband, she added, had just brought from the vineyard. These, in consideration of the fruits and other provisions which they had conveyed thither, were politely refused; and the baskets being opened, some of the most delicious sweetmeats were offered to the cottager, of which she modestly consented to partake; some wine was then produced by the hostess, which, more from courtesy than inclination, was accepted.

This simple repast being concluded, the Signora desired her young companions would leave her to the care of her humane entertainer and the female domestics who had accompanied them, and continue their ramble.

At first Laurette objected to the proposal, being unwilling to leave her friend in a state of indisposition; but her arguments were overruled by those of the Signora and Enrîco, who could not forbear joining in the request.

As they were retiring from the cottage, the entrance of the mountaineer, who was its possessor, prevented their design; not being prepared to expect visiters, his looks expressed surprise and pleasure, but without making any enquiries, he drew chairs for his young guests, and desired they would be seated. They obeyed, and the peasant addressing himself to his wife, desired her to prepare some refreshment. The Signora, who understood his meaning rather from his gestures than his words, not being perfectly conversant in the German tongue, informed him they had just been regaling themselves with some fruits, and concluded with thanking him for his attention and hospitality.

The party then alternately explained the occasion of their visit; expatiating, at the same time, on the neatness and simplicity of the cottage, the fineness of its situation, and the pure and exalted felicities of rural life.

Enrîco beheld, with an equal degree of curiosity and pleasure, the peculiar form and countenance of the mountaineer: from some lines in his face, his long beard, which characterizes the inhabitants of Saltzburg, and the silver hairs which were thinly scattered among his fine chesnut locks, he might have been supposed to have been upwards of fifty, did not his light carriage, his glowing complexion, and his fine dark speaking eyes, seem to contradict the supposition. An inexpressible serenity of soul was pictured upon his brow, whilst the whole contour of his face, which was regular, exhibited a certain dignity of mind inseparable from a virtuous character. There was indeed something altogether in his figure and deportment not easy to describe; and our hero regretted his want of sufficient skill in the provincial dialect, which prevented the agreeable communication with him that this circumstance would have afforded.

Enrîco having reminded Laurette of their intended ramble, they arose to depart; and informing the Signora that they would call on her again before they returned to the castle, they repeated their acknowledgments to the host and his benevolent companion, and ascended the summit of the mountain.

The prospect from this eminence was more extensive and picturesque than they had ventured to imagine; and as they gazed alternately on the surrounding objects, and on each other, they yielded to the exquisite sensations of the moment; forgetting in the happiness of the present, the unpromising aspect of the future, the approaching separation, and the despondency they had so lately indulged.

The village consisted of a number of cottages, built of stone, and straggled amid the rocks, without the appearance of design or order; a few wooden huts, inhabited chiefly by shepherds and vine-dressers, with the ruins of an abbey, standing lonely and solitary nearly at the foot of the mountain, and what had formerly been the conventual church, but was now left open for the devout accommodation of the unlettered rustics.

The extremity of the eminence commanded, on one side, the wide part of the valley which ran between two beautiful hills, parts of which were cultivated to their summits with the vine and pomegranate, and other parts covered with rich dark woods, encircled with lakes, whose effect was not less singular than charming; on the other side were large masses of yellow granite, rising in the most grotesque forms, and the deep glen through which they had at first ascended, whose rocky points were yet sparkling in the rays of the sun, whilst the depth below was veiled in perpetual shade and obscurity. A vast chain of hills bounded the horizon, which were scarcely to be distinguished from the clouds which rested upon them, and which gave grandeur and sublimity to the landscape.

Being somewhat fatigued with traversing the mountain, Enrîco and Laurette seated themselves upon a rock, and in cheerful unrestrained conversation, disregarded the lapse of time, and even the unequalled magnificence of scenery which was every way presented.

As Enrîco fixed his eyes tenderly upon Laurette, he thought she never before appeared so beautiful as at that moment; her dress was more than ordinarily negligent, and the wind, which had disordered her fine hair, had given a soft bloom to her complexion, which no vermilion could emulate. Whilst he continued to regard her elegant form, which for grace and proportion might have been taken as a model for perfection, and listened to the sweet accents of her voice, his soul was resigned to the fascinating influence of love and beauty; but when he reflected upon the Marchese, who, he was assured, could not behold such inimitable perfections with indifference, he fell suddenly from the most animated discourse into fits of musing and dejection, to which a mind, less interested in his happiness than Laurette's, could not be insensible.

She recollected what had passed in the pavilion, and also the conversation of the preceding evening, when he mentioned having had another conference with the venerable Carthusian, but was prevented from acquainting her with the result by the appearance of the Signora.

The person from whom he had obtained information concerning the Marchese, she believed could be no other than the Father Benedicta, who, from his looks and manners when she presented him with the letter previous to her quitting her former abode, and from some hints he had then dropped, was evidently concerned on her account; and it was equally certain that he was not much prejudiced either in favour of the epistle or the writer.

Anxious to be acquainted with the extent of his fears, that she might administer all possible consolation, yet fearful of increasing the uneasiness of Enrico by reverting to the cause of it, she at last ventured to ask how long Anselmo's indisposition had detained him at the monastery? and whether the Monk had mentioned any thing in which they were materially interested?

Enrîco did not instantly reply; for it was difficult to command his feelings, and the eyes of Laurette being fixed upon his with an expression of earnest and tender solicitude, tended to heighten his distress.—Finding, at length, that suspense was becoming painful, he assumed an appearance of composure, and then began as follows.

CHAP. IV.

"Love only feels the marvellous of pain,
Opens new veins of torture in the heart,
And wakes the nerve where agonies are born."

YOUNG.

"My first visit to the Father was short, for it was long past midnight when I entered his cell. What happened at that interview I have already related. He appeared at first much affected, but afterwards became more tranquil; and a message from the Superior, who politely accommodated me with a bed, put an end to all farther discourse.

"I was then conducted to my apartment by one of the lay brothers, whose office it is to attend upon pilgrims, and being weary and exhausted with grief and fatigue, obtained a transient forgetfulness in repose. I had not slept long, before I was alarmed by the tolling of a bell, whose hollow and heavy sound vibrating through the buildings, produced a melancholy and solemn effect. Knowing that this was not the usual summons to the early matins, I conceived it portended some extraordinary event, and being desirous of learning the occasion of it, arose and dressed myself in haste. These suspicions were confirmed by the shutting and opening of doors, the murmur of distant voices, and of the number of footsteps which were heard passing and repassing the cloisters.

"I endeavoured, for a considerable time, to arrest the attention of some of the Friars by calling at the door of my apartment, but without success, and was retiring to my bed without being acquainted with the cause of this alarm, when one of the brotherhood, whom I afterwards discovered to be the same who had given me admittance on my arrival, entered the chamber, and informed me that the bell I had heard announced the departure of a soul that was just fled to its eternal home.

"I started, and without giving myself time for reflection, demanded whether the person he alluded to was Father Benedicta.

The answer was a negative; it was Father Marco, who had been long ill, and whose death had been some time expected. Thanking him for his attention, he withdrew; and, glad to find my fears respecting the worthy Monk were not realized, I endeavoured to compose myself to rest.

"In the morning I was introduced to the Prior, who received me with much cordiality and friendship. We conversed for some time over the morning's repast upon different subjects, which he discussed with much ease and fluency, though it was not without reluctance that I entered into a conversation, which, however animated on the part of the Superior, was in my present tone of spirits, tedious and uninteresting.

"Having obtained his permission to revisit Father Benedicta, who I was assured was in a state of convalescence, though not sufficiently recovered to attend prayers in the chapel, I availed myself of the indulgence, and repaired to his cell.

"On opening the door, I observed this devout Monk, being newly arisen, was engaged in the performance of his devotions. He was kneeling at a square stone table on the eastern side of the room, that was covered with a black cloth, on which were placed a human scull, and other mementos of mortality; a small ivory crucifix stood in the centre, over which was suspended a painting, representing the resurrection of Lazarus.

"Fearing I had obtruded myself into his presence at an improper hour, I apologized for my intrusion, and would have retired, but he prevented my design, and leading me to a seat, "You are welcome, my son," said he, with his accustomed mildness; "a visit from you can never be unseasonable; it is a gratification which I have long anxiously desired, and for which I have waited perhaps too impatiently."

"Here he hesitated; and, on looking up, I thought I discovered something more in his countenance than its usual expression: the fire of devotion was still in his eyes; his face, which was marked with the lines of penitence and sorrow, was animated with a faint glow that crossed his cheek and disappeared, leaving upon the features it thus transiently illumined, that kind of dignified tenderness which we generally attribute to beings of a superior order.

"You are doubtless acquainted with some unfortunate events that have taken place since you last joined your regiment," resumed the Father, "but possibly have not been able to ascertain the cause of the compulsive and arbitrary measures employed; or to form any conception as to what part of the Continent Madame Chamont, your excellent parent, is conveyed."

"After assuring him that I had but recently received this unwelcome intelligence, and was unable to form any conjecture concerning it, I demanded eagerly why the castle was deserted; and whither you and the rest of its inhabitants were removed?

"They are removed, I think," returned the Monk, meekly, "to a castle in the principality of Saltzburg."

"Think, Father!" I replied, "gracious heaven! do you then only think? If you are not certain they are there, or in some place of security, I shall suspect that there remains another calamity to be unfolded, another attack upon my peace, perhaps severer than the last."

"You are impetuous, my son," returned the Monk, "but these are trials that put our virtues to the proof, and frequently render ineffectual the most vigorous efforts of reason and fortitude. Though we must endeavour to endure as christians, we must feel as men; nor can we expect to see always the warm affections of youth corrected and regulated by the calmness of discretion. Laurette, the subject of your enquiry, is still under the protection of the Marchese de Montferrat, though not under his eye; the Marchese being still resident at the Castello St. Aubin, in the neighbourhood of Turin."

"You have at last relieved me, holy Father, I replied, from a state of perplexity and suspense that was becoming almost insupportable; and which, I hope, will, in some measure, excuse that extreme impetuosity of which you have justly accused me, and which the most perfect esteem for your character would, on any common occasion, have prevented me from discovering."

"Father Benedicta bowed; then asked if I had been introduced to my patron, and, if not, whether he had never intimated a desire, either by message or letter, of being personally known to me? On my convincing him of the contrary, he was evidently much amazed; and enquired, with some appearance of confusion, if I was acquainted with the nature of the connection which had so long subsisted between the Marchese and Madame Chamont?

"I informed him that I was not; for every thing that could lead to the subject had been as much as possible avoided, and that whenever I had ventured to introduce any thing likely to have this tendency, my mother appeared chagrined and unhappy; that she never on any account mentioned my father, and scrupulously concealed every circumstance of her past life; that the name of the Marchese seldom escaped her lips, though I was compelled to believe, from the earliest period of my existence, that my only dependance was upon him; and that, from the native generosity of his disposition, he had sent to the protection of my mother a lovely little girl, who was supposed to be the orphan daughter of a deceased friend: from which circumstance, as well as from the conversation of his steward, I was taught to reverence him as a father, to respect him as a friend, and to consider him as a man of stainless honour and unblemished reputation, to whom only I could look as to the patron of my future days.

"Would to heaven you was not mistaken, my son!" returned the Monk, mournfully, "perhaps I am not justified in advancing any thing which may serve to counteract principles so heedfully instilled into your mind in early youth, but I fear you have been miserably deceived. Is it possible that you are unacquainted with the unfortunate story of the Conte della Croisse?" resumed he, sighing deeply, and pausing to await my answer. "You have not, I think, been stationary at the Castle of Elfinbach since a certain strange and, I may say, providential discovery."

"On my requesting to know what was the discovery he alluded to, he betrayed many symptoms of astonishment, and then added, "You are, I find, designedly kept ignorant of the affair; and since, by extending your knowledge, I might possibly injure your repose, an explanation would be unpardonable.

"Indeed," continued the Monk, seeming to recollect himself, "I may have been too uncandid in my conjectures; we are apt to reflect upon our own frailties and imperfections with partiality, and to judge too unfavourably of the conduct of others. The Marchese may have some virtues."

"Here the father was silent; and, being anxious to comprehend the extent of his suspicions, I acknowledged myself much interested in what had already been recited, and besought him to indulge me with an explanation, and inform me who was the Conte della Croisse, and with whom his story was connected. A violent emotion seemed to agitate his frame as I repeated this request, and, without answering me, he arose and paced the room for some time with quick and perturbed steps; and then, after regarding me with a look of fixed and earnest attention—

"My son," cried he, "this subject is too painful; neither my health nor my spirits will allow me to continue it; and, since it will inevitably endanger our mutual peace, we will defer it till some future period, when, should an explanation be necessary, whatever torment it may inflict upon myself, I will give it you.

"Watch over Laurette with the tender solicitude of a brother; for she is young, artless, and beautiful, and may have need of a disinterested protector. I wished to have had some conversation with that dear child, but she was taken suddenly from the castle, and every precaution I had formed for her future welfare was, by this means, rendered ineffectual."

"Having thanked him for the zeal he had discovered in your cause with the ardour natural to my disposition, the Monk cast upon me a look of tenderness, and continued—

"It is needless to exhort you to exert your most strenuous endeavours to inform yourself of the destiny of your unfortunate parent; but let me request, nay command, that, should every effort prove inefficacious, you will not allow yourself to sink into despondency; but remember the duty you owe to your God, to yourself, and to your country. Recollect that wherever she is, she is equally under the protection of heaven, who never abandons the virtuous; and that your utmost exertions are necessary as well for your own preservation and advancement, as to support the unprotected innocence of your adopted sister."

"Here the father remained silent; and the entrance of a Monk, who came to enquire into the state of his health, put an end to all farther discourse upon the subject. Having no hopes of renewing it, I took my leave; and, with a mind but ill at ease, repaired to the cottage to fulfil my engagement with Anselmo.

"I found him considerably better, and much more cheerful

than on the preceding evening. He told me he was in readiness to accompany me, though his looks did not agree with the assertion, for he still appeared pale and enervated.

"Having continued with him some hours, I availed myself of the Prior's invitation to return to, and remain in, the monastery, till Anselmo was in a situation to travel. During this period, my time was chiefly devoted to the society of Father Benedicta; but nothing could prevail on him to renew the discourse. He seemed to repent having touched upon it at all, and we parted mutually dissatisfied; he regretting that he had said so much, and I that he had explained so little.

"The rest of the narrative may be concluded in a few words: I left him considerably recovered, and received his heavenly benediction, mingled with tears and gentle remonstrances; and, having obtained a direction to the Castle of Luenburg, set forwards, attended by Anselmo, for Saltzburg. No material incident happened on my journey, and with the rest you are acquainted.

"I introduced myself to the Signora d'Orso; she received me with courtesy, and instructed me where to seek you. Contrary to my expectations, you was beyond the boundaries of the walls. At the time that you passed near the shrubbery on your return, I was conversing with Ambrose, who, I was in hopes, might have seen what road you had taken, but who was unable to give me any satisfactory intelligence.

"I have now, my Laurette," continued Enrîco, "acquainted you with all; and, from the circumstances I have related, you may guess all I feel, and all I fear. We must part—a temporary separation is unavoidable. I must go in search of my much-injured mother; and if she has not been seized by banditti, but has been torn from her home, her family, and all who are dear to her, by the daring machinations of designing villany, I will not rest till I have discovered the authors of this premeditated cruelty—till I have restored her to her tenderest connections, and have exposed the artifice of her persecutors. There are laws, and if they cannot be enforced, I have a sword, never yet drawn but in the exercise of justice, but which shall be raised against the heart of the oppressor, in the cause of defenceless innocence.

"But, Oh Laurette! before I am compelled to quit these heavenly regions, dear to me, because consecrated by your presence, and, in compliance with my wayward destiny, prepare to bid you a long, and if obliged to engage in any desperate enterprize, perhaps a last adieu; tell me, I conjure you, that I am not indifferent to you, and that the recollection of our juvenile felicity will endear to your remembrance him who was a sharer of it—the companion of your earliest days; since this is the only reflection that can soften the rigours of my fate, and dissipate the cloudy atmosphere of my future prospects?"

Laurette, who had marked with concern every circumstance which he had related, and had been comparing them with those that had fallen under her immediate notice, now yielded to the softness that oppressed her mind; and, leaning tenderly upon his arm, covered her face with her handkerchief, and wept unrestrainedly.

"By heaven this is too much!" cried Enrîco, endeavouring to command his emotions, "forgive me, dearest Laurette, if, in the attempt of drawing from you a mutual confession, I have renewed that grief I ought to have mitigated.—Say but that you love me and, from this moment, all the energies of my soul shall be exerted in your cause, and for the security of your happiness."

"Is it possible, Enrîco," replied Laurette, "that you can doubt the sincerity of my friendship—a friendship I have so long, so tenderly indulged; or believe that the son of my amiable benefactress, who supplied to me the place of a parent, and deprived of whom, I now feel the wants of one, can be reflected upon without esteem and gratitude."

"Esteem and gratitude!" repeated Enrîco, "and is this all I must expect or hope for—is the cold sentiment of friendship a sufficient reward for inviolable affection—is this all you can bestow as a recompence for the innumerable cares and anxieties I have endured?—rather hate and abandon me at once—teach me to think of you, and adore you no more—and let me wander over this desolated earth, without a hope to stimulate exertion, or an object to endear existence.—There was a time when I indulged the transient, delusive idea that I could have insured your affection; but I have been deceived, unhappily deceived, and you have assisted in the deception that has undone me."

"You wrong me, indeed you wrong me," replied Laurette, in a voice scarcely audible, "how have I deserved this censure? and why, by affecting to misunderstand me, will you thus add to my distress? Enrîco, you are not calm—you do not listen to the dictates of reason, nor resign yourself to the guidance of discretion. By endeavouring to work upon my feelings, in thus appealing to my heart, you have been striving to wrest from me a confession, which perhaps I ought not to make.

"I am not insensible to your merit, nor do I affect to be so; but the peculiarity of my situation forbids any advances but those of friendship and brotherly affection, which I have ever tenderly cherished. To enter into any engagement without the sanction of those under whose protection I am placed, would justly expose me to censure, and would appear, to the unprejudiced and discerning, as the height of indiscretion and ingratitude.

"Besides, would not such conduct lessen you in the estimation of the person, on whom your dependance, as well as mine, is placed? Would not the Marchese openly resent the want of confidence we had betrayed, and consequently withdraw his patronage, not only from me, but from you; and should I not then consider myself as the author of your misfortunes, and feel acutely the uneasiness such a reflection must occasion?"

"Has he not withdrawn it already?" returned Enrîco; "has he ever expressed a wish to see me, or exerted his interest to procure my advancement? How slender would be my hopes if they rested entirely upon him!—But are you determined, Laurette, to resign yourself to the power of the Marchese?"

"Alas! on whom can I depend?" replied she, sighing; "I have no friend but him on whom I can rely for immediate support, no relation living, at least not to my knowledge, and am totally unacquainted with the authors of my existence. If the Marchese proves himself unworthy of my confidence, and I find any thing in his conduct which may eventually prove injurious to my peace, it will then be time enough to relinquish his protection, and to secure another asylum in a less splendid and dangerous situation."

Finding that she was too firm to yield to the force of a premature attachment, and was too strictly guarded by delicacy

to avow more than a sisterly affection, till it was sanctioned by
those who had a right to the disposal of her; Enrîco only ventured to request that, should her present abode be less eligible
than she expected, and he sufficiently fortunate in his military
department to secure an independence, or at least the prospect
of one, that she would then allow him to resume the subject, and
in the mean time permit him to write to her; and that she would
continue to think with tenderness upon him, whose whole
existence was dedicated to her service.

To this she cheerfully assented, and giving him her hand with
the most charming frankness, reminded him of the time they
had been absent from the cottage, and proposed their returning
to it immediately.

Having watched, for a few moments, the sun sinking slowly
upon the surface of the water, they gradually descended the
extreme point of the mountain, and entered the cottage.

The Signora had been expecting them some time and, as her
ancle was still very painful, had sent one of the servants to the
castle to order Ambrose to bring a horse, for the purpose of
conveying her home.

As no animal, except a mule, could traverse without danger
the steep ascent of the eminence, she was compelled to go near
half a league round; which obliged Laurette and Enrîco to return
without her by what way they should think proper.

Ambrose soon appeared; and the Signora being mounted behind him, our young wanderers took leave of the kind-hearted
peasantry, and agreed, as the difference in the length of the way
was inconsiderable, to return by the other side of the mountain,
and to visit the solitary ruin.

Having descended the eminence by a lone and entangled
sheep-path, frequently turning aside to mark the purple tints of
the western sky, to listen to the last flutter of the breeze among
the half leafless trees, or the distant sound of a flute, or a vesper-
bell, they arrived at the long-neglected and forsaken abbey.

The deepening glooms of the twilight, which fell fast around
them, rendered the solitary grandeur of this lonely ruin still
more impressive and sublime, whose interesting appearance was
materially increased by the correspondent melancholy of the

scenery. A clump of dark firs, on one side, cast an almost impenetrable shade, whilst the other opening upon an extensive heath, was exposed to the merciless beatings of the not unfrequent storm. All here wore an aspect still more dreary and deserted, from the total want of vegetation which was every where visible.

"The thistle was there, on its rock, shedding its aged beard; the old tree groaned in the blast; the murmur of night was abroad*."

The abbey was originally built round a quadrangle, in the manner of a fortified castle, with spires instead of turrets. The entrance into the court was rugged, overgrown with long grass, and scattered with the fragments of the fallen edifice. The walls which marked the circumference, wore an appearance of great antiquity, and of such ponderous strength, that they contemplated with astonishment the invincible attacks of time. The ivy and the elder had taken root in the crevices of the stones, which were encrusted with moss, night-shade, and wild gilliflower; and from the loop-windows, which were fringed with weeds, a solitary sprig of the ash and the arbeal were occasionally seen waving mournfully in the wind, and replying to the murmurs of the rising blast.

The spires of the building were crumbling fast into dust, and the body of this once massy structure was nearly sharing the same fate. Indeed the whole of the remains were in so tottering a state, that Laurette could scarcely prevail upon Enrîco to allow her to enter what had once been a door, to examine it more minutely.

> "A pile stupendous, once of fair renown,
>   This mould'ring mass of shapeless ruin rose,
> Where nodding heights of fractur'd columns frown,
>   And birds obscene in ivy bowers repose;
>
> "Oft the pale matron, from the threat'ning wall,
>   Suspicious, bids her heedless children fly;
> Oft, as he views the meditated fall,
>   Full swiftly steps the frighted peasant by.
>   LANGHORNE.

* Ossian.

On the eastern side of the court was a small chapel, which was less ruinous than the rest of the fabric, though the narrow Gothic windows, once filled with painted glass, that cast a dim and fading light, were now shattered and decayed; whilst the pavement leading to the entrance, which once resounded only to the foot of devotion, was now rude and grass-grown.

Impressed with the awful scene of desolation that surrounded her, Laurette felt a sublime and tender melancholy stealing upon her mind; and as she surveyed the venerable pile sinking slowly into oblivion, her imagination reverted to its former inhabitants, now long since mingled with the dust.

The door of the chapel being made of the most lasting materials, retained somewhat of its primitive appearance; a large stone, by way of a step, was placed at the entrance, which being broken, and covered with moss and fallen leaves, exhibited an aspect of gloom, neglect, and silence.

The door was not quite closed, and desiring Enrîco to follow her, Laurette entered the chapel. It was dark, and was considerably larger than she expected to have found it. A narrow window, at the farther end, just discovered its extent; and turning round she distinguished, in that part of it where the altar had been formerly erected, a figure in the dress of a white friar, kneeling, and deeply engaged in devotion.

The idea of the mysterious Monk darted instantly across her mind, and not being sufficiently tranquil to endure new scenes of surprise and terror, she seized the arm of Enrîco, and would have hurried him from the place, without farther explanation.

Astonished at the alarm she expressed, and the sudden paleness of her looks, he endeavoured to learn the occasion of her fears, and to quiet them; informing her, in a low voice, that she had nothing to apprehend, since it was doubtless some Friar from a neighbouring monastery, who, walking round the ruin, had been suddenly inspired to offer up his evening prayer at that once holy altar.

Laurette acknowledged the apparent probability of the remark; but at the same time repeated her resolution of retiring, in a manner which sufficiently displayed how much of terror was mingled with amazement.

Smiling at what he believed to be merely superstition, yet secretly touched with the earnestness of her manner, he was leading her towards the door, when the Monk, who either did not hear, or did not regard the murmur of their voices, arose and advanced with quick steps towards the entrance.

They stopped for a few seconds by the side of a pillar to let him pass; and as he swept by them, as if before unconscious of witnesses, he turned aside his cowl to survey them. It discovered a thin spare face, marked with age and affliction; a ray of light that fell upon it, gave life to a large, full, melancholy eye, that was lifted up with an expression of mingled pity and sadness. There was indeed nothing in his figure or countenance expressive of severity or austere devotion; and Laurette thinking she recognized the person of her mysterious visiter, clung still closer to Enrîco, and endeavoured to conceal herself behind one of the columns.

As he passed, Enrîco bowed, and would have addressed him; but he drew his cowl close, and heaving a deep sigh, left the chapel.

When they crossed the court, they beheld him standing by the side of the building, as if surveying it, and frequently turning to see whether he was observed. As they pursued their walk, Enrîco gently rallied her upon her superstition; for his mind, being somewhat reassured by the promise she had made him of accepting his protection, should she be obliged to relinquish that of the Marchese, he felt more disposed to cheerfulness.

When they had arrived near the castle, Laurette turned, and perceived the Monk, at some distance, apparently following them. Her suspicions concerning it being the identical Friar who had delivered the portrait, were now more strongly confirmed; but not seeming to regard him, she hastened her steps, and, faint and fatigued, arrived at the castle.

The Signora was already there, waiting with the evening's refreshment; and after relating to each other the incidents of the day, they separated and retired to their rooms: Laurette to reflect upon the conversation during their ramble, with the strange adventure at the abbey; and Enrîco, upon the charming object of his regard, who was never absent from his thoughts.

CHAP. V.

"When morn first faintly draws her silver line,
    Or Eve's grey clouds descend to drink the wave;
When sea and sky in midnight darkness join,
    Still, still he views the parting look she gave."
                                                ROGERS.

Enrîco had remained some days at the castle of Luenburg before
he had collected a sufficient degree of fortitude to enable him
to endure the idea of quitting it; till the dutiful impulses of
his nature directing his harassed thoughts towards his mother,
determined him to fix an early day for his departure.

This intention being imparted to his Colonel by letter, who
was still resident with his regiment, he began to reason himself
into composure, and to mark the limits of his intended route.
No places, he believed, were so likely to afford information as
the hotels and village inns on the borders of the Rhine, which
made him resolve to let none of them escape his enquiries.

Now secretly accusing himself of inattention by this transient
delay, and now yielding to apprehensions he could not possibly
eradicate, the mind of Enrîco endured the most painful conflict;
and so acute were his feelings, that it was long before he could
assume serenity enough to acquaint Laurette with the day which
he had appointed to leave her, and to conjure her never to forget
him.

On the evening preceding the time fixed for his journey, he
detained her for some hours longer in the saloon than was his
custom; inflicting new torment upon himself, by reflecting upon
the fleeting nature of his happiness, and the anguish of being
compelled to leave her innocent and defenceless beauty exposed
to the rigours of a destiny so full of danger; and the melancholy,
but not improbable conjecture, that they might meet no more.

These sad presages, which Laurette found it impossible to
dispel, she endeavoured to assuage, by representing the cause-
lessness of his surmises, and the indispensible necessity of

exercising the virtues of resignation and fortitude.

Enrîco listened, and attempted to profit by so bright an example of meekness and patient endurance, internally suffering from disappointment and uneasy apprehensions, yet suffering with the most collected firmness; but though his mind was naturally strong, noble, and vigorous, it required an effort beyond it to bear to leave her alone to contend with the adversities of her fate, without the possibility of his being able to overlook the conduct of those in whose power she was placed, or of investing himself in that authority, which would give her a claim upon his immediate protection.

She had, however, promised to correspond with him, to remember him with the affection of a sister, which recollection, at the same time that it operated as an antidote to his present inquietude, permitted him to look forwards to the future with less regret and solicitude.

On the morning that was to separate him from her, in whose society he enjoyed all the felicity he was capable of experiencing, he arose, pale and unrefreshed by sleep, long before the sun had risen upon the hills that bounded the eastern horizon, and paced as usual, with slow and thoughtful steps, the grand terrace walk, which was under the range of apartments occupied by Laurette, the Signora, and other branches of the family.

None of the domestics being arisen except Ambrose, who had opened him the door of the portico, a deep and universal silence prevailed, disturbed only occasionally by the distant sound of a cataract, the stroke of a wood-cutter, or the distant and mellow tones of a flute, to call the sheep from their nightly folds.

At length the sun emerged gradually from the waters into a clear and cloudless sky, spreading over the whole extent of ether a meek and silvery glow. The grey mists that had dimmed the summits of the mountains, crept slowly into the interstices of the rocks, and the gentle responses of the birds were heard feebly from the neighbouring woods.

With a mind too much absorbed in its own reflections to be able to feel the full force of sylvan beauty, or to listen with pleasure to those simple and rural sounds so dear to the heart of the enthusiast, Enrîco continued to walk along the terrace with perturbed and unequal steps, till he was roused from his thoughtfulness by the opening of a casement. He turned—it was Laurette; she did not instantly perceive him, and he retreated a few paces backwards to observe her motions.

She looked pale, and seemed to have been weeping, but her beauty was nothing impaired by the sorrow she appeared to have indulged. A loose robe was negligently thrown over her lovely person, without care or art; it was of the purest white, long, and open at the bosom, displaying to advantage her fine disordered hair, that wandered about her neck loose and unconfined. Her eyes, which were yet filled with tears, were directed towards the heavens, and her thoughts seemed to have ascended with them.

Enrîco was at present undistinguished, for he had placed himself behind the spreading branches of a larch, and was sensible only to the charming object of his affection. She sighed, and in the same moment he heard his own name pronounced in a soft and tremulous accent, accompanied by some words too indistinct to be heard. Unable to endure the increasing tenderness that was stealing upon his mind, he sprang forwards from the deep shade that had afforded him concealment, and requested that she would descend, and walk with him in the gardens.

Confused at being thus unexpectedly exposed to the gaze of her lover, she blushed, and drying away the tears that had fallen unrestrainedly upon her cheeks, she forced a smile upon her features, and agreed to meet him at the portal.

Having bound her beautiful locks with a turban, which she usually wore, not because it was authorized by custom, but as it was a mode of dress recommended by Madame Chamont, who imagined that it became her, which was ornamented with a wreath of roses and violets, worked by her own delicate fingers; she threw a thin shade upon her shoulders, and left her apartment.

She met Enrîco at the door of the great hall, who was impatiently waiting her arrival; and, on observing with pity the extreme sadness that was depicted upon his countenance, held out her hand to him, and asked him, with a soft yet melancholy smile, if he was ill?

Transported with the tenderness of her manner beyond the

powers of expression or utterance, he could only press it eagerly to his lips, and then hold it to his heart, as if he would never part with it again. At length Laurette gently disengaging herself, asked him how long he had been in the gardens, and whether he was inclined to prolong his walk, or to wait in the terrace parlour till the Signora was risen?

"Have you not promised to ramble with me," returned Enrîco, "and would you deny me a pleasure——" here he paused, "the last I may ever experience" he would have added, but his voice faltered; and Laurette perceiving his emotions, without attempting a reply, took his offered arm, and walked with him along the lawn.

The door of the pavilion being open, they involuntarily entered it; and proceeding to the last of the apartments that opened into the shrubbery, seated themselves upon a small sofa at the extremity. A large marble table was placed before it, which was scattered over with leaves of music; at one end of it lay a small lute, the property of the Signora, who sometimes, when alone, had resorted thither, that she might be enabled to beguile the moments of solitude with a song.

Laurette took it up, and played a little melancholy air; it was a cantata from Metestasio, but too applicable to her present feelings to bestow the charm of content. It breathed the sorrows of disastrous love; and as she played, "she waked her own sad tale from every trembling string."

At the conclusion of it, her lips faltered, the colour forsook her cheek, and forgetting the lesson of fortitude which she had been so lately instilling into the mind of Enrîco, and the resolution she had made to wear, at least, the appearance of it in his presence, she was compelled to lean upon the side of the sofa for support; and tears, which she could no longer suppress, fell in large drops upon the lute.

Enrîco, who had been lost to every other circumstance in the harmony of her voice, now thought she had fainted, and would have caught her in his arms; but an effort of fortitude revived her, and disengaging herself from his embrace, she would have spoke to have quieted his fears, but the entrance of Anselmo prevented her. He had been for some time in quest of his master, and finding that the door of the pavilion was unfastened, had ventured to intrude. His business was to inform him that the horses were in readiness, and to know if he had any further commands.

Enrîco started as if he had received a summons for death; and after walking to the other end of the apartment with hasty and agitated steps, paused for an instant to recompose his disordered spirits. In a few moments he assumed an appearance of composure, and returning again towards Laurette, who had just risen from the sofa, he fixed his fine eyes upon her's, with a look too expressive to be misunderstood, and then added—

"The moment of separation, which has been long painfully anticipated, is arrived; and nothing but the sweet consolatory hope that I shall still live in your remembrance, could reconcile me to this cruel exile."

Laurette was unable to reply; and having led her from the pavilion, he reminded her again of her former promises, and, with an aching and oppressed heart, gazed tenderly upon her pale but lovely face, and heard her innocent farewel.

The Signora, who was but just arisen, came forwards to meet them at the outer gate, and wishing Enrîco much happiness with the appearance of much sincerity and kindness, he mounted his horse; and, after lingering some time for one more look at the beautiful Laurette, till the white folds of her robe were lost in distance, he left the boundaries of the castle, and pursued his journey.

Overcome with grief for the present, and sorrowful presages for the future, our heroine returned pensively towards the mansion; and being unable to conceal the uneasiness that preyed upon her heart, retired to her apartment, that she might weep, and indulge it in secret. The hope that Enrîco would succeed in his enterprize, was too feeble to sustain her; for the length of time that had elapsed since Madame Chamont was forced from the castle, and the many ineffectual measures that had been already employed, promised nothing of success to any future ones that could be adopted. Sometimes she imagined that the Marchese was materially concerned in it; and at others, though many collected circumstances seemed to justify the opinion, she dismissed it, as uncandid and illiberal.

What the Father Benedicta had uttered, agreed but too well with the words of the mysterious Monk, though those of the latter were of more dreadful import; and she remembered and reflected upon them with increasing emotion. That he was the person whom she had seen in the chapel of the ruin, she believed nearly amounted to conviction; both from his dress, the height of his stature, and the attention with which he had regarded them; this, added to the circumstance of his following them, as if to be assured of the exact place of their residence, was sufficient to confirm the suspicion.

It appeared reasonable to suppose, from the former conduct of the Father, that he would loiter about in the evenings, in the hope of meeting with her; but whatever symptoms of curiosity she had formerly betrayed respecting her birth, and of being acquainted with the manner in which he had obtained the possession of the picture, so much of terror was mingled with it, and so little did she believe it would avail her any thing as to her future happiness, to be informed of her birth and con- nections, since she had no relation to claim, or to protect her, that she resolved rather to avoid than precipitate an interview, which could be productive of no real good, and might possibly augment her uneasiness.

Accustomed from earliest youth to place an unlimited con- fidence in the wisdom and goodness of Providence, she deter- mined to act in every respect with caution and dignity, and to endure those temporal and unavoidable evils, which are the common lot of humanity, with patient firmness.

Had she not been so strictly enjoined to secrecy as to preclude the advantage arising from the advice and participation of disin- terested friendship, she would have met him without reluctance; but thus situated, another conference, even could it have been effected with ease and safety, she was aware might lead to future inquietude and danger; and therefore resolved to take no direct measures to further his scheme, but rather to avoid any future opportunity of conversing with him, unless some succeeding event should make another interview necessary or desirable.

The violent emotions Enrîco had betrayed, when he related the conversation that had passed between himself and the pious

Carthusian, would have determined her, had she not already by a solemn promise bound herself to perpetual silence upon the subject, not to disclose what she had seen and heard, lest they should confirm his worst and most terrible surmises. From the words of the mysterious Monk she had every thing to fear, and nothing had happened, or was likely to happen, at present, to obviate or remove the painful impressions which they had left upon her mind.

But thus being prepared to encounter calamity, she resolved, if possible, not to yield to its influence; but, by opposing the most vigorous efforts of her fortitude, to endure what could not be remedied, and to gain at least, by her most strenuous endeavours, the applause of her own heart.

The picture which he had delivered, she wore constantly in her bosom, suspended by the small string of brilliants to which it was fastened, though she so entirely concealed it in the folds of her robe, that it could not be perceived.

That it was really the portrait of her mother, was beyond a doubt. The resemblance that it bore to herself she was perfectly aware of, for the mild pensive cast of the countenance, the soft cloud upon the brow, the smile that played upon the lip, and the expression of the whole, were too striking to escape the penetration of the most transient observer.

As Laurette fixed her eyes upon the portrait, some portion of her former curiosity returned; she was anxious to be informed of the destiny of her parents, though it was probable they had been long since numbered with the dead. Her tears streamed anew when she reflected upon her hard unhappy lot, the obscurity of her birth, her family (if any of them were still in existence) unknown to her; commanded to beware of the only person whom she had been taught to revere as a protector; deprived of the guardian of her infancy and childhood; and with no human being, except Enrîco and the Father Benedicta, to interest themselves in her welfare; and these, from the peculiarity of their situations, precluded from affording immediate assistance, however necessary.

The Signora had indeed hitherto behaved to her with uniform kindness, and she had no reason to apprehend that it was likely to be of short continuance; for she appeared to possess a strong and well-informed mind, a correct judgment, not easily to be led into error, and much feminine grace and softness, which rendered it unlikely that she should be misled by the sophistical arguments of designing falsehood, or be induced to yield to the influence of decided wrong. The pains she had already taken to console and re-assure her, were striking proofs of her friendship; and this being one of the most substantial comforts that her lot afforded, she resolved to endeavour to conciliate her esteem by every gentle attention which her situation allowed.

To this conduct the natural sweetness of her disposition would have directed her, unbiassed by other motives; but she now saw the necessity of securing one friend, at least, in the place destined for her future residence, who might be inclined to assist her on any future emergency.

A gentle tapping at the door roused her from these deep and melancholy reflections, and arising hastily from the side of the bed, on which she had been sitting, she opened it, and beheld the Signora, who being desirous of diverting her thoughts from the subject of her grief, proposed a walk along the grounds. She could not, she added, alluding to her late accident, undertake an extensive ramble beyond the boundaries of the castle; but the day was too fine to be allowed to pass without taking advantage of it, and she hoped she would indulge her with her society, as she was anxious to have her opinion respecting some intended improvements.

Laurette instantly assented, and succeeded so well in the endeavour of tranquillizing her spirits, that she appeared little less animated than usual. The fineness of the weather assisted her efforts; and the vivacity of her companion, who exerted herself to soften the affliction of her friend, tended to comfort and re-assure her.

There was something in the manners of Laurette at once so endearing and fascinating, that no one could be acquainted with her without feeling for her the most lasting affection; she entered with so lively an interest into the joys and sorrows of others, and mingled such an amiable concern with her assiduities, so entirely divested of art or unnatural refinement, that she appeared to the Signora, who had been also schooled in adversity, and whose native levity of disposition had been checked, though not entirely annihilated, by the correcting hand of Misfortune, as one of the most perfect creatures she had ever seen. The amiable sentiment she had conceived for her fair young friend, induced her to dwell upon the affecting incidents of her past life, which she had before briefly and imperfectly related, and upon the remembrance of those sorrows, which time had softened, but not thoroughly erased; that, by convincing her that she was not singularly unfortunate, she might teach her to endure her calamities with patience, and convince her also of the possibility of finally triumphing over them.

By a long course of useful and extensive reading, united to an uncommon strength of memory, she was enabled to recollect many anecdotes in real life, and many passages from the most polished writers and historians of the age, which made her not only an entertaining, but an intelligent companion, every way formed to engage the affections of our heroine, and to deserve her confidence.

Having wandered for some time through the lawns and shrubberies, and taken a general survey of the improvements, they discontinued their walk; and music, conversation, and other innocent amusements shortened the cares and fatigues of the day. In the evening, Laurette avoided taking her accustomed stroll, lest she should see her ghostly visiter, whom she determined, for the present at least, sedulously to avoid, since so little comfort could be expected from intelligence which she was not permitted to disclose.

CHAP. VI.

"Nor peace, nor ease that heart can know,
Which, like the needle true,
Turns at the touch of joy or woe,
But, turning, trembles too."

GREVILLE.

Some weeks passed before Laurette heard from Enrîco, and being alarmed at this delay, she became anxious and dispirited; sometimes fearing that the warmth of his disposition had led him into some dangerous enterprize, and at others, that he was ill, or had met with some unexpected obstacle in his pursuit. She was at last, however, relieved from this painful suspense by a letter bearing his signature, which contained no other unpleasant intelligence than that he had been at present unsuccessful in his enquiries, though he was not yet without hopes of obtaining the welcome information; and concluded with desiring that she would write to him immediately, and relate every thing that had happened.

She had stepped into an anti-chamber to read the epistle, and was deeply engaged in the perusal of it, when the trampling of hoofs drew her attention towards the window, and she perceived in the gloom of the evening, for it was nearly dark, two men on horseback advancing towards the gate. In one of them she imagined she recognized the person of Paoli; but the dim grey of the twilight prevented her from being certain that she was right in her conjecture, till she heard him call loudly for Ambrose, and then saw him alight from his horse, and, attended by a stranger, whom she believed to be one of the inferior servants belonging to the Castello St. Aubin, cross the second court, and enter the private door, where she had gained admittance on her arrival.

The return of Paoli, thus suddenly and unexpectedly, to the castle, indicated, she supposed, the approach of his Lord; and willing to be assured of the truth of the conjecture, she gained the top of the stairs, meaning to descend and inform herself of the whole, when an universal trembling seized her, and being unable to proceed, she leaned upon the spiral balustrade, in that state of breathless suspense which frequently precedes some new and much-dreaded event. Soon afterwards she heard a passing footstep in the hall, and saw through the iron rails, over which she bent, the Signora ascending the foot of the stairs. Knowing that she would afford her the gratification she desired, Laurette returned to the room she had quitted, and seating herself on a small settee by the fire, endeavoured to prepare herself for what might happen.

The looks of the Signora as she entered, announced some hasty intelligence, and before Laurette had power to request to be made acquainted with the nature of it, she was told that the Marchese was already within a day's journey of the castle, and meant to reach it on the following day; that he had sent his steward and one of the inferior servants to apprize them of his intention, that all things might be in readiness for his reception, and was proceeding on his way with all imaginable speed.

Though this was little more than Laurette expected, the moment she was assured it was Paoli, the certainty that the Marchese was really upon the road, and already so near the end of his journey, almost overcame her; and she turned suddenly so pale, that the Signora was compelled to throw open the case-ment, and to lead her towards the window. In a few minutes she revived; and after thanking her amiable companion for her attention, consented to walk into the air.

Leaning upon the arm of her friend, she descended slowly the marble stair-case, and crossing the hall, stood for a few minutes at the portico, surveying the placid face of the heavens, illuminated with innumerable stars, and then proceeded along the court. When she had passed through the great gate, she turned a fearful and enquiring eye amid the trees of the avenues, expecting every moment to see the white robes of the Monk glaring among the dark branches of the fir or the mountain-ash, and fancying she heard the deep tones of his voice in the hol-low murmurs of the wind, amid the faded and almost leafless woods.

A small repast was prepared for them on their return, of

which Laurette scarcely partook, and soon afterwards retired to her bed. The night was spent in broken and uneasy slumbers, the intervals of repose were short and disturbed, and the visions of her sleep were confused and terrible. Unrefreshed by this transient respite from real calamity, and unable to gain any comfortable repose, she arose by the dim light of early morning, and amused herself for some hours in her apartment, with reading that fine, melting, and descriptive kind of poetry, for which the bards of Italy are so highly and justly celebrated.

A summons for breakfast broke in upon her solitude, and descending into the breakfast-room, she was received by the Signora with more than her accustomed tenderness, who mingled the most refined compassion with her solicitude; and after a short consolatory address, which was delivered with the most attractive gentleness, besought her to rely upon her friendship, which she might rest assured would never be withdrawn from her, but should be ever exerted most sedulously for her security and happiness.

Laurette could only answer with her tears, for her heart was too full for utterance, and her gratitude far beyond the powers of expression.

The day was passed, as usual, in a variety of simple occupations, but with less tranquillity than many of the preceding ones; and towards the close of it, our heroine being in hourly expectation of the arrival of the Marchese, repaired to an anti-chamber adjoining the Signora's apartment, where she frequently passed many hours in the morning, in reading, drawing, embroidery, or other works of taste and fancy.

As she was amusing herself in the arrangement of some books that were placed in a recess in the wall, she discovered, amongst the rest, a manuscript volume bound in black, the property of the Signora, containing a number of Poems written by herself, chiefly of the elegiac kind, from which she selected the two following little pieces of poetry, apparently composed by the Signora in her affliction, after the loss of Lorenzo d'Orso and her infant son.

TO DEATH.

Hail, awful Power, no human heart denies,
Who com'st unsought for, and when ask'd, denies;
Thou, who did'st give this bosom ceaseless woe,
Repress the tears which thou hast taught to flow.
Was't not enough, with direful hand, to wrest
A beauteous infant from a mother's breast;
But must a husband, and a father, feel
Thy arm, relentless as the murderer's steel?
When first, Oh Tyrant! thy sad work began,
How thro' my veins the thrilling horror ran;
Awhile entranc'd in speechless grief I lay,
This heart forgot to beat, each pulse to play,
Till ling'ring, near her home, the vital flame
Faintly revisited her mortal frame;
These eyes, reluctant, met the op'ning light,
And long'd for slumbers of eternal night.
Oh! thou, at once the foe and friend of man,
In pity finish what thy rage began.
Oh! come, I hail thee now a welcome guest,
And with thee bring that long-sought stranger, Rest.
I ask no strains of elegiac woe,
No pensive tear on my cold urn to flow;
But young Delight shall clap his cherub wing,
And soft-ey'd virgins Hymeneals sing,
With freshest flowers shall strew the gladsome way,
And choral music melt on every spray;
Their vestal hands my hallow'd tomb prepare,
Whilst sounds celestial float upon the air.
When loosen'd from her mean companion, clay,
The soul, exulting, wings her heavenly way;
Quicker than thought, through constellations flies,
Leaves the gross air, and anchors in the skies.

Ah! come, Lorenzo, from thy bright abode,
Smooth the rude path, and lead me to my God!
Descend in all thy blaze of heavenly charms,
New woo me now to thy celestial arms;
Prepare thy roseate seats, seraphic bowers,
Nectarious sweets, and never fading flowers.

Fancy presents thy beauteous image now,
The amaranthus blooming on thy brow,
Whose varied tints surpass the Tyrian hues,
Sweeter than perfume of Arabian dews.
When the bright God of Day retires to rest,
And softly sinks on Ocean's silver breast;
When hush'd in night the stormy winds are laid,
And gentle moon-beams tremble through the shade;
If yet thy Emma claims thy guardian care,
In slumbers soft, etherial whispers bear;
Hush the rude tumults of each rising sigh,
And wrap my soul in visionary joy.

SONNET.

Ah! why, sweet Philomel, that plaintive song,
    Why dost thou shun the day star's glitt'ring light,
To mourn, unseen, the woodland glades among,
    And tune thy vesper to the Queen of night?

Art thou too widow'd? has relentless Fate,
    From thy fond breast, thy sweet companion tore?
Does faithful Memory every charm relate,
    And tell of raptures thou must know no more?

If such thy woes, sweet bird, ah! yet again
Pour through the shades of Eve the liquid strain;
Still dwell like me, on long-regretted hours,
    Till Morn, bright sparkling through the murky gloom,
Sheds on the zephyrs' wing her wild perfume,
    And wakes, to light and life, the op'ning flowers.

The distant rolling of a carriage at last announced the approach of the Marchese; and, in a state of mind that partook of
terror, Laurette advanced towards the lattice, and in the same
moment beheld a splendid chariot stop suddenly at the gate, and
soon afterwards the Marchese alight. The dusk of the evening,
for it was past twilight, prevented her from distinguishing his
figure, any otherwise than that he was tall, and appeared stately.
    He did not address any of the domestics that were crowded

about to receive him, except Paoli, and then walked silently through the courts.

She now waited impatiently for the Signora, anxiously listening to every approaching footstep till near an hour had elapsed, when she ventured into the corridor to listen if she could hear her voice.

An universal stillness seemed to prevail through the castle, except in that part of it which was inhabited by the servants, from which a loud and coarse laugh occasionally proceeded. At last the long-expected step was heard ascending the spiral stair-case, and Laurette, overjoyed to be released from this state of inquietude, sprang forwards to meet her beloved friend, and to ask if any enquiries had been made relative to herself.

"My Lord," returned the Signora, "being fatigued and indisposed, means to retire early to his room. He has mentioned you, but has not intimated a desire of being introduced to you this evening; you may therefore compose yourself, my dear friend, and be assured you have nothing to fear. In the morning I shall be enabled to give you some further information upon the subject, and in the mean time I request you will endeavour to fortify your mind, and not allow yourself to yield to imaginary distresses."

The Signora was in fact unacquainted with the principal cause of her uneasiness, and consequently was not capable of forming a judgment upon the matter; but her valuable advice was not lost upon Laurette, who always endeavoured to profit by the virtuous precepts and examples of others, which she always received with gratitude, and beheld with admiration.

Thankful for this temporary release, and re-assured by the words of the Signora, the night passed with less agitation than the preceding one; and having yielded to the sweet influence of undisturbed repose, she awoke more refreshed and tranquillized than before, and after offering up her meek and plaintive devotions, waited patiently for the Signora, who promised to visit her in the morning, and to breakfast with her at the accustomed hour.

She entered at the appointed time, and observed, with pleasure, that Laurette appeared less dejected than when she saw her last; and that she was able to converse with ease, though not with vivacity, upon indifferent subjects.

A summons for the casiera to attend upon the Marchese in the saloon, put an end to all farther discourse; and Laurette requesting that she would return to her as soon as she was again at leisure, remained in her room, occasionally amusing herself with reading, drawing, or in taking a survey of the rich and glowing landscape from one of the balconies.

The Signora found the Marchese busily employed in looking over some papers, which had been delivered to him by his steward, which he laid aside as soon as she entered, and politely offered her a chair. After some general conversation, concerning the furniture and recent improvements at the castle, he asked carelessly about Laurette, if she seemed satisfied with her new situation, or lamented being removed from the Castle of Elfinbach; and then, without waiting for an answer, reverted to the former subject, and enquired how she had disposed of the paintings and other ornamental effects; and then proposed taking a view of the whole range of apartments, that he might give some directions concerning them.

The greater part of the day was passed by the Signora in attending upon her Lord, who was apparently highly gratified with her judgment and taste; though she seized every interval of leisure, and dedicated it to the society of her lovely friend, who now determined to confine herself to her chamber, till the Marchese should intimate a desire to see her; secretly wishing that moment might never arrive, which had been so long anticipated with terror. Thus devoted to solitude and silence, she employed her time in writing to Enrico, frequently destroying what she had written, lest it should increase his uneasiness; and then beginning other letters, and throwing them aside, because as little to her satisfaction as the former ones.

Towards the evening she entered again into the balcony, and saw, at the farthest extent of the terrace, the Marchese in conversation with Paoli. They were a considerable distance from her apartment, but being unwilling to be seen by them, she retired; and closing the casement, stood for some minutes leaning pensively over the back of a chair, which was placed directly under the windows, contemplating the fine features of nature, and the beautiful variety of objects it commanded, till she saw them descend from the terrace, (which, after extending the whole length of the edifice, wound round the western turret, and then terminated in a gentle slope); then ascending a winding path, hewn in the rock below, which was shaded from her view by thick groves of fir, acacia, and pomegranate, they glided into obscurity.

The Marchese, from this transient survey, seemed to be listening to the discourse of his steward with much deference and attention, whilst Paoli talked much; though, from distance, she could only distinguish a faint murmur, which was accompanied with much eagerness of gesticulation.

As soon as they were gone, she retired from the window, and, stirring up the almost decayed embers, sat down by the fire, and endeavoured to finish her epistle; but it was nearly dark, and being compelled to defer it for the present, she resolved to conclude it on the following day.

In about an hour the Signora returned to her room, with a message from the Marchese, who desired to see her immediately, as he was waiting to receive her in one of the lower apartments.

Knowing the necessity of obeying him, and having been in continual expectation of a similar address, she summoned all her spirits to her aid, and prepared to comply with the command.

They found him in one of the saloons, lounging carelessly upon a sofa, with a book in his hand, which he appeared to be reading so attentively that he either did not, or affected not, instantly to observe them. The Signora's voice, however, roused him from his abstraction, and fixing his eyes upon Laurette, with a look expressive of surprise, he arose involuntarily as they advanced, and led her to a seat. A silence of some moments ensued, which none seemed disposed to interrupt, proceeding rather from embarrassment than any other cause, till the Marchese, with many symptoms of confusion, began to make an enquiry concerning the old castle she had quitted; at the same time avoiding making any mention of Madame Chamont, and then suddenly changing the discourse, as if fearful it might lead to a subject that would be entered upon with reluctance.

If he was charmed with the beautiful form of Laurette, which, though pale with apprehension and terror, was infinitely more charming than any thing his imagination could have portrayed, he was not less so with her manners; and the silent admiration with which he regarded her, though it tended to heighten her distress, increased the natural loveliness of her person.

Susceptible even to weakness, the mind of the Marchese became entirely absorbed in the contemplation of so much delicacy and sweetness, which no recent hint had prepared him to expect; and as he continued to observe her with an earnestness that evinced the power of her attractions, he soon became insensible to every other object.

Anxious to put an end to an interview, rendered painful by embarrassment, Laurette arose soon afterwards, and would have withdrawn; but this the Marchese so ardently opposed, that she was compelled to relinquish the design, and to return, though reluctantly, to her seat. There was something in her appearance and demeanour so different from what his imagination had suggested, that he continued to gaze upon her with augmenting surprise. But what was his astonishment when that timid reserve, that retiring delicacy, which had hitherto veiled many natural perfections, being now in some degree conquered, she discovered what had only been transiently obscured, a highly cultivated and accomplished mind, whose strength, softness, and elegance gave power and energy to beauty. How much unlike the poor, unpatronized, neglected orphan, which his fancy had delineated; nurtured in solitude, and consigned early to grief and misfortune, with a mind unstored with virtuous principles, and features marked with no other expression than that of dissatisfaction and regret, perhaps with rustic coarseness and vulgarity.

Nor was the interesting person of the Signora d'Orso, or the polished ease of her manners, unobserved or beheld with indifference, so little expected in the humble capacity in which she had engaged; and, as conversation awakened the powers of her mind, her superiority over the greater part of her sex was so striking, that he resolved almost instantaneously to make a companion of her, as well as of Laurette, whom he now began to reflect upon with increasing partiality.

When the supper hour drew near, the casiera, not forgetting the humility of her station, arose to depart; but the Marchese prevented her design, by desiring that she would continue with him the evening, which request he concluded by ordering a repast to be immediately prepared in an adjoining room.

This was a proposal which contained too flattering a proof of her Lord's esteem and condescension to be received without pleasure; and had she been disposed to have rejected it, the expressive look conveyed by her lovely young friend, would have counteracted the intention. Being again seated, she joined in the conversation, which now became general, with more than her accustomed vivacity; and Laurette, though somewhat chagrined at not being permitted to retire when she ventured to make the attempt, being considerably re-assured by the Signora's continuance in the party, insensibly lost much of her reserve, and though her lovely countenance retained the same pensiveness of expression, it was occasionally enlivened with smiles, and lighted up with intelligence.

As an Italian and a woman of birth, the Signora was acquainted with several families of consequence in Italy, which were personally known to the Marchese. This circumstance led to much unreserved communication, and the frankness and ease with which she delivered her sentiments, entirely divested of that servile kind of fear which frequently accompanies conscious inferiority, so exalted her in his estimation, that his behaviour was at once attentive and respectful.

After having partaken of a slight but elegant repast, with the addition of some dried Italian fruits, by way of dessert, the ladies were allowed to retire, but not without first promising to breakfast with the Marchese on the following day.

As soon as they had quitted the room, the Signora could not forbear speaking of her Lord in the highest and most respectful terms, and awaited impatiently Laurette's opinion upon the subject, who confessed he was more agreeable and condescending than she expected to have found him; but it was easy to discover that her former prejudices were not entirely removed, and, though she acquiesced in the sentiments of her friend, her apprehensions relative to his future conduct were not dissipated.

CHAP. VII.

"In each wild song that wakes the vale around,
    My fair one's fascinating voice I hear,
And Fancy bids the soft lute's silver sound,
    Waft her mild accents to my ravish'd ear.

"Deep grav'n by Love, thy image ne'er shall fade,
    While Memory in this breast maintains her seat;
And when for thee it beats not, lovely maid,
    Each trembling pulse of life shall cease to beat."

                                        SALMAGUNDI.

In the morning the ladies met in the breakfast parlour somewhat
later than the accustomed hour, and were soon afterwards joined
by the Marchese.

He was more animated than on the preceding day, discoursed
with ease and elegance upon every subject that was introduced,
and directed his attentions so peculiarly to Laurette, that her
confusion and distress were evident.

Before she had been introduced to him, her imagination had
suggested that he was much older, and that he possessed more
gravity, and dignity of deportment. She was therefore not a little
surprised when she beheld a tall, graceful figure, of an insinuating and fashionable address, apparently not more than forty;
for the spirit and vivacity of his countenance, when actuated
by gaiety and good humour, counteracted the effects of time,
and his whole behaviour, when solicitous to please, assisted in
carrying on the deception. To the Signora he was polite and
attentive; but when he addressed Laurette, there was an air of
tenderness in his manners which he did not attempt to disguise,
and which it was impossible not to understand.

The apprehensions that Enrîco had suggested were now
communicated to her own heart; the temporary vivacity that
had enlivened her features soon vanished, and was succeeded
by a kind of thoughtful and tender dejection, which, so far from

detracting from the natural graces of her person, bestowed an additional delicacy and softness.

The Marchese, who watched every change of expression with undeviating assiduity, imputed this pensive cast of character to perpetual retirement, and dwelt with energy upon the advantages arising from an unrestrained intercourse with the world. This sentiment was warmly applauded by the Signora, who, by enlarging upon the subject, endeavoured to place her favourite persuasion in the most favourable light; for if she had a weakness, it was certainly that of possessing too great an attachment to the fashionable elegances of life, which had lost nothing of value, but had rather gained additional importance in her estimation, from having been long withheld from her. It was this growing and seductive passion, so early implanted in her nature, aided by that love of liberty so natural to the human mind, that occasioned an invincible aversion to a conventual life, and which taught her to submit her duty to her inclination, by accepting the protection of a husband, without the knowledge or acquiescence of her only surviving parent; which conduct nothing but his unjustifiable severity could have excused.

The day passed without any material occurrence; the attentions of the Marchese rather augmented than decreased, and he attempted, but not always with success, to detach Laurette from her friend, that he might more effectually insinuate himself into her favour and confidence. But the melancholy he thus strove to dissipate, was by these measures increased. She received his assiduities with coldness, and sometimes with terror, which it was impossible to conceal or subdue; and the animated emotion of displeasure with which she repressed the familiarity of his advances, when respectful attention yielded to the ardour of ungovernable passion, wounded and offended his pride.

But he was too well initiated in the arts of intrigue to suffer himself to give words to his resentment; and, as he attributed this uniform reserve to the cause of offended delicacy, since it appeared not to be merely the effect of solitude and inexperience, he resolved, if no possibility existed of contaminating the angelic purity of her mind, since she was not only the most beautiful, but the most interesting object he had ever beheld, finally to offer her his hand. The rank to which she would be elevated by so splendid an alliance, he imagined, could not fail to attract and dazzle so young and charming a creature; who, if in the slightest degree conscious of the perfections she possessed, would doubtless be anxious to place them in a situation where they would meet with deserved admiration, and not continue, if an opportunity offered of placing herself eligibly in the world, to shroud herself in silence and obscurity.

On the death of the Marchesa he had indeed hastily, and too rashly determined not to submit to what he termed the shackles of matrimony; but other reasons, besides the extreme beauty and innocence of Laurette, now influenced his conduct—reasons which he reluctantly avowed even to himself; they were however sufficient to unfix his wavering resolution; and the more he reflected upon this newly-concerted plan, the more fascinating it appeared.

He still ventured to believe, that a considerable portion of flattery, judiciously administered, might prove efficacious, as few minds, if feminine, could resist its power. And as sophistry was not likely to be detected by so young and inexperienced a girl, unremitting attention to her desires, assisted by the most lavish praises he was empowered to bestow, would eventually triumph over that retiring diffidence of deportment, that guarded delicacy of conduct, which was so strikingly featured in her character.

But, however sanguine his expectation, the artful means he employed for the accomplishment of his purpose, not only retarded, but prevented the success of the enterprize. What had been darkly and mysteriously hinted, recurred frequently to her thoughts; and the image of Enrîco, noble, respectful, and tender, being presented with all its interesting accompaniments to her mind, rendered the solicitude of the Marchese still more unpleasant and disgusting.

She remembered, with satisfaction, the promise she had given him previous to his leaving the castle; and was determined, if her new lover deviated in the smallest degree from the nice rule of propriety, to accept of his protection. Nothing, indeed, could prevail upon her to alter her resolution respecting a marriage with Enrîco, before he was enabled to provide for her without involving him in new difficulties; for though she could have been satisfied with a very slender provision, if shared with the object of her affections, yet her apprehensions of entering into life with embarrassments, which might finally lead to sorrow and repentance, when the romantic enthusiasm, peculiar to youth and inexperience, subsided, repressed every yielding principle of her nature; and she thought only of consigning herself, with his assistance, since she had so little to expect from the exertions of the Marchese in his favour, to a convent, or some other temporary place of security, till she could fix upon some more eligible abode, or till the bars which prevented their union were removed.

The letter, which had been conveyed to Enrîco, did not remain long unanswered, and she was agreeably surprised on receiving one much sooner than she imagined it possible. This was delivered to her by the Signora when she was alone in her apartment, and with mingled joy and curiosity she perused the contents.

He informed her, in the first place, of his own situation, and want of success in his undertaking; and then of the necessity of his quitting Germany, at least for a short time, at the desire of the Marchese de Martilini, his Colonel, who was prevented by indisposition from remaining with his regiment, and was then resident at his seat near Mantua. He had reason to fear, he added, from some recent accounts, that his disorder was of a severe and dangerous nature; and, from its frequent attacks, had so injured and debilitated his constitution, that but little was to be expected from medicinal applications.

An epistle, penned by an unknown hand, had acquainted him with some circumstances which made his attendance necessary, particularly that of the strong desire which his Colonel had expressed to see him, and his many anxious enquiries respecting his future destination.

He likewise informed her, that since his departure from the Castle of Luenburg, a cessation of hostilities had actually commenced; and that, in consequence of this measure, a speedy termination of the war was universally expected, which would probably precipitate his return, and prevent the indispensability of his future absences.

He then reverted to the subject of her last epistle, expressing his astonishment at the intelligence conveyed, which was that the Marchese de Montferrat, contrary to his original intention, meant to reside during the winter in Germany.

But this was a topic too productive of uneasiness to be dwelt upon; and that part of the paper which contained it was written over with so disorderly a hand, that the characters which attempted to convey those undescribable sensations of tenderness that pained and agitated his breast, were scarcely legible.

Then desiring that, should any thing happen to render her present situation unpleasant, she would recollect her former promise of accepting his protection, whatever distance might divide them, he gently withdrew her from the immediate cause of their mutual uneasiness, by reverting with tender concern to those blissful moments of juvenile felicity, which once made existence happiness.

"How often, Laurette," he continued, "is your image presented to me in the visions of my fancy! How often, since I have been wandering in unsuccessful pursuits, have I dismissed Anselmo, that I might indulge my melancholy in secret, and fastening my horse to the sapless branches of an oak, have rambled about in the still and silent hour of evening, endeavouring to recal the exact expression of your countenance, to recollect the tones of your voice, and every word you have uttered, in those charming moments of unrestrained and mutual confidence which we have enjoyed together. Sometimes I seat myself under the spreading branches of a larch or a sycamore, and gaze upon the mild splendour of the setting sun, sinking gradually from my view beneath the faded and half-foliated woods, in the sweet hope that the same object is engaging your attention, and that I meet you in idea.

"In the course of my enquiries," continued Enrîco, "I was imperceptibly led into the neighbourhood of your former residence, I may also add of my own, in the days of childhood. Finding I was within a league of the castle, an irresistible inclination directed me to the place; and dismissing my servant on some trifling pretence, I indulged the pensiveness of my feelings, by wandering through those now desolated shades, where we have once held unrestrained communication.

"To gain admittance into the interior of the edifice was denied me; but with a melancholy pleasure I was enabled, through the high gothic casements of the lower apartments, to discover dimly in the gloom the scenes of our earliest happiness.—The furniture, every thing remained the same, and methought I saw you indistinctly through my tears, seated in one of the recesses in the saloon, where we have so often sat, marking the fine tints of the sky, when the last ray of the retiring orb had empurpled the sublime summits of the mountains, and the blue mist of the twilight was overspreading the plains. Do you not remember how often, in that mild and placid hour, we have rambled over the dewy hills, marking the winding course of the river stealing slowly along in the most romantic directions, or listening to the sighing of the wind amongst the trees? Do you not remember, but is it possible you can forget, how frequently we have lingered under your favourite tree, till only the tinkling of a sheep-bell, or the mellow tones of a flute were heard faintly from the margin of the river or the plaintive orisons of the nightingale were warbled sadly from the woods?

"Oh Laurette! the melting recollection of those moments overwhelms me;—I sought out this spot, so tenderly endeared to me by the grateful memorials of the past, and throwing myself on the rudely carved bench, which was formerly so familiar to me, sat lost in pensive reverie. Your image again presented itself to my fancy; I saw you in that white robe which you usually wore, without any other ornament than a knot of wild flowers, gathered from the interstices of the mountains; a lute was in your hand, you bent over it, with one of those smiles which are at once so seductive and fascinating, and as the rising breeze wafted aside your locks, a blush ripened on your cheek. How strong, how chimerical is the imagination of a lover! methought you touched a chord of the instrument, which was answered faintly by an echo. The sound communicated to my soul—I started from my seat—but the angelic vision was no more; it came only for a moment to console me, and then vanished from my sight.

"I know you will condemn these wild and romantic effusions of a disordered mind; but you do not know what tender and interesting reflections your idea imparts to it; I would not part with it to be occasionally less wretched, because I should then lose all that can make life desirable."

In another part of his letter he adds, "I am resolved to see you before I visit Italy, whatever danger it may expose me to; I will encounter the coldness, perhaps the displeasure of the Marchese, for I find it impossible to quit Germany without one consoling glance. In a few days after the receipt of this I may probably be with you; do not mention my intention to any one; I wish it was possible to see only yourself, for the necessity of my speedy arrival in Italy will prevent my being stationary. I would desire to see you alone, and without the knowledge of the Marchese, if I was not in danger of hazarding your displeasure. You will not, I fear, adopt this mode of conduct, however requisite, because it discovers a want of openness.

"But why, Laurette, will you forget that I am your brother? Why would you deprive me of the sacred power of protecting you, the primary wish of my soul; of defending you from future injuries, or of redressing them if committed?"

Towards the conclusion of the letter he gave her an account of the convents he had visited, and of the unsatisfactory intelligence he had received; and then finished with a request, that she would indulge him, if possible, with a private interview, since, contrary to his original design, he was resolved to see her immediately.

Laurette perused the former part of this epistle with a painful interest, and a ray of consolation was communicated to her bosom when she arrived at that part of it which treated of his intended visit. But the interview, for which he pleaded so forcibly, she feared could not be easily obtained; as the Marchese seldom left her even for a moment, and consequently that retirement, which had been long familiar and dear to her, could only be enjoyed in the solitude of her own apartment.

Laurette was roused from these reflections by the ringing of the dinner-bell, and before she had descended the stairs, the Marchese, who thought every moment of her absence an age while she had been engaged in the perusal of the letter, came forwards to conduct her into the room which was appropriated for that purpose.

The empassioned glances which he cast upon her, as he advanced forwards to lead her into the room, covered her with confusion; and as he took her hand, on their way through the hall, it trembled so excessively, that the animated expression of his countenance suddenly changed, and surprise, mingled with displeasure, succeeded.

He would have demanded the cause of this alarm, but to avoid interrogatories she hurried into the apartment, and seating herself by the side of the Signora, endeavoured to conceal her chagrin by an ill-assumed appearance of composure.

During the dinner hour, the Marchese, contrary to his custom, remained totally silent, and seemed unusually thoughtful. As soon as the cloth was withdrawn, without offering any thing of an apology, he arose from the table, and traversed the room with a gloomy and disordered air, regardless of the Signora and even of Laurette, though the conversation of both was more than once directed to himself.

The repulsive coldness which was so evident in the deportment of the beautiful orphan, in spite of all his insinuating efforts to secure her affections, at once wounded his feelings, and exasperated his pride.—What he formerly imagined proceeded merely from native timidity, and that chilling reserve, which usually accompanies rigid delicacy of sentiment on the first advances of freedom, he now attributed to a different cause.

Paoli having been informed of Enrîco's visit at the castle, did not fail to communicate this intelligence to his Lord, who received it with no sensation of pleasure. From what had been related to the steward, he appeared to have been a favoured lover; and his person and manners being spoken of in the most flattering terms, assisted in justifying the surmise.

As Paoli did not conceal the smallest circumstance from the Marchese relative to Enrîco, he soon succeeded in his intention of inspiring him with jealousy and aversion towards the amiable young Chevalier, which now added keenness to the various and conflicting passions that agitated his breast.

Had his rival been any other than his own son, he would probably have meditated some dreadful revenge; but the ties of blood, however feebly cemented by the bonds of affection, prevented him from exercising any actual cruelty, though it tended not to mitigate his resentment, but rather added warmth to the violence of his unrestrained passions. He had before determined to disown and abandon him, notwithstanding his former promises were delivered with a degree of solemnity which would have awed a mind less strong and energetic than his own.

At an earlier period of existence, could he have allowed himself time for reflection, he might possibly have shrunk from this act of undeserved barbarity with the abhorrence it merited; but he was now grown too familiar with vice to be shocked at, or even to detect its natural deformity; and his love of virtue, of which it was evident he possessed no larger a portion than what is inseparable from, and inherent in, our natures, was so weakened by a long course of debauchery and immorality, so secretly practised as to deceive superficial observers; who, allured by his apparent generosity and public benevolence of conduct, easily gave him credit for the reality of every perfection which he found it necessary to assume; and being thus satisfied with the outward semblance of goodness, he wanted not only resolution, but inclination, to become virtuous.

Though the Marchese did not relax from his resolve respecting Laurette, he discovered that it was requisite to adopt some new plan for the accomplishment of his design; he easily perceived that she regarded him with the most stoical indifference, which she now did not attempt to disguise;—he was also conscious, that the spark of gratitude which had once faintly beamed from her countenance was extinguished; and, instead of appearing flattered by his attentions, she carefully avoided giving him any opportunity of bestowing them.

CHAP. VIII.

—————"Some strange commotion
Is in his brain, he bites his lip, and starts;
Stops on a sudden, looks upon the ground,
Then lays his finger on his temple; straight
Springs out into fast gait, then stops again,
Strikes his breast hard, and anon he casts
His eye against the moon: in most strange postures
We've seen him set himself."

SHAKESPEARE.

The Signora, who observed this almost immediate change in the deportment of the Marchese, attributed it to the right cause. She perceived, on his first interview with Laurette, the commencement of his passion and saw, with extreme concern, the visible coldness of her manners, and the air of unusual dejection which was delineated on her countenance, when his assiduous attentions were more particularly directed to her.

It was easy to discover, even on a superficial acquaintance, that the passions of the Marchese were strong and invincible; and though the Signora was totally unacquainted with his excesses, and was equally a stranger to the insatiable cruelty of disposition he had formerly displayed when any one dared to oppose him in his interests or his pleasures, she had sufficiently penetrated into his character to be aware of the danger of irritating his pride, and ventured gently to remonstrate with her friend upon the subject.

She suspected the attachment which had so long tenderly subsisted between our heroine and the handsome young Chevalier, even before she was personally known to him, though the native delicacy of Laurette's sentiments and feelings prevented her from openly avowing any extraordinary prepossession in his favour. Yet as she no longer retained, in any eminent degree, that enchanting frankness of expression which once gave new charms to her conversation and demeanour when in the presence of the

Marchese, whose attentions could not be misunderstood, what before was only conjecture, now ripened into conviction.

The solicitude that the Signora discovered for the welfare and happiness of her lovely favourite, was received with the most attractive gentleness, and repayed with almost filial affection. But when she reverted to the Marchese, dwelling upon the ardour of his passion, and the unhappy consequence of such a rejection; which, considering his rank, fortune, and accomplishments, could only be occasioned by a premature attachment, a throbbing emotion agitated the bosom of Laurette, and her tears flowed silently and fast. Since she was now wholly in his power, the danger of exasperating his vengeance was too evident to escape her notice, yet she could not, however necessary, submit to the meanness of disguising her sentiments for the sake of future advantage, or to the policy of apparently encouraging hopes, which could not finally be realized.

The Marchese was now less frequently in the society of the ladies than on his first arrival, and even in their presence, the deep musings of his mind so entirely abstracted him from conversation, and threw at times such a deep gloom over his features, that Laurette could not observe him without a sensation of awe, mingled with terror. He was frequently closeted with his steward for many hours in the day; and when he returned into the saloon, his dark piercing eyes assumed a ferocious and dreadful appearance, so different from their former expression, that no one presumed to address him, except Paoli, who possessed over his Lord an unlimited power; and, by constant and unremitting perseverance, was enabled to prosecute his purposes with all imaginable ease and success.

The aspect of the Marchese now indicated the most restless inquietude; he often started wildly from his seat, without any apparent cause, answered widely from the subject if a question was directed to him, which was never unnecessarily the case, and threw his eyes strangely around the room, like a man newly awakened from a dream, as if his whole soul was absorbed in some desperate and important enterprize, which he was alarmed lest any one should penetrate.

It was after one of these secret interviews with the steward,

that the Marchese informed the Signora of his intention of
visiting the old castle on the Rhine; having some thoughts of
rendering it habitable, that he might occasionally retire to it
as a summer residence: at the same time requesting, that she
would prepare to accompany him thither on the succeeding day,
as he wished to have her opinion and assistance respecting the
alterations.

He slightly asked Laurette if she would consent to be of the
party; and, on her modestly declining it, left the room to give
some farther orders to Paoli, without repeating the invitation.

Having betrayed no symptoms of anger or resentment, the
expected consequence of her refusal, a ray of comfort was conveyed to the bosom of Laurette; since she had been for some days
in hourly expectation of Enrîco, and had now an opportunity of
seeing him alone without the knowledge of the Marchese.

To remain at the castle during his absence was a privilege
so unhoped for, that she could with difficulty conceal her satisfaction. But how must she inform Enrîco of her new cause of
apprehension, without augmenting his distress? though to avoid
entering upon a subject, in which he was so nearly interested,
would be utterly impossible, since he would assuredly introduce
it, and reluctance on her part would naturally kindle curiosity
and lead to conjecture.

When the morning arrived, the family assembled early in the
breakfast room, and, as soon as they had partaken of the usual
repast, the carriage being in readiness, the Marchese informed
Laurette that they meant to return at the expiration of a week,
and seating himself by the side of the Signora, drove from the
gate.

As soon as the chariot was out of sight, though she had
reason to lament the absence of her friend, the beautiful orphan
felt as if released from a long and mournful captivity; joy once
more played about her heart, and forgetting for the moment the
presaging aspect of the future, she yielded to the new and sweet
emotion.

The only unpleasant circumstance with which this indulgence
was attended, arose from the presence of Paoli, who, contrary to
her expectation, received no orders to attend his Lord; but as he

did not often obtrude himself into her company, she reflected upon it with less uneasiness, and, being alone, began to form some plan as to her future conduct.

It was now the beginning of November, and the winds blowing chill and bleak from the mountains, prevented her from frequenting her favourite solitary walks; she sometimes, indeed, strolled along the lawn, or through the thick shades of the shrubberies; but the cold and drizzly rains, and the thick mists that pervaded the atmosphere, made her fearful of continuing her rambles. When the weather did not permit her to extend them, she observed, not without some astonishment, that she was followed at an inconsiderable distance by Paoli, who seemed to watch her movements whenever she advanced along the grounds with the most uniform scrutiny, as if anxious to avail himself of every opportunity of observing them, when she was the least apprehensive of his intention. He never, however, attempted entering into any conversation with her, even when aware of her notice; but this restraint upon her actions, which was evidently the result of design, confined her almost constantly to her apartment.

With somewhat of impatience she now awaited the arrival of Enrîco, and when several days had elapsed, began to reflect upon his absence with grief and disappointment. Something might have happened since he had last written, to have prevented the execution of his design; but his not acquainting her with the occasion of his absence, when he had so expressly declared his resolution of visiting her, was an omission for which she could by no means account.

The week now drew rapidly to a close, yet still he did not appear; and, as she was hourly apprehensive of the return of the Marchese, she began rather to dread, than to desire the performance of his promise.

One evening when it was nearly dark, as she was standing at the window of her apartment, she perceived, at some distance, a tall figure in a white garment, stealing slowly through a copse beyond the boundaries of the castle, as if desirous of concealment.—This she was convinced could be no other than the Monk who had formerly forewarned her of the danger of her situation, and whom she had of late studiously avoided.

As she continued to observe him, he advanced nearer, and entering a small gate, at the extremity of the walls, swept hastily along the grounds till he had reached a thick grove of evergreens which led to the southern side of the building, when he suddenly stopped, and remained stationary.

It now occurred to her mind, that the reason why she was so narrowly watched by Paoli was, that by this means he might be enabled to prevent a future interview with the Monk, which, from some cause, she was incapable of investigating, and which was known only to the Marchese and himself, was thus carefully to be hindered from taking effect.

Curiosity, from a second review of the subject, triumphed for the moment over every other consideration, and she felt an irresistible inclination to descend, and hear him unfold the important secret, which he was before prevented from disclosing.

As she still ruminated upon this singular event, new fortitude was communicated to her mind; and leaving the room with an assumed appearance of calmness, she resolved, if by any means the vigilance of her tormentor could be eluded, who, as it was night, would probably not suspect her of rambling from the castle, to go immediately to the place.

Scarcely had she descended the stairs before her resolution forsook her, and fear and terror took possession of her faculties. The little advantage that might possibly attend such a discovery, and the dangers which might arise from this mode of procedure, in the calmer moments of reflection, compelled her to abandon the design; and she was returning pensively to the apartment she had quitted, without attempting to gratify her curiosity, when the rolling of a carriage announced the arrival of the Marchese.

Paoli ran instantly to the gate to welcome his Lord, whilst Laurette, who experienced a slight degree of surprise and disappointment, remained fixed to the spot.

In a few moments he entered the great hall, attended by his steward, whom he hastily called aside, without apparently observing any other, whilst Laurette waited to receive the Signora at the door of the saloon.

Surprised that she did not appear, she proceeded towards

the portal, and made an enquiry of one of the servants, who informed her, to her unspeakable grief and astonishment, that she was left at the Castle of Elfinbach, and was to remain there till the ensuing week, for the purpose of overlooking the repairs.

The glaring impropriety of her situation now filled the unfortunate Laurette with new terrors; she trembled, lest the Marchese had adopted this plan that he might continue his persecutions successfully, and more than ever distracted with tormenting apprehensions, she entered the saloon, and throwing herself upon a sofa, which was fixed in a recess under a window, burst into an agony of tears.

Having remained there some time, she heard steps in the hall which advanced nearer, and believing it to be the person whom she most dreaded to see, arose hastily, and endeavoured to open the window which descended to the ground that she might effectuate an escape; but the attempt was in vain, and the presence of the Marchese prevented her from retreating by any other means.

He entered with an air of easy confidence, and as Laurette tremblingly advanced forwards to welcome him, he led her courteously to a seat, and then placed himself by her side. A deep blush now took possession of her features; she cast her beautiful eyes upon the ground, and a sigh, that refused to be suppressed, agitated her bosom.

The Marchese, after gazing upon her for some time with a look of earnest tenderness, took her hand, and would have pressed it to his lips, but she withdrew it hastily from his grasp, and a look of displeasure awed him into forbearance.

"By heaven this is too much!" cried the Marchese; "Laurette, you are cruel—you are unjust;—you know I love you; my passion I have never attempted to conceal, though it has been chilled with the most provoking indifference. But, in spite of all your reserve, I cannot believe you mean seriously to reject me; and to convince you that the proposals I mean to make are as honourable as advantageous, I now offer you my hand. Consent then, beautiful Laurette," resumed he, softening his voice, and regarding her with a look of ineffable tenderness, "to become the Marchesa de Montferrat, and to accept of a situation which every other woman would embrace with transport."

Keener agony now suppressed her utterance; her silence encouraged the hopes of the Marchese, who watched every turn of her countenance with the utmost impatience, and taking again the resisting hand she had withdrawn, besought her to determine immediately.

Her answer was at once gentle and decisive: she acknowledged the honour he was solicitous to confer, but conjured him not to distress her by a repetition of his request, which would inevitably be productive of uneasiness, and could never be attended with success.

The firmness of her tone and manner surprised and offended him; the attachment, which he suspected had early subsisted between her and Enrîco, could only account for this conduct. Anger was again kindled in his breast; the submissive tenderness of deportment which he had assumed, vanished, whilst resentment and ungovernable pride struggled for concealment.

He did not, however, yield without reflection to their influence, but with all the eloquence he could command, pleaded forcibly his cause, assiduously endeavouring to remove every obstacle which her imagination could suggest. But to each new argument she replied with the same decisive coldness, without assigning the reasons that actuated her, though he frequently demanded them in a tone of authority and displeasure.

Finding that she was not to be wrought upon by any means that had been hitherto employed, resentment, no longer to be restrained, burst forth with unbridled energy; his breast heaved with contending emotions, which he found it impossible to resist, and a deep indignant glow animated his expressive features.

"You are then determined to reject my suit," resumed the Marchese, rising hastily from his seat, and fixing his eyes upon her's with a keen and penetrating glance.

"You have already received an answer, my Lord," replied Laurette, "and why should I irritate you by repeating it? You have hitherto protected me, and have, from that circumstance, a claim upon my gratitude. I was taught, from the earliest period of my existence, to consider you as my only surviving friend;

and, when personally unknown to you, to honour and revere
you as a parent;—forgive me when I say no other sentiment can
be excited; and permit me also to add, that if you wish for my
esteem, you must instantly desist from farther persecution."

Rage and exasperated pride now deprived him of utterance;
and as he still continued to pace the room with a perturbed and
agitated step, Laurette, willing to take advantage of this silence,
arose and would have retired. But this he resolutely opposed,
and fastening the door to prevent a similar attempt, compelled
her to return to her seat.

New terror now took possession of her mind; but knowing
that resistance would be vain, and remonstrance equally ineffectual, she ventured not to dispute his authority. As he still
continued to traverse the room, apparently musing upon some
new project, an universal trembling seized her, and scarcely
dared she to raise her eyes from the ground, lest they should
meet his dreadful and indignant glances.

A Venetian mirror that was placed on the opposite side of
the saloon, over which was suspended an Etruscan lamp, dimly
reflected his figure, which was altogether more stern and terrible
than her fancy could have formed:—His cloak hung loosely from
his shoulder, his plume waved haughtily over his brow, whilst his
darkened countenance, that expressed all the energies of a soul
refusing to be subdued, was strongly marked with rage, jealousy,
and revenge. In a few minutes he started from his reverie, and
placing himself upon the sofa, again demanded her reasons for
rejecting him.

"You have already heard them, my Lord," replied Laurette,
mildly. "My answer, I think, was sufficiently decisive; and, as
I have no more to add upon the subject, I must request your
permission to retire."

"Presumptuous girl!" interrupted the Marchese, in a voice
half stifled with resentment, "will you still persist in this daring
obstinacy? Do you dispute my power, or is it that you have a
young Chevalier at hand to protect you?"

As he uttered these words, which were accompanied with a
disdainful and sarcastic smile, a faint glow tinged the cheek of
Laurette; the tremulous sensation that was stealing upon her

spirits prevented her from framing an immediate answer; but the integrity of her mind invested her with new fortitude, and as he paused with his eyes fixed upon her innocent and blushing face, as if awaiting her reply, she endeavoured so far to command her feelings as to give it with dignity. When she had regained some portion of her native composure, she attempted to convince him of the impossibility of gaining her affections by this arbitrary conduct, or indeed by any other mode that could be adopted; at the same time requesting him not to compel her to lose all esteem for his character, as she should unwillingly relinquish the favourable impression, and this could only be prevented by a promise on his part never to resume the subject.

"Do you forget," returned the Marchese, emphatically, "your orphan and dependant state? Do you forget that you are without friends, fortune, or connections? that there is not a being existing on whom you have any claim for protection—none who, from any other motive than that of common humanity, would preserve you from the miseries of neglect and poverty? Have I not hitherto defended you from these; and have I not a right to be obeyed?"

"I am not insensible to these obligations," replied Laurette, weeping, "and I would not willingly have any thing happen to cancel them; I would fain consider you as a tender and disinterested friend, still honour you as the guardian of my helpless infancy—but as a lover, my Lord, I must not, indeed I cannot return the affection with which you have honoured me."

"You must not, and you cannot!" repeated the Marchese, with deeper emphasis, whilst jealousy and rage lent all their fury to his countenance: "But your reason for persisting in this refusal is evident; some wretch has pilfered those affections which ought to have been mine; and by heaven he shall not escape my revenge. Laurette, you either accede to my wishes, or you are thrown from my protection, not into the arms of your lover (for I will pursue him with unabating vengeance), but into a situation sufficiently remote to elude his most arduous researches; where, after lingering in obscurity, you will live and die unknown and unlamented. Recollect that I will no longer be trifled with; I have dedicated too much of my time already to the indulgence of your caprice; and from henceforth, if you still continue to practise it, I will assume the tyrant. Hitherto I have meanly descended to supplicate, in hopes of inspiring you with a mutual attachment, but my mind has regained its energy; consider me then no longer as your slave, but remember I expect, nay command your obedience, and that a contrary conduct will be attended with the punishment it merits."

Laurette heard not the latter part of the sentence, for she had fainted; the assurance that Enrîco would be involved in her misfortunes, to whom he certainly alluded, quite overcame her, and she sunk lifeless upon the sofa.

The Marchese, unwilling to call for assistance, made many fruitless attempts to recal her to life; and taking her into his arms, ventured to open the folds of her robe for freer respiration. Whilst he continued to support her, with his arm encircling her waist, anxiously gazing upon her colourless form, and impatiently awaiting the glow of animation which had formerly added such loveliness to her person, the string of brilliants, that was suspended round her neck, attracted his attention; and, not doubting but the portrait of Enrîco was fastened to it, he snatched it hastily from her bosom, and starting, as if he had seen an apparition, let it fall involuntarily from his hand. A faint struggle now indicated returning life, and the Marchese taking immediate advantage of it, demanded how she had obtained the possession of that picture.

"The picture, my Lord," replied Laurette, "what picture?"

"That which was concealed in your bosom," returned the Marchese, sternly, "by whom was it delivered? Speak, I command you, instantly."

"Alas! I know not," sighed Laurette, scarcely knowing what she had uttered; "it is the portrait of my mother."

"The portrait of your mother," repeated the Marchese; "and who informed you that the Contessa della Caro was your mother —who has dared to utter such a falsehood? tell me this instant from whom you have received this intelligence, or expect the severest inflictions that rage and disappointment can suggest?"

The deep and dreadful tones of his voice when ascending the climax of passion, so agitated and alarmed Laurette, that she relapsed into a state of insensibility, and the Marchese having employed many ineffectual means to restore her to life, was compelled to call for assistance.

In this lifeless condition she was conducted to her apartment by one of the women of the castle, and, gradually reviving, retired to her bed. When she was alone, and began to meditate upon the Marchese, dislike arose into abhorrence; and though she felt that she must inevitably suffer, she trembled less for her own fate than for that of Enrîco. If she persisted in refusing the hand of her persecutor, she knew there was nothing to be expected from his clemency. He had threatened to convey her to some remote and dreary solitude, where she was to be left, without pity, to all the horrors of her wayward destiny. To what place did he allude when he assured her, with menaces, that it was beyond the reach of her lover? The astonishment and terror that was delineated on his countenance, on the discovery of the picture, was also food for conjecture. He declared that it was the Contessa della Caro, but denied that it was her mother with a degree of vehemence which tended rather to frighten than convince. Unable to solve this inexplicable mystery, she endeavoured to find comfort in repose; but it was long before she was relieved by slumber from these harassing and tormenting apprehensions.

CHAP. IX.

> ————"Whither should I fly?
> I've done no harm! But I remember now
> I'm in this earthly world, where to do harm
> Is often laudable, to do good, sometimes
> Accounted dangerous folly; why then, alas!
> Do I put up this womanly defence
> To say I've done no harm! what mean
> These faces?"
>
> SHAKESPEARE.

Laurette arose with the first blush of early morning, and not daring to quit the apartment, sat pensively by the side of her bed, meditating upon a train of anticipated evils, which it was impossible either to conquer or dispel. The melancholy sensation which the conversation of the preceding evening had excited, having obtained a transient respite by repose, returned to her waking faculties with severer poignancy, and grief of the most corrosive nature overwhelmed her heart.

Enrîco, suffering for her offences, was incessantly presented to her tortured imagination. She perused his letter again and again, endeavouring, though without success, to inform herself of the occasion of his absence, and still more of his unaccountable silence.

A strange and fatal presage told her they should meet no more; she pressed the paper to her bosom, sighed, and wetted it with her tears, and then breathing a prayer for his preservation, arose from the bed on which she had been sitting, and attempted, in the contemplation of the variegated scenery which was exhibited from her window, to abstract her thoughts from those agonizing reflections that could no longer be endured.

The morning was chill, and the sun shot only a pale and uncertain ray, yet it was peaceful and serene; and as none of the inhabitants of the castle were visible, she descended into the balcony, and gazed upon the tranquil face of the heavens with a devout and tender emotion.

"The season, like her fortunes, had fallen into the sear, the yellow leaf;" yet, though the glow of maturity was past, some remains of vegetation appeared groves of fir, laurel, and other evergreen shrubs, were thinly scattered upon the hills that inclosed the walls of the mansion, whilst the spires of distant convents, seen only from the woods when divested of their honours, added grandeur and beauty to the landscape.

All was serene and gentle; yet tinged with the melancholy that assailed her bosom, all appeared desolate and mournful. With a pensive and dejected air she leaned over the rails of the balcony, endeavouring to find some single object that might fix her attention, and soften the acute pangs of piercing reflection; but the woods, the rocks, and the mountains were too familiar to her eye to have the wished-for effect, and, except the low warblings of the autumnal songsters, no sound, not even the pipe of the goatherd, broke upon the stillness of the morning.

Finding no possibility of soothing herself into a transient forgetfulness of her present sorrows, or of softening the recollection of those hours now fled for ever—hours, in which she had enjoyed happiness as exquisite as pure, she yielded to the softness that oppressed her feelings, sometimes pronouncing the name of Enrico in accents so tremulous that she was scarcely conscious of having uttered it, and at others that of Madame Chamont, the amiable guide of her inexperience, whose ill-starred destiny she still severely, though secretly, lamented.

Resolved not to quit her room without the express orders of the Marchese, she attempted to amuse herself with sketching some of the finest features of the landscape before her; but enervated by affliction, her trembling hand was unable to direct the pencil; she endeavoured to read, but her attention wandered from the subject, and she was finally compelled to resign every former source of gratification, because they had lost their accustomed power.

The picture, which seemed to have led to some fatal discovery, still hung in her bosom. She often drew it from its place, and gazed mournfully upon the sweet expressive face, and having no doubt but it was her mother, and from what had involuntarily escaped the lips of the Marchese, that it was the Contessa della Caro, though he positively denied that it was the portrait of her unknown parent.

But however the practice of guilt and hypocrisy may enable a man to wear the mask of falsehood so successfully as to deceive the greater part of the world, events for which he is totally unprepared, frequently, by their suddenness, may surprise him into confession. The language of nature is indelibly engraven on the human countenance, and however the slave of vice and insincerity may hope to seclude it from the eagle eye of Truth, there are moments when the mask of dissimulation will drop, and the unfortunate being who has taken refuge under so weak a subterfuge, if not totally abandoned to irremediable guilt, will be covered with the blushes of shame and dishonour.

The Marchese, for the moment off his guard by his own inadvertency, betrayed a secret which the wealth of the world could not have wrested from him; for though his selfish love of pleasure was unbounded, and his schemes for the means of obtaining it were deep and unsearchable, reputation was the leading principle of his mind, the soul of his existence, and none but the immediate victims of his cruelty were thoroughly acquainted with his excesses.

When Laurette considered the various inconsistencies of the Marchese's conduct, her candid and inexperienced mind found it difficult to analyze his character: one moment he was solicitous to please, the next haughty and reserved; his countenance now beaming with tenderness, and lighted up by gaiety and animation; the next instant, if not meeting with that attentive regard which he considered as his due, darkened with anger, vexation, and disappointment.

Had no prior attachment removed a marriage with so capricious a tyrant almost beyond the bounds of possibility, she would have instantly rejected him; for her mind was too pure and unambitious to barter the treasures of contentment for wealth or precedence, and to forsake the substance of happiness for the shadow; though she was too prudent to enter into a matrimonial engagement, even to save herself from the present evils of her destiny, till there appeared a probability of effecting it without involving the object of her tenderest attachment in new and severe difficulties.

Laurette had remained the greater part of the day alone in her apartment, without receiving any orders to leave it; in which time no one intruded upon her retirement, except the servant who conveyed her food, of whom she ventured to enquire if the Marchese was below, and whether any thing had been mentioned relative to herself.

The young woman informed her, with many symptoms of compassion, that her Lord had been, for the last half hour, in private conversation with Paoli; that his thoughts seemed to be employed on some important concern, as he scarce partook of a morsel at dinner, and as soon as it was removed, called again for his steward, in whose society he had spent some hours in the morning, and whose presence appeared more than usually necessary.

Conceiving herself to be the subject of their discourse, Laurette answered only with a sigh; and not doubting but that some new misery was preparing for her, endeavoured to arm her mind with a sufficient portion of fortitude to sustain it with serenity.

Next to the hated marriage with which she had been threatened, nothing seemed so dreadful to her terrified imagination as a removal, without the knowledge of Enrîco, to a remote and dreary solitude; yet more than ever convinced, that if she persisted in her resolution of rejecting his proposals, this, or some other situation not less hopeless, would be selected for her, she once half resolved to attempt an escape from the castle, and to endeavour to gain admission into a convent; but the little chance of success which this method of proceeding offered to maturer reflection, prevented her from putting it into practice. Could she be so fortunate as to elude the vigilance of her haughty protector, the Argus-eyed Paoli would detect her design before it was carried into execution; and even was it possible that she should so far succeed as to gain some religious retirement, few Superiors, she feared, were sufficiently disinterested to receive a poor unpatronized female, however unhappy her situation, without a friend to speak in her behalf, or the possession of any property by which she might be enabled to pay for her maintenance. And was she to throw herself upon the compassion of strangers, of an humbler rank of life, who would dare to admit her, and much less to harbour her, when the danger of incurring the displeasure of the Marchese would be the price of their hospitality? And even should any one be so blind to their immediate interests as to listen to the soft pleadings of humanity, could she, wrapped in temporary security, act so inconsistently with her own exalted sentiments, as to expose such benevolence and refined generosity to his unbridled resentment?

These considerations determined her to abandon the design, and to wait with humility for the interposition of Providence in her behalf, in whom, she had been taught early, to place an unlimited reliance.

"Why do I tremble at the future," cried the beautiful sufferer, with that firmness and dignity inseparable from true greatness, "when I know that there is an Omnipotent Power who governs the world with wisdom and equity, and who frequently turns the dark designs of the wicked from their original bias, to the advantage of oppressed and unrepining innocence.

"Forgive me, holy Saint," resumed she, falling meekly upon her knees before a small image of Saint Rosalie, "forgive me if I have dared to murmur; and Oh! infuse into my heart that pure and heavenly virtue which taught thee to endure calamity with patience, and even with transport. Shall I presumptuously repine when I look around, and, in the narrow sphere of my observation, see others suffering the extreme of misery, and expect exemption from the common lot of mortality?—No, let me rather endeavour to fortify my mind with those invaluable principles of religion which were instilled into my heart, from the earliest period of my existence, by my first and dearest friend. And may I, as the only proof of gratitude I am enabled to bestow, cherish her inestimable precepts as much as I revere her memory! and if she is already released from the shackles of mortality, and is become the companion of angels, may she look down with compassion upon her adopted child, strengthen her weak resolves, and lead her, by secret inspiration, to that excelling and unassuming piety which dignified her character!"

With a mind elevated above the narrow boundaries of the earth, Laurette arose from her knees, and walked again towards the lattice. The day was still fine, and her feelings being somewhat tranquillized with these meek effusions of devotion, she surveyed the placid face of Nature with a sensation of pleasure.

Knowing that the Marchese, when in secret conference with his steward, frequently remained some hours in his closet, she resolved to descend, by a private stair-case, and, if she was fortunate enough to escape unobserved, to amuse herself with a ramble through the grounds.

Having executed her purpose unperceived by all, except the lower order of domestics, she bent her steps towards the pavilion, and entering the banqueting-room, seated herself upon a small settee that was placed under a canopy.

Every thing remained the same as when she left it last, which was on the morning when she parted with Enrîco. The Marchese and the Signora had been there in the interval, but nothing appeared to have been displaced. The leaves of music still lay scattered upon the table, the lute lay neglected upon a corner of the sofa, and her imagination could have almost portrayed the form of Enrîco sitting pensively in the place which he had so recently occupied. His looks, his words, his attitudes, returned with all their pathetic interest to her memory, and connected his idea with more than usual tenderness.

Till the moment when she was taught to feel the most dreadful apprehensions for his safety, she was not wholly acquainted with the extent of her attachment; she had deluded herself into the suggestion, that she loved him only with the affection of a sister, as the companion of her infantine felicities, and as the son of her maternal friend. But now that danger was suspended over his head, which threatened finally to crush him, she acknowledged a warmer and more tender sentiment in his favour.

Unable to continue long in a place, rendered too interesting by sadly pleasing recollections, she reached the extent of the building, and found in the apartment, beyond the room of state that she had quitted, a small pocket volume of Italian miscellanies, which she remembered to have seen in the hand of Enrîco on the morning preceding his departure. She opened it with an emotion of joy, and as his name, which was inserted in the blank leaf, met her eye, resolved to avail herself of what she esteemed an inestimable treasure, by securing it in her pocket.

Afraid of being observed if she remained longer in her present situation, she would have retreated by the way she had entered, but voices approaching the pavilion prevented her design; and, before she had time to recover from the breathless agitation of spirits this unexpected incident occasioned, she distinguished the tones of the Marchese, and soon afterwards those of Paoli.

Alarmed lest they should enter the apartment she occupied, and her inadvertency by these means expose her to new evils, she endeavoured gently to open the door leading into the shrubbery, in the hope that she might be able to secret herself among the trees, till an opportunity offered to favour an escape. But it was locked, and the key being removed, she was compelled to remain in the pavilion, carefully avoiding any noise which might lead to detection.

Though Laurette could not descend to the meanness of

voluntarily overhearing conversation supposed to be private, there being only a thin partition wall between the room she had chosen, and that occupied by the Marchese, it could not easily be prevented, and she was obliged, however reluctantly, to submit to what appeared unavoidable.

When apparently in the most earnest discourse, they spoke low, as if afraid of being overheard, though unconscious that any one was near; and some disjointed sentences, which seemed to be of dreadful import, were occasionally communicated to her ear.

Soon afterwards she heard her own name hesitatingly pronounced, followed by Enrîco's; and curiosity triumphing over the nicer feelings of her mind, directed her involuntarily towards the door.

A short silence succeeded, which was at length broken by Paoli, who uttered something in a low key which she could not clearly understand, and then exalting his voice, he added—

"You are well aware, my Lord, of the necessity of this measure; why then do you hesitate to adopt the only possible means of ensuring your safety and reputation? Some discovery fatal to your peace has been made—her silence, as well as her indifference, confirms the justice of the suspicion; she is treacherous, my Lord, and every thing is to be feared from the artifice of a designing woman. That softness of character, which she assumes at discretion, is it not worn as a veil to conceal the blackness of her intentions? and is happiness to be obtained in a state of continual fear?"

"To what would you advise me?" replied the Marchese, in a voice agitated with contending passion; "have I not already given orders for her removal; to what further would you urge me?"

"To secure your own safety beyond the reach of circumstance," returned the steward; "to teach you to act consistently with those exalted ideas of independence, which have hitherto aggrandized your character. Do you cease to remember, my Lord, that self-preservation is one of the first laws of Nature, that it is wisely interwoven with our existence for reasons too forcibly to be rejected, and becomes the master-spring of all our

actions? If a venomous insect assaults us, do we not annihilate
it? Who, but a maniac, would feel the sting of a serpent, and not
endeavour to release himself from its grasp?—Would any one,
not divested of reason, endanger his own life by listening to the
plea of humanity? If an assassin attacks us with the weapons of
death, and we succeed in disarming him, do we not instantly
sheath the stiletto in his breast; do we feel any thing of remorse
or pity, when we behold it reeking with the blood of an enemy?
I need add no more, my Lord; you must assuredly understand
me; there are means to prevent the evils which threaten you—it
is you that are to apply them."

"There are means," repeated the Marchese, "but they are
dreadful ones; yet, if it must be done, let it be done quickly; I
would fain not think of it again till it is beyond recal. Let me
be acquainted with the time and place, and then let the subject
drop for ever."

"About seven leagues from this spot," continued Paoli, "is a
house every way fitted for the purpose: it stands in a lonely and
dreary forest, and is fenced out from the civilized world by wild
and almost inaccessible woods. These are sometimes infested by
banditti, but never with any other human being; the beasts of the
deserts are their only inhabitants, and scarcely a vestige of man
is to be found. Here Silence has fixed her abode, disturbed only
at intervals by the howling of the wolf, or the cry of the vulture.
In such a situation actions have no witnesses; these woods are no
spies. You understand me, my Lord?"

"I do," returned the Marchese, with seeming emotion; "but
the time, have you thought of that?"

"Any time, my Lord, to-morrow."

"To-morrow!" exclaimed the Marchese; "Ah to-morrow, or
to-night, it cannot be too soon. I leave this business to you; but
I command you, let me hear of it no more till it is executed—I
would fain escape from the recollection."

They now quitted the pavilion; and Laurette, anxious to hear
the whole of the conference, since she was certainly the subject
of it, listened in hopes of catching another sentence; but their
voices, after being imperfectly heard from the opposite side of
the building, grew fainter, and were soon lost in distance.

With trembling limbs, that could scarcely support her agitated frame, she gained the door of the pavilion, when a death-like faintness prevented her from proceeding, and she was obliged to lean against one of the pillars of the portico for support. Somewhat revived by the cool breeze, she looked fearfully around, and being assured that the Marchese and Paoli were returned to the castle, began to reflect upon the dangers with which she was surrounded, and to consider if there was any possibility of eluding them.

Death, in its most terrifying form, was presented to her affrighted imagination; and being convinced that, if she continued longer in the power of her persecutors, it would be inevitable, she determined to attempt an escape. Fear gave new swiftness to her motions, and with rapidity, almost incredible, she ran, or rather flew to the small arched door, which was usually unfastened, and was the direct road from the castle. But this being locked, hope, the only balm of affliction, forsook her, and had she not felt the indispensible necessity of actual exertion, this new disappointment would have overthrown her purpose. But the certain danger of delay animated her resolves; and, however improbable it appeared that she could effectuate an escape, unobserved, from the principal entrance, she ventured to make a similar attempt. But here also she was denied admittance; and being unable either to proceed or to return, in a state of inconceivable suffering she threw herself upon a grassy acclivity, under the shade of a larch, and endeavoured to reflect upon some probable means of avoiding the horrors of her destiny. But she was unable to direct her thoughts to any point that was likely to lead to preservation; the gate of mercy seemed to be closed against her, and the knife of the assassin ready to be plunged into her innocent and unoffending bosom.

As Paoli, for what cause she was incapable of ascertaining, appeared to be a more formidable enemy than even the Marchese himself, who seemed, from the conversation in the pavilion, to have betrayed some symptoms of remorse and pity, she once half resolved to throw herself at the feet of her haughty lover, to convince him, if possible, that she was innocent of the crimes alledged against her; and that no attempt, on her part, to investigate circumstances intended for concealment, had justly rendered her an object of resentment. But the knowledge of his disposition, which she had already obtained, was sufficient to dismiss the forlorn hope which had been recently conveyed to her heart. For even was she allowed to see the Marchese, which was an indulgence the wary steward was not likely to grant, lest it should unfix the wavering purpose of his Lord, there appeared but a small degree of probability in the supposition that she would be enabled to interest his compassion, without making another sacrifice more dreadful to her than that of life itself.

No prospect of effecting her safety by her own efforts, nor any human assistance appearing, she could not acquire resolution to stir from the place; but continued to sit, with her pale cheek resting upon her still whiter arm, till the whole scene was involved in almost total darkness, without her having fixed upon any plan that was likely to lead to security.

The chill winds of the east now blew cold from the mountains, and scattered the few remaining leaves from the half-desolated branches, whilst scarcely sensible of existence, she continued to muse upon what she had heard with undescribable anguish, till a deep and hollow knell, proceeding from a conventual church at an inconsiderable distance from the castle, at length recalled her to consciousness. She started—it was the bell of death; and seemed, to her weakened and almost deranged faculties, to foretell her own immediate dissolution. Pale and breathless as a statue, she clasped her hands eagerly together, and uttering a deep convulsive sigh, proceeded from the place.

Voices were now heard approaching towards the tree she had quitted, and a pale uncertain light was dimly seen through a grove of dark firs which led nearly to the spot. In the next moment she perceived two men, apparently in pursuit of her, bearing torches, whom she soon discovered to be Paoli and Ambrose. She was not long unobserved; and the former accosting her in a rough voice, demanded whither she had been, and what had induced her to ramble so far at that late and perilous hour? Being incapable of framing a reply, he seized her by the arm with the fury of a barbarian, and finding from the livid paleness of her countenance that she was near fainting, commanded Ambrose to assist in supporting her. In this manner she was conveyed to the castle, more dead than alive, and soon afterwards into a kind of garret, never before occupied by any of the family, and far removed from her former apartment. To this place she was carried by Paoli, who, having seated her upon an ancient leather settee, which was placed at the extremity of the room, left her a lamp, and retired, not forgetting the precaution of fastening the door, lest his dark designs should be frustrated.

No doubt now remained in the bosom of Laurette but that the desolate apartment to which she was conveyed by her inexorable enemy, was to witness the perpetration of his bloody designs; and that the wretch who was hired to commit the execrable deed, was to take the advantage of night and of silence, the hour when all but herself were resigned to the influence of repose. Her meek, her inoffensive life, was given into the hands of an inhuman monster, a wretch incapable of pity, dead to every principle of benevolence and virtue. He had appointed the morrow for the execution of his villany, in a dreary and unfrequented forest; but as she was unable to learn the result of the conversation, from not having heard the whole of it, he seemed to have yielded to the request of the Marchese, and meant to execute his purpose instantaneously.

Though Laurette's apprehensions of death were too terrible to be sustained with uniform fortitude, the sufferings of Enrîco when he should be informed of her destiny, was a reflection more difficult to be endured; and this, aided by the probability of the persecutions of the Marchese being extended to him, should one victim be insufficient for the gratification of his resentment, completed the number of melancholy sensations that pained and corroded her heart.

The more she endeavoured to unravel the mystery that had involved her in such a series of calamities, the more inexplicable it appeared; and being incapable of investigating the subject with the minute attention it required, it seemed, from a cursory survey, to be the effect of some deep-laid scheme, formed by the malicious disposition of Paoli, for the accomplishment of her destruction, rather than the result of a combination of casual occurrences, as she had formerly imagined; since something had been evidently laid to her charge which no part of her conduct could justify.

A thousand times she blamed the weakness, the cowardice which prevented her from availing herself of the many opportunities that had offered themselves of obtaining another interview with the Monk. But this was beyond recal, and she was soon going to expiate this error, the only one she ever remembered to have committed, with her blood.

It was now past midnight, and though she was at too great a distance from the inhabited part of the castle to hear what was passing below, she had reason to believe that all were retired to their beds.

A deep and mournful stillness seemed to reign throughout the mansion, and being in hourly expectation of her murderer, she betook herself to prayer, that she might prepare her mind, as much as possible, for the awful change that awaited her, by soliciting the protection of Heaven in the moments of dissolution, which she was well assured could bestow comfort even in the agonies of death, and teach her to sustain them with dignity.

As soon as her plaintive orisons were concluded, she took the volume of poems from her pocket which she had found in the pavilion, and connecting with it the idea of Enrîco, bathed it with tears newly come to her relief, and then opening it, accidentally met with one of the beautiful sonnets of Petrarch, composed after the death of Laura. Not daring to trust herself with the perusal of a poem whose subject was so destructive to fortitude, she instantly closed it, and taking the fatal picture from her bosom, whose saint-like countenance so finely imaged her own, she pressed it to her lips, and breathing an eternal adieu, replaced it in her bosom; and then throwing herself upon the bed, endeavoured to await, with something like resignation, the doom which she considered as inevitable.

As the morning advanced, her fears gradually subsided. If that desolate apartment was intended for her death-room, the bloody deed, she believed, would have been executed in the silence of the night; and with no small degree of consolation she beheld the first dawn of early day peep through the high lattices of her prison.

Somewhat re-assured by this unexpected clemency, and nearly exhausted with fatigue, she yielded for a short time to the sweet influence of sleep; but her slumbers were broken and disturbed, and dreadful foreboding visions terrified her fancy.

She thought she saw Enrîco with a wild unsettled look, haggard countenance, and every symptom of suffering, dart into a forest, whither she was conveyed for the purpose of being massacred, who, after many ineffectual efforts to accomplish her release, was obliged to resign her to her murderer. She was then conducted through unfrequented woods, followed by Enrîco, till they had reached a place still more dreary than the last, when the assassin drawing a stiletto from beneath his cloak, which he had previously concealed, gave her the mortal stab; then, as if not sufficiently glutted with the sight before him, he drew the instrument from her bosom, yet reeking with her blood, and plunged it into the heart of Enrîco.

This horrible dream, occasioned by the excessive agitation of her spirits, had such an effect upon her mind, that, uttering a faint scream, she started wildly from the bed, and saw, by the dusky light which the narrow casement admitted, a tall figure, whose stature her imagination heightened to a being of gigantic size, standing by her side, apparently watching her as she slept. Not having courage to cast her eyes again towards that part of the chamber where they had met the object of her terror, to be convinced that it was not an illusion, she uttered a deep and dreadful scream, and again fell senseless on the bed.

No means being employed to recal her to life, she remained in this state of insensibility till she found herself in the arms of the steward, who had already conveyed her, assisted by Ambrose, beyond the walls of the castle.

Paoli having mounted a mule that was in readiness at the outer-gate, commanded Laurette to be placed behind him, and ordering her to be tied to the animal, to prevent her from effecting an escape, hurried from the place; when he had somewhat relaxed from the pace with which he had set out, she made a gentle, but hopeless, attempt to interest his compassion.

"Oh save me! save me!" cried she, weeping, "if ever you have known what it is to suffer, or have felt the soft touches of sympathy; if ever you have considered the value of existence, or have trembled at the thoughts of losing it."

"To what do you allude?" replied Paoli, sternly; "what reason have you to indulge yourself in fanciful conjectures, and what is it that you fear?"

"Alas! I fear every thing," returned Laurette, mournfully; "and it is you only that can save me."

"Is there any thing so very terrible in a removal from the castle," replied Paoli, angrily—"a place that you entered so reluctantly; are you never to be pleased?"

"Ah! but I know——" cried the fair sufferer, weeping.

"What do you know?" interrupted the steward, turning round fiercely upon his saddle; "and what is it that you apprehend since you know it to be the will of the Marchese?"

"Ah! but to be conveyed, I know not whither; to be carried into a dreary wood, and to die; to have the rights of burial denied me, and to be left a prey to the wolves of the desert—have I deserved all this? and can I reflect upon it without fear?"

"Banish these ridiculous suspicions," returned Paoli, with surprise, "who has told you all this? who has imagined it for you? or what cause have you to indulge in these improbable surmises?"

"No one has informed me of my danger," replied Laurette, tremulously; "Alas! I had no friend left in the castle to inform me of it. It was myself only that heard it in the pavilion, when you was in conversation with the Marchese."

"And what demon," interrupted the steward, "has instructed you in the art of overhearing secret conferences? what did you hear? tell me instantly, as you value your safety."

In hopes of being able to excite his compassion, Laurette acquainted him with the circumstance of her having been in the pavilion previous to their arrival, and of the fruitless attempts she had made to leave it, that she might not be obliged to overhear conversation intended to be secret. Then disguising some part of the discourse, lest it should irritate him the more, she related what she had heard.

Some symptoms of confusion appeared in Paoli's countenance at the recital, though he positively denied that it had any reference to herself; and after endeavouring to convince her that no harm would befal her, he sunk again into his accustomed reserve; whilst Laurette, with a heart palpitating with terror, was compelled to proceed on her journey.

END OF THE THIRD VOLUME.

THE

ORPHAN

OF THE

RHINE.

———➤ * ◄———

𝔄 𝔯𝔬𝔪𝔞𝔫𝔠𝔢,

IN FOUR VOLUMES.

═══════

BY MRS. SLEATH.

═══════

Sweet are the uses of adversity,
Which, like the toad, ugly and venomous,
Wears yet a precious jewel in his head.
SHAKESPEARE.

VOL. IV.

═══════════

LONDON:

PRINTED AT THE

𝔐𝔦𝔫𝔢𝔯𝔟𝔞-𝔓𝔯𝔢𝔰𝔰,

FOR WILLIAM LANE, LEADENHALL-STREET

1798

CHAP. I.

"How oft the sight of means to do ill deeds
Make deeds ill done! Hadst not thou been by—
A fellow, by the hand of Nature mark'd,
Louted, and sign'd to do a deed of shame,
This murder had not come into my mind:
Hadst thou but shook thy head, or made a pause,
When I spake darkly what I purposed,
Or turned an eye of doubt upon my face,
Or bade me tell my tale in express words,
Deep shame had struck me dumb, made me break off,
And these, thy fears, would have wrought fears in me."

SHAKESPEARE.

THE lovely orphan was no sooner conveyed from the castle, than the Marchese appeared to labour under such an oppression of spirits, as no change of circumstance, or of place, promised to remove.

Though he would willingly have spared himself this new cause of remorse, by confining Laurette in a convent at the instigation of the inhuman steward, he had at last determined upon her death. Offended pride and disappointed hopes taught him at first to reflect upon it with indifference, whilst the apparent necessity of committing this horrid deed, to conceal the perpetration of another not less criminal, actuated him still more powerfully; yet, probably, even these arguments would not have possessed a sufficient portion of energy and persuasion to have effected so sudden a resolution, had he not beheld in the person of Paoli a wretch, whose mind, as well as aspect, indicated him a villain, marked and selected by Nature for the accomplishment of the most daring and bloody purposes; who being entirely unrestrained by conscience, was ever ready to espouse the cause of iniquity, for the sake of temporary advantage; and from a long acquaintance with all the arts of intrigue, was enabled to direct the weaknesses and vices of others to his immediate interests.

Three days had passed since Laurette's departure from the castle, during which period a thousand internal conflicts destroyed the repose of the Marchese, and lacerated his guilty bosom. He awaited with a dreadful kind of impatience the return of Paoli. The sun of the morning arose to him without exciting one sweet or pleasurable emotion; and, as if anxious to escape from his penetrating and reproachful beams, he frequently retired into the deep clefts of the rocks, or the rude narrow glens of the mountains, as if alarmed lest his very thoughts should have witnesses; but, though he dared not trust himself to visit those scenes which were once rendered interesting by the soft form of her, who was now the patient victim of his cruelty, her beautiful image, adorned with all its innocent and unassuming graces, was continually presented to him, even in the wild and lonely recesses he had chosen. Since she had now paid so dear for her offence, remorse and tenderness rapidly succeeded each other; and sensations, as new as they were agonizing, were excited in his breast. Conscious that to the mind diseased, no state is so insupportable as that of suspense, he became still more impatient for the return of his steward, though it was impossible he could communicate any intelligence of a cordial nature, since he equally dreaded to hear that Laurette was assassinated, or had effected an escape, as such an event could not take place without the interference of another, which must inevitably lead to a discovery productive of the most alarming consequences.

Four days had now elapsed, and still he did not return; something the Marchese imagined must have happened to occasion this delay, and sensations still more afflictive and terrible passed through his disordered mind. Unable any longer to endure the pressure of his uneasiness, which was now rendered still more acute by a thousand memorials of her whom he had thus sacrificed to ambition and unjust resentment, he adopted the resolution of repairing to the castle of Elfinbach, in hopes that a new succession of objects might effect a change of idea. This plan, as soon as formed, was communicated to Ambrose, who was commanded to attend him thither, and leaving orders for Paoli to follow him immediately on his return, the Marchese proceeded on his journey.

After a dreary and melancholy ride over barren heaths and rugged precipices, the travellers arrived at this desolated castle, which, from the heavy rains that had recently fallen, and the high winds which had blown down the rampart-wall, and shattered the easements, appeared more than usually gloomy. The Marchese surveyed it for a moment in silence, and then alighting from his horse, asked eagerly for the Signora, and was directed into one of the saloons.

He found her alone, engaged in some household employ-ment; and being surprised at his sudden return to a place not at present rendered fit for his reception, she looked chagrined and embarrassed. The restless agitation of mind that was so strongly delineated on the features and manners of the Marchese, did not elude the observation of the Signora, though the cause was inexplicable. She would have demanded the reason of this conduct, but the reserve, with which he repressed every inquiry she ventured to make that could lead to the subject, occasioned her to desist.

She did not mention Laurette till the following day, fearing lest this mysterious sadness was the effect of her coldness, and might be increased by reverting to the cause; but anxiety to gain some information respecting her lovely young friend overpower-ing every other consideration, directed her simply to interrogate him concerning her health. The name of Laurette, uttered by the Signora, roused him from that state of stupor into which he had fallen. He started, and confusion for the moment prevented him from framing a reply, till at length recalling some portion of that studied composure, that masterly command of feature, for which he was once so deservedly eminent, he informed her, without recollecting that he had not answered her first question, that Laurette had proved herself unworthy of his future protec-tion, by having escaped secretly from the castle, unknown to and unobserved by any one.

The Signora now imagined that she was acquainted with the whole: every thing that the Marchese had uttered relative to her escape, appeared probable, when she recollected the boldness, and even aversion, with which she had uniformly repressed the ardour of his passion. But in what part of the province could she find an asylum that would defend her from the power of her lover, or elude the vigilance of his researches, should he be disposed to continue his persecutions, was unanswerable. Her unprotected situation filled the mind of the Signora, as she reflected upon it, with new terror; but afraid of betraying too much emotion in the presence of her Lord, she abruptly quitted the apartment, that she might consider it more deeply in secret.

The Marchese now believing that he had convinced his Casiera that Laurette had deservedly forfeited all claim to his protection from having voluntarily quitted the castle, less frequently came into her presence than before, still endeavouring to find that repose he had lost amid the wildest scenes of Nature, which his dark discoloured imagination rendered still more dreary.

Day after day passed in a state of mournful solicitude, yet Paoli was not announced; "the attempt, and not the deed," was dreadful! If the bloody business was transacted, what could have detained him? A thousand terrible surmises now agitated his breast; his nights continued to be sleepless, and, before he had been a week resident at the castle, his pallid countenance, and his emaciated limbs, foretold alarming consequences!

A strange account of noises heard in different parts of the mansion, and of spectres being seen gliding through the galleries at the dead hour of the night, was now circulated among the domestics! The Signora was informed of it, and, willing to remove what she termed causeless superstition, endeavoured to convince them of the absurdity of allowing themselves to be deluded by imaginary terrors; but the arguments she made use of to quiet their apprehensions were ineffectual. Ambrose averred, that he had met a figure clothed in white, gliding through the corridor, who, without accosting him, vanished apparently into one of the deserted apartments! The female servants, who were procured by the Signora from the nearest village, to assist in cleaning the castle, each declared they had seen the same spectre, exactly answering to his description, in different situations, and had all formed the resolution not to stir alone in the night, nor even in the dusk, each declaring that she had rather meet a wild beast than a spirit!

The Signora's woman, being the only one among them who had not caught the contagion, proposed, if any one would accompany her, to explore every room in the castle; but no individual in the family being courageous enough to assist her in her researches, she was compelled to abandon the design, though not without branding all, particularly Ambrose, with the imputation of cowardice.

The Marchese in the meantime, though kept in total ignorance of the affair, through the express orders of the Casiera, appeared to suffer more internal horror than any of the servants. His meals were short, and his answers, when any one addressed him, were far from the purpose, and usually uttered with an aspect of displeasure. At some times he seemed lost in the gloom of silent thoughtfulness, whilst at others his strong expressive features were distorted by emotions; and with his arms folded upon his breast, and his eyes fixed with a vacant stare upon some object he was unconscious of beholding, his whole frame appeared to suffer some dreadful convulsion. He usually retired early to his room, but seldom to his bed: he never courted the sweet influence of sleep, for he knew that it shunned the blood-stained couch of the murderer, and descended only on the lid of unoffending innocence.

CHAP. II.

"What man dare, I dare;
Approach thou, like the rugged Russian bear,
The arm'd rhinoceros, or Hyrcanian tyger;
Take any shape but that, and my firm nerves
Shall never tremble."————

SHAKESPEARE.

The room, which was selected by Ambrose for his Lord immediately on his arrival, was on the northern side of the edifice, and from its remote situation, as well as from the circumstance of that range of apartments having always remained locked during Madame Chamont's residence in the mansion, had long fallen into disuse. It was a large dreary-looking chamber, partially hung with tapestry of no common workmanship, representing a group of grim and ghastly figures habited as knights, with their spears, bucklers, and other implements of war. The bed, which was composed of crimson damask, was so much faded and discoloured with age, and the curtains that hung loosely from the high canopied tester, had been so long a prey to the moths and the night-flies, that the windows were no sooner opened, after having been closed for near twenty years, than they fell into fragments. A few faded portraits, in the costume of the thirteenth century, and a large old-fashioned mirror, whose massy gilt frame appeared to have withstood the assaults of ages, were the only ornaments this apartment contained, if those could be called ornaments, which, instead of relieving the eye, tended to make the correspondent gloom of the whole more dreadfully impressive.

This room Ambrose endeavoured to convince the Signora was less exposed than any other to the fury of the winds, and upon the whole a more comfortable asylum than any other which the castle contained.

The Marchese, in any other frame of spirits, would have been shocked at its desolate appearance; but horrors were now become familiar to him, and taking a lamp and book, he usually retired to it early; and if he ever closed his eyes, this transient repose was obtained in a large antique chair, covered with green damask, that was placed by the side of the fire.

The Signora, believing that this increasing malady was chiefly the effect of sleepless anxiety, ventured one night, unknown to him, to put something in his wine of a soporific nature, whose effect being almost instantaneous, occasioned him to retire to his chamber still earlier than before.

Scarcely had he entered the room before he perceived a soft composure stealing upon his spirits, and contrary to his late custom, threw himself upon the bed, and yielded to a transient slumber. But the comfort of serene sleep was denied him; for his guilty soul conjured up strange and dreadful images, not less appalling than his waking terrors. He imagined that, for some crime committed against the ecclesiastical powers, he was consigned to the dungeons of the inquisition within the authority of

Rome, where he remained in hourly expectation of being summoned to the secret tribunal—a tribunal where mercy, and even
justice, are for ever excluded, to confess what must doom him to
immediate death, or have that confession extorted from him, by
means more dreadful than the human mind could conceive, by
inflictions more excruciating than the annihilation of existence.
He awaked; it was but a dream, and sleep still overpowering
him, he closed his eyes, and again yielded to its influence. The
dreadful vision still continued; he was now conducted by two
of the officers belonging to this hopeless prison, through dark
subterranean passages, to the secret tribunal. The grand inquisi-
tor, with the three persons that formed the tribunal, were seated
on a lofty elevation. He arose when he entered, and eyeing him
with a dreadful kind of minuteness, proceeded to judgment. The
charge against him was read; it spoke of murder and sacrilege.
His accuser was called; it was a Monk, of a meek and saint-like
appearance, clad in the holy vestments of his order. He came
forwards; the trial proceeded; the facts alledged against him were
incontrovertible, and the tribunal, in a loud voice, demanded
his confession. The excessive agitation of his mind now released
him from the fetters of sleep, and starting from the couch, in
an agony not to be described, he pronounced the word "Confess." "Confess," repeated a voice apparently proceeding from a
distant part of the room, in a tone at once deep and impressive.
The Marchese's alarm increased; a sound was certainly heard
that echoed his words, and surprise and terror for the moment
deprived him of utterance. But a desperate kind of courage was
at length communicated to his mind, and in an accent not less
firm, though more furious, he retorted, "Confess what?" "Confess what?" returned the same voice, delivering the last word in a
tone of deeper emphasis—"Dost thou ask what?" The sensation
which the Marchese now experienced, was little short of distraction; it could not be an illusion, and he would have sprang from
his couch to have investigated this mysterious affair, and to have
discovered, if possible, from whence the tones proceeded; but
throwing his eyes wildly around, he perceived a tall, dreadful-
looking figure moving slowly from one of the angles into a remote part of the chamber. The lamp was extinguished, and the

dying embers refused to administer the smallest portion of light; but the moon-beams that penetrated through the half-decayed curtains, dimly discovered the figure.

With a countenance, on which extreme agony of soul was faithfully delineated, the eyes of the Marchese continued to follow the terrifying phantom, who, without appearing to observe him, moved pensively along beneath the dim Gothic arch of the casement, in a kind of white robe or cassock, which descending beneath the feet, swept mournfully along the ground. A hood of the same colour covered its face, and shaded the ghastliness of its features. The castle bell now tolled one; the spectre stopped, turned, and in a few moments advanced with a quickened movement towards the bed. The desperate courage which the Marchese had assumed, now vanished; he threw himself back upon the pillow, his breath shortened, the cold dews paced each other down his forehead, he veiled his face, which exhibited a cadaverous paleness, with the coverture; and stifled groans, and irregular respiration, were all the symptoms of remaining existence!

In a few minutes he heard a rustling kind of noise towards the feet of the bed; the curtains were soon afterwards undrawn, and had not the alarm attendant on conscious guilt, wrapped him in obscurity, he might have seen distinctly the form of the spectre bending silently over his couch.

In this situation he remained till the light of the morning dissipated the gloom that had veiled his dreary apartment; when venturing to divest himself of his temporary covering, he perceived that the phantom, which had excited such alarm, was vanished, though the door of the chamber was still fastened.

This remarkable incident now completely engaged his attention; and having communicated the affair to Ambrose, who was become a kind of confident since the departure of Paoli, he contrived, with his assistance, to remove the tapestry with which the apartment was hung, that by these means they might be enabled to explore every part of the wainscot, and to discover if any secret entrance was concealed behind this grotesque covering; but no door, or any other possible method of gaining admission, appeared, or any thing that could act as a clue to conjecture. Still more perplexed and agonized, the mind of the Marchese became a prey to superstitious terror. Afraid of being alone, yet ashamed of acknowledging his weakness, he suffered a tumult of distracting apprehension, which no effort of fortitude could subdue.

CHAP. III.

"Ah me! for aught that ever I could read,
Could ever hear by tale or history,
The course of true love never did run smooth;
But either it was different in blood,
Or else misgrafted in respect of years,
Or else it stood upon the choice of friends,
Or if there were a sympathy in choice,
War, death, or sickness, did lay siege to it."

SHAKESPEARE.

Enrîco had been prevented from visiting Laurette according to his promise by a second letter from Italy, which acquainted him with the increasing indisposition of his Colonel, and convinced him of the necessity of his quitting Germany immediately, if he was desirous of preventing the danger of seeing him no more. The grateful heart of the young Chevalier felt a severe pang of self-reproach when he perused this epistle, and willing to repair this fault of omission with all imaginable speed, he wrote to inform Laurette of the occasion of his absence, and commenced his journey. As the Signora was removed from the castle at the time this letter arrived, it unfortunately fell into the hands of the steward, who, after intercepting and reading it himself, discovered the contents to his Lord. Thus the two lovers mutually upbraided each other without any actual cause, and felt, through the meanness and vices of others, the most poignant regret and solicitude.

As soon as Enrîco had reached the borders of Italy, he made the best of his way to Pietola*, the customary residence of the

* This place is celebrated by ancient historians under the name of Andes, and is rendered famous from its having given birth to Virgil. It is only a small village, or hamlet, about a league from Mantua.

Marchese de Martilina when disengaged from the duties of his station.

Here he arrived but just in time to receive the last sigh of his revered patron, and to bathe the almost lifeless hand that was extended to welcome him with his tears! Perfectly sensible, though unable to give his thoughts utterance, the Marchese gazed with silent tenderness upon his young favourite, till the vital spark, which had been long expiring, was extinguished, and he fell into the arms of death as into a quiet slumber. The serenity displayed by this great and good man at the hour of death, sufficiently evinced that his life had been blameless: it was the cloudless evening of a tranquil day; no ruffling gales disturbed the calm of his soul; all was comfort and repose.

The affectionate Enrîco felt as if he had lost not only a friend, but a parent; and when he followed the adviser and protector of his youth to his last mournful receptacle, he suffered an agony of distress, which required a more than ordinary effort of fortitude to subdue. Endowed with that exquisite perception of pain, or pleasure, which is annexed to extreme sensibility, he found it difficult to tear himself from the place which contained the sacred remains of his friend; till anxiety to gain some intelligence relative to Laurette's silence, which was as mysterious as alarming, determined him to remove from Pietola without further delay, and to set forwards for the castle of Luenburg.

Having given orders to Anselmo for the horses to be prepared, which were to convey them into Germany, he visited, for the last time, the grave of his much-revered Colonel; and after having indulged the sacredness of his sorrow in secret, was walking silently from the spot, when he was accosted by the nearest relative of his deceased friend, who, with much courtesy of address, requested an audience.

Enrîco bowed assent, and following his conductor to a place appointed for the purpose, was informed that the Marchese di Martilina had bequeathed to him a thousand Louis-d'ors per annum, as a pledge of his friendship and esteem. The heart of the noble Chevalier overflowed with effusions of gratitude, which no eloquence of language can express, as this event was recited; tears of tenderness and regret rushed into his eyes, and having thanked the Signor for his information, with a gracefulness of expression peculiar to himself, he retired to indulge the luxury of his feelings in secret. Enrîco had accidentally heard that his much-lamented Colonel had accumulated a considerable share of personal property, besides those ample estates he possessed in many parts of the Continent, which devolved to the male heir; but he never flattered himself into the supposition that he should be remembered in his will, though on former occasions he had experienced many proofs of his benevolence. A mind more sanguine and disinterested than his own might, indeed, have collected some circumstances to favour such an opinion; as the Marchese had no near relation living, and consequently his immense possessions descended to a distant branch of the family, to whom he was not much attached, whilst the ever-increasing partiality he had discovered for the amiable Chevalier wore the most promising aspect in his favour.

This worthy Nobleman had never formed a matrimonial connexion, owing to his having experienced a severe disappoint-ment in the early part of his life, which directed him, as the most effectual way of subduing it, into the service of his country.

New avocations now retarded the journey of Enrîco for a few days; but more than ever anxious to behold the charming object of his affections, whose fair form too frequently obtruded itself into his thoughts, as well as to learn the cause of her silence, as soon as suitable arrangements were made respecting pecuniary affairs, he proceeded on his journey.

The tender melancholy which pervaded the heart of our hero, was not unmixed with pleasing sensations, when he con-sidered himself as advancing towards that mansion, which he had reason to imagine was inhabited by her, whose presence was sufficient to compensate for the loss of every other valuable con-nexion, and who, he flattered himself, would mingle the breath-ings of affection with the blushes of retiring diffidence.

He recollected that he now possessed a competency adequate to all the comforts, if not the luxuries, of life, which, though by no means equal to the merit of the person beloved, was yet, he was convinced, far beyond her desires, as it would, at least, place them, would she deign to listen to his proposals, above mediocrity; but when his mind reverted with painful concern to his lost parent, whose destiny was yet veiled in obscurity, a cloud of premature sadness overshadowed his future prospects. Was she present to congratulate him on his new accessions, and at the same time to confer upon him her orphan charge, how pure, how unmixed, would have been his felicity; and how exquisite would have been her sensations when empowered to bestow such happiness!

Lost in these reflections, Enrîco proceeded silently along; nor could the loquacity of Anselmo, who endeavoured to direct his attention towards those "cloud-capped" temples, decayed edifices, and lofty columns, which on every side decorate the Italian landscape, giving sublimity to beauty, withdraw him from thoughtfulness.

Having proceeded for many leagues along the winding borders of the Po, by means of a gondola they crossed the Adda that communicates with the Lago di Como, celebrated by Virgil under the name of Lake Larius, which issuing out at the extremity, loses itself in that river, the grand receptacle of all others, except the Adige, that washes the vernal and fruitful soil of this romantic country. Had Enrîco's mind been entirely disengaged from nearer interests, with what solemn emotions of awe and admiration would he have contemplated the scene before him? The vast range of Alps, which serve as a barrier to divide France and Germany from the Italian states, rose in irregular and misshapen forms, some towering till their summits were lost in perpetual obscurity, whilst others were broken into so many steeps and inaccessible precipices, that the traveller, surveying them with that kind of enthusiasm which is peculiar to the admirers of stupendous imagery, feels an affecting kind of horror stealing irresistibly to his heart.

After passing with much difficulty these dangerous acclivities, the soul of Enrîco became more animated. Every step he conceived brought him nearer to Laurette; and though still far distant, he imagined the wintry landscape, as he passed the boundaries of Germany, exhibited a less saddened appearance. Hope again brightened his prospects, and scarcely submitting to the delay of stopping for necessary food, he redoubled his speed.

A few days brought them within three leagues of the castle, and having proceeded thus far, the travellers were compelled, from the darkness of the night, to put up at a small cottage on the road, meaning to prosecute the remaining part of their journey on the ensuing morning; but Enrîco had of late suffered so much mental, as well as bodily fatigue, that he was obliged to remain at the cottage some hours longer than was his intention, and also to take something of a medicinal nature before he was enabled to proceed; though his impatience arose almost to agony when he recollected how inconsiderable was the distance which separated him from Laurette, and yet that he was prevented from being with her, without having even obtained an assurance that she was still in safety. Towards evening, however, the symptoms, which had threatened him with severe indisposition, abated, and, unable to endure the idea of procrastinated happiness when his lovely enchantress was so near, he determined to proceed; and, after bestowing upon the owners of this little asylum many testimonies of gratitude, they continued their journey.

It was night when the travellers arrived within sight of the mansion, and new sensations assailed the mind of Enrîco as he surveyed it. From what had passed, he had every reason to believe that he must encounter the displeasure of its possessor by venturing into his presence without a previous invitation, who had never once hinted a desire of being known to him on any former occasion; but the force of his attachment soon weakened these unpleasant surmises, and as nearer interests succeeded in his thoughts, he wondered how they had ever troubled him. When Enrîco had reached the high wall which encompassed the castle, his heart beat high with expectation. He attempted to open the arched door which had before given him admission; it gave way to his touch; and desiring Anselmo to attend to the horses till he received orders to the contrary, he advanced rapidly through the grounds. The moon, which before gave only a pale and uncertain light, now shrunk beneath a cloud, and it was with much difficulty that he was enabled to proceed through the numerous shrubberies and low coppices, which were every where scattered around. The path he had chosen, though the most direct one leading to the portico, was winding and irregular, frequently intercepted with small clumps of juniper, almond, and pomgranate, or with knots of variegated evergreens, which, in a more favourable season, perfumed the air with their fragrance. When arrived at the principal entrance, he knocked, but the summons was unanswered; he listened, but no step was to be heard; fear and mistrust, with a thousand melancholy accompaniments, were now communicated to his mind. He surveyed the front of the edifice; no lights appeared at the windows. He ascended the solarium*, and looked through the glass door that opened into the terrace-parlour, which the Signora d'Orso and her fair friend formerly occupied when alone; but it was deserted, and even the lamps, which used to be hung in the balconies, were removed. Impatience now arose to the most painful solicitude; he knocked again and again, but without better success, and at length becoming desperate by this cruel disappointment, endeavoured to scale the wall inclosing the court which led to the portal. After many ineffectual attempts, he succeeded in his desires; but the enterprise was a dangerous one, and as he alighted on the other side, something placed there for the purpose lacerated his leg. The pain, though acute, was disregarded; but the blood, which flowed fast from the wound, obliged him to apply his handkerchief as a bandage to the part till assistance could be procured. This accident, though it retarded the execution, tended not to subdue the energy of his resolves. He bounded instantly towards the door, and knowing that a bell, resounding through one whole wing of the building, was here the signal of approach, he repeated the alarm, and in a few minutes had the consolation of hearing footsteps approaching slowly along the hall. The door was now opened by a male servant, whom Enrîco never remembered to have seen during his former residence in the castle, who, after surveying him with surprise, demanded his business. In a voice rendered tremulous by emotion, he inquired for Laurette, and was informed that she had eloped from the mansion without the knowledge of the family, and was gone no one could tell whither.

To describe the sensations of the unfortunate Chevalier at

* Terrace walk.

this moment, would demand powers of expression beyond the utmost eloquence of language. He rushed into the castle in spite of the efforts of the domestic, who endeavoured to prevent his design, and hastening along the hall, stopped at the door of the saloon. He attempted to open it, but it was locked. The Marchese and the Signora were then assuredly removed, and whither must he go for information. The servant, by whom he was admitted, having never seen him before, being entirely ignorant of his intentions from the circumstance of his scaling the wall, as well as the wildness of his looks, took him for a maniac, and had left him to pursue his own inclinations only whilst he acquainted his fellows with the adventure.

Lost in bewildering conjecture, Enrîco stood with his eyes unconsciously fixed upon the deserted apartments in a state of total inaction; for surprise had deprived him of the power of exertion, and made him sensible only of his own misfortunes and disappointment. One solitary lamp, suspended from the ceiling in a central situation, which cast a dim and partial light, scarcely dissipated the gloom that was every where visible; but his mind was too much wounded to feel the effect of accidental events, though all around appeared melancholy, hopeless, and blank as his destiny.

The few remaining domestics now crowded about the forlorn traveller, some to demand his business at that lone and silent hour, and others to prove the truth of the assertion, by discovering whether he was really touched with insanity. Extreme agony of mind prevented Enrîco from immediately undeceiving them; but recollecting the necessity of recalling some portion of that resisting fortitude, which love only could have weakened, he repeated his inquiries with all the calmness he could command, and finally, by declaring his name, endeavoured to make himself known. This avowal roused one of the women that followed in the rear, who elevating her lamp as she advanced nearer, for the purpose of examining his countenance, let it fall suddenly from her hand, exclaiming, in evident astonishment, that it was indeed the Chevalier Chamont. Somewhat animated by the certainty that he was remembered, at least, by one of the domestics, Enrîco made a second attempt at recomposing his spirits; and having requested that she would indulge him with a few moments' conversation alone, she opened the door of the terrace-parlour to give him admittance, whilst the rest stole silently away.

Fanchette, which was the name of the servant, possessing much natural kindness, was easily prevailed upon to give him an audience; and when she beheld his wild, unsettled appearance, and the many symptoms of distress which marked his dejected features, compassion was so warmly excited in her bosom, that, had it been in her power to have offered him consolation, she would have bestowed it with pleasure.

The Marchese, as well as Ambrose, had confidently affirmed that Laurette had voluntarily escaped from the castle ever since her departure, and had taken much pains to circulate this report among the servants; and as she had not been seen by any one but Paoli and Ambrose after having left the pavilion, the probability of the assertion was apparently justified; though Fanchette observed, that the steward's quitting the castle at so early an hour in the morning, without giving some previous intimation of his intentions, appeared somewhat mysterious. The sudden removal of the fair orphan, in whose fate all were interested, had been a subject of surprise and conjecture in those apartments appropriated to the use of the servants ever since the event had taken place. Various opinions were received and propagated, which were faithfully recited by Fanchette; but from these nothing was to be gathered that might lead to a future discovery. Plunged still deeper in despair, the disconsolate Enrîco could scarcely be prevailed upon to continue in the castle during the night, so anxious was he to commence his pursuit of Laurette, however hopeless the attempt.

Having at length reluctantly assented to Fanchette's wishes, who kindly applied something of an healing quality to his leg, which was found upon examination to be very slightly injured, Anselmo's horses were ordered into the stable, and he into the kitchen, to partake of a comfortable repast, and the warmth of a blazing fire. Enrîco's mind was too much disturbed with internal conflicts to attend to the wants of Nature, and throwing himself upon one of those sofas, on which in happier times he had often sat with Laurette, he yielded to all the melancholy forebodings of his agitated breast.

CHAP. IV.

"Oh thievish night!
Why shouldst thou, but for some felonious ends,
In thy dark lantern thus close up the stars
That Nature hung in Heaven, and fill'd their lamps
With everlasting oil, to give due light
To the misled and lonely traveller?
For their way
Lies through the perplex'd path of this drear wood;
The nodding horror of whose shady brow
Threats the forlorn and wand'ring passenger."

MILTON.

Unable to obtain even a moment's repose, Enrîco arose with the dawn of early day, and being determined to go instantly in search of Laurette, roused his servant from a comfortable sleep into which he had recently fallen, with orders for him to prepare to accompany him on his new expedition. Anselmo hastily obeyed the summons, and the unfortunate travellers, being again mounted, commenced their hopeless journey.

It was a dreary December morning, and the grey heavy mists that loaded the atmosphere brought on a cold and drizly rain. The woods were now disrobed of their honours; no choral harmony resounded through the desolated branches; all was melancholy, repose, and silence! With no guide but chance, and without having obtained any intelligence that could serve as a clue to discovery, the wretched Enrîco traversed the barren hills and humid vallies, in a state of mind that partook of agony. A thousand vague conjectures passed across his mind as he continued to ruminate upon the subject. Sometimes he imagined that the Marchese had conceived a passion for Laurette, and had adopted this plan at once to separate her from the Signora, and to deceive the domestics; at others, he conceived it probable that she had made a voluntary escape to avoid falling a victim to his artifice, which, he naturally believed, had been already exerted for the accomplishment of her destruction. But why was the promise she made to him on parting disregarded? Why did she not inform him of her danger, and accept of his protection? A slight emotion of indignation accompanied this reflection; she might be false, her affections might be another's, or, what was still more probable, they might never have been his.

This apprehension brought with it a pang more acute, but it was only momentary. He recollected the touching expression of her countenance when he tore himself from the castle, the sweet languishment of her charming eyes as they followed him towards the portico, and the tears and speaking blushes that graced her last innocent farewels. These had been indelibly impressed upon his memory ever since he had parted from her in every distressing emergency; and amidst all the cross accidents and unexpected calamities which he experienced, these sweet remembrances conveyed a cordial to his wounded spirits.

Thinking that some information might possibly be obtained from the peasantry, should they have providentially taken the same road as the lovely young fugitive, they did not permit a village or town to escape their inquiries;—but no one had seen any person the least answering to the description; and a few incoherent words, accompanied by a stare of idle curiosity, was frequently the only answer they received. Wounded where he was the most vulnerable, the distracted Chevalier suffered the keenest anguish that circumstance could inflict: it was too deep for utterance; but the wildness of his aspect, and the settled paleness of his countenance, discovered the inward working of his mind.

As it advanced towards mid-day, the rain gradually ceased, the sun looked meekly from the south, and a cold driving wind assisted in dissipating the mists, which had enveloped the faded features of the landscape. As Enrîco surveyed the cheerless face of Nature, and contrasted it with its summer appearance, he could not forbear applying this melancholy change to his own more desolate situation; and sighing deeply as the idea occurred, he turned involuntarily round to contemplate the whole of the prospect, and observed, as his eyes glanced towards those vast mountains that rise in all forms and directions in this picturesque country, that which he had once rambled over with Laurette, crowned with the rustic church. A thousand mournful reflections were now communicated to his mind:—where was the sweet wanderer gone, who appeared like the Hebe of that secluded retreat? If alone, how could she avoid danger? And if conveyed away by stratagem, how was it possible she should escape from it? The more he reflected upon the subject, the more improbable it appeared that he should ever meet with her again; yet he steadily resolved never to relinquish the pursuit, since life without her, who could only make it desirable, would be a tasteless potion.

Several leagues had been traversed without any material event, in which time no intelligence had been obtained, though they stopped at all the inns and cottages on the road, as well as at the convents, to renew their inquiries.

Anselmo, who was naturally volatile, preserved throughout the whole of the journey a respectful silence. He perceived that his beloved master's uneasiness was too deep to be diverted from its source, and could only be removed by the success of the enterprise, or by the slow, but certain, effects of time. Knowing with what reluctance he stopped to obtain a sufficient portion of food, the wary servant had procured unknown to Enrîco three flasks of Florence wine, the best that part of the country afforded, which he secured in his wallet, to be in readiness in case of emergency.

About the middle of the third day the travellers left the direct road, and struck into one which took a different direction. This path was more rugged than the one they had left, lying for a considerable way among gloomy forests, desert heaths, and rocky precipices. No human abode, except a few solitary huts, appeared within the reach of vision, whose rude inhabitants were chiefly employed in leading their goats from the shrubby tops of the mountains to the tinkling of a bell, or the soft breathings of a flute, or in seeking for the moss-lined nest of the marmot amid the clefts of the rocks. These wandering rustics were frequently addressed by Anselmo; but his interrogatories were usually answered with rudeness, or at best with incivility.

The scene now gradually became more barren; yet, though

destitute of the accompaniment of trees, it was still highly interesting and charming to the admirers of romantic imagery. Large
masses of granite scowled beneath the eye, and mountains,
whose crested summits penetrated into the clouds, considerably
augmented that sensation of solitary sublimity that overwhelms
and astonishes the mind of the spectator.

The melancholy air of neglect and depopulation, which was
on every side discernible, unenlivened by sun, threw a melancholy calm over the spirits of our hero, though they tended not
to subdue the energy of his soul. As the evening advanced, a
dark line of threatening clouds, rolling in vast volumes round
the heads of the eminences, were productive of an effect, at once
awful and sublime, which was heightened by the scream of the
eagle returning to her lofty abode, or the repeated cries of the
kestril, or the wurchangel*, sated with the triumph of rapacious
pursuit.

Anselmo, alarmed and intimidated at the gloomy appearance of Nature, aided by the approach of night, looked wistfully
around for some hospitable retreat; but they had now passed
near a league beyond the huts of the peasantry, and no place of
security was to be seen. The path, which had long wound among
the mountains, now directed them by a precipitant descent into a
deep and extensive valley, bordered with wood, and interspersed
with lakes. Though this new scene afforded more appearance of
vegetation than those they had quitted, the entangled thickets
being occasionally intermingled with a variety of dark firs and
evergreen oaks, still it wore an aspect of melancholy and desolation; the luxuriance that clothed the lofty side of the glen being
no where else perceptible, whilst the uncultivated mountain and
the frowning precipice were still the principal objects of this
lonely, yet sublime landscape, rising into the most majestic and
yet terrifying forms that imagination could conceive. A branch
of the Danube, rushing impetuously over several large fragments
of broken rock, only disturbed the universal silence, rendering
the effect of the whole more awfully impressive, as it foamed
with dreadful and inconceivable rapidity through the intervals

* Or, great butcher bird.— See Pennant.

between the masses of rock that formed the bed of the torrent. It was with much difficulty that they were enabled to proceed through this deep and rough glen, rendered dangerous by the advance of night, and the motion of this boisterous stream, which rushed impetuously in a series of broken cascades, till it precipitated itself, with the force of a cataract, into the bosom of the parent river. They now continued their way, through long and winding sheep-walks, towards the extremity of the valley, till they reached the border of a small clear lake, which again intercepted their path. Here amid long grass, weeds, and rushes, the solitary bittern had long fixed her abode, who having shaken off her autumnal indolence, was seen rising in a spiral ascent, filling the air with her cries, till she was lost in the immensity of distance. Night, which now closed in, brought them to the edge of a forest, dark, dreary, and almost inaccessible. As they advanced, the gloom became more profound, and the clouds, which had long been gathering over their heads, discharged their humid contents: even Enrîco felt appalled, and turned to descry, if possible, some place of security. Anselmo was still more anxious to obtain an hospitable shelter, but no vestige of habitation was to be seen; and the latter, encouraged by the example of his master, ventured, though reluctantly, to proceed. A path cut in the forest directed them along till they had reached that dreary and unfrequented spot, known to the traveller by the name of the Jammer Holtz, or Wood of Groans, situated near the Ghorde. This place, which cannot fail of exciting in the occasional visiter a sensation of fear and horror, did not lose its accustomed effect, and they were each for the moment irresolute whether to venture into the interior of the forest, or to return towards the skirts of it, and await the approach of morning.

Anselmo, though he disdained the imputation of cowardice, pleaded warmly for the former plan, observing that there were several trees, whose interwoven branches were capable of affording them security from the storm; and that in such a situation they would be in less danger of becoming a prey to banditti, or to the beasts that infested the deserts. Impatient of delay, Enrîco did not yield immediately to the proposition; but was giving it a second review, when Anselmo perceived a light glim-

mering through the wood at no considerable distance from that
part of it in which they were stationed: it cast only a faint gleam,
and from the waving of the trees was seen only at intervals; yet
they were soon convinced that it proceeded from a taper, and
not from one of those watery exhalations, which in low boggy
grounds frequently leads the traveller astray. Elated by this unexpected adventure, they dismounted, and tying their horses to
the stump of an oak, advanced towards the place. The storm was
now past, and the moon, emerging from a cloud, threw her soft
light upon the tops of the trees, and discovered half hid, among
the unfoliated branches, the shattered wing of a hunting villa. It
appeared to have been once a stately structure, but now exhibited an air of extreme neglect and desolation. Part of the portico
was still visible; but the pillars, which were broken and decayed,
scarcely supported its roof. A small court led to the door, which
was scattered over with masses of the ruined edifice. It had once
been paved; but the stones were so much broken, that several
self-planted trees had established themselves in its area, which
exalted their tall heads above the mouldering walls that inclosed
them. A light still gleamed from a window, and having with
much difficulty made their way through the heaps of rubbish
that on every side obstructed their path, they arrived at the entrance, hoping in this long-neglected spot, which, doubtless,
from the circumstance of the taper, contained some solitary inhabitant, to gain admittance for the night. Anselmo advancing
first, heaved a large rusty knocker, whose sullen sound was awfully reverberated through the building, but no answering footstep approached. Again they repeated the summons, but no one
appeared; nor was any sound to be heard but the deep murmurs
of the wind, which blew in rising gusts round the decayed mansion, and the loud roar of a distant cataract. In a few moments
the light receded, but no human being was visible; and half-
despairing of success, the unfortunate travellers walked round
the edifice to discover if it was possible to obtain admission at
another door; but no other entrance appeared, and they were returning hopelessly towards that which they had quitted, when a
deep groan, proceeding from a kind of grate, or loop-hole, again
riveted their attention.

"Some one is suffering here," cried Enrîco, recalled from his abstraction by this new incident, "and Providence has, perhaps in mercy, conducted us to this place for their deliverance. Let us make another attempt, and if we are still unsuccessful, we will address the prisoner, and, if possible, afford assistance."

Anselmo did not wait for a second command, but sprang hastily round, whilst Enrîco lingered for some moments behind, with his eyes fixed in astonishment upon the ivyed arch of the window, in hopes, as the moon still shone full upon it, of being able to discern the unfortunate sufferer who had thus interested his compassion. The groan was not repeated; but, assured that it was not fancy, having heard it distinctly in the pauses of the wind, he determined not to leave this melancholy abode till the affair was investigated. Grown desperate by delay, Anselmo again thundered at the door, and on hearing a slow measured step advance towards the entrance, called loudly to his master. Enrîco instantly appeared, and the door being opened by a being, whose aspect indicated the extreme of guilt and wretchedness, they were asked who they were, and what had directed them thither? Enrîco, after informing him that they were benighted travellers, who requested a lodging for the night, put a ducat into his hand, and besought admittance. The haggard wretch, whose meagre countenance was distorted by a long connexion with vice and misery, having already the splendid present in possession, would have closed the door upon his necessitous guests, had not our hero, who was aware of his design, assured him that if he would allow them to remain there during the night, he would present him with twice the sum on their departure.

This was a bribe too considerable to be rejected, and having thrown open the door, which he had held half closed in his hand, they were admitted into the interior of the structure. They then proceeded through a long dark passage, in which opened two doors in contrary directions, that on the right leading into a large desolate hall, and the opposite one into a kind of kitchen, which the stranger observed was the room usually inhabited by himself, and the only one with which they could be accommodated during their continuance in the mansion. This miserable apartment contained no other furniture than a few broken chairs, an old worm-eaten cupboard occupying one of the angles, a Norway oak table, whose grotesque frame was cut into numerous devices, and an ancient time-piece, which was erected as a fixture, and seemed, from the antiquity of its appearance, to be nearly co-existent with the building. There was no fire, though it was the middle of winter, and the room consequently rendered intensely cold by several apertures in the wall, which admitted the bleak winds of the east. Anselmo complaining of the chill air, besought the stranger to kindle a fire upon the hearth, and also to prepare them some refreshment. Maschero, which was the name of the host, eyeing him askance as he made the request, replied sullenly that he had no food in the house, except a few barley cakes, and a dish of goat's milk, which were both of them stale and unpalatable. Enrîco desiring that he would bring these, and also some wood to kindle a fire, the stranger took the lamp from the table, and withdrew. Anselmo knowing that his master's thoughts were partly absorbed in a new subject of astonishment, proposed that they should engage their host in conversation during the greater part of the night, and take an opportunity of searching the mansion when he was overpowered by sleep.

"How can this possibly be effected?" replied Enrîco, hastily; "if he has an important secret in his possession, it is unlikely he should be so little on his guard as to disclose it. Force is the only means that can be adopted with success: and though I should unwillingly spill the blood of a wretch like this, if innocence can by no other method be released from the grasp of oppression, we must submit to necessity."

"I have something in my wallet though," returned Anselmo, rising with a look of self-complacency, "which, if properly applied, may be of use notwithstanding, as it sometimes brings to confession as completely and instantaneously as the most acute tortures of the inquisition."

Enrîco turned to him with a look of inquiry, and could not forbear smiling when he saw him select from his store two flasks of wine which he had thus fortunately procured. The matter was now hastily determined; the liquor was to be presented to Maschero, who would doubtless receive it with pleasure, and if it failed in the design of making him sufficiently communicative, it would, at least, from its inebriating qualities, lull him into a state of insensibility, till they had explored the different apartments in the ruin, and had accomplished their design.

In a short time the gloomy and sullen inhabitant of this miserable abode returned with a log of wood, and a bundle of sticks. There was no grate remaining; but throwing the fuel upon the hearth, a fire was instantly kindled, and his guests, who had been long shivering with cold, drew close to the blaze. The barley cakes were then placed upon the table, with a small bowl of goat's milk, and a large old horn, to be used as a drinking vessel. Anselmo, who was too hungry to be nice, eyed them with satisfaction, whilst Enrîco, though little inclined to partake of this coarse, unpalatable fare, attempted to eat. The wine was then produced, and the stranger was requested to taste of it. He assented. It was a liquor he had been long unused to. The lineaments of his face seemed to lose their hardness, and he began to join in the conversation. Enrîco demanded if the mansion contained any other tenant? and being answered in the negative, discontinued the inquiry. Finding from his name, as well as from his accents, that he was an Italian, Anselmo availed himself of this discovery, by claiming him as a countryman, and asking several questions concerning his family and former residence; but the recluse was too wary not to elude his inquiries, and soon convinced his guests that he had previously determined never to unfold any particular with which they were at present unacquainted. The wine now went cheerfully round; Maschero drank plentifully, and was soon so much elevated as not to perceive that Enrîco and his servant, after having taken a very small quantity, were satisfied with only raising it to their lips. Accustomed only to spare and meagre diet, it soon arrested his faculties, and before he had drained the second flask, he fell back on his chair, and closing his eyes, sunk into a fast sleep. The success of the design elated the spirits of our travellers, who anticipated with pleasure the full accomplishment of the project they had so artfully imagined. Anxious to commence the pursuit, Anselmo arose from his seat, and taking the lamp from the table, moved it slowly towards the corner, in which Maschero was placed, to observe if his slumbers were sound. The lids of his eyes did not move, and being convinced that he was perfectly insensible, he was going to make a sign for his master to proceed, when he perceived a small dagger just appearing beneath the cloak of the stranger. The policy of securing this instantly occurred, and drawing it carefully from its concealment, he presented it with an air of triumph to his master, telling him, at the same time, in a low voice, that he was ready to accompany him. Enrîco, having extended his arm to grasp this instrument of death, started when he examined the blade, which was apparently rusted with blood. He, however, repressed the expression of his astonishment, and desiring Anselmo to follow him, quitted the room, without neglecting the necessary precaution of fastening the door on the other side, which was easily effected by means of a bolt. This, from long disuse, could not be managed without some little noise; but the loud breathings of Maschero convinced them that he still slept. Having previously secured the lamp, they advanced along the hall, and departing through a contrary door, which directed them into a long vaulted passage, they were enabled to find their way through many intricate windings to a stone stair-case. These steps, which were mouldering into ruins, led them into a wide dreary gallery, in which opened several rooms. Anselmo, being naturally superstitious, followed slowly behind, and as the hollow gusts of wind hurried through the deserted passages, expected every moment to see the form of a spectre gliding into the remote corners; but ashamed of confessing his fears in the presence of his master, he remained silent, whilst Enrîco took a general survey of the old chambers through which they passed. All that had hitherto fallen under their observation were unfurnished. The casements were gone, the walls were in several places decayed and mouldered into dust, whilst the yarrow, the nettle, and other weedy shrubs, which had taken root in the interstices of the broken stones, were seen waving through the apertures. Birds of prey had long lived unmolested in this dreary building, and seemed, from long possession, to have laid claim to the most considerable part of it. The sight of the lamp, however, put many of them to flight, whose screams resounding through the whole range of apartments, had a dreadful and solemn effect. Unappalled by these terrors, Enrîco reached the extent of the gallery, and undrawing a rusty bolt, opened the door of the only room which had not before fallen under his notice. This chamber was of a triangular form, low, gloomy, and extensive, containing nothing like furniture except a small mattress at the farther end of it, a stool, and a broken table. A high narrow grate was the only means of admitting the light, and from the whole of its appearance, it seemed to have been originally intended for a prison. Being well assured, from the direction of the window, that this was the room from whence the groan proceeded, Enrîco desiring Anselmo to wait without the door, advanced towards that corner where the mattress was laid, and beheld, to his unutterable astonishment, the figure of a female, whose face was covered with a veil, apparently asleep! Enrîco's breast now throbbed with new emotion; his heart beat quick, his limbs trembled, and a feverish heat pervaded his whole frame. Having proceeded within a few steps of the bed, he placed the lamp upon the floor, and turning the veil gently aside, beheld the pale, yet lovely, countenance of Laurette! She started, but did not awake, and never did Enrîco discover so much self-command as at this moment. Rapture and tenderness struggled in his breast, and scarcely could he stifle those feelings which would have prompted him to clasp her wildly to his heart, and awaken her to a sense of unexpected happiness. But a moment's reflection was sufficient to convince him that such a conduct might be attended with danger; joy might operate too powerfully upon a frame enervated by sorrow, and he prudently resolved to send Anselmo to watch by her till she awaked, and gently to prepare her for an interview; yet, after having thus determined, he could not deny himself the luxury of gazing once more upon her beautiful face. Her slumbers seemed now to be tranquil, yet mournful visions had recently been presented to her fancy, for her cheek was still wet with tears.

As he stooped to take up the lamp, which he had placed by the side of the mattress, he observed a small book, bound in red leather, that he instantly knew to have been his own, and which he recollected to have left at the castle of Luenburg. He took it up, and saw on the blank leaf that she had been attempting to sketch his likeness. Memory had been too faithful to its task not to portray his exact resemblance, and charmed with this new proof of her affection, all his senses were absorbed in delight and rapture.

Fearing Laurette should awake, and endure an agony of surprise, which, during her present state of indisposition, might overpower her faculties, and plunge her again into insensibility, he receded towards the door, and calling Anselmo gently forwards, who had remained in the passage whilst his master explored the apartment, he informed him who the prisoner was, and instructed him in what manner to proceed.

The delighted servant could scarcely suppress the acknowledgment of his joy, and taking the lamp, with a heart bounding with rapture, promised strictly to observe the rules which had been prescribed; and entering the chamber, placed himself as far as possible from the mattress, but in such a situation, that he might easily observe her motion. Enrîco, in the meantime, waited impatiently in the gallery, whilst love, tenderness, and astonishment took possession of his mind. How she had been conveyed thither, by whom, and for what purpose, was as marvellous as inexplicable; and the more he reflected upon the subject, the more intricate and wonderful it appeared.

"The wretch," cried he, "who occupies the mansion, is undoubtedly an assassin! The dagger, rusted with blood, is an undeniable proof of it: was it then intended that her innocent life should be sacrificed? If so, who could instigate the wretch to so horrid a deed—a deed so disgraceful to humanity, that none but fiends could reflect upon it without shuddering!"

Unable to solve this mystery, the mind of Enrîco suffered a tumult of distracting surmises, till the soft voice of Laurette, that dear, that well-known voice, wrapped him in attention. She was uttering something in a tone of supplication, but the words were undistinguishable, for they were low and inarticulate; yet it was easy to ascertain that Anselmo was offering something of condolence, which she did not clearly understand. Still he listened in hopes of distinguishing her words, till he heard a faint scream, not expressive of terror, but of mingled surprise and rapture, which was instantly succeeded by the name of Enrîco, pronounced in those sweet, those melting accents, which had ever possessed such powers of enchantment over him. Unable to endure longer suspense, he did not wait to be recalled; but rushing precipitately from his concealment, darted into the room, whilst joy of the most ecstatic kind pained and agitated his breast.

Laurette had just risen from the mattress when he entered, and being weak, almost to fainting, was obliged to lean against the wall for support. As soon as she beheld him, from whom she believed herself separated for ever, her soft bosom throbbed with new emotion, and the powers of utterance forsook her; but as Enrîco, with all the enthusiasm of affection, called wildly upon her name, her beautiful eyes were turned towards him with a look so full of affection and tenderness, that his feelings arose almost to agony.

"And is it possible," cried Enrîco, pressing her gently to his heart, whilst his words were almost stifled with transport, "that I have at last found her whom I so hopelessly sought? Oh Laurette! from this moment one destiny shall unite us; we will separate no more."

The fair captive attempted to reply, but tears of joy prevented her utterance; and as Enrîco surveyed her pallid cheek, her thin emaciated form, and every symptom of alarming indisposition, solicitude succeeded to rapture, and anxious as he was to be made acquainted with every particular relative to this mysterious event, he forbore making any immediate inquiry concerning it. As soon as the first tumults of joy were subsided, Laurette, who was unable to move without assistance, and whose delicate frame was still more weakened by this sudden, though joyful, surprise, sat down upon the mattress, whilst Enrîco, after having dispatched Anselmo to convey the remaining part of the wine, and some of the barley cake, which had been left in the room where Maschero was confined, seated himself by her side, supporting her with his arm, which encircled her waist, whilst tears of tenderness and compassion fell copiously from his eyes, as he marked the ravages grief had already made upon her angelic countenance.

As soon as Laurette had taken a small quantity of the wine

and cake, which Anselmo had fortunately removed without awakening his host, and had received fresh assurances from Enrîco that she was safe from the power of the assassin, and that no danger was likely to befal him or his servant on her account, she felt considerably revived, and joined with her enraptured lover in returning thanks to Heaven for having thus sent her a deliverer. Anselmo could not forbear weeping for joy; his master's happiness was inseparable from his own, and he could not, nor did he attempt to conceal his transports.

Laurette, having convinced Enrîco that her indisposition entirely proceeded from want of rest and necessary food, besought him to leave her alone, and in the meantime to endeavour to procure some sleep in one of the adjoining apartments, as she was assured from his appearance he was in want of repose, promising on his return she would gratify his curiosity respecting her present confinement. As it yet wanted some hours of day, he assented, observing it was more for her sake than his own that he was prevailed upon to leave her. Laurette rewarded his acquiescence with a smile, and pressing her hand to his lips as he bade her adieu, he quitted the chamber.

Anselmo recollecting that, in one of the unoccupied apartments, he had seen a large old piece of tapestry lying at one corner of it, which appeared formerly to have been used as a floor-cloth, assured his master that this would make a most excellent bed, and that he would engage, with the assistance of an old blanket that lay by the side of it, to make him a more comfortable one than he had enjoyed for some time. Enrîco remarking that the assertion was by no means improbable, since his couch, in whatever situation, had of late been a thorny one, desired him to prepare it; adding, with a smile, that the knight, who came to relieve distressed damsels, must not be afraid of a few temporary inconveniences.

The tapestry being spread in several folds upon the broken floor of a remote chamber, which was selected by Anselmo from the rest, because the walls were more entire, Enrîco lay down to rest; but as joy is as great an enemy to repose as grief, he did not feel the least inclination to sleep. His servant, at his desire, partook of the bed he had so judiciously formed, as well as of the tattered blanket, which served them both as a covering.

In this situation they remained till the morning dawned faintly through the narrow shattered lattice of their room, which was so fringed with weeds, that the sun was scarcely ever admitted.

CHAP. V.

> "Can such things be?
> And overcome us like a summer's cloud,
> Without our special wonder!
>   Blood will have blood;
> Stones have been made to move, and trees to speak:
> Augurs and understood relations have,
> By magpies, and by choughs and rooks, brought forth
> The secret man of blood."
>
> SHAKESPEARE.

Anselmo's mind not being harassed with such a variety of strange surmises as his master's, he sunk into a quiet slumber, from which he did not awake till it was light; when, having forgotten the reality of his situation in the visions of his fancy, he could not forbear uttering an exclamation of astonishment; but soon recollecting the past, he turned round to inquire of Enrîco in what manner Maschero was to be disposed of, who would probably soon become sensible to his confinement, when he beheld with amazement that his master had quitted his side. Starting instantly from the bed, he hastened into the gallery, where he soon discovered him taking a general survey of the building; endeavouring by these means to beguile the tedious moments that must elapse before Laurette would again admit him into the interior of her prison.

As they passed along one of the apartments, whose barred casements looked into the court, they perceived a board to shake under their feet, which, on examination, was found to be loose and unfixed.

"This is surely a trap-door," cried Anselmo, with evident astonishment, "which leads into some strange, and still more dreary, place. Let us explore it, Signor; who knows but we may find some hidden treasure."

Enrîco made no reply; but desirous of being convinced whether it was really a door, and if so, to what part of the ruin it led, attempted to unclose it. He was not long unsuccessful, and on heaving up the board, discovered that it opened upon a flight of steps, which being steep, broken, and decayed, perfectly corresponded with the rest. These they immediately descended, and soon found themselves in a dismal old chamber, which contained, amongst a considerable quantity of lumber, a large oak chest.

This, on opening, they perceived to be empty; but the lid was no sooner closed, than it occurred to Enrîco, that, from its external appearance, it probably contained a false bottom. Having communicated his thoughts to Anselmo, the chest was again examined, and the suspicion ascertained not to have been groundless. The artfully-contrived board was speedily removed, and our travellers beheld, to their mutual astonishment, the plumed helmet of a warrior, a military habit, with several other articles of dress, stained with blood; an unsheathed sword rusted by time, and a cross of the order of St. Julias. Enrîco started with an emotion of horror as he surveyed them, whilst Anselmo observed, with a shuddering sensation, accompanied by an expressive shake of the head, that there had been some foul play there.

"Gracious Heaven!" exclaimed Enrîco, recovering from the stupor of amazement into which he had been plunged, "What do these garments mean, and with whose blood are they stained?"

Anselmo, who had been examining them severally as his master spoke, took up a piece of linen, which seemed to be connected with the rest of the apparel; this was literally dyed in gore, and as he extended his arm to display it to Enrîco, it dropped into pieces with age.

"The unfortunate being who owned these things," cried Anselmo, piteously, "has long since been at rest. Can you conjecture, Signor, whose they could have been?"

"Your question is a strange one," returned Enrîco, "since I cannot possibly ascertain to whom the ruin belongs, much less can I form any idea of its present possessor; and even could that be discovered, I should still be as far from the point as to the murder committed in it."

"But one may form some kind of a notion about it, Signor?"

"Indeed! then you have more penetration than I have, who am unable to form any judgment upon the subject."

"I do not mean to insinuate that I have more penetration than you, Signor. Do not mistake me; but it is reduced to a certainty that blood has been spilled—ah! and in this very place; the garments are here to attest the truth of the assertion."

"There is sufficient testimony of that," returned Enrîco; "but I thought you was endeavouring to discover the authors of this assassination, and was applying to me for assistance."

"That was not the case, Signor; you never will understand me without I speak directly to the purpose. The whole of the affair then is this: If you think as I do, you will from these evidences believe, that this old building belongs to some great man, who keeps it as a kind of slaughter-house, that when any one offends him, or stands in the way of his advancement, he may send him to an eternal sleep without making any one the wiser."

Enrîco appeared thoughtful, but made no reply; and Anselmo, having replaced the bloody garments in the chest, disposing them in the same manner as before, followed him up the steps. Scarcely had they reached the trap-door leading into the chamber, before a loud knocking at the outer gate filled them with new astonishment.

"Mercy upon us!" cried Anselmo, "the ghost is surely coming to revenge himself upon us for disturbing his old clothes; for what human being would think of coming to such a place as this? If it is man, I can soon do for him; for I have a weapon here," resumed he, taking the rusty dagger from his girdle, "that will do his business quickly—ah! and one too that, by the appearance of the blade, seems to have been well employed; but, if it should be a spirit, Oh Sancta Maria! Signor! what can we do with that?"

Enrîco, without waiting till Anselmo had concluded his harangue, walked towards the window which opened into the court, and beheld, to his unspeakable surprise, four armed men taking a survey of the edifice. At first he imagined them to have been banditti, who infested the woods in the night, and were accustomed to inhabit a part of the building during the day; but the appearance of him who seemed to direct the motions of the rest, indicated nothing of the kind.

The alarm was now repeated, which being aided by the yells of Maschero, who had just discovered his confinement, had altogether a dreadful effect. Afraid that Laurette, from being ignorant of the cause, might be disturbed and affrighted, Enrîco ran hastily to her room. She was just awake, and seemed better. The knocking still continuing, she inquired the cause; and on his assuring her that nothing was the matter, and that he would speedily return to her, she consented to be left.

Not knowing whether the intentions of the strangers were hostile or otherwise, Anselmo took the dagger from beneath his cloak, whilst Enrîco, clapping his hand upon the hilt of his sword, in an attitude of defence, proceeded towards the door.

The person, who appeared to be the leader, advanced first with a stately and dignified air. He seemed to have passed the autumn of life, for locks of grey shaded his forehead, and his face was marked with the lines of age. Struck with the benignity of his aspect, Enrîco raised his hand involuntarily from his sword, and courteously bowing, offered him admittance. The stranger, after surveying him a moment in silence, turned to the men, and said, "There must be some mistake; this is not the person we were taught to expect."

"May I be allowed to understand the motive of this visit?" cried Enrîco, addressing himself to him who was evidently the superior, "possibly I may be enabled to solve this difficulty."

The stranger gave an assenting nod; and then desiring the men, who had accompanied him, to await his orders in the wood, followed his conductor into the hall; not without frequently turning an inquiring eye towards the place from whence the cries of Maschero proceeded.

"I will unravel this mysterious affair immediately," resumed Enrîco, finding his new acquaintance was much interested in these expressions of distress, "when we have reached a place convenient for the purpose." His guest again bowed, and continued to follow him.

The only seats they were able to find, were two large stones which had fallen from the ceiling at the farther end of the hall, but by these they were tolerably well accommodated; and the stranger having again fixed his eyes upon the intelligent countenance of our hero with new astonishment, requested to be made acquainted with his name; and since it was impossible that neglected solitude could be his residence, by what strange combination of circumstances he had been directed thither.

Enrîco did not keep him in suspense. He related his name, at least the only one he had ever known, that of Chamont, and informed him briefly of the most interesting events of his past life, as far as was connected with the subject upon which they had touched; including the mysterious manner in which his mother had disappeared, Laurette's residence with the Marchese, her precipitate retreat from the castle, though in what manner had not been investigated, and how strangely, how miraculously she had been discovered in the prison of the ruin; which little narrative he concluded, by declaring the means that had been employed to intoxicate the assassin, who, he had every reason to believe, meditated her death, though he had at present taken no desperate method to accomplish it.

The stranger could scarcely wait for the conclusion; but throwing his arms round the neck of Enrîco, he exclaimed, in an agony of joy, "Are you then the son of Madame Chamont, the noblest, the most amiable of women? And shall I, by presenting you to her after this long, this hopeless absence, be enabled to discharge some part of that vast debt of gratitude which I owe her. Behold in me the Conte della Croisse, the once wretched La Roque, who, but for her interference, must have perished in a dungeon."

Enrîco's amazement increased; he had never heard the name of Della Croisse uttered by any one except Father Benedicta; and the little he had been able to gain from what that Monk had inadvertently dropped, was so wrapped in obscurity, that no opinion could be formed upon the subject. But as the Conte's exclamation indicated that he was not only formerly known to his mother, but was actually acquainted with her present place of residence, his raptures could not be repressed; and falling at the feet of his venerable guest, he besought him with tears to inform him immediately where his revered parent was removed, and whether he could not instantly be with her. Della Croisse's heart melted within him when he beheld these effusions of affection; and so much was the sensibility of his nature excited, that it was some time before he could command his feelings sufficiently to comply with the request. But finding his auditor could no longer endure a state of suspense and anxiety, he informed him that Madame Chamont was in a place of security not many leagues distant from the wood; and that he might soon have an opportunity of being introduced to her, and of bestowing upon this excellent parent that unexpected and exalted happiness which his presence would inevitably confer.

"Having been recently apprized," continued the Conte, "of the alarming situation of the lovely young captive, with whose fate I find you are already acquainted, I brought a carriage to convey her from this place to the convent in which Madame Chamont has found a secure asylum."

"My mother is then safe in a convent," repeated Enrîco, rapturously.

"She is," returned the Conte; "and not having remained resident there long enough to have commenced Nun, according to the established rules of the Institution, will have no objection to remove from it.

"I have many circumstances to unfold," continued Della Croisse, "in which you are materially interested, and must therefore request you will allow me a patient hearing."

Enrîco bowed assent; but fearing lest Laurette should be uneasy at his absence, excused himself for a moment before the Conte began his recital, and hastened to her apartment. She had been expecting him for some time with a degree of painful anxiety; but his presence soon relieved her from uneasy apprehension, and after having taken, at his desire, a small portion more of the wine and cake, which had been left on the preceding night, he again quitted the room, with an assurance that he would return to her as soon as suitable arrangements were made relative to their intended departure.

The cries of Maschero still continuing to resound through

the edifice, producing a melancholy and dreadful effect, Enrîco found it necessary to silence him, by asserting that, since his criminal intentions were discovered, his only hopes of obtaining that mercy he had so little reason to expect, rested upon the compassion of his judges, and the purity of his future conduct.

This had the desired effect, and Enrîco, being anxious to hear the important incidents which were shortly to be unfolded by the Conte della Croisse, again seated himself upon the stone by his side, and besought him to proceed.

"As it is necessary," replied the venerable guest, "that we should remove from this place as speedily as possible, I shall relate all briefly. You are, doubtless, informed that your birth is supposed by all, even by your mother, who is, notwithstanding, Virtue herself, to have been illegitimate." Enrîco shuddered, and looked surprised.

"You are, I say," added the Conte, "universally considered as the illegal offspring of the Marchese de Montferrat."

"Impossible!" returned Enrîco impetuously. "Who dares to asperse the character of my mother?"

"None, none," replied the Conte, "can cast a shade upon her spotless reputation: I would myself defend her with my life from the shafts of calumny and malice; grant me but patience, and you shall hear the whole. The Marchese de Montferrat is your father; you are his lawful child, and consequently the next heir to his title and possessions."

"Great Heaven, is it possible!" cried Enrîco, lifting up hands and eyes in astonishment; "and is this mystery but just unravelled?"

"The death of a wretch," returned the Conte, "who has been long initiated in all the arts of cunning, and who has long secretly sought my destruction, could only have unravelled it. The monster to whom I allude, is the Marchese's steward; you are assuredly acquainted with his character?"

"Is Paoli then dead?" interrupted Enrîco.

"The same," replied Della Croisse. "That death, he so long meditated against me, he received at my hands: I met with him by accident, or rather by the direction of an interposing Providence; for to attribute such events to blind chance is impious.

He attacked me; I was fortunately armed, and being aware of his infamous design, before he could disengage the stiletto from his cloak, plunged mine into his heart. He groaned, and fell; but his breathing convinced me he was still alive. Little as he merited compassion, I found my breast was not steeled against its influence; and ordering my servants, who were not far behind, to convey the assassin to an inn, I followed him, and sent for assistance. The wound was pronounced mortal; but the effect was not instantaneous, as it allowed time for the confession of his crimes. He informed me that Madame Chamont was placed in a convent, whither she was to have remained for life; in which seclusion more than ordinary restrictions were exercised over her. That, by the express orders of the Marchese, she was not permitted to write from the cloister; and the more effectually to prevent the circulation of letters between her and her son, she was taught to believe that he had been killed in an engagement, and that Laurette, her adopted daughter, was already united to a young Nobleman, selected for her by her guardian.

"He then informed me," resumed the Conte, "that this fair young creature was the daughter of the Conte Della Caro, whose father was murdered in a wood by a wretch hired for the purpose by order of the Marchese de Montferrat, who, if he died childless, was the next heir to his estates; but as the Contessa brought forth an infant soon afterwards, it was necessary that this also should be removed. Some qualms of conscience seizing upon the Marchese at this time, prevented him from sacrificing the child; but as to secrete it was indispensably requisite, he found means of doing this so efficaciously, that no one suspected his design, every body supposing that the infant expired with its mother, who lived only to give it birth. Some peculiar circumstances had, he added, induced the Marchese to believe the mysteries respecting her origin had been unfolded to Laurette; but who the person was who had obtained and conveyed this intelligence could not be ascertained, as no one, he had imagined, had gained any certain information upon the subject. This, together with her beauty and inimitable accomplishments, instigated him to offer her his hand, as a means of securing the secret to themselves; but, contrary to his expectation, this was resolutely refused, and finding from another conversation with her, and the discovery of a picture, bearing the resemblance of her mother, the Contessa della Caro, that she had been previously made acquainted with the secret of her birth, he had at last determined upon her death.

"He then declared to me," continued the Conte, "whither she was conveyed; at the same time giving me so minute a description of the assassin employed, as to render a mistake impossible. Not expecting, therefore, to meet any other being than the forlorn and guilty wretch I was in search of, you may easily conceive my astonishment when I beheld you, apparently an inhabitant of the ruin, at the time of my arrival."—Here the Conte remained silent, and Enrîco, after acknowledging his gratitude for the active part he had taken, and expressing his surprise at the interesting events that had been recounted, demanded in what convent Madame Chamont was now resident, and how the legality of her marriage with the Marchese de Montferrat was to be proved, since the person, by whom the confession had been made, was removed by death.

"The convent in which your mother is placed is not far from this place," returned the Conte; "she is in a society of reformed Benedictine Nuns, of the congregation of Mount Calvary, and has probably before this time entered into her noviciate state. As to the priest who officiated at the marriage, being already acquainted with his name and place of abode, there will be no difficulty in securing him as an evidence, who will bring undeniable proofs of the truth of the assertion.

"As to the murder committed on the body of the Conte della Caro," resumed the Conte, "it must, if possible, be consigned to oblivion, the offender being not only the husband of Madame Chamont, but your father; and as the fair orphan may easily assert the justice of her claim, without making so dreadful a disclosure, through the evidence of the woman who acted in the capacity of nurse, the wife of Paoli, whose testimony will be sufficient to vindicate the proceeding, and who will be ready to appear in case of necessity."

Enrîco shuddered at the idea of the Marchese de Montferrat, who, he was now convinced was his father, being brought to justice, and inquired eagerly if it could not be prevented.

"Easily," replied Della Croisse, "if the offender will criminate himself in a private confession, and restore Laurette to her
rights, by bestowing her upon you, and by investing you in his
possessions, at least the principal part of his property, on your
nuptials, and in the rest on his decease. But from what I was
enabled to gather from the last words of Paoli," continued the
Conte, "the Marchese does not consider your mother as his lawful wife; the steward having expressly received orders from him
to procure a person under the assumed habit of an ecclesiastic
to solemnize the marriage, instead of which, from some secret
motive, he applied to a secular priest, probably from this consideration, that should the Marchese be induced to deny him
pecuniary assistance, he might, by disclosing the affair to him
after his union with the lady whom he afterwards married, procure large sums by keeping the important secret. But this never
happening in the course of his stewardship, the Marchese, he
confessed, was yet ignorant of the truth; but the priest being yet
alive, to whom I might instantly apply, the fact would easily be
proved. The unfortunate wretch also acknowledged," resumed
the Conte, "that he had artfully instigated the Marchese to the
murder of Laurette for some time before the measure was adopted, fearing lest he should succeed in gaining her affections,
and by another connexion involve him in new difficulties, as he
had, he declared, suffered continual fear and apprehension during the lifetime of the reputed Marchesa, lest the former marriage, through the confession of the priest who united them,
should be publicly attested. The person, he likewise informed
me, who was employed to assassinate Laurette, was his brother,
a native of Italy, who had consented to execute the bloody business, according to his engagement, in consideration of a splendid reward. That it was their intention to have murdered her, as
she slept, on the night of their arrival at the wood, but that grief
and terror had prevented her from yielding to repose; and being
each unwilling to undertake the task allotted to them, during
his continuance with Maschero, they had mutually agreed to
leave her to perish by famine, having previously determined in
what manner the body was to be disposed of, which was to be

entombed in an obscure part of the forest. The wretch, who was necessary to the crime, whom he had acknowledged for his brother, he commended to my mercy; and having particularly directed me to this place, soon afterwards expired in inexpressible agony and horror."

Enrîco, who had listened with increasing amazement, now arose from his seat, and stood for some time transfixed in astonishment. The scenes of complicated guilt and depravity, which had been thus wonderfully unfolded, quite overpowered him; and when he connected the tender name of father with these enormities, the blood crept cold through his veins, and a chilling sensation disordered his whole frame. But as soon as his thoughts glanced upon Laurette and his mother, dwelling upon the rapture the latter would experience on seeing him, tears of affection and tenderness fell fast from his eyes; and requesting that the Conte would liberate Maschero, and deal with him as he thought proper, being in haste to depart, he flew again to Laurette, who had been long impatiently awaiting his return.

Lost in doubt and perplexity, her spirits were now nearly exhausted; and unable to form any conjecture concerning the person below, from what she had heard, besought him to acquaint her who he was, and what was his business. Unwilling that she should suffer even a transient suspense, Enrîco, after some little preparation, informed her all that he deemed necessary for her to know, concealing every thing for the present which could excite uneasiness, and even disclosing the joyful part of the intelligence with the utmost circumspection. But when she was convinced that her dear-lamented friend was in safety, and that there was a probability of her soon being with her, joy could no longer be restrained, and tears of tenderness and affection flowed fast upon her cheek.

Fearing the effect of these indulged transports upon so delicate a frame, Enrîco endeavoured to calm them by an assurance, that nothing should prevail upon him to remove her immediately, but a promise on her part to become more tranquil.

Whilst Enrîco remained in the prison with Laurette, Maschero was released from his confinement by the Conte della Croisse, on his solemnly declaring that he would never again participate in a crime of such magnitude. The punishment for capital offences by the German laws, being so much worse than death itself, was held in utter abhorrence by his lenient accuser, the wretch who has committed them being doomed to wear that external brand of infamy which precludes, through a miserable existence, the possibility of a return to virtue; that probably, had he been instigated by no primary consideration, he might have been tempted to have declined a prosecution without reflecting that by this clemency he would be espousing the cause of vice, and violating the laws of justice.

Enrîco had hitherto mentioned nothing to the Conte of the strange discovery made in the old chamber previous to his arrival; and having now every reason to believe that the Marchese, his father, was materially concerned in the murder, evidently committed either in or near that place, determined to avoid it. The bloody clothes found in the chest were once, he imagined, the property of the Conte della Caro, who was said to have been massacred in a wood, and whose body was either buried or concealed in some part of the ruin. But Anselmo, not being aware of his master's intention, and being anxious to disclose to the stranger all the wonders of the place, conducted Della Croisse, in his absence, through the trap-door leading to the apartment, and displayed to him the object of their mutual surprise.

The Conte examined the sword, helmet, and garments severally, without being able to ascertain the unfortunate possessor; but he no sooner discovered the cross of the military order of knighthood, than he was convinced that they originally belonged to the Conte della Caro, who, he recollected, from Paoli's confession, was declared to have been assassinated in a wood or forest. Deeming it imprudent, however, to give Anselmo admission into the secret, he ascended the steps, observing that the person, to whom those bloody garments had belonged, was probably murdered by banditti, who, after having interred the body in some adjacent place, had secured the clothes of the deceased to prevent detection.

Anselmo appeared not perfectly satisfied with the conclusion, but made no reply; and Della Croisse having returned again into the hall, desired he would inform his master that the carriage had been waiting for a considerable time at the skirts of the wood; and since all preliminaries were adjusted, he was in readiness to depart.

Enrîco, attended by the beautiful Laurette, soon entered the room; and as she leaned gently upon his arm for support, there was something so lovely, so interesting, in her appearance, that as Della Croisse continued to gaze upon her with a mixture of pity and admiration, his eyes were suddenly filled with tears; and scarcely could he subdue his feelings sufficiently to answer the meek effusions of her gratitude, which she bestowed upon him.

The party now quitted the ruin, and the armed men, who had attended the Conte for the purpose of securing the assassin, were discharged without executing their design. Enrîco remembering the ducats he had mentioned to Maschero as the price of their admission, on a promise, solemnly delivered before them all, that he would quit his present residence immediately, and endeavour to become an useful member of society, did not withhold them. Laurette being supported, or rather carried through the wood, was placed in the carriage with the Conte and Enrîco; the horses were consigned to the care of Anselmo, and the whole party, thus relieved from fear and anxiety, commenced their journey.

They travelled leisurely through the day, frequently stopping for refreshment, as Laurette's weak state required the most strict care and attention. In the evening they arrived at a small inn on the road, not more than two leagues from the convent, where they were enabled to procure a suitable person to attend upon Laurette, and comfortable accommodations for the night.—During their continuance in this place, Della Croisse acquainted Enrîco with the melancholy incidents of his past life. He also related the manner of his having met with Madame Chamont at an inn, as she was travelling from the hills of Mount Jura into Germany; expatiated with gratitude upon her amiable conduct towards him and his daughter; the still greater obligations she had conferred on him afterwards by saving him from a miserable death; which little recital he concluded with a relation of that part of her story which was immediately connected with his own.

Enrîco listened to all with a painful concern, and thought every moment an age till he could throw himself at the feet of that beloved parent, from whom he had been so long, so strangely separated.

CHAP. VI.

"Bring the rath primrose that forsaken dies,
The tufted crow-toe and pale jessamine,
The white pink, and the pancy freaked with jet,
The glowing violet,
The musk-rose, and the well-attir'd woodbine,
With cowslips wan that hang the pensive head,
And every flower that sad embroidery wears."

MILTON.

Rest and nourishment had so happy an effect upon Laurette, that she was enabled to prosecute her journey on the ensuing morning without much apparent fatigue. The vehicle which had conveyed them thither, was stationed at an early hour near the door of the inn, and our travellers felt their hearts bound with new sensations of pleasure when they entered it.

As soon as they were seated, Enrîco besought Laurette to acquaint them with all that had happened to her previous to her quitting the castle; and also by what chance the letter which he had written to her, remained unanswered.

The epistle he alluded to, she assured him, was never received; and as letters very rarely miscarried, they were both internally convinced that it had been intercepted. She then proceeded to inform him of the strange events which had taken place during his absence; what she had suffered from the unremitting assiduities of the Marchese, his cruelty, his threats, when she repeated her resolution of rejecting him; the conference overheard in the pavilion, and the unaccountable manner in which she had been forced from the chamber.

Enrîco listened with the most earnest attention as she continued her little affecting narrative, which was frequently interrupted by her auditors with exclamations of surprise and horror, particularly in that part of it which treated of the conversation supported between the Marchese and Paoli in the room of state.

When the steward had conveyed her, she added, about a league from the mansion, he endeavoured to dissipate her fears by an assurance of protection, solemnly declaring that the Marchese had no intention of sacrificing her life; but had determined to place her in a convent till he could think of some other method of disposing of her more congenial to his inclinations.—This, she acknowledged, had the desired effect, as she now imagined that a new plan had been adopted, less terrible than her former surmises had suggested, and the circumstance of being confined for life in a cloister, since she now believed herself separated for ever from her earliest and tenderest connexions, produced reflections unattended with regret: but her late sufferings occasioned such languor and indisposition, that they were obliged to alight at a small inn upon the road. A fever was the consequence of these repeated alarms, which confined her for some days to the place, during which time she was attended only by a woman of a very unpromising aspect; a surgeon, resident in an adjacent village, and Paoli, who expressing the utmost impatience for her recovery, seldom quitted the room.

"Ah Laurette!" interrupted Enrîco, "how providential was this illness! But for such an event, the benevolent exertions of the Conte della Croisse, as well as my own efforts, to inform myself of your situation, might have been fruitless." The fair narrator directed a look of gratitude towards Heaven, and then continued her recital.

"As soon as I was able," resumed Laurette, "to leave this inn, which presented very indifferent accommodations, we pursued our journey; and firmly assured, from what Paoli had advanced, that I was going to be secluded in some religious retirement, I made no farther attempt to interest his compassion, or obstruct the prosecution of his purpose.

"On the evening of the second day after our departure from the inn, he informed me, that I should be at the end of my journey that night. Again my fears began to take alarm; I looked wistfully around, but no convent appeared. Night hung her glooms upon the landscape, but still no hospitable asylum was

to be seen. I now began to imagine I had been deceived; apprehension succeeded to hope, and a thrilling sensation of horror
almost deprived me of reason. We then entered the precincts of
the wood, whose wildness and extent appeared dreadful. The
sterile sublimity of the rocks, which I had hitherto contemplated with awful admiration, receded from my view. The deaf-
ening sound of the cataract softened in a sad murmur; the wind
moaned among the trees, and the hollow sighs, that it sometimes
uttered, seemed to lament my approaching fate. As we entered
the wood, the moon threw a pale, uncertain light upon the eminences; but no sooner had we arrived near the centre, than her
beams were entirely excluded; briars and entangled thickets frequently intercepted the path, rendering it not more dreary than
dangerous, and voices, heard at intervals in the silence of night,
filled me with new terrors. At length a light was seen streaming
through the trees, proceeding from a distant window. I inquired
to whom it belonged, and was informed it was a house not far
from the convent, which would accommodate us with lodgings
for the night. Thither, incapable of making resistance, I suffered myself to be conveyed. Maschero gave us admittance; and
having conducted us to the habitable part of the ruin, brought
some food. I attempted to eat, but could not; and pleading las-
situde and indisposition, requested to be directed to my room.
Maschero led me to an apartment, and after eyeing me with a
malignant kind of curiosity, withdrew, leaving me, at my desire,
the lamp he had carried, which I considered as an invaluable
treasure. As soon as he had retired, I began to examine the door,
in hopes of discovering some possible means of fastening it; but
none appearing, I yielded without restraint to the impulse of
my feelings, which were now too violent to be subdued. When
I had indulged the first paroxysms of my sorrow, I advanced
towards the window, to take a minute survey of my situation,
and to ascertain if there was any apparent possibility of escaping
from it, should I be deserted by my artful conductor, and left in
the power of Maschero, whose unprepossessing appearance had
given me justly the idea of an assassin.

"After a night passed in the utmost distress and anxiety, I was
again visited by this emaciated figure, whose aspect had excited

at once pity and terror. He entered without seeming to recollect that the room contained any other inhabitant, and after setting a pitcher of water and a cake upon the floor, would have instantly withdrawn; but I prevented his design by inquiring whether Paoli was arisen; and being answered in the affirmative, ventured to ask if he had mentioned any thing relative to our intended departure?"

"You are at the end of your journey, I believe," replied Maschero, with a malignant smile; "and since the person who brought you has thought proper to leave you, must make yourself contented where you are."

"What I suffered from this intelligence cannot be easily imagined, or rather what I suffered a short time afterwards; for having fainted, I was not immediately conscious of what had passed. As soon as I recovered, I found myself again alone. The door was fastened, and the pitcher and the barley-cake were placed by the side of the mattress upon which I had fallen. My distress now admitted of no increase, death appeared unavoidable, and I now began to consider in what manner it was likely to be executed. Sometimes I conceived it probable that Paoli had only absented himself for a few days, for the purpose of transacting some business in that part of the province, and meant to return at the expiration of that time, and to fulfil his intention. At other times, I imagined it likely that I was designedly left to perish, either by poison or famine; and that the steward intended to wait at a convenient distance, till after my decease, that he might have the satisfaction of conveying the intelligence to his Lord.

"Two whole days passed in this manner without any material event, in which time no creature approached the melancholy chamber selected for my apartment. Hunger had obliged me to take a small portion of the cake, with which my inhospitable host had supplied me; it was coarse and unpalatable; but being ready to sink for want of food, I was compelled to have recourse to it. The next day this pittance was exhausted, and I soon discovered that it was not the intention of my gaoler to present me with more, who having closed the door upon me when I was in a state of insensibility, meant never more to break in upon my solitude with a repetition of his services.

"As night advanced, I felt my indisposition considerably augmented; a death-like faintness was communicated to my heart, and placing myself again upon the mattress, I endeavoured to resign myself to my lot. At last a loud knocking at the outer door roused me from my seat. I started, and proceeded towards the grate; but the gloom prevented me from distinguishing any object, though I had no remaining doubt but that it was Paoli, who was come to witness the completion of his dreadful purpose.

"Some hours passed in the utmost solicitude, till wearied Nature could no longer resist the attacks of sleep. With what succeeded this period," resumed Laurette, "you are already acquainted; but the extent of my gratitude you cannot easily comprehend."

The look, which accompanied the conclusion of the narrative, was perhaps more expressive of her feelings than any thing she could have uttered: and those bestowed upon her by Enrîco displayed more of compassion, affection, and tender concern, than the most forcible language could have conveyed.

The spires of the convent were now discovered above the tops of the trees, and the most pleasurable emotions succeeded. It was a stately Gothic edifice, inclosing an extensive area. The walls, which were at a considerable distance, were strengthened at the angles by small square towers, which were partly in ruins; and these, together with the whole of the out-works, though formed of the most ponderous materials, were crumbling into dust, and were overrun with mosses, lichens, and other weedy incrustations, which gave it rather the appearance of a deserted than an inhabited mansion.

When the party had arrived at a large stone arch, leading into the grounds, they alighted from the carriage; and having crossed the lawn, were met by a Friar at the gate, who came forwards to receive them. Of him the Conte della Croisse made an inquiry concerning the Superior of the convent, and learned from him that the greatest part of the building was inhabited by a society of Monks, who were also Benedictines. This he considered was no unfavourable circumstance, as Enrîco and himself might easily gain admission into their order, should their enterprize not be conducted with the facility they desired: whilst Laurette might remain resident in the convent till Madame Chamont had obtained permission to leave it, and could do it without a breach of propriety.

Whilst the Conte continued in conversation with the Friar, the tolling of a bell, proceeding from the chapel, which was situated somewhat remote, fixed the attention of the travellers. Della Croisse inquired the occasion of it, and was told that a Nun was going to be professed.

"You will find some difficulty in gaining an introduction to the Superior," resumed the Monk, "till the ceremony is performed. Would it not be better to defer the execution of your intention till afterwards; and in the meantime, by mixing with the multitude, you may be gratified with a view of the solemnities. Some of the sisters are already proceeding towards the chapel, and if you will grant me permission, I will accompany you thither."

From what the Monk had declared, it appeared probable that the Abbess would not indulge them with an audience till the profession was over; and after thanking him for his courtesy, they agreed to the proposition.

The congregation was not at present assembled, and the Friar having conducted them along the eastern aisle, placed them on a bench of black marble, which was fixed near the altar, and then left them to join a procession of Monks, who were commissioned to attend.

As soon as this religious had retired, the party contemplated, with surprise, the magnificence and beauty of the chapel. It was supported by pillars of Carara marble, of the most exquisite workmanship. The niches of the walls were adorned with images of the saints and martyrs, the performances of the most celebrated artists, and taste and greatness of design were every where evident.

The organ was loftily situated in a gallery built for the purpose: it was composed chiefly of ebony, and ornamented with curtains of crimson velvet, which were curiously wrought with flowers of gold and purple. The altar was decorated with a profusion of wax-tapers, interspersed with vases, containing frankincense, and other costly perfumes. The table was covered with an embroidered cloth, which was worked by the ingenious hands of the vestals in the most chaste and sacred devices. A large crucifix was erected in the centre, which was supported on one side by an image of the Virgin, and on the other by that of Saint Agatha. The altar-piece was the last supper, by Michael Angelo, which was surrounded by a number of large medallion-paintings, by the most admired artists, representing the deaths and sufferings of the martyrs.

When they had paused for some minutes, to take a general survey of these splendid decorations, they observed two of the Friars hastening towards the aisle, to which they had been conducted on their arrival. They were habited as Benedictines; but their garments being made of coarser materials, bespoke inferiority of rank.

One of these religious spread a carpet, which he had brought for the purpose, in the centre of the chapel, whilst the other laid a pall at the steps of the altar. Soon after this preparation was over, a multitude of spectators assembled, which curiosity, or some not less active principle of their natures, had directed thither, who, having placed themselves in the most eligible situations, awaited the commencement of the sacred rites.

The funeral-bell, which had been for some time tolling, now ceased, and the loud peals of the organ were heard in its stead. A train of Monks, attended by their Superior, then advanced, who moved slowly along the aisle; and the ceremony of the entrance, which was not more striking than impressive, began. First came the novices, strewing the floor with the most beautiful evergreens, preserved and reared for the purpose; then the Lady of the convent, attended by the Nuns, according to their order, with her mitre, and in robes of state; and lastly, the fair devotee, who was come to take the sacred, the indissoluble vow, which was to seal her inevitable doom. She was conducted, or rather supported, by two of the sisterhood, who, with a slow and solemn pace, led her towards the centre of the chapel, each bearing a lighted taper in her hand. The music now ceased. A buz of indistinct voices was heard for the moment, which gradually grew fainter, and then died into silence. Our travellers, having eyed the procession with a kind of painful curiosity, now left the place on which they had been seated, and mingled with the throng. In vain did Enrîco endeavour to recognize the features of his mother; for the veils of the novices were so artfully folded, that their faces were entirely concealed.

As soon as the procession had reached the steps of the altar, the Superior of the monastery addressed the devotee in an exhortation replete with unaffected grace and eloquence, to which she gave the most fixed and earnest attention. The easy dignity of his manners, the deep pathos of his voice, and above all, the sublimity of his doctrines, so affected his audience, that the whole congregation listened to him with devout astonishment.

As soon as this was delivered, the sister, who was to take the veil, advanced between two others of the Nuns, to make her profession. Her voice was at first tremulous; but as she proceeded, it naturally regained its powers; and having answered some questions which were proposed by the priest, respecting the time of her initiation, she knelt before him, and made her profession, which was delivered with the most admirable articulation, and classical elegance.

The prayers appointed for the occasion were then read, in which the Abbess and the rest of the Nuns, as well as the Monks who attended, joined with much fervency, and apparent devotion. As soon as these were concluded, the officiating priest came forward, and having laid the proper dress of the order upon a small marble table erected on one side of the altar, began to assort them; whilst the Lady Abbess took the noviciate veil from the fair devotee, and prepared to enrobe her in black.—When this covering was removed, the eyes of the spectators were withdrawn from the priest, and fixed with a gaze of curiosity on the sister. It discovered a very lovely face, full of the most interesting expression. It was pale, but it was beautiful, and received lustre and character from a pair of dark blue eyes, whose fringed lids shaded a complexion of the most dazzling whiteness; whilst the extreme delicacy of her form was rendered infinitely more attractive from being finely contrasted with the long sable robe descending far beneath the feet, the garb, in which the reformed Benedictine Nuns of the congregation of Mount Calvary are clad.

As soon as the eternal veil was substituted in the room of the noviciate one, and the broad belt and the rosary were adjusted, the priest dipped the consecrated brush in the holy water, and, after having repeatedly crossed himself, sprinkled the devotee, who being then reconducted to that part of the chapel where the rest of the sisterhood were assembled, remained for some time at her devotions. Whilst this ceremony continued, the most solemn breathing strains issued from the organ, which seemed to wrap the souls of all present in a divine enthusiasm. These were succeeded by the choral voices of the Monks, whose deep tones were softened and harmonized by the sweet sound of female strains occasionally joining in and improving the melody.— These rites being over, the professed arose from the place in which she had been kneeling, to undergo that part of the solemnity which appeared to the spectators more awfully impressive than the rest. She was attended as before by two of the sisters, who having led her into the centre, receded a few paces back, whilst she threw herself, with a degree of collected earnestness, upon the carpet. Thus humbled to the dust, she imprinted a kiss upon the earth, to express her humility and lowliness of heart, as well as to signify that she had now totally relinquished the pomps and vanities of the world, to whose follies she was henceforth dead. The body of the fair votarist was now covered with a pall, as if the spark of life, which had animated it, was extinguished for ever; whilst the burial service was chaunted to the notes of the organ, assisted by the vocal powers of the Nuns, Priests, and Friars, whose wrapt souls seemed to be as much elevated above the world, and its trifling concerns, as if they had already shaken off the gross mould that inclosed them.

As soon as these lofty strains had ceased, the vestal was reconducted to her place; and after some time spent in prayer, in which she was devoutly joined by the Priests, Sisters, and whole fraternity of Monks, the consecrated wafer was administered, and the awful solemnities of the church in the rites of the Sacrament began. The devotee having received it with an aspect of collected meekness almost angelic, arose, and having kissed the robes of the officiating Priest, she bowed herself, with inimitable grace, before the crucifix, breathing at the same time a repetition of her vow. She then embraced the rest of the sisterhood, and was conducted by them to the Lady Abbess, who saluted her with a maternal smile, and afterwards to the novices, who received her with the most cordial affection; while a number of rose-lipped girls, fair and beautiful as angels, who were resident for a convent education, strewed flowers over them as they passed along to the last ceremony, that of the coronation, emblematic of that crown of glory, which is promised as a reward to those who, after suffering continual trials and mortifications, are admitted into the regions of felicity.

When this was over, the bleeding cross of Mount Calvary was hung in her bosom, whilst the chaunted hymn, which seemed to utter forth celestial sounds, rose into deep and choral harmony. All present, being wrapped in undivided attention, appeared to have forgotten that they were among the inhabitants of that world, above which they felt so strangely elevated. As the strains died into cadence, which seemed to have proceeded from no mortal touch, the procession of Nuns and Friars, attended by their Superiors, retired in the same order in which they had entered; and our travellers, who during these ceremonies had secluded themselves as much as possible among the crowd of spectators, emerged from obscurity. As the novices, who followed in the rear, moved slowly from the chapel, Enrîco observed them with peculiar attention, endeavouring to discover Madame Chamont, but without success. Many were tall and graceful like her; but there appeared so great a similarity, from being dressed exactly the same, that one was scarcely to be distinguished from another.

Delay now became painful, and the whole party being anxious to obtain some information relative to the best manner of proceeding, walked rapidly from the chapel; and having reached the great gate leading to the principal court belonging to the brotherhood, soon beheld, to their satisfaction, the Friar who had given them admittance on their arrival, standing with two of the Fathers of the Benedictine order in the portico of the monastery.

The Conte instantly advanced to them, and after politely interrogating them concerning their rules and institutions, repeated his former inquiry respecting the Abbess. The Monk received him as before with the most easy courtesy of manner; but on his requesting to know if there would be any impropriety in desiring an immediate audience with the Superior, was advised to defer it till she had given her charge to the sisterhood—a ceremony never dispensed with.

"If you have any thing important to learn from, or to disclose to the Abbess," resumed the Monk, "your arrival this day may be termed unfortunate; as when the solemnities of our church are over, the day is uniformly dedicated to innocent festivity, in which the Superior herself condescends to join. A feast is always prepared on this occasion in the refectoire of the convent, at which she also presides, and a number of Friars, particularly those of the Benedictine fraternity, and pilgrims are admitted. No business of any kind is allowed to be transacted this day, which is rendered not only sacred, but glorious, from its having entitled a beautiful spirit to that eternal reward, which will be conferred upon those, who, from motives of piety, resign the follies and vanities of the world."

"But if I only interpose in the cause of oppressed innocence," returned the Conte, "and endeavour to steal some hours of sorrow from the heart which has too long felt its influence; if my business is to bestow comfort upon those, from whom it has been long withheld, surely this cannot be called an intrusion upon the rites of their festivity."

"These arguments will have but little weight on the present occasion, I fear," replied the Monk, thoughtfully; "and, perhaps, if your request is forwarded with so little discretion, it may meet with a refusal, or, if otherwise, not with that degree of attention which it may merit. If you will take my advice, you will remain here to-night. In this monastery the stranger and the pilgrim are always received with hospitality; and, although the mode of life we have embraced excludes us from what are generally esteemed the comforts of life, we have at least the power of bestowing them upon others. And as to the Lady," continued the Friar, turning a look of inquiry towards Laurette, "I will introduce her to the convent, where she will be allowed to remain till the morrow."

Laurette courtesied meekly, and having thanked the Father for his attention with that elegance of expression peculiar to herself, awaited the result of the conference. Upon mature deliberation, the plan, which was marked out for them by the Friar, was adhered to; and the carriage being stationed at the outer gate, it was mutually agreed, that the party should remove to some inn, or cottage, capable of affording them accommodations till the evening, when they proposed to accept the kind invitation of the Monk, who promised to introduce them on their return to his Abbot, a man of exemplary goodness and piety. Doomed a little longer to suffer the pangs of procrastinated happiness, our travellers again entered the carriage, and soon arrived at a small, but cleanly, hotel, in which comfortable situation they obtained the rest and refreshment they required.

Laurette being much fatigued, at the joint request of Enrîco and the Conte della Croisse, consented to retire, and to endeavour, at least, to obtain some repose; but the exquisite sensibility of her nature prevented the approach of sleep; the idea of Madame Chamont, and the scene she had just witnessed, which called forth all the soft, as well as all the sublime emotions of her soul, pressed too much upon her thoughts; and though she wished to steal into a transient forgetfulness, that by salutary rest she might be better enabled to meet, with becoming fortitude and composure, the tender scene that awaited her, she found it could not be effected; and when informed that the carriage was in readiness to convey them to the convent, she arose without having once yielded to repose, and prepared to obey the summons.

Having satisfied the master of the hotel, they drove from the door, and arrived at the gate of the monastery just as vespers were concluded.

The benevolent Friar, who had been some time in waiting to receive his guests, advanced forwards to meet them, and having conducted them into a lofty apartment adjoining the refectoire, introduced them to the Abbot. By him they were welcomed with that superior kind of courtesy, which is not always attached to the manners of the recluse; offering them at the same time an asylum in his monastery till the business which had directed them thither was accomplished; and also to conduct Laurette to that part of the convent inhabited by the Nuns, where, he assured her, she would meet with all due respect and attention, which, he observed, alluding to her languid appearance, seemed to be necessary. Laurette, who considered that if she prolonged her stay at the monastery after what the holy Father had said, she might be looked upon by the fraternity as an intruder, after many acknowledgments of gratitude, consented to accompany him. As they crossed the spacious area, which directed her so near to her long-lost friend, all composure forsook her; and she looked round with solicitude, in hopes of being able to distinguish her among a party of novices, who, with their veils partly drawn aside, were walking, as if in earnest conversation, along the winding paths of the shrubberies.

As soon as she had gained admittance into the interior of the cloister, a message was sent from the Abbot to the Superior, requesting that she would take a female stranger under her protection till the ensuing morning. An answer was immediately returned expressive of the most hearty welcome, which was delivered by one of the pensioners, who, attended by a Nun, came to conduct her into the parlour of the convent.

Music, heard from a distant part of the edifice, convinced Laurette that the festivities were not over; and being unwilling to detain those who were constrained by situation to endure a life of austerity and mortification from the means of occasional enjoyment, she besought them to leave her alone; assuring the Nun, who was the most assiduously attentive to her, that she should be enabled to procure a sufficient degree of amusement from the novelty of the objects.

As it had been previously determined, that the Conte della Croisse, after having gained an audience with the Abbess, should unfold his welcome intelligence to Madame Chamont with all imaginable care and circumspection, Laurette resolved to conceal herself as much as possible from the rest of the Nuns; and having failed in her design of dismissing the sister, whose office it was more particularly to attend upon strangers, she pleaded weariness and indisposition, and requested to be conveyed to her apartment.

CHAP. VII.

"Come, pensive Nun, devout and pure,
Sober, stedfast, and demure,
All in a robe of darkest grain,
Flowing with majestic train,
And sable stole of cyprus lawn,
Over thy decent shoulders drawn;
Come, but keep thy wonted state,
Even step, and musing gait,
And looks commencing with the skies,
Thy wrapt soul sitting in thine eyes."

MILTON.

As soon as Laurette arose, she received an invitation from the Abbess to attend her in the breakfast-parlour, which was delivered by the Nun who had directed her to her chamber on the preceding night, distinguished from the rest by the name of sister Monica. Having returned this mark of politeness with her accustomed grace, she followed her conductor down the principal staircase, and was ushered into the presence of the Superior, who arose on her entrance, and, with an air of dignified gentleness, offered her a place by the fire. Laurette blushed deeply at the awkwardness of her situation, being thus led into the presence of a stranger without any previous introduction, who, she considered, might possibly form an opinion of her by no means to her advantage.

Having accepted her offer with a degree of modest diffidence, which rather augmented than detracted from the natural elegance of her manners, she awaited, with mingled anxiety and impatience, the arrival of the Conte della Croisse.

Her wishes were not long protracted; for scarcely had they partaken of the morning's refreshment, before the Conte, attended by the Abbot, after a short message to signify their intention, entered the room. Laurette being aware of the necessity of leaving them alone, and observing that some of the Nuns, among whom was sister Monica, were walking in a grove of

acacia and mountain ash, that overshadowed the edge of the
lawn, which the window of the convent-parlour commanded,
gained the Abbess's permission to retire, and hastened to join
them, rather wishing for the moment to avoid Madame Chamont than to meet with her, lest the sudden surprise might be
too powerful to be sustained with fortitude.

It was a clear frosty morning in the beginning of December;
the air was excessively chill, but the range of hills that almost
encompassed the monastery, as well as the high walls which
bounded the gardens, sheltered its inhabitants from those bleak
and petrifying winds, which are so much dreaded in mountainous countries. The party of Nuns seemed to regard Laurette
with a gaze of curiosity as she approached, frequently turning to
observe her as she moved pensively through the avenues; whilst
sister Monica, who was apparently solicitous to conciliate her
esteem by the gentle offices of courtesy, advanced forwards to
meet her, offering at the same time to show her all that was
worthy of notice in the gardens, as far as the austerity of her
rules permitted her.

Though secluded in this religious retirement from earliest
youth, this Nun understood and respected the laws of politeness; and though there was much in the appearance of her new
acquaintance to excite an interest in her concerns, she forbore
to infringe upon them by minute interrogation. The rest of the
Nuns having taken a contrary direction, Laurette was left alone
with sister Monica, who beguiled the moments of suspense by
leading her through the grounds allotted to the vestals, which
displayed through the neglected wildness of the whole some
vestiges of antique taste, perfectly in unison with the whole of
the structure, which, she was informed, had formerly belonged
to a suppressed society of a less modern institution than that of
the reformed Benedictine Nuns of the congregation of Mount
Calvary, which she learned, upon inquiry, was newly founded by
Madame Antonia, of Orleans, Princess of France.

By this communicative Nun Laurette was made acquainted
with many anecdotes connected with the lives of several of the
present inhabitants of the cloister, to which she listened with
eager attention, being in momentary expectation of obtaining

some intelligence relative to her maternal friend; but on her sad story the sister never touched, from which it appeared that she was either totally unacquainted with it, or that some primary cause prevented her from reverting to it. Though sister Monica possessed nothing of that childish levity, with which the manners of youth are sometimes infected, there was a certain vivacity of expression and a certain correspondent look attending it, unobscured by the gloom of a convent, which rendered her a very interesting and pleasing companion; and Laurette, who, from the natural gentleness of demeanour she displayed on a first introduction, had beheld her with partiality, now experienced an increasing sentiment of affection in her favour.

As they walked slowly through the gardens, Laurette could not forbear expressing her surprise at the wildness and neglect which was every where visible; at the same time remarking, that those places consecrated to religion which had hitherto fallen under her observation, had generally exhibited a very different appearance.

"This will easily be accounted for," returned the Nun, "when you are informed that the Superior of this convent, though in other respects almost unexceptionable in every species of goodness, allows her mind to be contaminated with one vice, whose baleful influence deprives her of that respectful regard which would otherwise be paid to her virtues; namely, that of an inordinate love of wealth. This feverish and ever-growing desire has been productive of many serious distresses, not only to those who are under her immediate protection, but extending also to herself. It has occasioned her to exist in a state of continual warfare between duty and inclination. She is sensible of the danger of this augmenting attachment; but wants firmness and zeal to subdue it. This foible, or this vice," resumed the sister, "for it deserves no softer appellation, has not only blunted the natural edge of her sensibility, which I have frequently heard her declare was too acute to be endured, but it has weakened her judgment, and by constant and guilty indulgence has checked the active benevolence of her nature, which might otherwise have been directed to the noblest purposes. But I am wandering widely from my subject," continued the Nun, sportively, "and must endeavour to return to it." She then gave Laurette an accurate account of every curiosity the gardens contained, which were numerous, and from the antiquity of appearance which the whole of them discovered, might be said to merit observation.

Having rambled over a considerable part of the grounds, a walk, conducting them through several little picturesque windings, directed them into what the Nun termed the wilderness, which, from its disordered and uncultivated state, might be allowed to deserve the name which the recluse had bestowed upon it. A path was, however, cut among the trees; and several recesses, in which were placed seats of wood, or wicker work, frequently presented themselves. Laurette, at the desire of her friend, took possession of one of them, and was informed by her that this little melancholy retreat was a favourite resort with the greater part of the society, who were probably walking towards the contrary end, or had seated themselves in one of those little summer recesses which were made for their accommodation. "Some of them I hear not far distant," resumed sister Monica; "speak low, or they will overhear our conversation."

She had no sooner made this remark than the sound of approaching voices proved the truth of the assertion; and two Nuns, the one in her noviciate state, and the other in her veiled one, moved slowly beneath the thick plantation of firs that guarded the entrance, and then advanced towards the arbour in which they were seated. Laurette did not immediately perceive them, till her new acquaintance pulling her gently by the sleeve, said, "They are here. This nearest the recess is she who was professed yesterday; and on the contrary side is sister Juliana; they are inseparables; if we remain here a moment we shall see them pass."

She had scarcely ceased speaking before they came up close to the arched tree under which Laurette and the sister Monica were seated. As soon as they had arrived within a few steps of the bench, the newly-professed Nun, after having given them a transient survey, courtesied meekly, and passed on; whilst her companion, who was much taller, moved pensively by her side with a mournful and dejected air, without once lifting her eyes from the ground on which they appeared to have been riveted. She had now, however, advanced many paces before she turned, and raising her veil, that entirely covered her features, discovered a face which Laurette imagined, from the cursory survey she had obtained, was Madame Chamont's. But the hasty manner in which the veil was replaced, and the obscurity of her own situation did not allow her to be certain. Scarcely had she recovered from the agitation this incident had occasioned, before one of the pensioners advanced with a hurried step towards the sisters, and addressing herself to the novice, informed her that she was wanted immediately in the apartment of the Superior, where a person, whose business was of moment, was in waiting to see her.

"To see me!" returned a voice, which Laurette instantly discovered to be that of Madame Chamont, though it was rendered tremulous by surprise; "who can want me?" The pathetic energy of her articulation, and the corrected sadness of her manners, as she turned towards the messenger, pressed forcibly upon the heart of Laurette; and but for the necessity of submitting her inclination to the dictates of prudence, she would gladly have thrown herself into her arms, and have acquainted her, without reserve, with the happiness that awaited her.

As soon as the Nuns had retired from the wilderness, Laurette ventured to inquire of sister Monica how long the novice, to whom the message was delivered, had been resident in the convent; and was informed somewhat above a year.

"Do you know any thing of her story?" rejoined Laurette, pausing timidly to await her answer.

"I am not in her confidence," returned the sister; "but this circumstance, as it does not detract from her worth, does not lessen her in my estimation, as she has doubtless some secret reason to justify the strict silence as to her former life, family, and connexions, which she has hitherto preserved; and, notwithstanding this secrecy, she is more beloved than the rest of the sisterhood, though I do not imagine any of them, not even the Nun to whom she is most attached, are better informed upon the subject than myself."

They had now passed through the wilderness, and were conducted by a gentle descent into a little rocky recess, which appeared like a natural cave. This perfectly coincided with the rest of the grounds; for the entrance was so wild, that it was with difficulty they were enabled to proceed. After some little exertion they, however, accomplished their design; and entering this little romantic dell, placed themselves upon a stone seat, which was encrusted with moss, whilst the number of weeds, and self-planted shrubs, that waved from the brow of the arch, contributed to the correspondent gloom of its appearance. Here they paused for some moments, listening, with tender, yet melancholy sensation, to the murmur of a tinkling rill, which was heard falling in gentle meanders among the channels of the neighbouring hills. There was something in this soothing sound which reminded Laurette of the past, of those days of juvenile delight, which she had spent at the castle of Elfinbach, whose spacious domain contained a wild and solitary spot not unlike her present situation, where she had often listened to the sad cadence of a waterfall in the stillness of the evening. This brought to her recollection the feelings connected with these memorials, the numerous hopes, fears, and anxieties that had oppressed and agitated her bosom, and the gloomy hours of retrospection which she had afterwards suffered when those days were remembered.

"Wherever we have a kindred melody,
"The scene recurs, and with it all its pleasures and its cares."

But the future, since she had now a generous protector who would never forsake her, presented only visions of happiness; and at times she found it as difficult to support that uniform calmness of mind, which ever accompanies true greatness in the midst of expected felicity, as to endure that appalling malignity with which fortune had hitherto treated her.

As soon as they had retired from this lonely dell, they proceeded through a vista towards the western lawn, which presented nothing worthy of attention, except a large ancient cross, which was erected in the centre. When arrived at the base of this sacred memento, sister Monica numbered the beads upon her rosary, and then prostrated herself before it; whilst Laurette, after bowing humbly as she advanced towards it, paused for a few minutes to examine the figures which were represented upon the pedestal, and the rudely-formed characters, which age had long since obscured, and now nearly obliterated. The steps, "which holy knees had worn", were almost sunk into the earth; the stones were fractured and discoloured, and overgrown with several vegetable encrustations; and though preserved by superstition from actual decay, were broken and deranged by time.

Whilst Laurette stood musing upon the impossibility of saving even these vestiges of holy record from the oblivious grasp of age, and the meek Nun with bended knees was invoking the shades of the departed, those long since mingled with the dust, to look down upon her, and to assist her weak endeavours after piety; a novice, unperceived till she had reached the side of Laurette, summoned her into the apartment of the Superior. Though she had been for some time in expectation of a similar address, a tremulous sensation took possession of her frame, and sister Monica observing the sudden change of her complexion, which from being more than usually pale, was instantly suffused with blushes, and that shortness of respiration proceeding from extreme solicitude, offered her arm, which Laurette gladly accepted, as she advanced with a quick, unequal pace towards the door leading to the cloisters. Having crossed these, she stopped for a moment to recollect her spirits, and heard, as distinctly as joy and agitation would permit her to hear, the voice of Madame Chamont, elevated into notes of transport. Impatience could now no longer be restrained, and pushing open the door with a kind of gentle violence, she soon found herself locked to the bosom of her long-lost friend. Any attempt to do justice to the feelings of the beautiful orphan, of Enrîco, or even of the Conte della Croisse, who had just witnessed a scene as tender, and if possible still more touching, when he introduced to his amiable benefactress a son whom she had mourned as dead, would be vain. Rapture broke forth into tears, and it was long before the charming Nun could believe the happiness that awaited her was not visionary, before she could assure herself that she was not still under the influence of some enchanting dream, from which she feared to be awakened to a sense of former distress. It was not immediately that Laurette was conscious that the room contained any other inhabitant than Madame Chamont: even Enrîco was absent from her thoughts, and the tender glances which he frequently conveyed to her whilst he saw more than filial affection expressed in the fine language of her eyes, were, perhaps, for the first time since they had been bestowed upon her, unobserved or disregarded.

CHAP. VIII.

"But let my due feet never fail
To walk the studious cloisters pale,
And love the high-embowed roof
With antic pillars massy proof,
And storied windows richly dight,
Casting a dim religious light."

MILTON.

The Conte Della Croisse, when admitted into the convent, after a formal introduction by the Abbot, was left alone with the Superior, who received him with that stately kind of politeness which is usually attached to the station she filled. As soon as he was seated, he began to open the occasion of his visit, and fixing his eyes upon her as he continued the subject, with the minute attention of a physiognomist, he perceived that her countenance relaxed with no symptom of pleasure when he mentioned the necessity of Madame Chamont's quitting her retirement immediately, to assert the legality of her claims, should any new difficulties arise to render her presence indispensable. Having entered into a full explanation of the subject as far as the nature of the case required, preserving at the same time a scrupulous reserve as to those events in which she was entirely uninterested, he requested an audience with his fair benefactress, and politely demanded her dismission, since he had already proved that all proceedings against her had been hitherto illegal. As soon as the Abbess had recovered from her surprise, she endeavoured to convince the Conte of the impossibility of yielding to his desires unless the intricacies of the affair could be unravelled, since she had nothing to depend upon but the bare assertion of a stranger, which she considered as insufficient to prove the justice of his claim. From the intelligence which the Conte had received from Paoli in his dying moments, he knew that a considerable sum had been paid into the hands of the Abbess on Madame Chamont's entrance into the convent, which accounted in some measure for the many insurmountable obstacles which were thrown in the way of her departure.

Being perfectly aware of this, he took the most effectual method of silencing her scruples, by convincing her that the sum, which was consigned to her care for the benefit of the sisterhood, would never be recalled; not forgetting to assure her, upon his honour, that he would himself indemnify her from any loss she might sustain; and, moreover; would venture to affirm, that if she would assist in forwarding their design, Madame Chamont, when reinstated in her rights, would richly compensate her for every proof of kindness and attachment she had discovered, since she was unequalled in generosity as well as every other mental perfection.

The Conte's arguments had the desired effect; and as the Abbess listened with complacency to these eventual advantages, she became gradually reconciled to the person by whom they were offered; yet, to enhance the value of the obligation, and also to persuade her new guest that she was not actuated by mercenary considerations, she thought proper to propose a few more objections, which being delivered with less energy than the former ones, were easily removed by the Conte, who anxiously availed himself of every turn in his favour.

After much courtesy of address on the part of Della Croisse, aided by a little well-timed flattery, agreeably and delicately administered, which the Abbess was too young to receive with displeasure, the requested interview was granted; and the noble Conte, whose generous heart overflowed with the most lively effusions of gratitude, was permitted to prepare Madame Chamont for that scene of delight she was shortly to experience, and afterwards to contemplate the effect of joy, the most exquisite in the completion of newly arisen hopes, when she clasped her long-lost son to her maternal bosom! Such scenes of ecstatic bliss cannot be justly delineated by the feeble hand that attempts to sketch them; nor can the mind, which has not been disciplined in the harsh school of adversity, form an adequate conception of them. A sudden alteration in the manners of the Abbess, after Madame Chamont's introduction to Enrîco and Laurette, was evident to all. The apprehensions which her avarice had excited being lulled to repose, there was room for the exercise of those sympathetic virtues which Nature had implanted in her mind; and now that her interest was no longer at war with her inclination, she did not arm herself against their influence. Anxious to remove any little prejudices which she considered might yet lurk in the mind of the Conte, she paid the most marked attention to her guests, giving Laurette an invitation with more than ordinary kindness to remain in the convent till all preliminaries were settled relative to their departure, not omitting to repeat her permission for Madame Chamont to resign her protection when the nature of her concerns rendered it necessary.

The Conte and Enrîco now began to form plans as to the best method of proceeding; and, after a second investigation of the subject, determined to leave the ladies at the convent, whilst they went in search of the priest by whom the marriage was solemnized, who they learned upon inquiry had left his residence in Turin, and had entered into an order of Franciscans not many leagues from Saltzburg. This was a circumstance much in their favour, as it prevented them from traversing a number of barren mountains and rocky precipices, which would have considerably impeded their progress. To prove the truth of Paoli's assertion, without taking this Friar as an evidence, whose testimony would alone be sufficient for the execution of their purpose, would, they knew, be impossible, even should they find the Marchese more favourably disposed towards them than, from his former conduct, they had reason to expect. To allow Madame Chamont and Laurette to attend them on such an expedition, unless the Marchese should intimate a desire to see them, would, they also considered, be highly imprudent, since their reception might be far from a pleasant one; though, by alarming the fears of the Marchese, it appeared probable, since he was now entirely at their mercy, that he would be glad to embrace any terms of reconciliation that would be offered him, rather than suffer his crimes to be exposed.

As soon as they had informed the ladies of their newly-concerted plan, they recommended them to the matronly protection of the Superior; and, attended by Anselmo and two of the servants belonging to the Conte della Croisse, commenced their journey.

As soon as Laurette was alone with Madame Chamont, she related every interesting event that had befallen her since she last parted from her; and requested, in return, that she would acquaint her with every thing that had happened to her since she had been forced from the castle, as this had long been a subject of painful surmise.

"You are already informed, my dear child," replied the amiable Madame Chamont, "of the principal incidents of my eventful story: and what I have to relate will, therefore, appear but like a repetition of what has before been recited; yet, as you desire it, I will indulge you with pleasure.

"You may possibly remember that, on the evening of my departure, Paoli proposed, as soon as vespers were concluded, that I should accompany him along the decayed side of the edifice, that he might consult me respecting the repairs; and you may probably recollect that I acceded rather reluctantly to the proposition, though at that time I was incapable of ascertaining his intention, which was, after conducting me to a remote part of the structure, to deliver me into the hands of three ruffians, who, having covered me with a veil so thick as to exclude every object from my view, placed me upon a mule, and conveyed me, regardless of my cries, through the deepest recesses of the woods, when, having arrived at a small inn, situated at the extremity of the forest, we stopped without alighting for refreshment. As soon as we had reached this place, one of the men, whose aspect indicated him less ferocious than the rest, assured me that I had nothing to fear, and promised, that if I would follow strictly the rules he should prescribe, that he would engage to conduct me to some place of security. This kindness, in a man of his profession, filled me with astonishment; and though I could scarcely believe him sincere, I ventured to assure him of my acquiescence.

'You have then nothing to do,' resumed the ruffian, 'but to remain silent. Any attempt to liberate yourself by your own exertion, or any endeavour to interest the compassion of others, whom we may accidentally meet with in our way, will render my scheme for your preservation abortive. Appear resigned to whatever may be your destiny, and leave the rest to me.'

"His companions, who had remained a few moments behind to finish their refreshment, now approached towards us, preventing by their presence all further communication; but being somewhat re-assured by these promises, my spirits gradually revived; and mindful of the injunctions I had received, I preserved an uniform silence. We travelled all the next day and the following one without obtaining any rest, till, from fatigue and indisposition, I could scarcely proceed. My companions frequently stopped upon the road to procure some food, of which they always offered me a part; but never ventured to alight, probably having some material reason for this precaution.

"It was not till near midnight that, after two days' harassing journey, we arrived at the place of destination, which was an ancient dreary habitation secreted in a wood. The impenetrable veil that was thrown over my face did not allow me to distinguish the road; but I was no sooner sat down than it was removed, and I found myself in a large grass-grown court, with three ill-looking men, whose persons I had only partially seen.

"Scarcely had I obtained leisure to reflect upon my situation before a loud halloo, given by one of my companions, brought to the door of this melancholy abode a being, whose appearance had more in it of savage ferocity than was expressed in the countenance of my conductors. Terror and consternation now almost overcame me, and so weakened was I for want of sustenance and rest, that, had I not leaned against the trunk of a tree, I must have fallen."

"You have no farther to go at present," cried one of the men roughly, "but if you will follow your host into the hall, he will give you some supper; for since you have eat so little upon the road, you must doubtless be in want of refreshment."

"Finding there was no alternative, I obeyed; and the men, having fastened their mules to a tree, entered the room into which my conductor had directed me. Obliged to submit to the necessity of mixing with this horrid group, I endeavoured to reconcile myself to my lot; but no sooner had I partaken of a small portion of the bread and milk, which was prepared by our host, than the indelicate jokes, that were occasionally mingled with their loud peals of laughter, determined me to abandon their society; and addressing myself to the person of the house, whose name was Maschero, I desired to be directed to my apartment."

"Holy Maria!" exclaimed Laurette, in a tone of astonishment, "was you then at the Jansmer Holtz, the abode of the assassin? Could it be the intention of the Marchese that you also should be sacrificed? If so, tell me briefly, I beseech you, how your escape was effected."

"From what has since happened," continued Madame Chamont, "I have no reason to suppose that the Marchese had any design upon my life; but not to keep you longer in suspense, I will hasten to the conclusion of my mournful narrative.

"I was then shewn into a large dreary-looking room, whose appearance was sufficient to impress terror upon a mind not already occupied by this dreadful sensation; but what more than any thing alarmed my fears was the certainty of not having any means of fastening the door. My conductor did not forget, however, to secure it, with the assistance of a bolt, on the other side.

"As soon as I was alone, a thousand melancholy conjectures passed along my mind; and unable to compose myself to sleep, I paced the room for some time in silent agony, frequently starting as the old boards shook beneath my feet; and imagining I heard other steps beside my own, and saw grim and ghastly figures gliding into remote corners. These apprehensions were augmented by other noises, for which I could not immediately account, but which struck me with more terror and dismay than I am able to express. Deep groans were apparently uttered from an upper apartment, and screams, which I was assured did not proceed from the nocturnal revellers, whose voices, which I could yet sometimes distinguish, broke upon the stillness that pervaded the room: I did not, however, long suffer these imaginary terrors, which were not less appalling than my real ones, being soon convinced that the sounds I had heard were occasioned by a considerable number of owls that inhabited the ruinous part of the building.

"I had not suffered more than an hour the forlornness of my situation before the man, whose unexpected compassion had awakened my gratitude, entered the apartment. I trembled as he approached; but my fears were gradually dispersed when he assured me, that if I would bestow upon him and his associates all the money and valuables I had about me, they would not leave me to perish as was their original design, but would convey me to a convent not far from the wood, where I might easily obtain admission.

"You were then employed for the basest of purposes," cried I, astonished at his having made this avowal; "and you have agreed, no doubt, for some considerable reward to take away my life, which, if not more than ordinarily useful, has at least been innocent. Can you, after such an acknowledgment, hope to obtain mercy?"

"The proposal I have made," interrupted the ruffian, "is at least merciful; and if you refuse to accede to it, you are no longer an object of compassion. But I have no leisure to parley, therefore be swift. What is that gem upon your finger?" resumed the ruffian; "take it off, and let me examine it."

"It was a ruby presented to me by my mother of considerable value, and unable to bear the idea of parting with this little sacred memento, I refused to yield to his wishes; at the same time delivering my purse, which contained no inconsiderable sum. He counted the ducats with a look of sullen dissatisfaction, and then demanded, in a stern voice, if I was determined not to relinquish the jewel. Afraid of irritating him by repeating my resolution, I endeavoured to interest his pity, by informing him that it was the gift of my last surviving parent, from whom I had been long separated, and as such was invaluable.

"If it is more precious to you than your life," replied the ruffian, maliciously, "you may assuredly keep it; you are certainly at liberty either to accept the conditions, or to reject them."

"Finding that nothing less than the ruby would bind him to my interest, since the sum in the purse was insufficient for the gratification of his avarice, I was compelled to yield to his threats, though not without shedding many tears at the sad necessity which obliged me to part with it.

"The light of the morning now dawned dimly through the grate of my prison, and soon afterwards I had the satisfaction of quitting my gloomy abode to pursue my journey. Melancholy as was the prospect before me, it was less dreary than on the preceding night, and a small portion of that hope, which never totally abandons us, returned with all its cheering accompaniments to my heart. When I arrived at the convent, the Abbess left her room to receive me; but what was my astonishment when I discovered from her conversation that I was an expected guest. It was now easy to investigate the truth even through the obscurity which veiled it. The men were employed by the Marchese, or rather by Paoli, in obedience to the commands of his Lord, to convey me by stratagem into this religious asylum; and the wretches, selected by the steward for the purpose, taking advantage of my fears and ignorance of their intentions contrived to rob me of the little property I possessed.

"Scarcely was I settled in my new habitation, when the arrival of Paoli was announced, who came to make some arrangements respecting my board. He was closeted for some hours with the Superior; but the result of this conversation was kept a profound secret.

"As soon as he was gone I discovered, from the behaviour of the Abbess, that she had been induced, through the insinuations of the steward, to form an unfavourable opinion of me, as she never addressed me with that maternal affection which characterized her deportment towards the rest of the sisters; and when her eyes accidentally met mine, I observed they were usually turned from me with an expression of contempt, and sometimes of horror, that penetrated my heart. That Paoli had uttered much to my disadvantage, to excuse the infamy of his proceedings, was evident; but of what nature were the aspersions he had thrown upon my reputation, was not easy to be discovered. Often did I half resolve to lay the case before the Abbess, as well to excite her compassion with a relation of my misfortunes, as to absolve me from the crimes imputed to me by my enemies. But an irresistible impulse withheld me for a time from putting this fluctuating design into practice; and another unexpected event relieved me from the indispensibility of again adopting a plan, which, from the probability of being accused of adding dissimulation to treachery, wore rather an unpromising aspect.

"One day, as I was sitting alone in my cell, a message was delivered to me by one of the novices, desiring my attendance at the grate. The surprise this incident excited almost overwhelmed me; hope had so long sunk beneath the horizon of my prospects, that I believed it impossible the morning of joy could ever more dawn upon them; a faint sickness was communicated to my heart, and it was with difficulty that I was enabled, even with the assistance of a Nun, to reach the appointed place. It was late in the evening when I was summoned to the grate; but the dusky hue of the twilight did not prevent me from distinguishing that the person in waiting was Paoli. His figure was too strongly impressed upon my mind to allow me to mistake it; and knowing that a tongue like his could convey no welcome intelligence, I surveyed him for a moment with a look of silent abhorrence, but without uttering a word, till at length disengaging something from his cloak, which I soon discovered to be a letter, "I am come," cried he, with a malicious smile, "to bring you news of your son; this paper will inform you of the whole"—I took it with a trembling hand, and desiring the Nun, who accompanied me, to elevate her lamp, opened it in haste. The first words which met my eye were these:—

"Your son, having been called into actual service, has lately died in consequence of a wound received at the battle of Prague; and your adopted daughter, in obedience to the will of the Marchese de Montferrat, her guardian and lawful protector, is contracted to a young Venetian nobleman. Any future inquiry after these persons will therefore be useless."—The paper now dropped from my hand, a dimness came before my eyes, and I fell lifeless on the pavement. The cries of the Nun who attended me, brought others to my assistance; and on recovering I found myself on a bed in one of those apartments which are allotted to the Superior, with two of the sisters, who were seated by my side. One of these I soon perceived was sister Agnes, the Nun who was professed the day of your arrival, and the only one to whom I had singularly attached myself.

"It was long before my health was re-established, and probably it would have been still longer, had not the Abbess, who soon learned the cause of my sorrow, assisted, with the utmost kindness and attention, in the recomposing of my spirits. During the first three months of my captivity, the use of pens, paper, and every other implement of writing, was denied me; and so strictly was I guarded, that had I been inclined to attempt an escape, I should have found it impracticable. But after this melancholy event I was treated with more gentleness than before; and not feeling any desire to be delivered from confinement, since every earthly tie was dissolved, I endeavoured to conciliate the esteem of my associates; and being entirely disengaged from all worldly concerns, resolved to dedicate the rest of my days to the exercises of religion."—

Here Madame Chamont concluded her recital; and scarcely had Laurette expressed her sense of the obligation, before the Lady of the convent entered the room. The conversation now turned upon more general subjects till the bell rang for dinner; when the party, retiring from the Abbess's parlour, joined the Nuns, who were assembled in the refectoire.

The rest of the day was passed by our heroine and her earliest friend in a state of tender thoughtfulness. The absence of Enrîco and the Conte, as well as the motive of it, now the raptures of the meeting were over, threw a soft shade upon the spirits of Madame Chamont. The interview, which was shortly to take place between them and the Marchese, had something in it peculiarly touching. Her son was gone to claim him as a father; her spotless reputation was shortly to be cleared from those cruel aspersions with which it had been tainted, and how these important matters were to be conducted was a subject for continual reflection. Laurette did not consider it so deeply; happiness was alone presented to her in the visions of her fancy; the Marchese, she believed, would not only confess, but repent of his crimes. What he had meditated against her was already forgotten; and unsuspicious of the murder of her father, she knew of little else that could be laid to his charge.

To walk together through the cloister in the calm hour of twilight; to wander among the massy pillars which supported its arched roof; to mark the holy devices upon the dim gothic windows, was a charm the most congenial to their feelings; and often did Madame Chamont and Laurette steal away unobserved to enjoy that melancholy kind of pleasure, which scenes of this kind never fail to excite in devout and susceptible minds. With what pious sensations did they pace the burial-ground of the convent, divided only from that appropriated to the Monks by a terrace-walk bordered with cypresses! How many of the sisters, who, after having lingered out a life of solitude and penitence in that religious retirement, were now, they considered, numbered with the dead!

The second evening after the departure of the Conte and Enrîco, the chapel-door being left open after the evening prayers, they went, attended by two of the sisters, to see an ancient stately monument, which was erected to the memory of the convent's Foundress, who from her exemplary conduct was reputed a Saint. It was composed of black marble, and was situated on that side of the chapel which was nearest the altar. It was almost encompassed with some others, which had since been erected to the memory of several of the former Abbesses, which, though less splendid, were also ornamented with a number of religious devices.

The privilege of being interred in the chapel was only granted to the Superiors, the Nuns, whatever might be their rank, being always buried without. Laurette could not forbear heaving a profound sigh when she reflected upon the vanity of human distinctions and as she returned slowly towards the cloister, she frequently turned to survey the simple graves of the Nuns, which were covered with high grass, and bordered with evergreens; it being one of the rules of the institution that, after the profession of a vestal (an event which had recently taken place) for the novices to replace the flowers and shrubs used in the ceremony in the same baskets in which they were originally gathered, and then to leave them at the foot of the altar till the vigil is at an end: as soon as the festivities are over, the train of Nuns proceed from the convent to the burial-ground, and being met at the chapel-door by the novices bearing the baskets, strew them upon the graves of their departed friends, chaunting at the same time a requiem for the repose of their souls. This being concluded, the vesper service is performed; after which the sisters are allowed either to return to their cells, or to remain in the gardens till the tolling of the second bell.

CHAP. IX.

"Better be with the dead,
Whom we, to gain our place, have sent to peace,
Than on the torture of the mind to lie
In restless agony."
SHAKESPEARE.

Near a week had elapsed since the departure of Enrîco and the Conte before any news respecting the success of their embassy arrived. During this painful interval Madame Chamont's mind became a prey to causeless anxiety. Joy and sorrow had so uniformly succeeded each other in her past life, that she could scarcely forbear dreading the future; for having enjoyed so lately the raptures of unexpected felicity, experience had taught her, that, in the general course of human events, she might probably suffer the reverse. Long schooled in affliction, her disposition, though it remained unsoured by disappointment, had lost much of its sanguineness; and she sometimes doubted if, when at liberty to return to the world, whether she should acquit herself to her satisfaction, whether her weakened spirits could support that elevation of rank to which she must shortly aspire, with the bustle of society, and all those accompaniments of greatness, which in high life are so seldom dispensed with. Respecting the interview between the Marchese and her son, she indulged a variety of vague conjectures. It was their first meeting; and what would be the result of such an event? Anxiety was increased by reflection, and all the tender, the indescribable sensations of the mother were called into action.

From this state of suspense she was, however, relieved by a letter delivered by Anselmo, who, as soon as he had entered the

gate, inquired eagerly for Madame Chamont, and was directed
to the convent parlour. Having received it with breathless anxiety, she retired to her apartment, and finding it bore the signature of Enrîco, unfolded and perused it in haste. It contained
only a few lines; but these were sufficient to quiet her fears concerning the effect of their journey.

"We have at present," says Enrîco, "met with no material obstacles to retard the success of our undertaking. The priest, who
was the principal object of our search, was easily found; and on
a strict investigation, we were mutually convinced that he also
had been made the dupe of designing villany, and was by no
means accessary to the plot, which appears to have been entirely
conducted by Paoli.

"The Marchese has already entered into a full confession of
his crimes. He seemed, on our introduction, to endure much
internal affliction; for never did I behold remorse and acute anguish more forcibly delineated than when his eyes met those
of Della Croisse. This self-condemning conduct induced us to
proceed in the affair with as much gentleness as possible, though
we did not omit the necessary information relative to the legality of his first marriage, and Laurette's providential release from
captivity and expected death! This intelligence, as it served to
assure him of her safety, seemed to take an oppressive weight
from his heart; though the starts of agony, which frequently convulsed his frame when his distracted mind reverted to his past
crimes, were altogether more dreadful than the imagination can
conceive.

"But I am wandering from my original intention," contin-
ues Enrîco, "which was only to state the policy or your leaving the convent immediately. Anselmo, who is the bearer of this
incoherent epistle, will procure you a carriage from the Kaiser*,
which will convey your charming companion and yourself to the
castle of Elfinbach, our present place of residence, and of late
the abode of the Marchese: perhaps it may be prudent to add,

* Caesar. The sign invariably used throughout Germany, which occasions it
to be generally substituted in the room of that word in the German tongue,
signifying an hotel, inn, or post-house.

that it is his request also, who, if we may judge by appearances, is anxious to obtain the forgiveness of those he has injured. I need not entreat you to prepare for an interview which may demand some exertion and fortitude, as I am convinced your own superior understanding will instruct you in what manner to act. I wish it was in my power to add, that the Marchese's sincerity and repentance are likely to be proved by the purity of his future conduct. But, alas! I fear it will be otherwise; his constitution seems to have yielded to intense sorrow, and much is to be feared from its baleful influence. I mention this," resumes Enrîco, "for the purpose of hastening your departure from the convent, as well as to acquaint you with what may happen. Let nothing prevent you from commencing your journey immediately."

When Madame Chamont had communicated the contents of this letter to Laurette, she gave orders for Anselmo to make every requisite arrangement; and being informed in about an hour that the carriage was in readiness, she took an affectionate leave of the sisterhood, and, attended by her fair charge, pursued her way towards the castle.

After a few days' journey, in which no event happened worthy of attention, they came within view of the mansion, whose rude, deserted appearance brought to the recollection of Madame Chamont the ideas it had first excited; and when they arrived at the great gate leading to the outer court, her tears flowed fast and unrestrainedly, as her memory reverted to the scenes she had witnessed since she last quitted it.

The death-like silence, which seemed to prevail throughout the castle as they advanced within a few paces of the portico, aided these uneasy sensations; and already had they reached the door of the great hall, which was thrown open for their reception, without having met with any inmate of the mansion. At last one of the servants belonging to the Marchese crossed the hall with a hurried step; and on being accosted by Laurette, stopped to hear her commands. She inquired for the Chevalier Chamont; and the servant having conducted them into one of the apartments which they had formerly occupied, ran to inform him of their arrival. They had not been many minutes in the room before Enrîco entered. His demeanour was mild, but dejected, and his face, "like to a title-page, foretold the nature of some tragic volume." Madame Chamont, who, from the hints dropped in the letter, too well guessed the cause, after a fruitless attempt to recompose her feelings, inquired tremulously if they had arrived too late?

"The Marchese is yet alive," returned Enrîco; "but we must not flatter ourselves with delusive hopes—he is evidently dying. To me and to the Conte he has made a full confession of his enormities, and may Heaven, in consideration of his sincere, though late repentance, pardon his atrocious crimes! A Carthusian Friar, who has been with him more than two hours at confession, is so shocked with what has already been related, that he has twice left the room without giving him absolution, though, as his decease is hourly expected, I hope he will be wrought upon not to postpone it."

Madame Chamont, who now found it necessary to resist the native softness of her heart with all the fortitude she could command, endeavoured to mitigate the keenness of her sensibility by the most vigorous exertion; whilst Laurette attempted to support the sinking spirits of her friend with an external appearance of firmness, the effect of painful effort. Since it was impossible for them to be introduced to the Marchese during his engagement with the Monk, the party resorted to the saloon, where they were soon joined by the Signora d'Orso, whose unbounded joy on beholding Laurette could only discover itself in tears. She would have made a thousand inquiries concerning her mysterious departure, and the events that had taken place since that memorable æra, could she have sufficiently commanded her voice; but surprise, for she had not been taught to expect her arrival, and the settled melancholy that was depicted upon the countenances of all present, prevented her interrogatories. After about an hour spent in painful reflection, the Conte della Croisse, with the permission of the Marchese, came to conduct Madame Chamont and Laurette into the chamber. Night and solitude combined to assist the pensiveness of their feelings, as they advanced with a slow, unsteady pace through the long winding galleries which led into the apartment; and as Della

Croisse laid his hand upon the door to give them admission, Madame Chamont's spirits so entirely forsook her, that she was obliged to lean against one of the pillars of the corridor for support. A look from Enrîco at length inspired her with new fortitude, who, taking a hand of each, led them to the side of the bed on which the Marchese was laid.

As soon as he was conscious of their presence, which was not immediately, a deep groan agitated his frame, and an expression of guilt and horror was marked in his wildly-looking eyes, which language can but feebly convey. "Great Heaven!" thought Laurette, as she surveyed, with mingled pity and astonishment, the emaciated form before her, "look down with compassion upon this afflicted being suffering in the last hours of existence the agony of an awakened conscience; and Oh soften the rigour of thy justice with the effusions of mercy!"

Madame Chamont's grief was silent, but it was deep; she frequently attempted to articulate, but could not; low sobs prevented her utterance, whilst her soft eyes were directed eloquently towards Heaven with a look that was almost angelic; yet, anxious to convince the Marchese that she came to offer him her forgiveness, and also to assure him that nothing of enmity lurked in her bosom, she extended her hand to grasp his, breathing at the same time a prayer for the repose of his soul. Charmed with the manner in which this favour was bestowed, he pressed it fervently to his heart; his ghastly countenance lost much of its dreadful wildness, whilst his hollow eyes, which before glared with deep and inbred horror, gradually softened till sorrow, deep and immoveable, was the only expression that remained.

As Madame Chamont and Laurette continued to kneel, though without addressing him, the Marchese gazed alternately upon each, but was unable to speak. They, indeed, appeared like two ministering angels come to offer consolation to a soul bowed down with the weight of its own irremediable crimes. But the awful distance at which he was thrown from them, sealed his lips in silence. Their countenances were irradiated by innocence, whilst his was depressed by guilt; and now that adversity had brought conviction to his heart, he experienced the weakness, the imbecility of vice when opposed to the innate dignity of virtue.

At length Madame Chamont broke silence, and in language the most simple and pathetic, pronounced her forgiveness; dwelling likewise with energy upon the promises of the Gospel in a stile so unassuming and elegant, that her auditors listened with interest and emotion, whilst the Marchese, at the same time that he found his whole attention irresistibly attracted by the consoling truths she had uttered, felt his hopes insensibly revive; and, after having received the pardon of all present whom he had injured, he became gradually more tranquil; though, when his eyes glanced upon Laurette, something was evidently brought to his recollection, from the influence of which he would gladly have escaped; and when he beheld the gentleness of her demeanour, and saw the anxiety she discovered for his happiness, he observed her with a kind of wrapt astonishment, as if he scarcely believed that a being so injured could bestow compassion upon its persecutor.

The interview was short, but affecting. The Marchese, as soon as his sufferings would allow him command of language, addressed himself to all present with the most pathetic energy, expressing forcibly the high sense he entertained of their unexampled goodness, who could thus bestow pardon upon a wretch whose crimes had been productive of such accumulated misery. Shortness of respiration, and sorrow at the recollection of the past, prevented the Marchese from proceeding, and being unable longer to support himself, he sunk back upon his pillow; a cadaverous paleness overspread his face, whilst his quivering lips, which were parched by the violence of his disease, appeared to be on the eve of closing for ever. The scene now became insupportably painful, and Enrîco perceiving that his mother and Laurette were much affected, would have conducted them from the room; but the Marchese being aware of his design, gently recalled them, and fixing his dim eyes alternately upon his son and Laurette, added, "You have long loved each other with an affection as pure as it has been lasting: I only have been the means of rendering this attachment unfortunate; and let me, as the only atonement I can offer for my past offences, bestow you on each other."

Laurette, not expecting such an address, bent her blushing cheek towards the ground, whilst Enrîco pressed her unresisting hand to his breast, as he leaned over the bed with an air of melancholy attention listening to the words of his father.

The Marchese paused for a moment, and then proceeded:

"Let him, whose crimes and weaknesses have clouded the days of juvenile affection with premature sorrow, now sanction your future happiness.

"Sanction did I say!" continued the Marchese, interrupting himself; "have I hitherto sanctioned any thing but vice; and is it not virtue to disobey a wretch like me? But can you not, Laurette, meek-suffering angel! as you contemplate the virtues of the son, forget the vices of the father?—the fiend, who would have been thy murderer, from having consented, after many struggles, to thy death, as well as to——." Here he stopped—his wandering eyes became fixed in horror—his limbs shook—he struck his hand forcibly upon his forehead, as if a pang had forced it there—and then, apparently exhausted, sunk again upon the bed!

Enrîco, finding that quiet and repose were necessary, conducted the ladies from the room, whilst the Conte della Croisse remained with the Marchese, who soon afterwards fell into a short slumber.

When they had descended the stairs, they were met by the Confessor, who, with his cowl over his face, was moving thoughtfully along on his way to the Marchese's chamber.

Enrîco first observing the Father, addressed him for a few minutes aside; whilst Laurette, hoping in this holy Friar to behold her early instructor, the father Benedicta, surveyed him attentively. The subject he had entered upon, seeming to engage all his powers of attention, prevented him from being conscious of the presence of any other than the person to whom he was speaking, till accidentally turning aside his cowl, she perceived, with amazement, the long pale visage of her mysterious visiter. Her presence, in the moment he beheld her, seemed to operate as powerfully upon his feelings; for his cheek reddened, and his whole frame suffered a slight convulsion; yet he remained silent, following her with his eyes till she had reached the door of the saloon, where the Signora was in waiting to receive her.

Had not the mind of Laurette been entirely occupied by the scene she had just witnessed, this singular incident would have excited her curiosity, and possibly she might have taken some pains to have unravelled an affair which had long engaged her in deep reflection. But compassion for the fate of the wretched Marchese, whose suffering she had so recently contemplated, was so forcibly impressed upon her memory, that the recollection of past events, as well as of past wrongs, were entirely obliterated from her heart.

As soon as Enrîco had ended his conversation with the Monk, he entered the room, and endeavoured, with an assumed composure of address, to bestow comfort and consolation on the rest of the party. The night was passed by all in a state of tender dejection, each retiring to their apartments with a persuasion that the Marchese could not survive the following day, as he every hour betrayed new symptoms of approaching death.

In the morning Enrîco and Madame Chamont were summoned into the Marchese's chamber as soon as they were risen; and Laurette, having disengaged herself from the society of the Conte and the Signora d'Orso, felt an irresistible inclination to take a solitary walk through the avenues, being willing to indulge the luxury of her feelings amid the scenes of her earliest youth—scenes which memory presented with more pathetic interest to her heart, when she compared what had happened when resident there, with the long train of adversities which had followed in the rear of her former felicity.

No sooner had she crossed the lawn, on her way towards the vista, than she observed the mysterious Monk moving slowly beneath the leafless branches of a chesnut in the attitude of deep reflection. The hints he had once given her on a subject of so much importance to her happiness, as he had so positively affirmed; the portrait he had delivered with such solemn injunctions, with the various inconsistencies which had hitherto marked his conduct, now crowded upon her mind; and since she had nothing to fear from the persecutions of those who had formerly been her enemies, she resolved, instead of avoiding him as before, to throw herself in his way, that she might demand what motive had instigated him to such a singular mode of proceeding.

This was no sooner determined on than she advanced with a quickened step along the avenue through which the Father had passed, and beheld him stationed at some distance apparently lost in thought.

The sound of her steps did not rouse him from his reverie till she had arrived within a few paces of the tree under which he was standing, when starting as from a dream, he seemed to survey her with astonishment and painful emotion, but without speaking. Laurette's newly-acquired courage now forsook her, and anxious as she was to have these mysteries unravelled, she was unable to address him, and slightly courtesying, passed on in silence. She had not proceeded many yards before a sigh, which seemed as if it would rend in sunder the breast that heaved it, again recalled her attention. She turned—it was the Monk, who, without moving from the place in which she had left him, stood gazing upon her with a rapt and earnest regard.

"He has certainly something to relate," thought Laurette, "which materially concerns me, and why should I fear to know it? His conduct has hitherto been inexplicable; but that by no means implies that it is always to remain so; besides, he seems to be unhappy, and who knows but I may have it in my power to comfort him?"—Thus released from the dominion of fear, she returned again towards the Monk, who observing her approach, threw his hood back upon his shoulders, and advanced a few steps forwards; then, as if a sudden pang had seized him, he stopped, fixed his tearful eyes upon the ground, and again drawing his cowl over his face, as if struggling to conceal an excess of tenderness, turned round, and leaned upon his staff.

Compassion, as well as curiosity, now warmed the heart of Laurette; and unable any longer to resist the amiable impulses of her nature, she ventured to intrude upon the sacredness of his sorrow by asking him why he wept. Her words seemed to have the effect of electricity, and so much of tenderness and pity was mingled with his astonishment, that Laurette felt her bosom throb with new emotion; and anxious, though fearful, to enter upon a conversation whose prelude appeared to have occasioned extreme distress, she at length besought him to inform her who he was, and why he bent his eyes upon her so piteously without unfolding the cause.

"Oh my daughter! my daughter!" cried the Monk, clasping her wildly to his heart, "Heaven, who alone is acquainted with my sufferings, knows what I have endured; since, without a possibility of assisting you, I have left you alone to contend with the adversities of your fate."

Amazed at a conduct she could by no means explain or excuse, Laurette disengaged herself from his embrace, and being terrified at the raptures he had betrayed, for which she could not account, was irresolute whether to remain with him till her curiosity was gratified, or to return to the castle; till the Monk, after having wiped away the tears that had fallen plentifully upon his cheeks, proceeded—

"Dear orphan of her whom I so early lost, canst thou forgive him who ought to have defended thee from the shafts of misfortune for having thus forsaken thee? And wilt thou, by listening patiently to his recital, acquit him of premeditated wrong?"

"Alas! what mean you, holy Father?" replied Laurette, interrupting him; "how have you wronged me, and what claim have I upon your protection who never knew you?"

"An undoubted claim," replied the Monk, emphatically— "the claim of a child upon a parent."

"Upon a parent!" exclaimed Laurette. "Oh Heavens! are you then my father?"

"I am not thy father," returned the Monk, mournfully; "but, as being the last surviving parent of thy beloved, yet unfortunate, mother, am bound to thee by the most sacred ties. From a long residence abroad I was supposed to be dead; and on my return from imprisonment and exile, was marvellously directed to this place."

Joy and astonishment now animated the features of Laurette. To find a relation of her mother in the mysterious Monk was an unexpected blessing; and the idea of having it in her power to soften the remembrance of the past, to tranquillize the future, and to sooth the infirmities of age with the sweet affections of her nature, was a source of immeasurable delight; and she besought him to inform her of those past events which he had described as replete with misery.

An advancing footstep, which proved to be Enrîco's, put an end to the interview; and the Monk, having given her his permission to acquaint her friends with what he had unfolded, immediately on the decease of the Marchese, she retired. As Enrîco attended her along the avenues, he perceived that her spirits had been much agitated; but fearing to distress her by an inquiry into the cause, he only rallied her gently on her love of solitude, and her secret confidence with the Father, and then conducted her into the terrace-parlour. Here she found Madame Chamont alone, and in tears; for her last interview with the Marchese had much afflicted her: having witnessed his repentance, she now lamented that death would so shortly prevent him from proving the sincerity of it. He had delivered her a packet with his dying hand, expressly commanding that it should be opened on his decease, as it contained papers conveying particular orders concerning the manner of his interment. This parcel he presented with his blessing, conjuring her at the same time to forget the unhappy wretch whose vices had proved so injurious to her repose, and to endeavour to prolong her life to augment the happiness of her children, who possessing the advantage of her precepts and example, would reach the summit of virtue.

The day now passed silently towards the close. The physician, by whom the Marchese was attended, having declared soon after their arrival that his patient could not survive many days, they were in momentary expectation of his death. The Monk, his Confessor, who had hitherto denied him absolution, was called in towards evening to administer the last Sacrament, and a few hours after midnight the soul of the Marchese, after repeated struggles, took its flight into the regions of eternity.

When this melancholy event was communicated to the family, they suffered for a time the severest distress; but knowing the necessity of exertion, each assisted in consoling the other, till by repeated endeavours they at length became reconciled and resigned, through the not presumptive hope that his repentance, though late, would be finally accepted.

CHAP. X.

"Now let the sacred organ blow
With solemn pause, and sounding slow;
Now let the voice due measures keep,
In strains that sigh, and words that weep."
                                    MALLET.

A few days after the death of the Marchese, Madame Chamont, now Marchesa de Montferrat, mindful of his last injunc-
tion, opened the packet, so solemnly delivered, in the presence
of the Conte, Enrîco, and Laurette, to examine the contents.
It contained several papers relative to the estates seized upon
in the lifetime of their rightful heir, the orphan daughter of
the Conte della Caro, the testimony of which was sufficient to
prove the legality and justice of her claim, and thereby to reinstate her in her immense possessions, should she refuse to unite
her fate with that of Enrîco. Other papers were also inclosed,
which were penned by Father Paulo, the priest, who attended
for the purpose during the illness of the Marchese, in obedience
to the will of the Conte della Croisse, acknowledging Julie de
Rubine, long known by the name of Madame Chamont, to be
the lawful wife of the Marchese de Montferrat; and the youth,
hitherto called the Chevalier Chamont, to be his legitimate son
and heir to the titles, as well as the estates of his deceased father. Then followed the will, which, after a proper arrangement
of the landed property, placed Julie, his acknowledged wife, in
undoubted possession of all the personal property, amounting to
an astonishing sum, excepting only a few legacies, which were
to be paid at the expiration of a month; one to the Conte della
Croisse, the rest to a small number of broken dependants, who
had hitherto partaken of his bounty. The rest of the writings
contained some particular orders relative to his funeral, which
he requested might be conducted with as much privacy as possible; and as he had no wish to be conveyed into Italy, for the
purpose of being entombed with his ancestors, he desired that

his bones might be laid quietly in the conventual church belonging to the Carthusians; that no monument should be erected to perpetuate his memory to futurity, but that every thing should be conducted with as little ceremony as possible.

As soon as all these affairs were properly adjusted, the remains of the Marchese were interred according to his desire in the church of the convent of St. Angelo, which was about a quarter of a league from the castle. The new Marchesa, Enrîco, Laurette, and the Conte della Croisse, attended as mourners. The service for the occasion was read by Father Benedicta, who delivered it in a stile so moving, that the least affected of the audience could not refrain from tears. When this ceremony was concluded, and the body consigned to the dust, a sermon was presented from the centre of the church, replete with all that simplicity and energy of expression which the solemnity of the subject required, and ornamented with all those peculiar graces of eloquence, for which the accomplished Monk was so deservedly eminent. It spoke of the reward of the just, and the excellence of all unpolluted conscience. The subject was of too affecting a nature to be introduced without exciting emotion. Laurette sobbed aloud, whilst the widowed Marchesa drew her veil over her face to conceal her tears from observation, as she leaned upon the arm of her son. The whole congregation, which consisted chiefly of Friars and Lay-brothers belonging to the monastery, and a number of the rustic inhabitants of the adjacent villages, listened with undivided attention as the Father proceeded, who dwelt upon the Divine promises concerning the fate of departed penitents in a manner that seemed to diffuse peace and comfort around. As he continued, the audience crowded still nearer; a saint-like devotion was portrayed on every countenance, and hope, which before had afforded only a pale and tremulous beam, now burst forth with unclouded radiance. The path leading to eternal happiness appeared no longer inaccessible; fear was succeeded by confidence, and sorrow by resignation. This discourse was followed by a deep and solemn strain attuned to the notes of the organ, which was full, harmonious and sublime, such as was calculated to impress deeply upon the mind the important truths which had been uttered.

This being over, the congregation dispersed, and the party returned to the castle in a state of tender melancholy, not altogether unpleasing, each disposed to reflection on the vanity of human desires, and human attainments.

On the following day Laurette availed herself of the Monk's permission, and acquainted her friends of what he had already disclosed relative to his mysterious appearances, and with every other event worthy of notice, displaying at the same time the picture of her mother, the Contessa della Caro, which she had till this period carefully concealed. However highly the fair orphan had been estimated by her amiable preceptress previous to this recital, the circumstance just mentioned, as it discovered that no threats or afflictions, however terrible, possessed sufficient influence to induce her to forfeit the promise thus sacredly delivered to the Father, was a convincing proof that she had early united all the winning delicacies of her sex with a certain dignity of mind not usually connected with youth and inexperience: that her son had made so excellent a choice was not the least of her comforts, and she looked forwards to the consummation of their happiness with a great degree of tranquil delight. Enrîco's eyes beamed with every virtuous sensation of which the human mind is susceptible as the Marchesa dwelt upon her praises, and anticipated with impatience that hour which would complete his felicity by bestowing upon him the charming reward of his fidelity.

Father Benedicta did not long delay his visit of congratulation and condolence, but came attended by the Monk, who had acknowledged himself the near relation of Laurette, whom he introduced to the Marchesa and the rest of the family by the name of Father Andrea. From this Friar the pious Carthusian had heard of the many strange occurrences which had lately taken place at the castle, and waited anxiously till he could clasp his dear friend, the unfortunate Della Croisse, to his breast without a breach of propriety. The meeting was joyful, yet affecting; for busy memory recurred with melancholy minuteness to the fatal incidents of their past lives, the follies which had disgraced their earlier years, and thus planted thorns in their future paths. So true is it, that the mind, though escaped from the dominion of vice, dwells with pain upon the recollection of those hours which have been dedicated to licentious pleasures.

In the edifying conversation of these devout Friars the family spent much of their time, and gained from their religious, as well as moral discourses, many solid advantages; Peace was soon established among them, and comfort and joy, the reward of virtuous endurance, came in her train.

The Signora, whose affectionate attention to Laurette, though she had been deprived through artifice of the power of assisting her, was remembered with gratitude, and detained not as a domestic, but a friend: and as soon as suitable arrangements were made, agreeable to the will of the deceased, the Marchesa, whose delicacy would not permit this truly-accomplished woman to consider herself as a dependant, presented her with a very considerable sum as a reward for her services to the Marchese, which she desired her to receive not as a bounty but a debt, gently intimating that the Marchese would have been aware of the justice of this measure, had his mind been sufficiently collected to have considered it properly. This piece of generosity was accepted as it merited, with unbounded gratitude; and in such society as she now enjoyed, the Signora felt that heaven had made her ample amends for all the former discomforts of her lot.

Nor was Dorothèe, the faithful servant of the Marchese, who had been so injustly discarded, nor Margeritte, nor Lisette forgotten; these had all taken refuge in obscure villages, which they gladly quitted to be again received into the service of their long-lost and much-lamented Lady. Blessed with an ample fortune, the Marchesa could now indulge with impunity the diffusive generosity of her nature; and it was with no common degree of delight that she beheld the same virtuous principles which she had early instilled into the minds of her pupils, now blossoming in maturity, bestowing upon their possessors those undescribable sensations of happiness, which exalted benevolence can alone experience.

After more than a month spent in the castle since the death of its former inhabitant, it was deemed requisite for Enrîco to be presented at Court, that he might take possession of the Ital-

ian estates annexed to the title; those in Germany being the sole
property of Laurette, now Contessa della Caro, in right of her
mother, the daughter of a Bavarian Noble, an heiress of immense fortune. The Conte della Croisse offered to attend him
on this expedition, which, in the present situation of affairs,
could not be dispensed with, and as soon as necessary arrangements were made, leaving the ladies at the castle till their return,
they quitted this ancient mansion, and commenced their journey towards Italy.

Father Andrea, who, in the person of Laurette, recalled the
image of her beloved mother, frequently gazed upon her with
tears; and so much acute anguish did her memory cost him, that
it was long before he could trust himself again with the subject,
or reply to Laurette's anxious request to hear something of his
story.

"We will waive it at present, my child," was his customary
answer. "Perhaps a short time may enable me to be more ex-
plicit."—This was sufficient to repress the inquiries of our heroine, though not to stifle her curiosity, who felt an ardent desire
of being acquainted with the destinies of her unknown parents.
As Enrîco wished her to remain in ignorance of the murder of
her father, he did not fail to signify this to the Monk previous to his departure, who strictly promised never to disclose it,
since distress, unattended by any advantage, would inevitably
be the result of such a declaration. But though averse to gratifying her desires immediately as to any particular events that
had befallen him, Father Andrea would oftentimes accompany
Laurette through the long galleries in the castle, which were
ornamented with the portraits of her family, and inform her for
whom they were designed. The painting in the oriel so strikingly resembled the miniature that she wore in her bosom, he
passed by in silence, but did not forget to explain the next which
was allegorical; and but for the apparent difference in the age,
strongly characterized the equestrian statue erected in the inner
court. This magnificent column, he informed her, was placed
there in honour of himself by his daughter, the late Contessa
della Caro, who having never heard from him since he had been
engaged in a battle, which had proved fatal to many, supposed

him to have been dead; and by means of an original portrait left
at the castle, which was drawn in the early part of his life, to
gratify her filial affection had ordered it to be copied agreeable
to her own design, giving it, instead of the wrinkles of age, the
blooming graces of youth. From this intelligence it was easy for
Laurette to account for the attitude of the figure which was the
next in succession, since it was evident, from the position of the
picture, that it was designed to represent the affectionate Contessa weeping over the tomb of her lamented Father.

"How elegantly is sorrow expressed!" thought Laurette, not
allowing herself to introduce so delicate a subject. "What languor—what softness is in those eyes—how beautiful is the tear
that trembles beneath the lid!"

Could the fair orphan have known, whilst she was internally
bestowing praises upon the portrait, the near resemblance that
it bore to herself; had she been conscious that her form was still
more attractive than that on which she gazed, and that her features, if not more exact and regular, were of a more bewitching
kind; that her eyes were not less brilliant, and the whole of her
figure not less lovely, she might have accused herself of vanity
as she lavished these deserved encomiums upon the insensible
object of her admiration. But she was the only person who remained ignorant of her external perfections, though, had she
known their extent, this conviction would not have detracted
from her worth, since she valued not too highly these accidental
advantages, either to be elated by the possession of them, or
depressed by the reverse.

Laurette, having received her education in the castle of Elfinbach, and spent, under the guidance of the present Marchesa,
some of the happiest hours of her life in this gloomy mansion,
retained for it an affection which she believed it impossible for
her to experience for any other residence, however evident its
superiority in point of beauty and accommodation. The shades,
the groves, and the mountains, had been familiar to her from
childhood, and a thousand tender memorials were connected
with them all. Nor was the Marchesa de Montferrat less attached to this dreary abode, though a considerable part of it
had fallen into ruins since she had quitted it last; and but for

its amazing extent, they would have found it difficult to have discovered a sufficient number of rooms for the accommodation of their household.

The rampart-wall had fallen entirely into fragments, and the northern side of the structure was crumbling fast into dust; yet the greatest part of the building, though not uninjured, was able to resist the inclemencies of the weather; and the rooms which they usually occupied, though they might have been presented to the curious as models of antiquity, when animated by the blazing fire and the social board, wore an appearance of more than modern comfort.

CHAP. XI.

"Beauty alone is but of little worth;
But when the soul and body of a piece
Both shine alike, then they obtain a price,
And are a fit reward for gallant actions."

YOUNG.

When Enrîco and the Conte had been absent some weeks, their return was daily expected; and as it was determined that the family should then remove to the mansion on the Saltzburg estate, till the castle of Elfinbach was made fit for their residence, Laurette besought the Monk, whose spirits were less oppressed than before, to perform his long-neglected promise before she quitted the seat of her ancestors.

"What relates merely to myself," replied the Father, "may be less interesting than you imagine. A life which has chiefly been spent amid the bustle of Courts and the clang of arms, though it may be marked with some affecting incidents, does not usually form a pleasing narrative: I shall therefore pass the greater part of it over in silence. I have before informed you that your mother was a native of Germany, and that my name was Ferdinand Baron Neuburg.

"It was in the reign of Rodolph, the son of Maximilian the Second, that I first entered into the service of my country, which at that time suffered not only from internal commotion, but was involved in wars with the Hungarians, and disturbed with the difference between this Monarch and Mathias his brother, to whom he finally ceded Hungary and Austria.

"Under the patronage of Rodolph, who regarded me with the most flattering attention, I became skilled in every military art, and received many enviable proofs of his attachment; but scarcely was I enlisted among the number of his favourites before an unfortunate affair deprived me of this flattering distinction. In the Empress's train was a young orphan beauty, whose name was Augusta, of a noble but reduced family, who had received her education under the sanction of her Imperial Mistress, and was introduced at Court much earlier than damsels of rank usually are. Any attempt to portray the extreme loveliness of this fair young creature, would convey but an imperfect idea of her charms, as it was not so much the graces of symmetry, or the bloom of complexion, though in these she excelled in an eminent degree, as it was a certain delicacy of sentiment and ingenuousness of mind, discovering themselves in every movement and action which diffused such universal enchantment.

"To see frequently the lovely Augusta, without feeling the influence of her charms, would have justly exposed me to the imputation of stoicism, particularly when I perceived that she bestowed upon me a decided attention whenever I presumed to address her, not less grateful to my affection than my vanity. As she was always about the person of the Empress, who distinguished her with peculiar marks of her favour, seldom a day passed at Court which was not rendered interesting by the object of my admiration; and I observed, with no common share of delight, when compelled, under the banners of the Duke of Bavaria, to lead a detachment of the Imperial armies into Hungary, that there was a transporting melancholy in her deportment, which seemed to intimate that she suffered the keenest apprehensions for my safety.

"My absence from Vienna was not long; the rebel armies were soon routed, and I returned once more to lay my laurels at the feet of my Master.

"You are brave, Ferdinand," cried Rodolph, rising graciously to receive me, "and I would fain think of something to bestow as a reward for your valour, something adequate to your worth: I know you are not mercenary, and either I mistake, or you are not ambitious, yet you would not disdain to receive a recompence from your Sovereign. I would raise you to the rank of General, did not your extreme youth stand in the way of your advancement; but this is a difficulty which time will remove, and an honour that may be conferred at some future period. If in the meantime I can serve you in any other respect, you have only to mention your request; and if it is within the bounds of possibility, it shall be granted."

"Deprived of the power of utterance by this unexpected generosity, I could not for some moments express the warmth of my gratitude. Rodolph perceived my emotions, and finding I had something to ask, conjured me not longer to deprive him of the power of obliging me, but to name my request.

"It was not immediately that I could form a reply; when I did, I touched upon the subject nearest to my heart, and asked, as the reward of my services, the hand of Augusta. Scarcely had I pronounced her name before I observed an expression of uneasiness and displeasure in his countenance which alarmed and perplexed me; and as I continued to expatiate on the ardent affection I had long conceived for this beautiful maid, he eyed me with a disordered air; and after assuring me that this was a recompence not in his power to bestow without the permission of the Empress, who would unwillingly part with her, and that these were affairs in which he always considered it prudent to remain neuter, he left me to all the chagrin and mortification that grief and disappointment could inflict.

"As soon as I was awakened from my astonishment to a sense of my hopeless situation, I naturally imagined that Rodolph was himself the lover of Augusta; and this surmise was soon afterwards confirmed.

"It was in commemoration of a victory formerly gained by the Emperor, Charles the Fifth, over the French King, Francis the First, that a society of German Nobility assembled to partake of a sumptuous banquet, given by the Duke of Bavaria in honour of this interesting event. Being included among the number of patriots, I endeavoured, as much as possible, to conceal the mortification I had lately experienced under an aspect of assumed gaiety. The conversation, though it was chiefly on the cabinet and the field, was lively and unconstrained; unbounded hilarity universally prevailed, and, after many attempts to obtain a temporary animation, I finally succeeded, though my heart was still occupied by one favourite object—the image of Augusta. As soon as the dinner was concluded, the wines sparkled on the board, and the exhilarating draught went round. The name of Rodolph was given—his praises echoed through the room. The flames of my loyalty had been somewhat extinguished, yet I accorded with the rest; I acknowledged him brave, noble, and warlike; I would have added disinterested, but my heart contradicted the assertion.

"The Empress was then given; her virtues were applauded, and encomiums, that would have enhanced the reputation of the immaculate Portia, were bestowed, or rather lavished, upon her. Then followed the Princes of the Blood, excepting only Mathias, whose disaffection to his Sovereign justly excluded him from this honorary attention; and then the Nobles in general, particularly those who had distinguished themselves in the Senate or the Camp.

"We have hitherto confined our attention to the brave and the virtuous," cried a young soldier, who was seated at the right-hand of the Duke, because accidentally related to him. "Shall not beauty come in for its share? has it not hitherto been offered as the reward of military glory, and shall we not exalt its praise? Let us then," resumed he, filling high the sparkling goblet, "drink to the matchless Augusta, the brightest gem of the Crown—the rose of Vienna!"

"I raised the cup to my lips, but scarcely could I keep it from falling; her name penetrated my soul, and brought with it a thousand uneasy sensations. The mirth of the assembly now became boisterous; the name of Augusta was frequently repeated, and it was easy to discover that she was universally considered as the favourite of the Emperor. My distress now became too deep for concealment, and without offering any apology for my conduct, I quitted the company abruptly, that I might converse with my own soul in secret, and reconcile myself, if possible, to my disappointment.

"In vain did I endeavour to combat my affection, or to convince myself that she merited the oblique aspersions that had been thrown upon her character; her modesty, her unexampled beauty, the dignity of her demeanour, the retiring delicacy of her manners—all pleaded eloquently her cause, and seemed to reproach me for having even listened to a conversation tending to deprive them of their influence.

"A few days after this event I was summoned into the presence of the Emperor, who received me with an affected satisfaction, which displeased me, because I easily discovered that it was not genuine. After having accosted me with his accustomed familiarity, he praised my former exploits, and concluded with making known his intention of sending me on another expedition into the precincts of Hungary. The coldness with which I received this proposal, for I was a stranger to the arts of dissimulation, offended him; but he cautiously avoided a verbal confession of his displeasure, still endeavouring to conceal it under an appearance of cordiality. He saw he had injured himself in my esteem, and considered that from the intestine divisions of his country, for many had secretly espoused the cause of Mathias, it would be a politic measure to regain it. Easily penetrating his design, I shrunk from the meanness of it with contempt; yet the strength of my local attachment determined me to defend my country, though I now no longer regarded with partiality the man who was reputed its father.

"Having acceded to his desires, I once more quitted Austria, but not till I had first accomplished an interview with my Augusta, by means of a confidential dependant. This was with difficulty effected, as native modesty for some time prevented her from according with my desires; but affection finally triumphed, and in accents which are indelibly impressed upon my memory, she acknowledged herself concerned in my welfare. Still, however, I was dissatisfied and restless; what I had heard at the banquet, with what had fallen under my immediate observation, gave room for conjecture; yet scarcely could I summon resolution enough to make it known. To hint my suspicions, to throw a shade upon her conduct which, if spotless, must so tenderly wound a heart incapable of depravity, would, I considered, be raising an insurmountable bar to my hopes. Yet to remain in a state of suspense, to endure the idea that her affections were devoted to another, to feel the possibility of doubting whether they were my own, was a reflection that brought with it the most acute anguish; and at length I resolved to free myself from these inquietudes by a disclosure of my half-indulged surmises.

"The result of this conference placed her worth and honour beyond a doubt, and occasioned me to depart with a full determination of returning as soon as possible to Vienna, and of renewing my suit. Released from these visionary distresses, I commenced my military tour. Success crowned our endeavours—the enemy retreated as far as Buda—the General of the Hungarian forces, after a severe and sudden attack, laid down his arms—victory seemed on all sides to decide for us—and, every way fortunate, we returned to the metropolis loaded with spoils and honours.

"Surely," cried I, "Rodolph will no longer refuse to bestow upon me the lovely Augusta. If my former deeds in arms have not entitled me to so rich a reward after this change in his favour, he will no longer slight my services but will confer upon me this estimable maid, the only return I shall require, or deign to receive.

"Full of these warm, these sanguine hopes, whose only tendency is to mislead the judgment, I arrived at Vienna, and took the first opportunity of throwing myself before the throne of Rodolph, whose arms were open to receive me. But before I had time fully to acquaint him with the extent of my good fortune, or to repeat my request, I perceived a fixed expression of melancholy in his countenance, so nearly connected with despair, that my heart glowed with every sentiment of compassion. He observed it, and endeavoured to force a smile upon his features, as he congratulated me on the success of my undertaking; but it was a smile that had more in it of internal sadness than of tranquillity. Finding that he listened to me with a divided attention, and being unwilling to probe the wound he seemed recently to have received, I left him with an intention of seizing a more favourable moment of winning him to my interest. Scarcely had I removed from his presence before Count Wallestein, a courtier in the train of the Empress, crossed my path. I inquired of him the cause of this universal silence which seemed to reign throughout the Court; and was informed, to my unspeakable grief and astonishment, that my Augusta was no more; that she had been attacked with a severe disorder soon after I left Austria, which in a few days proved fatal! The anguish I endured at this moment can be scarcely conceived; the Count saw it, and offered something which he meant for consolation, at the same time convincing me by his manner, rather than his words, that he had been acquainted with the attachment subsisting between me and Augusta.

"This unexpected calamity occasioned me to consign myself to solitude for the space of some weeks, during which time I allowed no one to intrude upon the rights of my sorrow, chusing rather to reconcile myself to my misfortunes in the solitude of my closet, than to attempt to procure consolation amid scenes of dissipation. Peace being soon afterwards proclaimed, I now felt disengaged from all earthly pursuits; and, after much consideration, determined to bid my adieu to my Sovereign, and to retire into one of those castles occupied by my ancestors in the Dutchy of Bavaria. This resolution was at first strenuously opposed by Rodolph, who held forth the most alluring promises to divert me from a project by no means favourable to his interests: but finding I was not to be wrought upon by the sophistical arguments made use of in his defence, he left me to pursue my own inclinations with many marks of displeasure, without even hinting any thing as to a reward for my former services. I had already made every necessary arrangement for my intended expedition, and was preparing to bid a long adieu to those scenes of illusion, which, from the prejudices of education, and the force of habit, had long occupied my thoughts, and was ruminating in silence on the new plan of life I was going speedily to adopt, when my reflections were disturbed by Count Wallestein, who having been long a concerned spectator of what was passing in my heart, besought me, instead of prosecuting my former intentions, to accompany him on a little rural excursion through Switzerland and Savoy.

'I know the nature of your feelings too well,' resumed the Count, 'to propose, what is usually recommended as a restorative to a wounded mind, scenes of levity and dissipation. These generally fail in their effect, and if otherwise, the remedy is too frequently a dangerous one; yet, though I mean to discountenance this method of subduing the pang of severe distress, I by no means approve the mode of conduct you have recently, and I may add, too hastily adopted. You are at present too young to bury yourself in total inaction; the duties of your station require exertion, and he who believes he can discharge them in solitude, suffers his judgment to be deluded. Much may be done, I acknowledge, in the narrow sphere of domestic arrangements; sorrow may be made to smile, and poverty to feel the diffusive power of benevolence. Virtue and content are said to inhabit the path of rural seclusion, and, like the wild flowers that decorate the forest, thrive best, amid the unfrequented shades of Nature; yet in situations like these, our sphere of action is too much contracted to lead to any high attainment in virtue. It is in society only that our power is equal to our inclination; and trust me, the blessings it bestows make ample amends for those little wayward accidents in human life, which will occasionally happen to the most fortunate, however ardently they may endeavour to escape from them. Let me then,' resumed the Count, 'prevail upon you to renounce a plan which secludes you from the participation of pleasure, without retaining power sufficient to indemnify you from partaking of that joyless portion of bitter disappointment, which inevitably lingers in the cup of human life.'

"These and other arguments, seducingly delivered, at last prevailed upon me to accede to the proposal, though I secretly resolved, on my return from this rural expedition, to quit Vienna, and to repair, at least for some time, to the seat of my ancestors. A few days after this event we commenced our journey towards Switzerland, meaning to perform it by easy stages, that we might occasionally loiter amongst the most picturesque scenes of this romantic country. It was now the beginning of June, and the heat not sufficiently intense considerably to retard our progress.

Every object that presented itself was enrobed in that sublime simplicity which characterizes these charming regions, whose imagery is at once lofty and impressive, filling the mind that contemplates it with the most exquisite emotions. Having coasted the Alps, whose snow-capped summits were half obscured in the clouds, viewing from these lofty eminences every unadorned beauty which the most glowing imagination could portray, we arrived at a beautiful village beneath the Alpine steep of a precipice, near St. Julian in Savoy, whose prospect was bounded by a fine range of hills retiring into remote distance, which, being covered on one side with fine woods and vineyards, formed a striking contrast with the naked sublimity of the uncultivated side, deformed, or rather aggrandized by huge masses of frowning rock, rising in the most romantic directions.

"We did not reach this village till near an hour after sun-set; for as we proceeded leisurely along the glen on our way thither, we frequently paused to survey the rich vermeil hue left upon Mount Blanc, long after the sun had receded from the horizon, which fired the whole western hemisphere with the most glowing tints, till the blue mist of the twilight stole meekly upon the scene, and the moon, sailing silently towards her destination, commenced her reign of tranquillity. Fatigued with traversing these immense mountains, which it was impossible to avoid, I proposed taking our nightly rest at a small inn, situated about a quarter of a league from the village, which, however, appeared to be near; but the Count objected to the proposition, assuring me that the village was an object of too much importance to be neglected, since it possessed more natural beauty than many others which had attracted our attention; and as we were now at such an inconsiderable distance, he must insist upon our reaching it that night, intimating a desire that, for the sake of variety, we should leave our carriage and mules at the inn, and descend gradually the mountain till we had gained the object of our ramble. Feeling no inclination to contend with him in a matter of so little importance, I acquiesced; and having disposed of our mules and attendants agreeably to his desire, we advanced towards the hamlet, which consisted of a number of small white cottages, remarkable for their neatness and beauty, almost sur-

rounded with mountains. In this sylvan spot the simple children
of Nature, whose habitations were enclosed by these almost inaccessible barriers, seemed to repose in uninterrupted quiet, and
to be equally removed from the cares and distresses of life. The
song of the herdsman, the bleat of the lamb, or the carol of the
hasty-footed passenger, tended to wrap the mind in that pleasing kind of melancholy, which rural sounds and rural objects
never fail to inspire, when the heart is sufficiently at ease to be
susceptible of these amiable impressions.

"Having examined all that had hitherto fallen within the
sphere of our observation, we proceeded, by a little winding
path, along a gentle descent, till we reached a cottage so peculiarly beautiful, that our senses were for some time absorbed in
admiration. It was small, and of exact proportion; and so much
taste was displayed in the grounds which inclosed it, that it appeared like the retreat of some sylvan deity, who had exhausted
all the beauties of nature to harmonize her favourite residence.
A little lawn led to the door, which was ornamented with several fanciful shrubberies, intermingled with a variety of those
many-coloured flowers, which enamel, and perfume with their
odours, the flinty bosom of Savoy. A wood wound along its side,
through which a stream, that had spent its fury among the rocks,
was dimly and but at intervals seen through the deep-foliated
branches that hung over it, whose sound died away in a gentle
murmur, as it retreated from this beautiful dwelling to form a
lake in front of the village.

"As we drew nearer to the cottage, a strain of music, so soft,
so sweet, that it seemed to proceed from no mortal touch, came
faintly to our ears in the silence of the night. It appeared to
possess the powers of enchantment, for we were unable either
to return or to proceed. Whilst we still listened, it paused, and
then, accompanied by a voice which was melody itself, struck
into another measure. The Count eyed me with a look of secret
triumph, and then desired me to follow him. I obeyed in silence
till we arrived within a few steps of the door, when I demanded
in what manner he intended to introduce himself to the fair
syren who had thus riveted our attention.

'Your curiosity will soon be gratified,' returned the Count, with a smile, which was attended by a look I did not comprehend. 'You have nothing to do but to follow my steps, and be assured the adventure will terminate to your satisfaction.'—While he yet spoke, the voice ceased, the music sunk into cadence, and low sobs, broken, but distinct, were heard in its stead.

"What can this mean?" cried I, interrupting him. "Can sorrow have found an asylum in this sweet abode? If so, where can we look for tranquillity?"—The Count, without vouchsafing a reply, advanced towards the window from whence the music was heard, and, encouraged by his example, I followed slowly along. The casement was thrown open to admit the cool breeze of the evening; but a shade of fine lattice-work, which was over-canopied with the *clematis integrifolia*, eglantine, and a number of variegated evergreens, concealed the inhabitants of this beautiful little cottage from the gaze of the passenger. Whilst we yet paused to observe the tasteful simplicity of its aspect, a rough breeze wafted aside the foliated covering, and discovered a female, clad in a white robe, bending gracefully over a harp. Her fine flaxen locks, which descended to her waist in the most luxuriant tresses, were simply confined with a ribbon passing over her forehead, and fastened, without the appearance of art, in a loose and airy manner. A thin veil, of the slightest texture, covered her face, to which imagination now gave all those charms of expression, all that softness of colour which glow in the mind of the painter, the poet, and the lover. In a few moments she arose, replaced the harp by her side, and then heaving a gentle sigh, advanced towards the window.

"Ashamed of being seen thus watching her movements, as the breath of the zephyr allowed me partially to observe her, I receded some paces back; but before I could conceal myself behind the interwoven branches of the *clematis*, she drew up the lattice-work with an intention of closing the casement, and gave us a full view of her person. Her veil was yet over her face; but as the Count approached nearer to the window she uttered an exclamation of surprise, and threw it back upon her shoulders. I caught the tones of her voice; but scarcely could I convince myself that I was still in existence, when, raising my eyes from the ground, I beheld in the beautiful recluse my beloved Augusta.

To convey a just idea of my feelings at this moment would be impossible; I shall therefore pass them over in silence, observing only that she received me with those speaking tears, and blushing smiles, which convey more eloquently than words the genuine force of affection.

"As soon as I was a little composed, I desired the Count would explain this eventful mystery, since it was evident that to lead me to this spot was a preconcerted scheme, and that he was acquainted with the strange circumstance which had given rise to the report of her death.

'You are right, my dear Ferdinand,' returned the Count, whose fine countenance was irradiated with a smile of benevolence; 'I have been the chief performer in this little drama, and if you will give me a patient hearing, I will instantly explain my motive for having thus led you from joy to grief, and from grief to happiness. You are not ignorant of the passion that Rodolph cherished for Augusta, which he, however, long concealed from her; but this unfortunate prepossession increasing with her beauty, he was led, by slow progressive measures, to the attempt of conciliating her affections, which he had some hopes of effecting. Your attachment to his favourite, and the benignant glances which she sometimes cast upon you, gave him more serious uneasiness than he had ever before experienced. This accounts for a behaviour which before this discovery was uniformly different, and for the manner in which he precipitated your departure into Hungary.

'No sooner had you left the Court of Vienna than the Empress observed his emotions in the presence of Augusta, and instantly guessed the cause. In this affair she displayed less of that exalted magnanimity of conduct than she had formerly discovered on every other occasion. Her affection for Augusta was transformed into the most deadly hate, which instigated her not only to withdraw her protection, but to inflict some punishment as severe as undeserved. hitherto I had been honoured with her confidence in affairs of equal importance; and fearing, lest the violence of her passions should plunge her into some unexampled error, I called a little dissimulation to my aid, and entering warmly into her feelings, promised to assist her design.

Fortunately at this crisis Augusta was so much indisposed as to be obliged to remain in her apartment. This was favourable to my purpose; and during her confinement I prevailed upon the Empress to allow me to spread a report of her death, and also to permit me to convey her into a convent, which would effectually prevent her from being either seen or heard of more. Having undertaken the management of this affair, I contrived to inform this fair victim of unjust resentment of these newly-concerted measures; at the same time assuring her, that if she would assist my enterprise, by wearing an appearance of joy in the presence of the Empress at being allowed to end her days in a religious retirement, instead of devoting her to a conventual life, I would only remove her for a short time to a little romantic retreat in a remote province till I had acquainted you with her situation, who, I was convinced, would gladly liberate her from solitude. Since to leave the Court had been for some weeks the primary wish of her soul, she gladly consented to the proposal, and was immediately conveyed hither. In the meantime the report of her death was circulated so successfully by the Empress and her confidential dependants, who had bound themselves by oath to an eternal silence upon the subject, in consideration of a great reward, that none entertained any doubt of its reality. A coffin, attended by all the ladies of the Court, who knew not but that it contained the body of their companion, was interred with all the rites of burial; and so artfully was every thing conducted, that the Emperor, the Nobles, and the whole Court, were completely deceived.

'As then, you must allow,' resumed the Count, 'that I have acted the part of a friend, you will pardon me for having permitted you to taste of calamity, since without the bitter ingredients of life, the sweets would be deprived of their relish; and as you will have the justice to allow that the few weeks of separation, which were necessary for the furthering of our scheme, have been more than counter-balanced by the joys of meeting, you have now nothing to do,' continued the Count, directing a playful smile at the blushing Augusta, 'but to obtain the hand of this fair wood nymph, who, if I have any skill in physiognomy, bestowed her heart upon you almost before she knew she had one.

A priest may easily be procured, by whom the ceremony may be performed, and your own prudence, as to secrecy, will instruct you how to act.'——

"The path being thus cleared, half the difficulties were removed; and having renewed my suit with all the ardency of the sincerest affection, she soon consented to bestow upon me the happiness I sought; and a priest being engaged, I was soon permitted to address her by the endearing appellation of wife."—The Monk now paused for a moment, to give a tear to the recollection of his former happiness, and then proceeded—

"As soon as the marriage was solemnized, we repaired, attended by the Count Wallestein, to this castle, in which I spent many years in uninterrupted felicity. Heaven blessed us with a daughter soon after our marriage, and the important secret remaining still undiscovered, I removed occasionally to Court during the reign of Rodolph; but my absences from the castle were never long, serving only to augment the happiness I enjoyed in the society of my wife and daughter. At last, however, it pleased Heaven to deprive me of my much-loved partner, though not till she had seen her daughter eligibly and happily united to the Conte della Caro, an Italian Nobleman, who accidentally saw her as he was making the tour of Europe, and who, on my consent to their marriage, promised to allow his bride to spend half the year in this castle, to which she was singularly attached. Thus deprived by death of my Augusta, I felt once more an inclination to travel, and to resume, if occasion required, my former profession, that of arms. Mathias had now succeeded to the empire; and though by no means attached to this haughty Prince, I determined to defend my country, now suffering from a confederacy called the Evangelical League, which was, however, counterbalanced by an host equally formidable, the assembly of the Catholics.

"Those who have courage to take an active part on either side when a kingdom is divided against itself, are encompassed with innumerable dangers, and few there are that escape persecution. Some trifling inadvertency, which I could never perfectly understand, was alledged against me, which was blackened with so many malicious insinuations, that, without any formal ac-

cusation, I was conveyed by stratagem from the kingdom, after
having rendered it many services; and having found means of
escaping from my persecutors, was confined in a prison by order
of Mathias, who recollecting that in the reign of his brother I
was no friend to his unjust pretensions, eagerly listened to the
calumnious reports which were circulated by my enemies for
the accomplishment of my destruction. In this miserable situation I remained near two years, and then, without any reason
being publicly given for this, or for my mysterious confinement,
I was as strangely released. Thus emancipated from captivity, I
resolved to leave the intrigues of Courts, and the uncertainty
of arms, to the young and the fortunate, and to return again
to my former residence. Having put my intention into practice,
of resigning for ever a military life, I returned to the castle of
Elfinbach, anxious to clasp to my heart a daughter from whom
I had been so unjustly separated. But what was my grief, when
I was informed that both she and the Conte were dead, the latter being slain by a party of banditti, or some other as lawless
wretches, which caused the death of the lovely mourner, his
widow, soon after she had given birth to a daughter, who, it
was supposed, had died with her! Though I had no suspicion
of the falsehood of the report concerning the fate of the infant,
having never heard any thing to the disadvantage of the late
Marchese de Montferrat, who I knew to be the nearest relative
of the Conte della Caro, and consequently the next heir to his
estates if he died childless; yet I could not forbear sometimes
listening to reports which were circulated, though not generally
believed, in the neighbourhood of Turin (whither I afterwards
repaired) respecting a female infant, which was sent to nurse
by the Marchese de Montferrat, believed by some to have been
the daughter of the Contessa della Caro. This instigated me to
call on the woman who had accepted the charge; but, except a
numerous family of her own, she had no child in her care; and
her replies were at once so simple and so artless, that I easily
credited her assertion, which tended to convince me that all reports upon this subject were founded in error. Weary of a world
in which I was left alone and unfriended, I finally determined to
find out some secure and peaceful asylum, where I might termi-

nate my days in peace and solitude; and at length fixed upon a little alpine spot amid the mountains of Switzerland, which was merely a cottage. In this melancholy retreat I remained many years under an assumed character and name, leading literally the life of a hermit, till a very singular dream, joined with an ardent desire of visiting my former dwelling, induced me to quit my retirement.

"It was one night, when I had fallen into a sleep much earlier than usual, that I thought a person approached me as I slept, and bade me to repair without delay to the castle of Elfinbach, for in that mansion the offspring of the unfortunate Conte della Caro was receiving her education, and that it depended upon myself not only to reinstate her in the possessions of her ancestors, but to save her from misery and from death. This visionary address was so deeply impressed upon my mind, that it was long before I could recompose my spirits, or convince myself it was but a dream. At the same hour the next night the command was repeated; the same figure appeared to me again in the visions of my sleep, bidding me depart, and watch unobserved the movements of the present inhabitants of the castle; not openly to declare what I had been told, but to wait the effects of time, which would eventually unravel all. This repetition of the last night's adventure determined me to adhere to the advice delivered; and having procured the habit of a white Friar, the better to protect me from danger and impertinence, I commenced, in the character of a ghost, my nightly watchings. I soon, however, discovered means of informing Ambrose that I was mortal, and from him gained an accurate account of what was passing in the castle, and what had happened before I reached its boundaries. From what he affirmed, I had every reason to believe that my dream was founded on truth, though it was not sufficient to lead to a certainty.

"To the chapel I had free access," continued the Monk, "at every hour of the night, and also to the burial-vault beneath, which I entered by means of an outward door opening behind the headless statue erected at the extremity, where I frequently spent some time in conversation with Ambrose, or, when alone, allowed myself the sad indulgence of weeping over the remains of my beloved Augusta, which were entombed in that place.

"When I beheld you, which was not, in spite of my utmost endeavours, till several weeks after my arrival, the resemblance you bore to your mother, convinced me you was her child; and thinking it necessary to warn you of your danger whilst in the power of the Marchese de Montferrat, I delivered you her picture, and meant to have disclosed the secret of your birth, and then to have offered you my protection; but was prevented by the interference of Paoli and your sudden removal. Not knowing whither you was conveyed, till after the return of Ambrose, which did not happen till a considerable time afterwards, I suffered the most restless anxiety for your safety. His presence, however, when he came to discharge the domestics, relieved me from apprehension, though the information he gave me determined me to go immediately in quest of you. Not knowing the exact situation of the castle in the principality of Saltzburg, I was obliged to repeat my inquiries; and being at first unsuccessful, was directed by chance, or rather by Providence, into the chapel of a forsaken abbey, which you afterwards entered, attended by a stranger of a dignified and amiable aspect, who proved to be the present Marchese. His presence prevented me from addressing you as I should otherwise have done; but by following you along the mountains, I had soon an opportunity of discovering your place of residence. After this event, I frequented the castle of Luenburg as I had formerly done this, but without obtaining the accomplishment of my desires. Soon afterwards I learned from Ambrose, whom I largely rewarded for this intelligence, that you was sent into a convent on the borders of Italy, and that the Marchese had retired in extreme perturbation of spirits and distress of mind to the castle of Elfinbach. Knowing, if this was the case, which I had no reason to doubt, that I might be enabled by some means, during your year of initiation, to contrive your escape, could I inform myself of your place of destination, I repaired again to this ancient and almost deserted mansion, entertaining some hopes that, with the assistance of Ambrose, I might repeat with success my supernatural appearances, and thus surprise and terrify the Marchese into confession; since it was now evident, from the whole of his conduct, that he had concealed, and usurped the rights of, a defenceless orphan. In this attempt I succeeded, and by the assistance of a trap-door, so artfully contrived as not to be perceived by the most careful observer, gained the interior of his apartment, and so well accommodated myself to his own guilty feelings, that the disorder of his mind hourly increased, and was followed by an alarming disease, attended with many dangerous symptoms. This occasioned him to send for a Confessor from the Carthusian monastery, that he might have an opportunity of unburthening his conscience.

"I was fortunately at the abbey of St. Angelo at the time the message arrived, in the society of Father Benedicta, with whom, under my assumed habit, I had accidentally formed a superficial acquaintance, and whose worth and goodness led me to esteem his character long before I was personally known to him. As to learn the substance of a confession, which appeared to promise much important information, was of the utmost consequence to my future interests, I formed the resolution of attending as Confessor, as I knew the severity of the ecclesiastical rules would effectually prevent my obtaining this knowledge, however necessary, by any other means. This induced me to make my intention known to Father Benedicta relative to my plan of personating a Carthusian, though without disclosing to him that I was not really a Friar; and with some difficulty, after making my reasons partly known, prevailed upon him to supply me with a habit of the order.

"As the Marchese had not signified a desire that any particular Friar should attend, I was readily admitted, and soon learned the cause of his remorse; but the purport of this singular confession I consider myself as bound, by the strictest ties of religion, as well as of honour, strictly to conceal, and should consider myself as culpable by the laws of justice, if I suffered myself to reveal it, as if I had taken the indissoluble oath administered in the period of initiation, which binds to eternal secrecy as to the nature of confessions.

"When the Marchese had completely unburthened his conscience, which was not till my third visit, and it was proved, after the arrival of the Conte della Croisse, that you was in a place of security, which appeared to take a considerable weight from his heart, I sent one of the brotherhood to bestow absolution, not being empowered to perform this ceremony myself, to whom also the substance of the confession was repeated in the same manner as before, though from the appearance of the Monk, which perfectly corresponded with my own, the Marchese was not conscious of the deception.

"As soon as these ceremonies were properly adjusted, I informed Father Benedicta of the artifice I had employed; and having thrown aside the habit I had formerly worn, substituted that adopted by the Carthusians; and entering into the convent of St. Angelo, agreeable to my former intention, took the name of Father Andrea.

"With all the rest, my dear child," rejoined the Monk, "you are already acquainted. I have now related to you all the material incidents of my past life, which for many years has been marked with severe misfortune; but Heaven, in your preservation and happiness, has bestowed some sweeteners of my melancholy existence, and I receive them with gratitude."

CHAP. XII.

"Swift o'er the lyre's harmonious strings
His magic hand the minstrel flings;
Obedient to the sprightly sound
The dancers' quivering feet rebound:
Diffusing wide their silver rays,
Aloft the sparkling lustres blaze:
While milder emanations flow
From love-enkindling orbs below."

SALMAGUNDI.

The Marchesa and Laurette did not neglect, amid the newly-acquired happiness that surrounded them, to visit their amiable acquaintance, the Abbess of the Order of Penitents, who received them with every proof of the sincerest affection. To her society they devoted many of the intervening hours passed in the absence of Enrîco and his venerable friend, finding in her conversation all that elegance of expression, and delicacy of sentiment, which rendered her as charming as respectable, even in the midst of age and infirmities.

It was now the latter end of May, and the season remarkably fine. The groves and the woods were again clothed in the most delightful verdure, whilst the hedgerows, which displayed that luxuriance of foliage ever perceptible in this fertile country, were now beautifully embroidered with honeysuckles, and overhung with the blushing wreaths of the rosa canina; all Nature seemed to have awakened to joy and harmony! With what emotions of delight did Laurette now wander along the borders of that river, whose bank had formerly been the scene of infant pastime, recalling fondly to her recollection the years that were past, and alternately weeping and smiling at the vicissitudes of fortune! How charming was it to bring back, with the aid of memory, every interesting event in that uninformed period of existence, when hope revelled in the heart unchecked by disappointment, and joy suffered no decrease from gloomy retrospection! It was after one of these sweet lonely excursions, which she had commenced in the absence of the Marchesa, who had taken an early walk to the convent, that she observed at some distance four horsemen advancing towards the castle, which on a nearer view she discovered to be Enrîco and the Conte della Croisse, attended by Anselmo and another of the domestics.

Tremblingly alive to every sensation of pleasure, she bounded swiftly from the mountains, and before the travellers alighted, arrived at the portico. As soon as Enrîco observed her, his eyes beamed with inexpressible rapture, whilst love, in the most lively colours, was depicted on his countenance.

The usual expressions of congratulation on meeting again being over, which were accompanied, on the part of Enrîco and Laurette, with those melting looks of unspeakable affection which lovers only understand, they were joined in the terrace-parlour by the Marchesa, and soon afterwards by the Signora d'Orso.

When the travellers had partaken of a little refreshment, they were requested to relate the success of their journey, which, they soon convinced their hearers had been every way fortunate;

since proofs of the legitimacy of Enrîco's birth had appeared sufficient to silence the claim of any other person, should an attempt to discountenance the justice and truth of the fact be hereafter made.

"Yet my happiness is at present incomplete," cried Enrîco, casting a look of tenderness upon the timid blushing Laurette; "will not she then, who has it exclusively in her power to bestow on me the felicity I ask, deign to confer it? Can she doubt the strength of my affection, or refuse to reward it, after having received so many testimonies of its permanency?"

"She does not mean to prevent, or even to procrastinate your happiness," replied the Marchesa. "She is above dissimulation; and as I have hitherto been allowed to influence her actions under the character of a preceptress, she will grant me the privilege of naming the day. Will you not, my lovely pupil," resumed the Marchesa, with a smile of ineffable tenderness, "give me this new proof of your dutiful acquiescence, the last I may have cause to demand?"

Laurette blushed deeply; and, having assured her beloved friend that any request of her's would have the force of a command, permitted her, after a little gentle reluctance, to name the same day on the following week.

Enrîco's joy on this occasion could only discover itself in tears; every wish of his soul was gratified, and it now appeared impossible, to his delighted imagination, that sorrow could ever again become an inmate of his breast.

The week now passed rapidly towards the close, which was employed by the Marchesa and the Signora in preparing for the intended marriage, which was to be attended with all that diffusive hospitality, so strikingly exhibited in the character of the former, and which she had now the power, as well as the inclination, to display.

Enrîco and Laurette, in the meantime, found an inexhaustible source of delight in traversing those sublime and beautiful regions in which the castle was situated. The trackless mountain, whose rocky glens were encrusted with moss, or enamelled with wildflowers; the impenetrable forest, sacred to the foot of the adventurer, were objects of curiosity and wonder, which they were never weary of contemplating or admiring, among which every day presented, from the variety of their productions, some new subject for investigation.

At last the long-expected day, which was to ratify these solemn vows already registered in heaven, arrived. The officiating priest was the Father Benedicta, who, at his own request, had the felicity of receiving the lovely bride at the hand of Father Andrea, in the chapel of the castle, by the name of Laurette Contessa della Caro, and of bestowing her upon Enrîco Marchese de Montferrat.

The ceremony being performed in the morning, the remaining part of the day was dedicated to rural festivity; and every luxury was procured in honour of this event, that the country, within some leagues of the mansion, could afford. The nuptials were, indeed, not celebrated with the lofty appearance of courtly personages, as none, except the family at the castle, could boast of a noble origin; the rest of the company being composed of the tenantry and uninformed inhabitants of those humble cottages, which were variously dispersed on the banks of the Rhine, who concluded the evening of this joyful day with a dance upon the lawn, to the lively notes of the guitar and the hautboy; each returning laden with presents to their homes, and pouring out blessings upon their hospitable entertainers.

Nothing could exceed the happiness of Father Andrea, when he beheld the felicity of his children thus hourly increasing. He seemed to have forgotten already all his sorrows, and looked up to Heaven with pious gratitude, which had thus recompensed his patience and sufferings, long after he had ceased to expect a temporal reward.

Inured to solitude, and naturally attached to it, the young Marchesa never wished to stray beyond her native mountains; she had formed no ideas of happiness beyond them, and it was not without some reluctance that she quitted the castle of Elfinbach, the abode of her childhood, to repair to the mansion on the Saltzburg estate till the former one was rendered more habitable. This was, however, a necessary measure, as a considerable part of the fabric was so much decayed as to form but an uncomfortable asylum. On this expedition she was attended by the whole of the family, except the Conte della Croisse and the Fathers, as the former had determined upon visiting his daughter at Augsberg during their absence from the castle, and the Monks were obliged to remain in the convent of St. Angelo.

In this modern and luxurious mansion, which to the elder Marchesa had all the charms of novelty to recommend it, they prolonged their stay till the castle of Elfinbach was made fit for their residence, which seemed, from having been long known, as well as from the circumstance of its having been the seat of Father Andrea when dignified by the title of Baron Neuburg, and of the late Contessa della Caro, to have a prior claim to their regard. Laurette had already resolved to return to it, and quit it no more; and Enrîco, whose every wish centered in her happiness, had adopted a similar resolution, being not less attached to it than the beautiful Marchesa.

During their continuance at the castle of Luenburg, the generosity of this noble family was so unbounded, that on leaving it they were followed for a considerable way by a large number of the peasantry, who crowded about their carriages with tearful eyes, showering blessings upon them as they repeated their adieus. How delightful were these simple effusions of gratitude to those on whom they were bestowed! And who that has a mind capable of reflection, and a heart of feeling, would exchange those noble impulses of our nature, which direct us to acts of Godlike benevolence, for the chillness of unsocial grandeur? And how can it be truly estimated what they lose, who suffer themselves to be deluded into an opinion that the bold pre-eminence of rank and state can compensate for the absence of those amiable affections, which teach us to conciliate and to deserve the love of others?

As the weather was more than usually favourable, they travelled leisurely towards the castle, Enrîco and Laurette occupying one of the carriages, and the elder Marchesa and the Signora the other, frequently stopping, and sometimes alighting; when any thing particularly attracted their attention.

On the evening of the third day they arrived at the castle of Elfinbach, which wore a much more comfortable appearance than when they quitted it last. The rampart-walls, the turrets, and buttresses, were repaired, and the fallen fragments, which before were only partially removed, were cleared from the courts, which, with the whole of the grounds, were new mown for their reception.

The Monks seized the first opportunity of welcoming them home, and a few days afterwards the happiness of the whole party was materially augmented by the presence of the Conte della Croisse, who informed Enrîco, soon after his arrival, that he had long secretly formed a resolution of entering into the convent of St. Angelo; and having taken leave of his daughter, was come purposely to fulfil his intention.

"The crimes of my youth," resumed the Conte, "stand yet in terrible array before me; and the only atonement I can now make for my offences, is to dedicate the remaining part of my life to prayer and penitence. Hitherto I have been irresistibly withheld from the execution of my intention; for the designations of Providence are uncontroulable. It was the will of Heaven that I should continue in society, to become an instrument of punishment to the guilty, and to rescue innocence from the grasp of oppression, relieving myself by these means from a debt of gratitude, which I should otherwise have found it impossible to have discharged; but the end being accomplished, why should I longer defer the prosecution of my purpose, since I am already bending with years, and, in the common course of nature, cannot reasonably expect to continue much longer an inhabitant of this world?"

Enrîco finding that his friend was bent upon this new project, and being secretly gratified on his having fixed upon the convent of St. Angelo for his future abode, did not attempt to dissuade him from his design; but gained, or rather wrested a promise from him, that he would remain in the family for the space of a month. Often in the society of Laurette and Enrîco did the penitent Della Croisse fix his eyes upon them with an expression of earnest tenderness, as he witnessed their mutual affection, whilst busy memory reverted to the scenes of his youth, and presented the image of his Helena, with all its amiable accompaniments, to his mind. When reflecting upon her, his thoughts would frequently glance upon Laurentina, she whose Circean charms had accomplished his overthrow, and dwell with painful regret upon the recollection of his complicated crimes and misfortunes.

"Learn from my fate, my children," he would sometimes say, addressing himself to the lovely pair, "the danger of venturing on the borders of vice. I was once virtuous as you are; but one fatal error, one unsubdued passion, plunged me into irremediable guilt; yet not aware of my danger, even when on the brink of a precipice, I believed I could return at discretion to the path of rectitude; but when once tempted to deviate from the principles of truth and honour, how soon is every amiable impression obliterated from the heart, how soon does vice by familiarity lose its deformity! Yet what an inexhaustible source of felicity is an untainted conscience, and how eternally connected are guilt and misery!"

Often, as he thus movingly addressed them, did he melt his audience into tears, who endeavoured, with all those gentle assiduities, which sensibility like their's knew so well how to bestow, to delude him into a transient forgetfulness of his past crimes; and sometimes attempted to convince him that the purity of his present conduct, aided by the sorrow he expressed for what could not be recalled, was sufficient to atone for the errors of his youth; and that the irregularities into which he had been precipitated through the artifice of others, were not so much to be attributed to his faults as his misfortunes.

Anselmo, whose faithful attachment to his master had rather increased than diminished, was, in consideration of his former services, exalted to the rank of steward, which the generous Marchese contrived to make both an easy and lucrative post.

Thus restored to joy and tranquillity, the inhabitants of the castle of Elfinbach enjoyed the most uninterrupted felicity.— Enrîco, whose dutiful impulses prompted him to the most benevolent exertions, set apart annually a third of his princely income for charitable purposes; and his mother, following his bright example, adopted a similar plan. None that entered the portals of this hospitable mansion departed without calling down blessings from Heaven upon its owners.

Della Croisse, at the appointed time, repaired to the convent of St. Angelo, and entered into the severe order of the Carthusians, where he found, in the purified conversation of his early companion, the pious Benedicta, and that of Father Andrea, all the consolation he was capable of receiving.—Whilst blessed with health, virtue, and innocence, the Marchese and Marchesa, in the bosom of their amiable family, experienced the most refined sensations of happiness; and anxious of possessing it themselves, felt a Godlike pleasure in dispensing it to others. They were blessed with a numerous offspring, lovely as themselves, and presented, in the whole of their lives to the reflecting mind of the moralist, a striking instance of the imbecility of vice, and of the triumphant power of virtue.

FINIS.

Printed in the USA
CPSIA information can be obtained
at www.ICGtesting.com
LVHW091021260823
756378LV00005B/66